More praise
SCALES OF JUSTICE
featuring the dragon familiar, Fanuilh . . .

"The characters are realistic and so are the situations, and it should appeal to mature fantasy and mystery readers looking for something different, as well as fans of the previous books." —*VOYA*

"Fans of Daniel Hood will rejoice at the arrival of the fourth in the series featuring the intricately woven exploits of Liam Rhenford and his dragon familiar Fanuilh . . . Those who enjoy a mystery set in another time and another place, one liberally laced with magic, will take this up with great anticipation." —*Kliatt*

KING'S CURE

Daniel Hood

ACE BOOKS, NEW YORK

KING'S CURE

An Ace Book / published by arrangement with
the author

PRINTING HISTORY
Ace edition / December 2000

The Penguin Putnam Inc. World Wide Web site address is
http://www.penguinputnam.com

Check out the Ace Science Fiction & Fantasy newsletter
and much more on the Internet at Club PPI!

ISBN: 0-441-00789-9

ACE®
Ace Books are published
by The Berkley Publishing Group,
a division of Penguin Putnam Inc.,
375 Hudson Street, New York, New York 10014.
ACE and the ''A'' design are trademarks
belonging to Penguin Putnam Inc.

PRINTED IN THE UNITED STATES OF AMERICA

10 9 8 7 6 5 4 3 2 1

CHAPTER 1

SITTING IN THE study while the scholar read his letter of introduction, Liam Rhenford reminded himself once again that he was no longer a student.

Then why are you sitting so straight? asked a small, cynical voice in the back of his head. *When you aren't fidgeting, that is.*

His fingers plucked at the seams of his breeches; he shifted in his chair and put his hands firmly on his knees, willed his face to assume an expression of polite expectation, and looked around the comfortable, book-cluttered study. Sea-coal glowed cheerfully in the small hearth, and a dozen candles flared in the ironwork stand by the scholar's chair, turning the raindrops that trickled down the study's single window into beads of gold.

This is ridiculous, Liam thought, the silence weighing on him. *You're not back at Pauper's.* He was sitting too stiffly, like a student called up for discipline, and deliberately slumped a little. The scholar read on unaware, face hidden behind the letter of introduction. *He's not your teacher, and you're not a student. You're here on the Duke's business.*

Nonetheless, he could not shake the feeling that he was suddenly younger by a dozen years, back at university, waiting for a robed tutor to scold him for his imperfect grasp of history, or his failure to attend important lectures, or his excessive drinking. And when the

1

scholar lowered the letter, Liam cocked his head like a dog anxious to please.

"Well and well," Master Cade said, smiling. He was a short man, plumpish, balding but possessed of an enormous white beard. His right leg was stretched out on a footstool, swathed in a blanket, and he wore a thick shawl around his shoulders. Though he lived in Torquay, the scholar's accent and dialect were southern. "This is a pretty introduction, Quaestor Rhenford. It is quaestor, is it not?"

Liam nodded. "It is only a temporary title. The Duke grants it to me from time to time." *When he has errands for me to run.*

"The Duke's not free with praise, yet he has more and to spare for you."

"He's very kind," Liam said, feeling foolish. *Why did you say that? He's not kind at all. Stop being such a lickspittle.*

Cade laughed and flapped the letter in Liam's direction. "Oh, come, Quaestor. The Duke of the Southern Tier has many parts, but kindness is not among them."

Liam blushed and grinned at the same time. "No, I suppose not." They shared a conspiratorial look, and his discomfort faded. The masters at his collegium had never laughed, and would never denigrate an important figure. *Not in front of a student, at least.*

"A kind man wouldn't't've sent you travelling with winter coming," Cade went on, eyes twinkling, "yet y'are here. Your journey could not have been pleasant."

Recalling the week spent clawing up the coast from the Southern Tier, with the fall storms worsening into winter gales, Liam shook his head. "It wasn't as bad as it could have been, but I think I'll return to Southwark overland."

"Small choice between the two," Cade pointed out. "The passes'll fair choke with snow in a month. And your errand here will run out that or more, I should think."

With a rueful nod, Liam agreed. The details of the project were laid out in the Duke's letter: a search among the many libraries of Torquay, and a survey of the city's countless scholars, for information on foreign lands as yet unvisited by Taralonian merchants. "He wants it as complete as possible. It's my own fault, I'm afraid: my business partner and I have had some success with new trade routes, and they came to the Duke's attention. He asked me about them, and I think I made them sound a little too attractive."

Cade chuckled. "And so he tasks you to find more. It seems a cruel reward, and untimely as well, unseemly in its haste. A trip to Torquay in late fall—could it not wait until spring?"

Liam spread his hands in resignation. "The Duke does not like to wait."

"Aye, patience is not among his parts either," Cade said. He considered the letter again, pursing his lips. "Well and well, I can arrange introductions with some proper scholars, and gain you entry to the appropriate libraries. I shall be glad to do so, for that the Duke is a sometime patron of mine; the work itself I shall leave to you." Squinting, he underlined a sentence in the letter with his finger. "I note here that you were at Prosper's Tower."

Liam nodded, though he usually referred to his collegium by its nickname, Pauper's. "I should say that I did not finish the curriculum." He paused, cleared his throat. "Family matters called me away."

Lost in the letter, Cade waved the admission aside. "I was at Whitetower," he murmured, reading. "A waste of time, for the most part. But it'll have prepared you for your task, I think." He turned the piece of paper this way and that, frowning. "He does not write where you will stay. Have you lodgings?"

"Yes, I arranged them this afternoon. At the Sober Student."

Cade stirred in his seat. "Mistress Tall's house, I believe? A goodly place, though she will gouge as to price. I shall write it down, lest I forget." He twisted and stirred, constrained by his blanket-wrapped leg; Liam jumped up and found quill and ink for the scholar, who scrawled the name of the inn on the Duke's letter and handed the quill back. "Y'are lucky to have lodgings. I'm told many houses are full up."

Resuming his seat, Liam admitted that it had been difficult. "I stopped at three places before I could find a room."

"It is the king's illness," Cade explained. Torquay was the royal capital. "Many are come to pray for his health—or to politick against its failing." His tone left no doubt as to his low opinion of the latter.

"Is he so bad as that?" The king had taken ill early in the fall, but word had not reached the Southern Tier that it was anything serious. "They were calling it a temporary indisposition in Southwark."

Frowning darkly, Cade shook his head. "It's more than that. How much more, none can say. Yet the carrion-eaters gather, to pick at his bones ere he's even dead."

If it's that bad, I'm surprised I got a room anywhere. Nicanor IV had no heirs; his death would bring pretenders and contestants for the throne from every corner of the kingdom. "I wondered why there were so many people on the Stair this morning."

"The Stair?" Cade jerked in his seat, startled. "You were on the Flying Stair this morning?"

Liam hesitated, surprised at the scholar's reaction. "Yes. From the City Below. We only docked today. I had to wait for the third ascent, or I would have been here sooner."

Wincing, Cade relaxed and settled himself, rearranging his leg on the footstool. "You must excuse me, Quaestor. The gout. Now, you say you only docked this day? And came directly here? Stopping nowhere on the way? Your despatch is admirable; the Duke will be pleased. But wait—you stopped at an inn. For long?"

Some of Liam's old student-feelings crept back, and his voice sounded defensive in his own ears. "Just long enough to secure a room and drop off my bags."

Cade nodded judiciously, as if that were the correct answer, and referred again to the letter in his lap. "The Duke notes here that y'have a familiar. And yet he asserts y'are not a wizard. Is it so?"

"It is." He cleared his throat, definitely feeling like a student. Cade's tone reminded him of the question-and-answer sessions his tutors used to impose to test his mastery of their lessons. "I inherited him from a wizard, but I am not one myself." He saw no point in mentioning that he had not received the inheritance entirely willingly—that the dragon had bound itself to him after its former master's murder— and the scholar did not seem overly interested in the circumstances, in any case.

"Hm. And is he with you?"

"He's waiting outside." Liam made a vague gesture.

"Ah. He must attract a deal of attention."

In fact, his familiar had done just that on his trip up from the City Below, Torquay's port. Liam had expected the opposite—mages were almost as common in the capital as scholars—but people had stared as he went by with the tiny dragon on his shoulder. "He does, as a matter of fact. Which I thought strange, I have to say. When I was here, you saw wizards and familiars on every street."

Again, Cade gave him an approving nod. "Aye, they were wont to be, until only a sevennight ago. But a Convocation's been called, by that Magister of Harcourt, Escanes. They've all gone to Caernarvon to hammer out their differences. Few are left in Torquay, and those only apprentices. So the world sees a familiar, and with him what must be a wizard, and wonders why y'are not in Caernarvon."

Put that way, Liam could understand the stares. He wanted to ask more about the Convocation—they were rare among wizards—but Cade was rattling the letter again.

"If you'd go unnoticed, leave your familiar at your lodgings or, better still, on your ship. And now I notice one last thing in the Duke's missive. He says y'have a packet for me."

"Oh yes," Liam said, remembering the paper-wrapped tube the Duke had pressed on him before his departure. He patted his chest, where it had rested for the past ten days, found nothing, and froze, one hand over his heart. *Hello.* Panic rose up briefly, then ebbed when he looked down at his hand and saw the green wool of his tunic. *It's in your coat, fool.* "I don't have it," he began.

"What?" Cade started, upsetting his gouty leg. He cried out and fell back into his chair, writhing in pain. Through gritted teeth, he asked, "You have it not?"

"No no no," Liam blurted, on his feet now, astonished at the scholar's reaction. He spread his hands in supplication. "Don't worry—I have it, I have it. It's in my coat. Your serving woman—"

"Fetch it!"

Liam hopped and raced out of the study, into the entrance hall of the scholar's small house. Cade's serving woman had taken his wet coat when he arrived, promising to dry it. *Where is she?* Beside a narrow staircase, an even narrower corridor led to the back of the house; he hurried down it, threw open the door at the far end— and heaved a sigh of relief, seeing his coat spread by the kitchen fireplace.

"Forgot something," he muttered to the serving woman, and went to the coat, grabbing the cloth and sighing again when he felt the familiar lump. He dug into the pocket—cunningly inserted into the breast by a clever tailor—retrieved the paper packet, and hurried back to the study. Cade had recovered from his start, and nodded graciously as he took the paper-wrapped tube.

"You needs must excuse me," he said. "It is a mere trifle the Duke was kind enough to send—a mere trifle, yet I had promised it to a friend, and would not disappoint him."

If that's how he gets over a mere trifle, Liam thought as he resumed his seat, *I'd hate to see how he'd act with something important.* Aloud, he said, "It's my fault entirely. I kept it in my coat, and forgot to take it out when I came in."

Cade hardly heard him. The packet was a cylinder the size of a man's index finger, wrapped in plain paper twisted at both ends and tied off with string. With greedy fingers, the scholar loosened the string and parted the paper just enough so that he—but not Liam—could see the contents.

Curious, but not too curious, Liam asked, "Is everything all right?"

The scholar smiled. "Aye," he breathed. "All's well. All's well indeed." He grew brisk suddenly, straightening in his chair, retying the paper. "I needs must beg a favor of you, Quaestor. My leg will not suffer much movement, and this must be delivered to my friend—the one to whom it was promised. Would you be so kind as to take it for me?"

Liam hesitated, thinking of the weather, then said, "Of course, Master Cade."

Smiles wreathed the scholar's face. "Ah, it's good in you, Quaestor. Passing good. I could send it with a street boy, but they're not to be trusted, and I would that my friend have it presently. I shall direct you."

Presently? Now? Keeping a frown from his face grew increasingly difficult as the scholar gave him directions to his friend's house: it lay on the opposite side of the city, and would mean a long walk in the cold and wet. "And you'll ask for Master Bairth," Cade finished. "You'll know him for that he's stout, with a very full head of black hair and only the thinnest of mustaches—no beard, mind you, only mustaches. Further, he's a slight limp, a hesitation in his stride. An ague in his joints, see you, and unmistakable. If you'd give him this, I should be ever in your debt." He held out the packet.

"It's no problem at all," Liam said, thinking that it was but determined to be gracious. "No problem at all. I'll just get my coat." He rose and took the paper-covered cylinder. "When may I call on you again about my research?"

"Why, this even," Cade said, with an expansive gesture. "You'll dine with me, once y'have delivered the packet, and we may get straight to the work."

Liam bowed. "Then I shall return as soon as I can." He went to the door and stopped, his hand on the knob, when Cade called his name.

"If you would go unnoticed," the scholar again advised, "go without your familiar."

Liam gave a slow nod and smiled uncertainly, then left the study and closed the door behind him. *What a strange old man.* Shaking his head, he went to the kitchen to get his coat.

Practical men would never have built a city like Torquay, Liam's tutors at university liked to say, and they said it with a certain pride, as if they were related to the men who had raised the place. The founders were religious men, the heads of the Seventeen Houses who came to Taralon in the mists of antiquity and imposed a king on the land. Practicality called for a royal capital on a major river, or in a central location, or with easy access to farmland, or with a decent natural harbor. Religion, however—in the form of omen-reading hierarchs and

their attendant haruspices, oneiromancers and scapulo-
mancers—said the new king must live near a particular
vale on the eastern coast of the new kingdom, where an
insignificant river rose out of the mountains and flowed
a short course to the sea. The vale they named Rentrillian, and by the priests' command, every king of Taralon
was required to be both crowned and buried there.

Over centuries, a royal city was carved out of the
mountains along the path of the insignificant river—
deemed sacred and named the River Royal—and if the
work was near-impossible, that was no concern of the
priests. If the river ran through a steep and inaccessible
valley, if it plunged over a towering waterfall before
reaching the coast, if nothing seemed to thrive there but
a hardy and all-engulfing type of ivy—that was not their
concern. The Seventeen Houses and the monarch they
chose from their number were religious men, and built
the capital where their priests told them to, regardless of
the difficulties.

So there were three Torquays: holy Torquay, in the
Vale of Rentrillian, where the priests maintained the
tombs of kings and held coronations; royal Torquay, below Rentrillian and above the great waterfall, where the
kings lived between coronation and death, along with
the wizards and scholars and administrators who served
them; and the City Below, a seaport built at the foot of
the falls so that ships from around the kingdom could
supply the capital with all that it lacked, which was simply everything. To bring everything up from the City
Below, there were only two paths: the Flying Stair, rising beside the falls seven times daily, for rich or influ-
ential people and small but valuable cargos; and the
Grain Climb, a switchback road hacked from the mountains, up which strained a neverending line of wagons
filled with grain, meat, wine, beer, cloth, coal, timber,
tiles, paper, glass, incense—everything.

Another road had been built in a valley some miles

to the south of the city, but it ran from the coast by a roundabout route to Rentrillian, and commerce did not travel it: only pilgrims on their way to the holy vale.

This is the stupidest damned city, Liam thought, standing beneath the eaves of Cade's house. Part of the judgment was based on the gloomy weather, part on the baffling conversation he had just had, and still another on the fact that he would have to walk halfway across the city in a still-damp coat. But most of it was based on the evident madness of building a city in inaccessible mountains. *Stupidest damned city.*

He jammed his hands into his coat pockets, cringed at the touch of clammy wool, and gathered a name in his head, shoving it out, projecting it into the rain: *Fanuilh!*

A reply appeared in his mind, a solid block like a newborn idea. *Yes, master?*

Where are you?

Here, master. His familiar dropped to the street in front of him: a miniature black dragon, wings folding neatly along its back. It shook itself, shedding rain like a dog, looked up at him, and sneezed.

"Have you caught a cold?" In the year or so they had been linked as master and familiar—the year since the night he had stumbled upon the fresh corpse of its master, the night he began his career as one of the Duke's investigators—he had never seen the dragon sick.

It sneezed again. *There is water in my nose.*

Liam eyed the gray sky and the steady, relentless drizzle, his mouth twisting in distaste. *You should stay out of the rain.*

I was hoping to hunt.

I doubt you'll find much in the city except rats, he told the dragon. *And I don't think you should eat them. I'll get you something later, unless you're starving.*

Fanuilh ducked its wedgelike head under its wings, rubbing its snout. *No, master. I can wait.*

Good. He glowered at the sky. *Because now we have a little errand.* Then he remembered Cade's advice; strange as it was that he should make such a point of it, it was sensible. *Rather, I have a little errand. I have to deliver something to King's Vale, on the other side of the river. You should find someplace dry to hole up for a while. All right?*

Satisfied that its snout was dry, the dragon withdrew its head from beneath its wing and looked up at Liam. *Are you sure you would not like me to come with you?*

He knew why it asked. it wanted to be close, to be able to protect him. It was a remarkably useful creature, a stealthy and clever spy with a small arsenal of minor spells, fierce in its loyalty, and the longer he considered the price he paid for his inheritance—a small piece of his soul lodged in the dragon, a piece he could not honestly say he missed—the more convinced Liam grew that it was a lucky chance that had brought him to the dead wizard's home. His glower faded to a rueful smile. *No, thanks. No sense in both of us getting soaked. I'm only delivering a package, not going to war. I'll see you later.*

So thinking, he stepped out from beneath the eaves into the rain.

Cade lived in a small alley off Craft Street, the main artery of Artisans' Vale. There were six vales in Torquay, cut by small streams feeding into the River Royal; Artisans' was north of the river, and the house Liam was headed for lay in King's Vale, on the south side.

Finding the river was easy: he went to Craft Street and headed downhill on the slippery cobbles, passing blocks of workshops. Their windows glowed warm and inviting, and he hunched in his coat, cold and unhappy. He was soaked to the skin by the time he reached the

Embankment. Brushing back his wet hair, he scowled at the river, hoping to hire a boat.

Few were about on the Royal, which was swollen and running high with late fall rains, and those he could see already had passengers. He cupped his hands over his eyes and tried to see the far bank, but it was obscured by the drizzle. Cursing, he turned right and headed up the Embankment.

Stupidest damned city. He remembered the first time he had come to Torquay, fresh from the countryside. The city had thrilled him then—the famous ivy-covered collegia in Tower Vale; the elaborate palaces of lords and members of the royal family in King's Vale; the impossible geometries of the towers in Wizards'; the hundreds of boats plying the river—and as he cast back in his memory, it seemed as if the sun was always shining.

It wasn't that good, he told himself, splashing through a puddle on the Embankment. *It wasn't.* And yet he could not shake the feeling that it had been: that he would like nothing better than to be seventeen again, free and irresponsible and a student in Torquay, his father alive and Rhenford Keep still standing. *I'd study harder,* he decided. *I'd go to more lectures. And drink less.*

Scowling, he shook his head, spattering rain from his hair and driving the idea away. He was not seventeen, his father was dead, and Rhenford Keep had long since been reduced to ashes. *You're here now, wet and miserable, errand-boy to the Duke of the Southern Tier. Get used to it.*

West on the Embankment he went, passing Gown Street, the entrance to Tower Vale. There were two large taverns at the foot of the street, the Jug on the left and the Bag of Nails on the right. His mood lightened at the sight of the familiar signs, and he thought fleetingly about dropping into the Bag to get warm and have a quick one; the Bag, because that was where he had gone as a student, it being customary for each collegium to drink at the tavern on their side of Gown Street.

Talk about stupid. He grinned at himself, thinking of his primary badge of success as a student: having been thrown out of the Bag not once or twice but four times. He shivered then, recalling the hangovers that had accompanied each ejection, and decided against stopping in.

Ten minutes farther on, a familiar shape emerged from the drizzle: the graceful arch of the Halfcrown Bridge. Liam patted the lump in his jacket pocket and quickened his step. The story ran that crossing had once cost the bridge's name; some time in the distant past, a munificent king bought it from the original builder and made passage free. Twin busts of the current monarch adorned both ends, and Liam rubbed the stone for luck, as everyone did—the statues were replaced each year, on Coronation Day.

The bridge was just wide enough for two on foot, and was usually busy; with the dirty weather, Liam had it almost entirely to himself, passing a single man as he crossed. Rain pocked the river far below, the sound strangely flat. What light there was, was fading: the afternoon waning, the clouds shading from dull gray to black.

On the far bank he turned west again, following the Royal to King's Vale, another fifteen minutes' walk. He was so far beyond soaked that he gave up huddling in his coat and walked freely, head up, the rain beating against his face. His nose ran and he wiped water from his eyes every few paces. The only consolation lay in his well-made boots: his feet stayed dry. *I have to get a proper cloak, an oilskin. This is ridiculous.*

Ridiculous, but not to last much longer: he could see the mammoth columns that marked the Processional, the main street of King's, and gathered around each a dozen or so people, shrouded in cowls and hoods against the

rain. Braziers lay at the foot of each free-standing column, a yard across and sheltered beneath wide awnings,
the glow of the coals painting the huddled groups orange. Liam heard their muttered prayers as he came up.

For Nicanor. He paused at the edge of the nearer
group to bow his head and add a wordless prayer, a
general hope for the king's recovery. Then he hurried
on, anxious to finish his errand, past the columns and
up the Processional. Even from the very bottom of the
vale, he could see the palace up at the top: thousands of
lights in the windows, twinkling through the drizzle. In
between were the houses of the wealthy; miniature palaces set behind ivy-coated walls. Rainwater foamed
down the gutters.

Cade's friend lived high in the vale, only three streets
below the palace. Liam climbed up the Processional,
counted off the intersections and turned, counted off two
smaller streets—and found the sizable stone house in the
middle of the block that Cade had described. Lanterns
cast a pool of light around the entrance, a welcome oasis
in the dark street, illuminating the bright red door and
the mounting block carved like a cresting wave.

Quite a house, Liam thought, jogging the last few
yards to the shelter of the doorway. *Cade's friend must
be someone at court.* A bronze knocker in the shape of
a porpoise hung in the middle of the door; above it was
a family crest worked in enamel: four porpoises on a
blue field, beneath the chevron that indicated royal service. Impressed, he shook himself out, trying to shed the
worst of the rain, slicked down his hair and wiped his
face, snuffled, and knocked. Then he waited, hopping
from foot to foot and blowing on his fingers to stay
warm. He was on the verge of knocking again when a
servant in blue-and-white livery opened the door.

"Yes?" The man looked him up and down, obviously
unimpressed. Tall and cadaverously thin, with a promi-
nent knot in his throat, he pursed his lips and waited.

"I've brought a package for Master Bairth," Liam said, straightening his shoulders and trying to look presentable, though the man's attitude annoyed him. "From Master Ossian Cade."

"Ah. Come in."

Liam thought it strange that it was the second name that gained him admission, but he was too eager to be done with his errand to complain. He stepped past the servant into a long, wide hall. Tapestries hung on the whitewashed walls, and a stand just by the front door held a number of hand-carved walking sticks, two with silver handles. Otherwise the hall was empty, doors to other rooms lining each side.

"Your coat." The thin servant held out his hand as if bored with the proceedings.

"I'll only be a minute," Liam explained, but the servant tapped his foot.

"You drip," he said, and Liam saw that he had, indeed, created a puddle on the red tile floor. He gave a guilty smile and shrugged out of his sodden coat, remembering at the last second to retrieve the packet before handing over the dripping mess.

With long-suffering patience, the servant dipped his eyes at Liam's belt. "Your blade."

It was only a small knife—he had never done anything more dangerous with it than spread butter—and Liam balked. "I'll only be a minute." *You swollen-headed ass.*

"You may not go before Master Bairth armed."

For a long moment Liam locked eyes with the servant, thinking that he should just hand over the packet and tell him to take it to Master Bairth himself. He wanted to—and then thought of Cade's description of the man. *I should give it to him myself. Servants have stolen things before.* He squinted at the irritating doorman. *And he's just the type.*

Making an angry sound in the back of his throat, he

drew the knife from its sheath and presented it hilt first.
The servant took it with his fingertips, as he had the
coat. "Third on your left." He indicated the door with
his eyes and waited, staring coldly, while Liam went
down the hall.

At the right door, he turned back and waved to the
servant, who stood with his coat and knife held at arm's
length.

"Thanks for all your help," Liam said, opened the
door, and stepped through.

The richly appointed chamber was empty, though a
wood fire burned in the fireplace and a cup of wine stood
on the oak writing table in the middle of the room.

Alone, Liam inspected the room with a critical eye,
and gave a low whistle of approval. The tapestries here
were better than those in the hall, the scenes more intri-
cate and colorful, and there was even a rug on the tile
floor in front of the fire. Beeswax candles in silver candlesticks lit the room, eliciting a mellow glow from the
polished panelling.

Cade certainly knows some interesting people.

He walked over to the fireplace. Wood fires were expensive in Torquay, since it was easier to haul coal up
the Grain Climb. He basked in the glow of the flames
and slipped the packet into the pocket of his breeches,
the better to warm both hands. The heat slowly seeped
through him, and though he was aware that he was being
kept waiting, he could not find it in him to care. *As long
as they have wood, I can wait.*

Even as he thought it, however, he heard a lock click
and spun guiltily away from the fire. There was a small
door in the far corner of the room, set flush with the
panelling so that he had not noticed it. It opened, and a
man stepped through.

He wore a snowy linen shirt and a slashed satin jacket
of canary yellow with hose to match; short, not thin but

by no means stout, his hair thin and receding deeply, a pointed goatee on his chin. He gave a friendly smile, and Liam frowned.

"I am Master Bairth," the man said. "You have something for me, I believe?"

But does he even limp?

Seeing Liam's hesitation, the man in yellow raised a hand to his lips, as if embarrassed. "I am rude. You have come a long way in the rain. Please, seat yourself." He indicated a chair in front of the writing desk.

And walked across the room to take the chair behind the table himself, his stride smooth and even.

CHAPTER 2

"MAY I OFFER you something?" the man who called himself Master Bairth asked, as he sat behind the table. "Wine, perhaps? Spiced and hot? It will lift the chill from your bones."

What's going on here? Liam took the seat opposite, using the business of sitting, of arranging his legs and making himself comfortable, to cover his confusion. For a moment he doubted his own memory; perhaps he had misheard Cade, or misunderstood his description. *No, you heard right. And this isn't the man. So—what now?*

The man in yellow wore an expectant smile, waiting for an answer to the question Liam had not heard. He repeated himself finally, and Liam blinked several times.

"Oh, no, thank you, Master Bairth." *I'm just a messenger. Why is he offering me wine?*

"You're sure?" The man had a charming smile, and his voice was pleasant, cultivated. "Come, it will do you good," he cajoled. "You must have had a long journey, eh? From, eh—" He twirled his index finger, as if the name of the place was on the tip of his tongue, expecting Liam to fill in the gap.

Instinct prompted Liam's answer. "Harcourt," he lied.

Mild surprise registered on the face of the man in yellow. "Really? From what Ossian said, I thought you from the south. But then, your speech is Harcourt."

"Just outside Harcourt," Liam elaborated, mind racing futilely. The man did not match Cade's description, but he seemed to know Liam's errand, and it was the right house.

"Ah." Another charming smile, as if Liam's exact origins interested him. "But the item you've brought me is from the south, yes? From Vespasianus?"

"Yes." The Duke's name startled him, and the answer slipped out before he could think.

The man in yellow sat up, his hand stealing to his chin to stroke his goatee. "You have it with you?"

What's going on? Liam almost ground his teeth, frustrated, unsure how to answer. *He knows why you're here.* He gave a slow nod, and the man across the table beamed.

"Excellent. I am relieved to hear it." He picked up a small silver bell from the tabletop and shook it. "We'll have some wine." The words were barely out of his mouth before the small door opened and another man entered the room. He wore a plain gray tunic and leather leggings, not livery, but he bowed like a servant. "Ah, Aldyne," the man in yellow said, about to give an order, then tapped his forehead and looked back at Liam. "I forget myself—you said you did not want wine. Excuse me." He waved a hand at Aldyne. "Never mind."

Aldyne bowed again and stepped back, but did not leave—he took up a position by the door. He had blond hair and a close-trimmed, reddish beard; an unremarkable face; broad, muscular shoulders tapering down to a small waist; and a short sword strapped on his right hip.

Cursing silently, Liam gathered a thought and projected. *Fanuilh!*

The man in yellow steepled his fingers. "Now, where were we?"

Yes, master?

"Harcourt," Liam stammered. "Or the south. I can't recall." *I think I may be in trouble.*

"Harcourt." The man in yellow chuckled. "Or the south. Yes, I catch it, I catch it. Very good."

I shall come at once. The dragon could find him wherever he was through their shared soul.

"Very good, indeed. May I see it?"

Liam faked stupidity. "See what, Master Bairth?"

The man's polite smile never wavered. "The item you've brought, my friend."

In the corner, Aldyne stirred a little, twisting his shoulders as if to work out a kink.

"Of course, of course." Liam patted himself down from shoulders to waist, as if he had pockets everywhere, and let his jaw drop. "I can't seem to—" Then he snapped his fingers. "I've left it in my coat. I'll just go fetch it."

He stood, and the man in yellow held up a hand to stop him. "No need." Barely raising his voice, he called, "Varro!"

The door behind Liam opened, and the thin servant from the hall entered.

The man in yellow smiled but all the charm was gone, and his eyes never left Liam's as he asked, "Is it in his coat?"

The thin servant spoke: "No, my lord."

Mock surprise washed over the man in yellow's face. "No? You must have overlooked it on your person, sir."

Fanuilh, things have gotten much worse here. Liam glanced around the room, gauging his chances. *Chances of what?* The man in yellow was seated, and thus no threat, but Aldyne had closed in, a hard, ready light in his eyes; worse, the thin servant was directly behind him. Liam sidestepped, trying to ease into a position where he could see both men.

I have just reached the river, master.

The thought was still fresh in his head, distracting, when the servant grabbed him from behind. Liam struggled but the man's arms were like steel. When Liam finally subsided, the servant said, "I have him, master." His breath stank, and was hot on Liam's ear.

"What's this all about?" Liam demanded, aiming for outrage but hearing a tremor of fear instead. "How dare you!"

The man in yellow rose lazily from his seat and gestured. "His pockets."

Aldyne strolled over, a sad smile playing on his lips. "Too easy, too easy," he muttered.

Liam cursed him. Aldyne stiffened and his arm shot out, snapping Liam's head back with a quick punch.

Pain exploded in his jaw, and with it the reality of the situation—how easily he had been caught, how little chance he had of leaving the room alive. *That sword's not for spreading butter.*

Aldyne put his hand on the hilt and warned, "There's more, if you would."

Liam worked his jaw, tested his teeth. *All there.* "No, thank you. I'm full."

"Wise, wise," the man in yellow chuckled. Aldyne began patting Liam down, and the small door in the corner burst open.

The man who came stumbling in fit Cade's description of Master Bairth—stout, black hair and mustache— but one eye was swollen shut, blood trickled down his cheek, and he reeled so much, unsteady on his legs, that it was impossible to tell if he had a limp.

"Murderers!" he shouted, slurring the word as if he were drunk. "Assassins!"

The man in yellow snapped, "What's this?" and Aldyne sprang away from Liam, crossed the room in a few steps, drawing his sword as he went. The real Master Bairth seemed not to notice: he caught sight of Liam, wrapped in Varro's embrace, and wailed:

"We're undone!"

The next few seconds passed too quickly for Liam, too many things happening at once: the man in yellow shouting, "Finish him, fool!" and Master Bairth wailing and Aldyne driving his blade deep into Master Bairth's

stomach. The servant shifted his grip slightly. Liam
gaped; Master Bairth stopped wailing and saw blood
spilling from his gut; he gasped and stumbled; he swept
Aldyne aside in a burst of strength, the blade coming
free, his hand going to his wound; he stumbled forward,
gasping for air; stumbled forward, impossible steps,
gasping. Varro shifted his grip again as the dying man
tottered toward them, fell, crashed against Liam, Liam
helpless, pinned, Master Bairth's blood and bulk crashing against him, and the three men fell back to the wall.

A few seconds, no more.

The servant grunted under the impact and Liam panicked, snapped his head back, smashing Varro's nose.
The servant's grip loosened and Liam thrashed, freed his
arms, shoved Master Bairth into Aldyne, coming up now
with his sword held high.

Liam spun, grabbed the shouting servant—there was
blood on his face—and threw him at Aldyne too,
jumped to the door, tore it open, and scrambled into the
hall.

Behind, shouts and curses, but he did not hear them,
only the blood in his ears and his own frantic, hissing
curses. He dashed the length of the hall, fumbled with
the door latch for terrible seconds, staining the metal red.
His fingers were tacky with Bairth's blood, and the latch
clicked.

He threw the door open and ran out into the rain.

Other houses had put out lanterns as night came on,
lonely outposts in the dark street. Liam ran right, away
from the Processional, toward the nearest corner. His
footsteps were precarious, the wet cobbles invisible and
treacherous beneath him, and he concentrated on letting
his feet touch the ground for the briefest time possible.
Fall and you're dead.

There were shouts in the street behind him before he
reached the corner; he ran to it, caught the edge of the

building, and paused for a quick look back. Aldyne was
first out the door, his sword aimed directly at Liam,
pointing him out for the others, the servant and the man
in yellow both with swords in their hands.

Where did they come from? There had been no swords
in the hall and none in the room, apart from Aldyne's.

"There!" Brandishing his blade, the servant charged,
and Liam waited for a long second because the others
did not. Aldyne spoke, received a nod from the man in
yellow, and set off in the other direction, toward the
Processional.

Circling, Liam thought, and pushed himself away
from the corner, running again, uphill now, deeper into
King's Vale. *He'll circle around the block, keep me from
the Processional.* He ran, thinking wistfully of the praying people at the foot of the main road, as if they could
save him.

Fanuilh!

There were other ways out of the vale, smaller streets
that would take him back down to the river. He ran
uphill, legs pumping against the steepening slope, and
came to another intersection. A lane opened on his left;
he ducked into it, going farther from the Processional.

I am coming, master. Five minutes, perhaps.

High, ivied walls all around, with only the occasional
lit doorway to orient him. Rain pelted his skin, soaked
his tunic, the wet sleeves flapping, weighing down his
arms. He ran on, his breathing ragged already, the air
cold in his lungs; his nose ran again, and he sniffled and
panted like a sobbing child.

There had to be another way to the river, but none
opened off the street he was on—the lantern-lit door-
ways stretched out ahead with no sign of interruption.
He lengthened his stride, running flat out, knowing he
could not keep up the pace for long.

The road sloped up, and a terrible thought hit him: if
there were no other streets, he would eventually come

up against the wall of the vale, the mountain-spur that separated King's Vale from Wizards' to the east. A dead end, then, with the servant and the man in yellow blocking the only way out.

There'll be another, he told himself, his legs beginning to ache as the street pitched up and up. He raised his head and there, ahead of him, a hundred yards farther on, the lights stopped at a blank wall. *Dead end.* He had run to the edge of the vale and the spur loomed overhead, a denser blackness against the black sky.

"We have him!"

He could not tell which of his pursuers shouted. He cursed and pressed on, thinking of a stand, a fight. *You won't last long.* The last bit of street was practically a climb, angling up to meet the spur, and he took it bent almost double, feet scrabbling on the rain-slick cobbles. There was a house to his left with colored lanterns on either side of the door, one green and one red.

He ran out of street, ran into the sheer stone wall of the spur, stopped himself with his hands and cursed, spun around to see the servant and the man in yellow slow as they passed a lit doorway. The servant huffed and puffed, but the man in yellow was grinning.

Liam bared his teeth at them, snarled, swiped a hand across his upper lip. *Don't want to die with a runny nose.*

The man in yellow stopped and put a hand on his servant's shoulder. "They come out by Tinian's; you know the place. Be quick, and we'll have him surrounded." The servant nodded and ran back the way they had come.

"You have me surrounded now, idiot," Liam panted, watching the servant go, and then, understanding, looked around himself more carefully.

"You'll not reach the bottom before Varro does," the man in yellow called. He was out of the light of the doorway, approaching through darkness. "Give in now, and it'll be quick."

A stairway in a corner to the south, barely three feet wide, carved between the last house on the road and mountain-spur. Dark as a mine tunnel, it was nonetheless the most beautiful thing Liam had ever seen, and he ran to it. Behind him, the man in yellow cursed.

There were no lights on the stairway and the steps themselves were uneven, so that he stumbled and nearly pitched headlong, recovered by pressing his hands to the cold stone that walled him in. Again he ran lightly, fingers trailing the walls, trusting to luck and speed, trying to ignore an image of himself lying sprawled at the foot of the stairs, neck broken.

There was light below him, a house door, but he could not tell how far below. He slipped, his feet shooting up, and dropped heavily on his back, the breath rushing from his lungs. Wheezing for air, he forced himself to his feet, starting shakily down the stairs again.

"Stop, man!" The false Bairth, his voice seemingly right in Liam's ear, and fear set him jumping, three or four steps at a time, too many. *You'll break your neck.* Three and four, tensing in the darkness with each leap, always on the verge of losing control, of falling. His arms scraped against the walls, shoulders struck with bruising force, he bounced from side to side—and finally fell because there were no more steps, only flat street, the stairs ended and his feet tangled up.

He sprawled onto the cobblestones with an explosive grunt and rolled over, scuttling on his elbows away from the stairs. There were lights here, two house doors close by, and from the ground he saw the man in yellow step out of the narrow stairway, sword angled down at him.

This is it? It was impossible, unimaginable. *Not on the ground.* He kept crawling away, crawled into a puddle. He could not seem to get his legs underneath him.

"My lord!" The servant calling, still a good way down the road.

"Tripped yourself up, have you?" The man in yellow closed the distance in two long strides and put the tip of his blade to Liam's throat. "You're not very good at this."

Liam goggled, incredulous. *This is it?* He could think nothing else.

The man slicked back his thinning hair with his free hand, grinned down at him. "Still, I'll be quick." Abruptly his eyes rolled up in his head, showing only white, and he slumped down on top of Liam. His blade slid wide, clattered to the ground.

Master? I am here.

Fanuilh hovered just overhead, marking time with downbeats of its wings.

Liam shoved the man in yellow aside and staggered to his feet, cast about for the lost sword. *Where's the other one?* He found the sword and snatched it up.

Down the street, master.

The servant was pounding on the door of a house a little way down the street, terrified eyes fixed on Fanuilh. "Please, help! Murder! Murder! They've murdered my lord!"

Slim-bladed and delicately balanced, the sword felt good in Liam's grasp. He hefted it, glaring down on the man in yellow. What looked like a sheath was stuck through the man's belt.

"Shut him up," he said, and Fanuilh darted away toward the servant. Liam bent and tugged at the sheath; it came free easily, and he saw that the sheath was wooden. *The walking sticks.*

The servant stopped shouting for help.

Liam suddenly remembered the packet and groped frantically at his pockets, then breathed in relief: still there.

Someone opened the door the servant had been

pounding on, and cried out at the man lying on his step, apparently dead. He was not dead, Liam knew, only asleep, put down by the same spell Fanuilh had used on the man in yellow.

I should finish him off, he thought, glancing at the false Bairth. But other voices had joined the first and people were spilling into the street, surrounding the sleeping servant. Three, four people, and then a man pointed in his direction.

"Look there. The murderer!"

Master, Fanuilh thought, *perhaps we should leave.*

The dragon was right—holding a sword in bloody hands, he would not be able to convince anyone that *he* was the victim—yet he could not tear his eyes away from the man in yellow. *I should finish him off.*

Master, the spell will not last long.

"Stop him! Stop, you!"

The man in yellow stirred at his feet.

Liam shook his head, growling, and ran back to the steps, disappearing into the darkness.

Plodding stolidly through King's Vale, Liam checked each street before he turned onto it and skirted the occasional pool of light from house windows as he made his careful, roundabout way down to the river.

If the rainy night made it practically impossible to see, it also made it impossible to be seen, and Liam took some small consolation from that. He shivered constantly, the sodden wool of his tunic more burden than protection; he was sore from head to toes, and in between he pictured his back as one enormous purple-yellow bruise. In the cold air, all the aches seemed to penetrate deep into his bones.

Small consolation, but he took it, along with his other: that he was still alive. *That's not so small. That's pretty big, considering.* He summoned the concentration to project: *Fanuilh.*

The dragon was scouting ahead for him, flying over the rooftops of the vale to check that the way was clear. *Yes, master?*

For back there. Thank you.

There was a long pause before the dragon replied. *You're welcome, master.* It let a shorter pause go by before asking: *What will we do now?*

Liam took a deep breath. He had been thinking about that very question, and had come to a few conclusions. *We'll need to find a Peacemaker and report Master Bairth's death.*

The Peacemakers were Torquay's constabulary, a force of a thousand men famous both for their black-and-white tunics and their incorruptible devotion to justice. They were named after the god of law—a bit of near-blasphemy the regent who chartered them five hundred years before had skirted by ordering the god to be worshipped locally under a different name, that of the Divine Judge—and their commander was called the Pacifex. Any doubts about the presumptious names had long since disappeared, as they had developed a sterling reputation for impartiality. During Liam's days as a student, the Pacifex had been a man named Hierbold Warden, and he had caused quite a stir by arresting a royal favorite, a rich and arrogant prince, for beating a beggar. Liam wondered if Warden was still the Pacifex, then shivered, and put aside thoughts of the Peacemakers.

Before we see them, I want to talk to Cade. I have a lot of questions for him. His fist clenched in his pocket, wrapped around the paper-covered tube. *A great many questions. We'll start with what this is,* he decided, squeezing the cylinder in his pocket. He had not opened it yet, and would not until he reached someplace dry and well-lit, where he could examine it at leisure. Besides, he had a vague idea that exposing it to the rain might damage it; he did not want to risk something that had already cost a man's life.

And very nearly yours, too. He was angry, furious in a stern, implacable way that was only exacerbated by his shivering and his bruises. Each discomfort reminded him that he had been used, treated like an errand boy, and sent ignorant into danger. *I'm no errand boy.* He was grinding his teeth by the time he reached the river, and he could feel the pressure all through his head as he waited in a dark corner while Fanuilh flew ahead. After a long minute the dragon promised him that the Embankment was safe; forcing the muscles in his jaw to loosen up, he stepped out from his sheltered corner and crossed to the river.

At the foot of the Processional, across from the columns and their brazier-limned groups of the prayerful, were the royal water stairs: a set of wide, white marble steps cut through the bank, their broad stone bannisters ornamented with dragons and lions. To north and south were the public stairs, plain stone, narrower and steeper, but blessed with canvas shelters and benches, so that commoners could wait for a boat without getting wet. The king would have servants with canopies and parasols—and would never have to wait.

Liam slumped onto one of the benches, keeping an eye on the river for passing boats while he combed water from his hair and wiped his nose on his sleeve. Fanuilh flew a wide circle above the shelter, watching for the man in yellow and his minions.

I probably shouldn't stay here. He was tired, though, cold and hurt, close to exhaustion, and feeling stubborn. *Let them find me.* He had Fanuilh with him, and the sword-stick. Sniffling, he gripped the wooden sheath and slipped the slim blade free. The steel would probably snap if it met a larger sword, but he liked the gleam of it in the light of the shelter's single lantern, and its tapering, wicked point. He made a few experimental passes, and the edge whistled nicely. *Let them come.*

They did not; nor did a boat, not for almost fifteen

minutes, during which he sat on the bench, shivering and staring dully at the sword in his hand. His mind skipped from idea to idea—the angry speech he would make to Cade; the way the man in yellow had stood over him; Fanuilh's uncomplaining loyalty, the sword-stick; Master Bairth stumbling; the letter of introduction; the cylinder in his pocket—but he could not concentrate on any of them. By the time a boat pulled into view, stroking down out of the west with a lantern bobbing on its high sternpost, he had given up trying to order his thoughts, and simply let them whirl.

"For hire," the waterman called through the rain, angling his boat in toward the bank. "For hire."

Liam climbed to his feet. "Here."

The man let his boat drift closer to the stairs and twisted in his seat to get a good look at his potential customer. He did not like what he saw. "Whither going?"

"Artisans' Vale."

The waterman backed oars, slowing down short of the stairs. "That's a long pull. Four princes. Have you coin?"

The suspicion was an insult; Liam muttered under his breath and flexed his numb fingers before reaching into the pouch at his belt for the four silver coins. He held them up and the waterman squinted, nodded, and drew his boat up to the stairs.

A hemisphere of wicker covered the passenger seat and Liam crawled beneath it with a sour grunt. The waterman sat opposite him, pulling out to the middle of the river with long strokes. He wore a voluminous cloak, mostly patches, with a deep hood, and over the hood a straw hat with a wide, ragged brim. He rowed easily, almost unconsciously, though he had an old man's face, lined and sagging and toothless.

Ordinarily, watermen on the Royal pretended not to notice their passengers, fixing their eyes on the river or the sky, but Liam's stared at him unabashedly, sucking his gums. The staring annoyed Liam, and he frowned and deliberately looked away. When they were out in the middle, with the current working for them, the waterman said, "You ought to have a cloak, master."

A mild observation, but it tapped Liam's cold anger. "You didn't ask if I had a cloak," he snapped. "You only asked if I had four princes."

The waterman shrugged without interrupting his stroke. "A cloak's good against the rain."

The shrug made him even angrier. "Yes, well, I had one, but I lost it playing forfeits up at the palace. And I thought it would be just delightful to walk home in the rain!" He did not know what had prompted him to include the palace in his sarcasm, but it brought a dark look from the waterman.

"They're not playing at forfeits in the palace now," he said, bringing Liam up short.

The king may be dying, you idiot. "No," he said, shaking his head. "No, I suppose not. I shouldn't have said that." He took a deep breath. "I was robbed. My jacket was stolen. I'm upset. Sorry." He offered a silent prayer for the king.

The waterman said nothing about his apology; he stopped staring, though, and when they had passed beneath Halfcrown Bridge, he pointed his chin at Liam's seat. "Bottle under there. For the cold."

Liquor of some kind, it burned going down and made Liam cough. The warmth in his stomach was worth it, and he thanked the waterman, who shrugged. After another small sip he replaced the bottle under the seat and leaned back, feeling better than he had in hours. He was still cold, still aching, and the liquor had provided only the illusion of warmth; nonetheless, he felt clearheaded, better equipped to deal with his situation. An irresistible idea occurred to him: there was a wineshop on Craft Street, almost exactly halfway between the river and Cade's alley. If he stopped there, he could have something hot to drink—the image of a cup of mulled wine appeared in his head, spice-fragrant steam misting above it—and get warm for just a few minutes. It would give him time to calm down and collect his thoughts.

No sense crashing in on Cade like this. You'll say something rash. Not that he had given up on his determination to know exactly what he had been thrust into, not at all; it was just that he knew he would get further if he was calm.

Mulled wine, and maybe something to eat, too. He cast back, trying to remember, and realized that he had eaten his last meal aboard the *Trade's Increase,* in the City Below, just after sunrise. If he stopped at the wineshop, he could get something to eat and a cup of mulled wine to warm him up—and also have a chance to examine the package. He clenched his fist, reassured himself of its presence. *I should definitely look at that before I see Cade. And have a quick cup.*

His mind was made up by the time the boat pulled up alongside the Artisans' Vale water stairs, and he gave the waterman five silver coins before jumping to the bank.

"Here now," the man said. "It's but four."

"For the drink," Liam called over his shoulder, thinking of a different drink. "Thanks."

The drizzle was as cold as before, and his legs were stiff from sitting in the boat, but he pushed ahead quickly, drawn on by the image in his head. *Just one. A fast one.* A small doubt nagged at him, a vague feeling that he should not stop, that he should go straight to Cade's, but the appeal of mulled wine was too much.

Fanuilh flew overhead, invisible in the rainy night, and Liam explained his plan. It raised no objections, and said that it would find a dry spot overlooking the street to keep watch.

You're the best familiar I've ever had, you know that? Yes, master.

Up ahead, he could see the sign of the wineshop, and warm yellow light in the two windows that flanked its door. He jogged the last few yards, threw open the door and ran in.

The wineshop was everything Liam had hoped for: dry and stuffy and hot, with two large fireplaces roaring at either end of the main room, and the smell of spices and wine in the air. Standing by the door, he sluiced water from his arms and chest and head, then threaded his way between the tables to the small bar at the back.

Eyes followed him as he went, and the clientele seemed too quiet. For a moment a wild thought flashed through his head—*You're covered with blood!*—but he dispelled it with a quick glance: the rain had taken care of that, washed the traces from his hands and stained his entire tunic so dark even he could not tell if anything remained of Master Bairth. *They're artisans. Sober, serious men. You're soaking wet, cloakless, and carrying a walking stick. Of course they're staring.*

Emboldened, he stepped to the bar and produced a couple of coins. "Have you any mulled wine?"

The barkeep, as sober and serious as his customers, took the coins and produced a wooden cup from beneath the counter. "The pot's on the hob. You serve yourself." A low sussurus of resumed conversation started up around the room.

Cup in hand, Liam made his way to the fireplace the barkeep had indicated and ladled his cup full from the iron pot. Steam misted over the cup, and the rich, heady smell of the spices made him sigh. He found himself a seat near the fire, on a bench whose far end was occupied by two middle-aged men with the overdeveloped forearms of smiths.

He savored his first three or four mouthfuls, the cold retreating from his bones, slowly sagging with relief. When he had finished half the cup, a blissful smile on his face, he set it down on the floor at his feet and pulled the package from his pocket. The paper was wet but not ruined, and he held the cylinder down between his knees and out of sight while he untied the string around one end. He peeled the paper halfway open, saw what was within and frowned.

A slim phial of ruby-colored glass, encased in an openwork frame of black metal. The frame completely covered the bottom half of the phial; four lozenge-shaped windows in the metal revealed the upper half. The stopper was a circle of the same metal, with six tapering points rising from its top; it looked like a crown. There was liquid inside, dyed red by the glass.

Still frowning, he tugged the stopper from the phial and bent his nose to it. There was no odor. He capped it again—the base of the crown fit snug and tight in the tube—and closed the paper. *Not perfume. A potion? Poison?* More likely a potion, he decided; poisons were not so rare that men needed to kill for them.

Baffled and disappointed, Liam slipped it back into his pocket and picked up his wine. Conversation had died again, and he saw a man standing by the bar, raising his cup. He wore a white smock daubed with paint, and there was paint on his fingers.

"The king, gentlemen."

Cups went up all around the room; "His health," in a ragged chorus. Liam joined in and bowed his head afterward, as everyone else did.

The painter drained his cup and left, shrugging into a cloak covered in stray pigment. Liam drank his wine with less relish, mulling over the strange phial, and when he was done he shook himself and took his cup to the bar. *Only one. Time to see Cade.*

At the bar he raised his cup as the painter had. "The king."

"His health," the wineshop chorused. It was the custom in Torquay, an automatic gesture lent new meaning

by Nicanor's illness. *The king sick, and without heirs,*
Liam thought, draining the last of his wine and handing
the cup back to the barkeep. *No wonder they're so serious.*

He left the wineshop.

Cold again, hugging himself to contain the fleeting
warmth of the wine, he jogged through the drizzle up
Craft Street and turned into Cade's alley. Fanuilh flew
beside him, and it projected a picture of the strange
phial. His familiar did not recognize it.

That is not to say that it may not be magical, the
dragon lectured. *Or that the contents may not be a potion. I know of no potions that require a special container such as that, but the maker may simply have
desired to make an impression.* It went on, explaining
why the phial might be anything at all, and Liam finally
interrupted the flow of its thoughts with a raised hand.

Don't worry about it. Cade can tell us.

The scholar's house was a short distance ahead, light
pouring from all of its windows, and Liam suddenly
stopped short. There was a man standing by the front
door, holding a lantern. He wore a cloak composed of
four black and white squares in a checkerboard arrangement, and a tunic of the same pattern. His free hand
rested on the short truncheon thrust through his belt.

What's a Peacemaker doing here?

CHAPTER 3

THE PEACEMAKER HEARD Liam approaching and barked into the darkness, "Who passes?" He was young and alone on a dismal night, but he held himself with authority and his voice was firm.

Liam jogged into the pool of light cast by his lantern. "I'm a friend of Master Cade's," he said, suddenly anxious. "Is something wrong?"

The Peacemaker looked him up and down. "Your name?"

"Liam Rhenford. Is he all right? Can I speak to him?"

Ignoring his question, the Peacemaker held out a hand, indicating for him to stay where he was. "I'll fetch the Pacifex."

Liam's jaw dropped as the young constable disappeared into Cade's house. *The Pacifex is here? Oh gods, what's happened?* He could imagine, however—did imagine. *While I sat and waited for a boat. While I dawdled over a cup of wine.* He cursed, hoping it was not true. *But why else would the Pacifex be here?*

His certainty grew until Cade's door opened again; instead of the man he was expecting—*How old would Hierbold Warden be now?*—a woman in a blue fustian cloak beckoned him inside. "Come," she said. "Unless you prefer the rain."

"I need to see Master Cade," he said, hurrying in. The woman stood in the hall, allowing him to come only so far. Beyond her he could see the closed door of the scholar's study. "Has something happened to him?"

36

She blocked his way quite calmly, despite his obvious agitation. Her hair was white-blond, her skin pale, and her large eyes were a washed-out, faded blue. She seemed like a ghost, somehow insubstantial, except for her patient expression and matter-of-fact tone. "I've some questions first," she began.

"Has something happened to him?" Liam interrupted. *While I sat guzzling wine and drinking to the king's health.* "Is he all right?"

"Who are you, sir?"

"A friend of his," Liam replied, bouncing on his toes, desperate to know. "Look, it's very urgent that I know if he's all right."

"Who are you, sir?" She repeated the question, singularly unimpressed with his urgency.

Liam made an angry sound in the back of his throat and gripped the sword-stick in both hands. *She's not even a Peacemaker!* "This is stupid. The other man said he was going to get the Pacifex— is he still here? Can I speak with him?"

She cocked her head, puzzled by the question. "Speak with who?"

His hands twisted on the wooden sheath. "The Pacifex! Can I please speak to the Pacifex!"

The woman glanced to the ceiling for patience, and then threw the left side of her cloak back over her shoulder. Beneath was a black-and-white checkered tunic, and around her throat hung a medallion with a gold border around a circle quartered into wedges, two black and two white. "You *are* speaking to the Pacifex."

Liam goggled at the medallion, knowing it for a badge of office. He stammered for a few seconds, unsure what to think, and while he did the Peacemaker who had been outside the house came downstairs. The woman heard him, and spoke without taking her eyes off Liam.

"Did you find the lieutenant?"

The young constable nodded, though she could not

see him. "He said he would come down shortly."

"Fine. We'll need a dozen men, Raker. Fetch them while I talk to our friend here."

The Peacemaker edged past the woman, careful not to brush against her, and then past Liam with considerably less care. When he had closed the door behind him, Liam pointed at the woman and finally managed to speak.

"But you— I thought—I was expecting Pacifex Warden."

She nodded. "I *am* Pacifex Warden."

"Warden's an old man. I know that."

"That Warden," she said, her lips compressing, "was my father. I have succeeded him. I am now the Pacifex Warden, and you have not answered my question. Who are you, sir?"

Incredulous, Liam rubbed his forehead, feeling feverish. "Liam Rhenford. I'm a quaestor for Duke Vespasianus." Quaestors were the Duke's investigators, his bloodhounds; it was a strange title, little used in the kingdom, but taken from the same ancient language as her own—and she seemed to recognize it.

She raised a skeptical eyebrow, taking in his sodden clothes. "A quaestor?"

"I know I don't look like one right now," he snapped, "but you don't look much like a Pacifex, either, and I'm willing to take that on faith."

With her left hand, she flourished two fingers across her tunic and medallion of office. "I have the uniform, and the badge."

Wasting time. The thought was like a dog's whine in his head. "There's a letter from the Duke in the study. It'll prove I'm who I say I am. I need to see it too; we can look at it together. Just please, tell me: What's happened to Cade?"

"Do you know him well?"

Now Liam looked to the ceiling for patience, stifling

a groan. *Wasting time.* "I only met him today. What's going on here?"

"You saw him earlier?"

"I met with him this afternoon," he burst out. "I left him just a few hours ago." Abruptly his throat closed around a lump, frustration, fatigue and guilt combining to confuse him, to reduce his thoughts to a mad whirl and his voice to a hoarse whisper. "He's dead, isn't he?" *While I drank wine.* "I think I know who did it." While he dawdled, the man in yellow and his helpers must have crossed the city in haste.

She waited a few moments before speaking. She was older than he was—there were fine wrinkles in the white skin around her eyes—but she seemed like a girl, so much smaller. The medallion was too large on her chest, and he noticed that her right arm hung rigid against her side, twisted unnaturally beneath the cloak. She waited until she heard the sound of footsteps on the stairs behind her.

"Master Cade is dead," she said at last. "He was murdered not very long ago. My lieutenant discovered him. Now, Quaestor Rhenford, please tell me, where is your knife?"

The footsteps paused.

At first he did not understand, and reared his head back. "My knife?"

The footsteps resumed.

Warden met his eyes and glanced significantly at his belt. He followed her gaze and saw the empty sheath where his dagger had been, the dagger he had handed over to Varro. He jerked his head up, and spoke the words as they occurred to him: "You think I did it!"

He saw her faded blue eyes blink, unmoved, and then, past her, the man whose footsteps he had heard coming down the stairs. Gray tunic damp, splatters of mud on his leather leggings, his fair hair rumpled and beaded with water: Aldyne.

"Lieutenant," Warden began, again speaking over her shoulder without losing sight of Liam, "this man—"

He moved out of panic, the walking stick coming apart in his hands and the point flashing to the Pacifex's throat. It wavered there, jittering beneath her chin. She gave a tiny gasp but otherwise held still. Aldyne froze, faced him with a wary, slit-eyed look. Both were far calmer than Liam, whose eyes danced back and forth from one to the other. "She called you lieutenant," he said to Aldyne, and then looked back at the woman. "Which means you—" He could not finish the sentence aloud. *The Pacifex? The Pacifex is part of this?*

"This is not wise," she murmured, barely moving her mouth.

"Shut up." *What are you into?* He ground his teeth. *What are you into here?* And then he remembered the other Peacemaker, the one sent to fetch a dozen more.

"You cannot get clear with this." Her voice, cool and reasonable, angered him.

"Shut up!" He needed time to think. The hilt of the sword was wet and felt slippery in his grasp; the point quivered wildly, never in one spot but always near her throat. *Fanuilh!*

Yes, master?

"If you don't kill me, I will find you." She made it sound a certainty.

Aldyne protested. "Pacifex!"

"Shut up, both of you!" *Is there anyone out there?* "I'm not killing anyone."

No one that I can see.

"If you will not kill us," Warden said, the logic obvious to her, "then you should put down your blade and surrender."

Liam barked a laugh at her. "So you can kill me? I don't think so." He took a stronger grip on the sword, held it firmly by her neck, and reached out behind him with his free hand, feeling for the latch. *I'm going to open the door, and I want you to put these two people to sleep.* Groping, he found the latch and pulled the door open.

Chin lifted to avoid his blade, Warden looked down her nose at him. "Don't be foolish."

Fanuilh trotted inside in a gust of rain, peering quizzically around the hall. Warden's eyes widened slightly at sight of the dragon; Aldyne whispered a curse, then glared at Liam with dawning comprehension. A moment later they both fell to the ground, asleep.

Liam sagged for a second, then pulled himself together and took a quick look into the street. A hundred yards away, just turning off Craft Street, was a group of men bearing lanterns. *Damn.* He looked back into the hall, wishing he had even a minute more. *I'd finish him off,* he thought, glaring at Aldyne. *But what about her?*

"If you don't kill me, I will find you." He lifted his sword, uncertain. *Gods, the Pacifex!* Outside, he could hear the sound of hobnails on cobblestones: Raker returning with his dozen Peacemakers.

One quick stroke. He held the blade over her head, and paused. Asleep, she looked even more like a child, fragile and vulnerable. He made a sound in the back of his throat, lowered the sword, and looked out into the street again.

The Peacemakers had covered half the distance to Cade's house.

Too late. To Fanuilh, he projected: *Let's go.*

Yes, master.

One of the Peacemakers called after him as he ducked out of the house; he ignored the man and ran. Behind him he heard more calling, shouts, and when he had turned two corners and was still running, the sound of whistles, shrill and piercing in the night.

The Peacemakers carried tin whistles, and it was said that the sound could spread from one end of Torquay to

the other in less than half an hour, alerting every constable in the city. *A thousand men,* Liam thought, sprint-
ing downhill and out of Artisans' Vale. *All of them
looking for me.*

Not just yet, however: it would take time for the Pacifex and Aldyne to spread the word, give instructions.
But they will. "I will find you." The Peacemakers would
be after him in force soon enough.

Master, what do you plan to do?

He ran out onto the Embankment and paused, bent
over with his hands on his knees, panting. Rain streamed
over his ears and down his cheeks, dripped from his chin
and his long nose, but his mouth was dry. *I don't know.
She'll set the Peacemakers after me. I don't know.* He
straightened up and started walking east before he had
really caught his breath. *I don't know what's going on
here.*

What was going on was impossible on so many levels
that it defied description, let alone understanding. He had
come to Torquay on a rather dull mission of research,
expecting nothing more than a few weeks of drudgery,
and somehow—in the blink of an eye, it seemed—he
was running for his life, pursued by murderous Peacemakers. Those two words alone, murderous and Peacemaker, were impossible to connect. Peacemakers were
incorruptible and impartial, famously virtuous.

Apparently not. The thought was too frightening to
contain any sarcasm. He wanted to tell someone; the
idea lurked in the back of his mind that if he told someone, he could get help. *Who would you tell? The Pacifex? She already knows.*

Most incredible was the fact that he had no idea why
it had all happened. His hand was wrapped around the
phial, and he could not imagine how it had sparked such
bloody events. *Who would kill for a potion? Or a poison?* He knew the sides—the Duke, Cade, Master Bairth
on one, the man in yellow, Aldyne and the Pacifex on

the other—but not why they were drawn up. He was the only person left on his side, but he did not know what they were fighting for, or what their goals were. He knew nothing.

Master, where are we going?

The inn, he thought. *The Sober Student.* He knew nothing, except that he had to keep out of the Pacifex's hands until he learned something. *They'll kill me if they catch me. Aldyne will cut my throat, and then they'll blame me for Cade's death.* Expressed, the thought shook him, and for a moment the whole thing seemed too much, an unbearable burden. Tears welled up in his eyes, and he screwed up his face to hold them back.

I think they will check the inns.

Fanuilh's thought was solid in his mind, a hard-edged presence stronger than panic. He focused on it.

Yes, he thought to himself. *Yes, they will. She will.* It was what he would do, if he were searching for a man who did not live in the city. He took a deep breath and scrubbed at his eyes, moving away from panic and tears. *I would send men to ask at the inns in the neighborhood.*

Taken that way, it was a small problem, a problem he could concentrate on and figure out. He needed his baggage, dry clothes, a proper cloak. Warden did not know where his lodgings were, so she would have to check every inn. And she would start in Artisans' Vale, near Cade's house. *So I have some time.*

The Sober Student was in the vale to the east of Artisans', called Stair for its proximity to the Flying Stair. *Grab some things. Not everything—just what you need.* He went through the list of necessities in his head, repeating it, refusing to consider what would come after. *Your good cloak. Dry clothes. Your sword. The rest of your money. A razor.*

Master, Fanuilh repeated, *I think they will check the inns,* and Liam realized that he had not responded yet.

I won't be staying long. We should have enough time.

Somewhere behind him, up in Artisans' Vale, whistles
blew.

*Dry clothes. Your razor. Forget the writing case.
Weapons, clothes, money. Maybe have them send up a
loaf of bread from the kitchen.* He remembered his
promise to Fanuilh. *Some raw meat.*

And after the inn, master?

I don't know. To himself: *Weapons, clothes, money.*

*If the Peacemakers are looking for you, you will need
a place to hide.*

I know. Put that way, he could allow himself to consider the idea. It was a simple problem: he was being
pursued and needed a place to hide—never mind why,
or from whom. A place to hide could be anything—an
inn, an abandoned building, someone's home. He ruled
out inns, since Warden could check them all. Abandoned
buildings were fine, but he did not remember enough
about Torquay to say with any certainty where he would
be likely to find one. *A private home would be best.*

Another whistle, far away.

*But you don't know anyone in Torquay, do you, you
idiot? A private home, gods.* He went back to his list.

The signboard of the Sober Student depicted a young
man in a gown poring over a book, while outside his
window other students drank and danced. From the
mouth of an alley farther down the street, Liam examined the sign and the door over which it hung. There
were no Peacemakers in sight, but he waited while Fanuilh flew around the inn and the nearby streets, checking.

It is safe, the dragon finally reported, and Liam left
the alley and ran across to the inn.

There were only two people in the common room
when he entered: the owner, a widow in clothes that had
once been fine but were now faded and threadbare, and
a merchant from Caernarvon, a thin, stooped, sour man

with improbably pendulous jowls, on whom the widow was trying to press another glass of wine.

"It'll do you good, master," she said, and then saw Liam at the door, soaking wet. "You there," she piped, voice shrill with instant indignation. "This's no public house. We only serve guests here."

The room was warm, and he closed his eyes to savor it for a moment before responding. "You rented me a room this afternoon, Mistress Tall."

Her eyes went wide. "Master Rhenford? Is it you? Whatever's happened?"

The Caernarvon merchant snorted and said, "The man's drunk." Verdict delivered, he applied himself to the bowl of soup before him, the smell of which was strong in Liam's nose and made his mouth water painfully.

"I'm not drunk," he promised Mistress Tall, and his earlier lie came easily to hand. "I was robbed."

"Robbed!" She pressed both hands to her cheeks in horror. "Oh, Master Rhenford!"

The Caernarvon merchant dropped his spoon. "Robbed, man?"

Be quick. "Yes," he said, words tumbling out. "I took off my coat to eat, and some thief snatched it away in a flash. I chased him but he was too fast, and so I had to walk all the way back in the rain." He spread his arms to display the sodden evidence of his clothes, but Mistress Tall no longer looked quite so horrified. In fact, she looked suspicious.

"You were eating?"

Meals were extra at the Sober Student, and she had stressed the quality of her kitchen. "Ah, yes. With a friend, who insisted. A great mistake—the food was awful—I couldn't eat a bite of it. If you'd be so kind as to send up some of your excellent bread and cheese, I'd be very grateful."

"I've something better," she said, sensing a moral advantage. "A pigeon pie, fresh made."

Humor her. "That'd be grand," he said, smiling and nodding for all he was worth. "Just grand. And if you could send along some raw meat, too."

Satisfied, she inclined her head. "Of course. Your . . . pet will eat as well." She had seen Fanuilh earlier, and made a great show of how little it bothered her to have the dragon in her house. "You go shift your wet clothes, and I'll send a girl along with the food, and to take the clothes to dry."

He bowed, smiled, bowed again, bowed to the Caernarvon merchant, and headed for the stairs to his room.

"Here," the merchant called, halting Liam on the bottom step. "Did you tell the Peacemakers?"

Liam's smile faltered, fell away, and then returned. "I plan to, as soon as I've eaten." Without waiting for the merchant to reply, he ran up the steps.

Weapons, clothes, money.

Clothing first: he peeled off his tunic and breeches, threw them on the bed, and dried himself with a blanket. He started digging through his dunnage bags for a shirt, then cursed and upended the two sailcloth sacks beside his wet clothes, snatching at the first shirt and pair of breeches that presented themselves. When he was dressed, he rummaged through the remaining clothes and chose his two warmest shirts, an extra set of breeches, and his spare tunic, a heavy thing of dark blue wool. He put the last on over his shirt, stuffed the rest into the smaller of his dunnage bags, and sat on the edge of the bed to pull on his boots.

At the sound of the knock he leapt to his feet, visions of Warden springing into his head. *So soon?*

"Master Rhenford? Sir?"

One of the Student's drudges, come to bring his dinner. Liam worked some moisture into his mouth and bid her enter. She deposited the napkin-covered tray on a small table in the corner with all the pomp and infuriating slowness of a religious ritual, curtsied, and said, "Your wet things, master?" Anxious to be rid of her, Liam bundled the clothes together and pressed them on her with a coin and hurried thanks. The drudge curtsied again and seemed to take forever getting to the door, promising to have the clothes back, ironed, before dawn.

"No rush," he said, as he shut the door behind her. *Unless you can have them back in five minutes.*

Money next: he opened his writing case and dug through the papers there—mostly scribbled ideas about the research the Duke had assigned him—until he found the notes-of-hand. Glossy squares of vellum blooming with ornate calligraphy in three different color inks, they would allow him to draw money from one of the temple treasuries in Torquay. *Anonymously, thank all the gods.* He rolled them up tight and slid the scroll into his boot, blousing his breeches to keep them safe. The writing case he discarded on the bed.

Weapons: there was a razor, a spare knife, and his hanger. The razor went into the small bag and the knife into the empty sheath on his belt. He hesitated over the sword. The stick he had taken from the man in yellow would draw less attention, and while it was not as sturdy, he did not expect to do much fighting. *Some running, and a great deal of hiding, but hopefully little fighting.* He discarded the hanger and uncovered the tray the drudge had brought.

Mistress Tall had sent along the entire pigeon pie in addition to the things he had asked for, and the aroma generated a rumble from his stomach. *You don't have time for this,* he growled to himself, wrapping bread, cheese, and raw meat in the linen napkin and stowing them all in his dunnage bag. He hefted the sack, decided it was not too heavy, and put on his cloak. Fine wool, with satin edging and a worked-silver clasp, he had brought it along on the off chance he was invited to some kind of formal event during the course of his trip. *Small chance of that now.*

Cloak secure, he gave a last look around his room to see if he had forgotten anything, and his gaze lit on the pigeon pie. The smell filled the room; he closed his eyes, sighed, and cut himself a slice.

Just be quick.

The pie was delicious, shy on meat but stuffed with mushrooms, the gravy thick and delicately spiced. He gobbled down his first slice, and was cutting another when the thought appeared in his head.

Master, there are Peacemakers coming.

Liam choked, spraying crumbs of pie crust, and ran to the window. He could see nothing but drizzle and an empty street. *Where are they?*

They have just turned the corner—perhaps a few hundred yards away. A woman leads them.

How could she find me so soon? He was deflating, folding in on himself. *How did she do it? I couldn't find someone that quick.* Abruptly, he stood straight. She had found him, but she had not caught him yet. With one hand he snatched up the sword-stick and his dunnage bag; with the other he drew a handful of random coins from his pouch and tossed them on the bed, then blew out the candles on the corner table and cracked the door to peek into the hall.

Empty. He slipped across to the door opposite, knocked softly and, when there was no immediate answer, opened it. He had excuses ready—misdirected, the wrong room—but it was empty too, and there was a window, as he had hoped. His room looked out on the street; this one on a small alleyway that ran behind the inn.

Where are they? The alley was pitch black. He eased the window open and received a faceful of rain.

Still approaching, master.

How many? He leaned out into the rain and dropped his dunnage bag, and the sword-stick after it.

Ten.

All together? No one's breaking off, or heading to the back? He sat on the sill and swung his legs outside, then wriggled around until he was lying on his stomach.

No, master.

Liam closed his eyes and dropped, hit the ground and sprawled backward, his feet tangled in the hem of his cloak. Scrambling to his feet, he shuffled in the darkness for a few seconds until he found his bag and the walking stick.

They are at the door.

At the same time he heard a distant knocking, the Peacemakers announcing their presence. *And not being shy about it, either.* If he could hear it all the way at the back of the inn, it must have sounded like thunder inside. Clutching his things, he sprinted down the alley.

Careful to avoid the Embankment, Liam worked his way out of Stair by sidestreets and alleys, heading west simply because that was the only direction open to him. The falls lay to the east, and Warden would have Peacemakers posted at the Flying Stair. Fanuilh scouted the streets ahead, choosing the best possible routes from the air.

The best possible routes where? Liam wondered. He needed to decide soon; the longer he stayed out, even with the dragon helping him, the more likely it was that he would run into a Peacemaker. *But where to go?*

Whistles shrilled behind him, like the distant call of some annoying bird. They had started up within a few minutes of his departure from the Sober Student. *Once Warden figured out I wasn't there.* How she had known to come to the Student in the first place nagged at him even as he tried to focus on finding a safe hiding spot. *What's safe? She picked the right inn out of a hundred.*

What makes you think she won't be able to pick out whatever hiding spot you choose?

Liam cursed, pulled his cloak closer around his neck, tugged the hood farther down. At least he was dry now, and relatively warm. *She got lucky, that's all. Lucky.* And she had not caught him yet. Torquay was a large city; there had to be countless places to hide, though the Pacifex would know them all better than he did.

Stop that!

He was well out of Stair now, walking quickly through the lowermost part of Artisans' Vale. A brisk walk, not a run, nothing to attract attention; he had the entire night to go to ground. *Just think—if this were Southwark, and you were chasing someone, how would you go about it?*

Checking the inns would come first—*How did she do it so fast?*—and posting men at any exit from the city. Warden had it easy there: three or four men could cover the Flying Stair and the Grain Climb, and another dozen could handle the roads to the west, to Rentrillian and over the mountains to the rest of the kingdom. So he was trapped in Torquay for the moment, and could not go to an inn.

How did she do it so fast?

Abandoned buildings, perhaps, if he could find one. The Peacemakers would start combing through them once they exhausted all the inns—*So fast!*—but that would take time; with any luck he would have a few days' respite. *And you're due some luck.*

Finding a suitable building would be difficult, but Fanuilh could help, flying over the city and looking for those with no lights in the windows or smoke coming from the chimney. *How do you think he's going to do that in the dark and the rain?* asked his cynical voice, but Liam was ready: if they found nothing tonight, he might be able to hide out in a wineshop or tavern, and hope for better weather tomorrow. And if all else failed, he could try to contact the Guild. *Only if all else fails,* he promised himself. *They'd be just as likely to turn you in as help you. There's no honor there.*

He projected his ideas to Fanuilh, and the dragon agreed that it was the best they could do at the moment. *I will look for places such as that,* it told him. *But what will we do after we find one? You will need to do something about the phial, and if the Pacifex is corrupt, we should inform someone in authority.*

Liam gave a sour laugh. *Any thoughts on who? Shall we just drop in on the king?* No one at court would listen to him, not with Warden swearing against him. *If I knew anyone here; if I had any friends . . . Friends.*

The name sprang to mind unbidden, a name he had forgotten, one Warden could never link to him.

Marcade, Liam said to himself. *Gods, Marcade! I haven't thought of her in years.* Then, projecting: *Fanuilh, we need to go to Tower Vale.*

CHAPTER 4

TWENTY-TWO COLLEGIA STOOD in the sinuous length of Tower Vale, each with its requisite gate, its cloistered quadrangle, its ivied watchtowers. They looked like fortresses, thick-walled and windowless, because the oldest ones—Whitetower and Blacktower and Bell's—had been just that, in the days when the colored gowns were uniforms, and swordplay was as important a subject as mathematics or law. Younger collegia, built in more peaceful times, had simply copied the style, and the students were given matching gowns to develop pride in their institution, not in order to distinguish their comrades in battle.

Ivy and tall towers to either side, broken up by the occasional tavern or bookshop, Gown Street and the collegia were home to students from across the kingdom, drawn by Tower Vale's renown as a center of learning. The place was steeped in centuries of lore, with hidden secrets lurking in the towers, forbidden knowledge whispering in the ivy, the wisdom of the ages waiting in the quadrangles.

And everyone comes here to drink, Liam thought, stepping around a freshly deposited puddle of vomit as the boy who had created it was dragged off by his friends. They wore purple robes with black sleeves, and seemed oblivious of the rain. *From Protector's,* he noted. *Naturally.* The tower had an ancient reputation for heavy drinking, assiduously maintained by every generation that attended it. A little way up the street, another boy was vomiting, urged on by his mates. He could tell they were from Bell's Tower by their simple brown gowns; Bell's, which boasted that it was the most serious of the collegia, with the most difficult curriculum. Liam shook his head, trying to remember if there had been this much public drunkenness on Gown Street when he was a student, and came to the rueful conclusion that there probably had been. Fortunately, his destination was not far. *I only hope Old Becca's still there. She'll be able to tell me where to find Marcade.*

Prosper's Tower was the youngest of the collegia, and thus had the worst location: neither far enough up the vale to be prestigious, nor close enough to its foot to be convenient to the Bag of Nails and the rest of the city. It was smaller than the other towers as well, and was called Pauper's in consequence; an entirely unjust nickname, since it charged the same fees as the others. That was the image that stuck, however, and students from other collegia had always found it amusing to warn barkeeps to make sure that a Pauper had enough coin to pay his score.

He had to pass only one more collegia to reach Prosper's, and he quickened his step, averting his eyes as he walked by the Tower of Surgeons. *Better to be from Pauper's than Bones,* he thought. It was considered the least of the towers, since its curriculum consisted solely of medicine, and its blue-and-red-gowned students were widely rumored ghouls, graverobbers, and worse. *And they don't have Old Becca.*

Surgeons behind him, Liam stepped out of the rain and into the gatehouse of Pauper's—the familiar tunnel lined with red brick, the torch brackets shaped like eagles' wings. Through the wrought-iron gates at the far end of the tunnel he could see the quadrangle, warm orange light in the windows all around it. It looked exactly the same as when he had left it, ten or more years before. *Was it raining then?* He could not be sure, but he thought it might have been.

After a few seconds Fanuilh fluttered to the ground beside him and Liam jumped, startled out of his reverie. *Is the woman here?* the dragon asked.

I hope so. I don't know how else I'll find Marcade. She would have to be there: Old Becca was a fixture of Pauper's. Then, remembering, he opened his dunnage bag and pulled out the napkin-wrapped bundle. *Before I forget.* He unwrapped the piece of raw meat and held it out. *Your dinner. You may as well stay here, out of the rain, while you eat.*

The dragon considered the meat for a moment before taking it in its teeth and trotting back toward the street. *I will go up to the roof, in case there are any Peace-makers about.*

Liam started to say that there was no need—they could not possibly have figured out that he would go to Gown Street, let alone Pauper's—and then thought better of it. *You didn't think she could find your inn, either.*

Get under the ivy, he told the dragon. *You'll be a little drier there.*

Yes, master. It leapt up, spread its wings, and flew out of the gate, leaving Liam to turn to the single door in the tunnel and pull the rope there. Beyond the door, in the gatekeeper's quarters, a bell jangled.

She'll know, he told himself while he waited. *Old Becca will know.*

Old Becca was the memory of Prosper's Tower. She had served as the collegium's gatekeeper for most of her life, and knew the name of every student who had ever passed through—their names, breeding, resources and doings, exactly how many times they had come home staggering and where they had gotten drunk. More im-pressive, she knew the history of the tower from its founding, and in greater and more interesting detail than any of the masters; her father had been gatekeeper before her, and his before him. *She'll know where Marcade is living now.*

He heard footsteps, and prepared a suitable story—that he lived in Harcourt, was just visiting Torquay, and wanted to look up his old friend Marcade. Old Becca would want to know such things, to keep her vast store of knowledge up to date.

A young man opened the door. "Yes?" He was fat and ill-kempt, with crumbs on the front of his tunic and small, unfriendly eyes. Liam stared at him blankly.

"You're not Old Becca," he said, when the young man began to look impatient.

"Am I not?" the man asked with a sneer. "No, I'm not. And unless you've an appointment—which I know you don't, as they're all written down within—I can't pass you into the collegium. Good night to you, sirrah."

He started to close the door and Liam, too flustered to register the insult, begged him not to. "No, please, wait —I used to go here, but I don't want to go in—please!" The surly gatekeeper relented, and rolled his fingers for Liam to get on with it. "I was hoping you could tell me where I can find a student who used to go here as well."

"The student's name, sirrah?"

Liam frowned, catching the insult this time. Old Becca had been sour and stubborn, but never openly rude. "Marcade. Marcade Vulgus. She was from Torquay originally. Her father held some office under the Lord Mayor. I can't remember what."

The gatekeeper did not even pretend to search his memory. "Never heard of her," he said, and tried to shut the door, but Liam's foot and arm were in the way.

"Think a little harder," Liam suggested, and shook the pouch at his belt so that the coins jingled. Old Becca had extorted tips to deliver messages or open the gate after hours, but never so blatantly, or with such open contempt. "Think a lot harder," he added, letting his voice drop low and giving the young man a hard, dangerous smile.

The gatekeeper switched instantly from rude to wheedling, his voice a singsong whine. "I can't—it's well before my time—I don't know her, I swear!"

"For which you're a useless, lazy, addled sack of dung," said a voice from behind him, an old woman's voice, cracking and wheezing. "Bring the gentleman in here," Old Becca commanded.

There were no candles or lanterns, just a tiny fireplace with a few lumps of sea-coal that cast a deep orange glow across the lower half of the bare stone walls and left the high ceiling in shadow. Buried in blankets, the old woman sat propped up in a bed just a few feet from the door, as if even in retirement she refused to be far from her gate. A milky cast obscured her eyes, but she lifted her head and fixed her blind gaze on Liam with uncanny accuracy.

"Don't mind my boy," she wheezed. "He's young yet, and a fool. I can tell you what you would know of Marcade Vulgus." She paused and sucked at her gums with satisfaction.

Liam brushed past Old Becca's sullen son to stand at her bedside; she tracked him with unseeing eyes. "I'm glad to hear that, mistress. And I apologize for disturbing your rest. If there's any way I can repay you. . . ." He let the sentence trail off, and she cackled.

"Aye, there's ways and ways. First tell me, why do you look for a student of Prosper's Tower?"

"She is, or was, a friend of mine," Liam said, and knowing that Old Becca would drag it out of him sooner or later, added, "I was here myself—we were here together."

"Aha!" she said, as if she had caught him in a lie. "And your name, sir?"

He told her, and she nodded as if she had known it

all along. "A Midlander lord. You came in the third year of Nicanor III's too-short reign, Mother pity him." She turned her head from side to side, trying to pinpoint her son, and when she could not—he was sulking silently by the fire—settled for raising her voice. "Hear you? In the third reign-year of Nicanor III, not so very long before you, and worth remembering! Third year, Nicanor III, Maid Marcade Vulgus and Lord Liam Rhenford, a Midlander. Repeat!"

Grumbling, her son repeated the information; as he did, however, his mother's jaw dropped, remembering. "You've a price on your head!"

For a moment, Liam was as astonished as she was. *How could she know? Warden couldn't have made an announcement already!* Then he realized what she was talking about, breathed a sigh of relief, and reached out to pat her shaking hand. "That was lifted a few years ago, mistress, in a Convocation of Lords."

He had mistaken the tremor for fear; she shook off his soothing hand and snapped, "I know that, you! But I never learned the cause. You shall tell me the whole of it, or not a word shall I tell you of Marcade Vulgus." She set her chin on her chest, determined.

With a different kind of sigh, Liam started to tell her how he had come to leave the collegium. He had hardly spoken a few words before she interrupted him.

"But all this is known to me! That your father took you away ere you had completed the curriculum, that your lands and castle were under attack, that you lost— all this I know. What I don't know is why you were under sentence of death, proscribed, with a purse to pay for your head." She waited, avid for details.

"Why?" Liam frowned. *For murdering a nasty old harpy in her bed.* "I killed the man who killed my father."

"And his name?"

"Lord Diamond."

She rubbed her swollen knuckles gleefully and snuggled into her blankets. "And how did you do the deed? With a knife in darkest night?"

Liam dropped his eyes to the ground and murmured, "Yes."

Abruptly suspicious, she sat up. "Don't make mock of an old blind woman. Tell the truth, now: how did you do it?"

"Just as you said."

She heard his grim tone, and grudgingly accepted the story. "Where've you been since?"

Anxious to be done, he spoke quickly. "I travelled for a while, the Freeports and their colonies, and when I heard about the amnesty, I came back to Taralon and settled in Harcourt, where I am a merchant in a small way. Now I think you've heard enough—what can you tell me about Marcade? Does she still live in Torquay?"

"Wait, wait," Old Becca whined. "I've more to ask. Do you know Rafe Powys? He was here some twenty-three years past, but I know nothing of him since he left."

"No more—"

"Or Bleys Travancore, that came seventeen years ago? They say he's head of his family now. Is it true he has a dozen mistresses, and the pox?"

"No more," Liam said again, raising his voice but keeping it level. "My questions now. Does Marcade still live in Torquay?"

Old Becca muttered unhappily for a few seconds before starting to speak, but when she did, she quickly warmed to the task, dispensing information with as much relish as she gathered it.

"Ah, Marcade Vulgus, as was. Came to the tower in the third year of Nicanor III, the first woman in my life to do so, though there had been others before my time. Can you name the others, you wretched boy, sulking by the grate?" Her son, caught, moved away from the fire and grumbled that he could, which seemed to satisfy her. "Her father was under the Lord Mayor, with responsibility for the sewers of the city—though she would never admit to that. Oh no, not her—always that he was close with the Lord Mayor, an intimate of the Lord Mayor, just come from an audience with the Lord Mayor. Oh, an arrogant young thing, was Marcade Vulgus, and proud of her few distinctions."

Liam, who remembered Marcade's name-dropping as a harmless affectation, started to protest that he knew all this, but Old Becca would not be stopped. It was as if she had the story memorized as a set piece, complete with commentary. "Ever greedy of advancement, she was, cultivating the acquaintance of all those with titles—including a certain young Midlands lord, with whom she spent the greater part of her spare time—that is, when she wasn't fluttering around the tutors, currying favor with them. Why, the way she hovered over poor Master Bahorel, flustering the poor grayhair so, and him a mere child where women are concerned—it was shocking!"

Fluttering? Hovering? He could not imagine Marcade doing either; in his memory, she wore a wicked smile, having just delivered some barbed witticism. She had a quick, stinging tongue, and never seemed to curry favor. *As I recall, at least.*

"She finished the curriculum with honors, and we all thought she'd go on to marry one of her fellow Paupers—two barons' sons from north of the King's Range'd have taken her happily, and an earl's boy from up by Caer Urdoch—but she aimed lower to rise the higher, and married a mere knight." The old woman gummed her upper lip, enjoying the apparent contradiction. "A mere knight, but in the king's service. The new king, that would be, Mother pity him in his illness, for our good Nicanor IV had been crowned but a year earlier. He was a mere equerry when she wed him, a companion of the Royal Hunt, but she's raised him up since, and's now a companion of the Household as well; one of dozens, true, but she now attends all the levees, and mixes with peers and princesses, and is fast on her way to becoming a lady-in-waiting to the Queen herself."

Her son grunted. "Much good it'll do her, if we have a new queen."

Old Becca gasped. "Hush! That you should say such a thing! Say a prayer this minute! If the Dark hears you—"

"Mistress," Liam interrupted, "what is this knight's name?"

"Eh? What knight?"

"Marcade's husband. And where does he live?" It would be King's Vale, if the man served at court, and the idea appealed to him. *Warden would never guess that I'd hide there.*

Worried that her son might have cursed the king, Old Becca had to be dragged back to the subject. "Nennius," she finally said. "Sir Ancus Nennius. So she's Lady Marcade Nennius." She was less clear about where they lived—in King's, certainly, and on Stable Lane, she thought, near the bottom of the vale, but she could not be more specific.

Close enough, Liam decided. He would cross the river and make discreet inquiries when he reached the neighborhood. Strangers asking for directions was not uncommon, and would arouse no suspicion; he had stopped two people himself on his way to Cade's that afternoon. Thought of Cade reminded him of the phial in his pocket, and of something Old Becca had said earlier.

"I'm sure I can find the place," he said. "It'll be good to see her again. Speaking of seeing people again, you mentioned Master Bahorel before. He was one of my tutors. Is he still in the tower?"

Old Becca shook her head. "Not these six years, no,

not at all. The mages discovered some talent in him, and apprenticed him to the Guild."

"Bahorel? You're joking." Liam could not imagine the frail old scholar as an apprentice.

She laid a finger alongside her nose. "It was not his talent for magic they wanted, but his knowledge of rare books on the subject." Bahorel had been an expert on texts of all kinds, and deeply versed in antiquities. "A shame it was, though I hear he's settled comfortably. He'll be in Caernarvon now, for the Convocation of Mages."

"Hm. A shame, definitely." He had seen Bahorel glance at the tiniest fragment of an ancient pot and identify its age to within a few years, as well as what part of the kingdom it had come from. He would have known what the phial was. "Who succeeded him in his chair?"

A man named Tollerdig taught Bahorel's subjects now, she told him, and with a show of indifference, Liam asked if he might see him. "I've a small question. A matter of no importance, really, but since I'm here . . ."

Becca's son was reluctant to go out in the rain, but at his mother's insistence he trudged out of the room to see if Master Tollerdig would receive a visitor. While he was gone, the old woman pestered Liam with questions about former students who had lived in Harcourt, prying for intimate details of their lives and offering up her own tidbits of gossip when he could not answer. The glee with which she related even the most tragic of stories—*Especially those,* he thought—soon grated on his nerves, and he excused himself.

"I'll just go see what's keeping your son." He closed the door on her pleas to stay, and took a deep breath of cold air.

Sad old woman. She had not seemed so when he was a student; he and his fellows had held her in a sort of awe, while her fund of stories, which now struck him as so much useless gossip, had seemed like valuable knowledge. *Then again, maybe it was just because she controlled the gate.* Old Becca had been known to refuse entrance to students who displeased her.

Liam went to the gate itself, at the end of the tunnel, and grasped the wrought-iron bars. Lights burned in the windows of the student wing to the east, glistening by reflection on the wet leaves of the shrubbery that lined the quadrangle. Two gravelled paths snaked and curved across the yard; one of Pauper's oldest traditions involved negotiating the paths blindfolded and drunk. He smiled, remembering, and then heard Becca's son, crunching gravel and muttering to himself.

"He'll see you," the young man said with ill grace, unlocking the gate and standing aside to let Liam pass. "He's in Bahorel's old chambers. Ring when you want to be let out." He jerked his chin at a bell-pull nearby and slipped out, swinging the gate closed with an echoing clang.

Going into the northwest tower, the domain of the masters, threatened to unleash a flood of memories—most of them involving standing at attention while one tutor or another droned on and on about his inadequacies as a pupil—and Liam deliberately squared his shoulders before leaving the quadrangle. *You're not a student. You're a grown man, a merchant, and a quaestor in the service of the Duke of the Southern Tier.* He went into the tower and started up the narrow, dark staircase, which led to the masters' private rooms on the third floor. *Not to mention a wanted criminal.*

For some reason, the last thought gave him confidence. If he could stand up to the Pacifex Warden and a thousand Peacemakers—*Which is a big if,* the cynical voice in the back of his head reminded him—if he could stand up to them, he should not be so nervous about approaching one lone scholar.

The dark panelling was the same, the splintery, uneven floors and the tall ominous doors, the hard wood of which hurt a knocker's knuckles. Liam bruised his on the door he remembered belonging to Bahorel, and a querulous voice bid him enter.

Space was precious in all the towers, and candles expensive for those on a scholar's stipend; Master Tollerdig's chamber was an irregularly shaped closet wedged into a corner of the building. A single taper burned atop a high secretary, before which the scholar perched on a stool, his head bent scant inches from a book. He looked up and squinted myopically at Liam.

"Ah! You are Master Rhenford?" He climbed down from his stool and offered a small bow. "Master Tollerdig, at your service." A spare man with a constant, uncertain half-smile and unfocused eyes, he gave an impression of vagueness that was at odds with the neatness of his clothes—maroon and green robes spotless and sharp-creased—and the precise order of the room—everything stowed away, books shelved in ranks by height, piles of paper squared off, quills and inkpot arranged just so. "You have a commission for me, I believe?"

"A commission? Oh, yes, yes. Well, nothing so grand as that, really. Just something I was hoping you could identify." He produced the phial in its paper wrapper, inventing his story as he went. "A friend, an acquaintance actually, found it among his father's belongings when he died. When the father died, that is. And my acquaintance wanted to know what it was. And what it might contain. If you can tell." He shut up and handed over the packet.

Tollerdig unwrapped the paper with care and held the phial up right in front of his nose, turning it this way and that. His nails, Liam noted, were neatly pared, but the cuticles were stained with ink—an occupational hazard. Finally, the scholar pooched out his lower lip. "Hm!"

"What?"

"It would seem to be." Without explaining, he went to his secretary, found a small knife in a cubbyhole and, before Liam could protest, scraped the blade along the length of the black metal frame.

"Hey!"

Tollerdig did not hear him. "As I thought," he said, raising both the phial and the knife for Liam's edification. "The blade is notched, and the metal untouched." The knife's edge was dented, and Liam gave a low whistle. "A sure sign of the true metal."

"The true metal?"

"Just so," Tollerdig said, though Liam had meant it as a question. "Now, the glass." The scholar brought down a mortar and pestle from a high shelf, laid the phial flat on his desk, and lifted the pestle.

This time Liam was quicker: he stuck his hand over the phial before Tollerdig could bring the pestle down. "What are you doing?"

The scholar blinked at him, confused. "A test, of course."

"You'll break it!"

Tollerdig smiled and shook his head. "If it is what I believe it is, I will not."

"And if it isn't?" *Two men died for that,* he wanted to say. *I'm not going to let some half-blind bookworm smash it.* He pried the phial from beneath the other man's fingers.

Abruptly stubborn, Tollerdig reached after the phial and insisted, "But it must be!"

"Must be what, Master Tollerdig?"

"True crystal, of course. And not just true crystal, but royal crystal." At Liam's blank look, he rolled his eyes and explained with elaborate patience. "It is also known as mage-glass, though no mage alive can make it. In

Taralon, none ever has. The secret of its shaping was lost before the Seventeen Houses came here, and what had already been made was forbidden to commoners." Both true metal and mage-glass were nearly indestructible, Tollerdig went on, and many of the kingdom's oldest treasures had been fashioned of them. "The Edaran Swords, for instance," he said, naming the twin blades that were the symbol of the reigning dynasty. "They are a thousand years old, and have seen countless battles, but bear not a single notch."

Royal crystal, his lecture continued, was simply mage-glass colored red; peers and princes were allowed any other kind, but red was the prerogative of kings. " 'I shall drink no sinful wine/from my cup incarnadine,' " he quoted. "King Galba the Pious. So your item, by rights, belongs to the king. And if you require further proof, there is the stopper."

The king? Liam frowned down at the phial, and the circlet of points around the stopper.

"It forms a crown, you see?"

Liam saw, but his frown deepened. *If it belongs to the king, how did the Duke get it?* "How would someone other than the king get hold of such a thing?"

"Theft," Tollerdig announced firmly, and then waffled. "Or by gift, on occasion. The king may dispose of such things at will, though it's rare. And rarely recorded—so little is." He sighed, as at an old complaint. "So little. Do you know there is no proper catalogue even of the Seventeen Treasures? Our most precious artifacts, and yet we know not where or, in some cases, what, they really are." He waved away a protest Liam had not made. "Oh, the Edaran Swords we know, and the Quintine Shield, and Psallant's Chariot—but what, I ask, is the Limb of Urdoch? Some legends call it a baton topped by a grasping hand, others describe a gauntlet; none agree. Or Pwyll's Larder, or Severn's Eye, or the King's Cure—we do not know; there is no catalogue!"

The scholar rambled on about the shocking lack of lists in the kingdom; Liam stopped listening to him, caught up in his own conjectures. The chevron of royal service had figured in the arms outside the house where he met the man in yellow and watched Master Bairth die, so it was possible that the Duke had meant for the phial to reach the king. *But why such an indirect route? Why all the sneaking about? Why didn't Cade just tell me?* And even if it were meant for the king, he would still not know why—though a wild idea did occur to him: Nicanor was sick, desperately so, according to some rumors. *A potion, or a medicine—something to restore him to health.*

As quickly as the idea rose up, he discarded it. *If you have a sick king's cure, you don't put it in the pocket of an errand boy and have him give it to an unimportant scholar to give to a casual acquaintance. You lock it in a chest and surround it with knights and blow trumpets as you go.*

Two men had died over the phial, however, and the Pacifex of Torquay was chasing him for it, so it had to be important. *But how? How?* The question, repeating itself over and over in his mind, made him grimace, and he only gradually became aware that Tollerdig was no longer speaking, and was in fact blinking owlishly at him.

"I'm sorry—my mind wandered. What were you saying?"

"I was saying," the scholar said, with a touch of pique, "I was saying that if you were to leave it with me, I might search through the tower's library, and see if it is mentioned in any of the histories. It would require some small outlay, in candles and ink and paper, but I may well be able to resolve your friend's question."

"Yes, yes," Liam said slowly, warming to the idea. "But I can't leave it with you. My friend made me promise to keep it with me. How long would it take?"

Tollerdig wavered, clearly unhappy about the condition, and finally gave in. "A day or so. But there'll be the outlay. Candles, ink, perhaps an assistant to make notes."

"Fine." From his pouch Liam took two gold coins, and the scholar's eyes lit up. "My ship leaves soon, so please look as fast as you can. I'll return in two days." *If I'm not in prison, or buried in an unmarked grave.*

The coins changed hands, and Tollerdig was all eagerness. "I shall draw it out at once, while it is fresh in my memory, and begin my research immediately after, Master Rhenford." He climbed back onto his stool, laid out a fresh sheet of paper, and began sharpening a quill.

"Grand," Liam said, looking down at the true metal and the royal crystal in his hand. In the light of the single candle, the glass was the color of blood. He thrust the phial deep in his pocket. "Grand."

Liam tipped Old Becca's son liberally, and interrupted the man's stammered thanks to ask for a length of string.

Fanuilh, he projected, *come down here.*

The gatekeeper had gone back inside by the time the dragon swooped into the gate tunnel and landed at Liam's feet.

Did you find out where the woman lives, master?

Yes. Kneeling, Liam held out the phial for his familiar's inspection. *Can you carry this?*

The dragon cocked its head, considering. *For a while, certainly. I would not drop it.*

Liam held up the string. *Actually, I didn't mean in your claws. I was thinking of your back.* There was a distinct pause, though Fanuilh neither moved nor thought a thing. *It'll be safer that way. They might catch me, but not you.*

Of course, master. It turned around and sat, presenting its back to him. *Between the wings would be best.*

Tying the phial in place only took a minute. The string

ran across the dragon's chest, over its narrow shoulders and down to the base of its wings, where it looped several times around the phial and through the points of the crown, and finally down to its tail, where Liam made the final knot.

Not too tight?

Fanuilh stood and stretched, arcing its head on its long neck to watch. It flared its wings and lashed its tail once or twice, then wriggled its hindquarters. The phial barely moved. *No, not too tight. And it seems secure.*

Liam blew out a long breath. "All right, then. Let's go find Marcade."

Where is she?

Across the river. And this is the last time I cross the Royal today, I swear.

CHAPTER 5

DRUNKEN STUDENTS STILL stumbled up and down Gown Street, but there were no Peacemakers, and the rain had diminished to a cold mist. Up toward the top of Tower Vale the bells of one of the collegia began tolling nine and soon after others joined in, both in the vale and, as a distant echo, in other parts of the city.

As Liam walked down toward the river, he told Fanuilh what he had learned from Tollerdig. *Have you ever heard of this mage-glass?*

Yes. It is fairly famous among mages, an insoluble riddle. Every few years someone claims to have worked out the necessary enchantments, but each solution proves false. Master Tanaquil once spent a week on it because of an obscure reference he found in an old text, but the reference was a dead end, and he quickly gave it up. Tanaquil was the wizard from whom Liam had inherited Fanuilh. *I was not aware that it was reserved for the king's use—and I doubt that any wizard who rediscovered the process would feel obliged to honor that.*

He could see the Jug and the Bag of Nails up ahead, blazing with light. There was a landing near the end of Gown Street, and with any luck it would not take too long to hire a boat to take him across the river. Peacemakers regularly patrolled the Embankment.

So, what is this? What's it for?

I cannot say, master, but I would expect that its im-

69

portance lies in the contents, not the container. True metal and mage-glass are extraordinarily durable, indestructible for all intents and purposes, but that is all. These are hardly qualities for which men kill.

Liam admitted the logic of that. *So I wasted two crowns on Tollerdig's research.*

I would think so. There is the possibility that the contents take their value from the container—that the phial has been enchanted to transmute whatever liquid is put into it—but that is highly unlikely. True metal and mage-glass were almost impossible to enchant, it explained; it was part and parcel of what made them indestructible. *Very few spells have been worked successfully on objects made from them.*

Which meant that the colorless, odorless liquid inside was what the man in yellow was after, and the only thing Liam could imagine being so valuable was some kind of magical potion. *But a potion for what?*

Could it not be a poison?

Poisons were relatively cheap, Liam told it, and easy to get. *Besides, why would the Duke be sending a poison to the king?*

Perhaps, Fanuilh suggested, *he sent the poison for the king.*

Liam refused to even consider the idea. The Duke was many things—arbitrary, quick-tempered, and old-fashioned all sprang to mind—but he was no regicide. In these days of weak monarchy, when the king was little more than a figurehead to most of Taralon and his actual power extended no farther than a day's travel from Torquay, the Duke of the Southern Tier was one of the few lords who bothered to pay his taxes in full. *Forget that,* he told the dragon.

Then it must be a potion. We would need to consult a wizard to find out what it is for.

Liam nodded, then vented a growl of disgust. *They're all away. Gone off to Caernarvon for their Convocation.*

And he could not wait for the wizards to return from their retreat. If the phial was meant for the king, he would have to find a way to deliver it, and that would be no mean feat. The king was not easily reached, even by men far more important than Liam: protected by layers of guards, swathed in courtiers, armored with palace servants, he was the least accessible man in Taralon. And if, despite his judgment, the phial was related to the king's health, if it contained some medicine or potion the ailing monarch required—he would not allow himself to finish the thought. *You have more pressing worries now, like crossing the river, and staying alive.*

He passed between the Jug and the Bag and reached the Embankment. Lanterns hung from stanchions at intervals along the waterfront, glowing in soft halos of mist. A few couples and groups of people walked the broad paving-stones, but neither he nor Fanuilh spied any of the distinctive black-and-white tunics. Less than twenty feet away, the Gown Street landing stood empty. Liam hurried across, hoping for a boat.

It was a bad night for it: the Royal was practically empty, wiser heads—including, apparently, most watermen—having stayed in out of the rain. Liam peered upstream and downstream, trying to distinguish boat lanterns from those hung on the riverbank, fuming silently while his hands clenched and unclenched in his pockets. Twice he was sure he saw a lantern approaching, only to find that his eyes and the mist had played tricks on him; twice more he was not deceived, but the boats already had passengers and did not pull into shore. Finally, he caught sight of a lantern that responded to his hail and started to make its way to the landing.

Master, Fanuilh reported a second later, *there is a Peacemaker approaching you from the west.*

Liam glanced wildly to his left, saw nothing, and looked right. There—almost a hundred yards away, a lantern bobbing toward him on the Embankment. Back out on the river, his boat was less than half that distance away.

Keep an eye on him, he told the dragon.

Ghostlike, the boat glided toward him, taking shape out of the mist. The waterman rowed with infuriatingly lazy strokes, whistling "Thorns of a Rose," a slow, sad ballad of lament. Liam cursed the man under his breath.

The Peacemaker is still approaching.

How far? He kept his head down.

Fifty yards. He does not seem to be paying any attention to you.

Concentrating more on "Thorns of a Rose" than on his rowing, the waterman bumped the prow of his boat into the steps of the landing and rebounded, then spent precious seconds coming in for a second try. When he was finally in place to his satisfaction, he smiled broadly up at Liam. "Whither going, master?"

Master, four men are—

"Step aside, man! We'll have that boat!"

Expecting the Peacemaker, Liam spun around. Four men stood on the steps above him, young rakes in their twenties, with slashed jackets of satin and velvet, gems flashing in their earrings, fashionable ruffs around their necks. *Not Peacemakers.*

"Excuse me?"

The leader leered down at him. "None of your insolence, sirrah. I said that boat is ours."

Master, the Peacemaker is almost upon you.

Gritting his teeth, Liam gestured at the boat and said, "My apologies, sir. Please, help yourself."

Master, the Peacemaker is watching.

The leader squared off against Liam while his friends laughed and piled into the boat. The rake wore a patchy mustache beneath a snub nose and wide-set eyes, and stared insolently up at him. "You're impertinent, dog."

Calm down, Liam told himself, but it was hard, the frustrations of the day welling up, tensing the muscles of his arms, whitening his fingertips on the stick. *You can't do this with a Peacemaker watching.* "My apologies, sir," he said, and came close to sounding as if he meant it.

The rake smirked and climbed into the boat, where he stood in the bow, facing Liam as the waterman unshipped his oars and pushed away from the landing. "That should teach you to keep a civil tongue in your head, dog." He kept his eyes locked on Liam's, meaning to threaten; Liam matched his gaze, unwilling to turn around.

Where's the Peacemaker?

On the Embankment, at the top of the landing.

Not far enough. Liam watched the boat with the rakes disappear into the mist, pretending that he was unaware of the constable.

"That was wisely done," the Peacemaker said, and it sounded so much like he was right there, speaking into Liam's ear, that Liam did not have to fake his startled gasp. He spun around, shaded his eyes as if to see through the mist, and let his mouth hang open.

"Eh? Oh—Peacemaker, I didn't see you there." He had the sword-stick, and Fanuilh was nearby. There was only the one man, smiling down at him.

"That was wisely done," the constable repeated, his smile approving and friendly. He wore the black-and-white tunic and a flat-crowned, wide-brimmed hat. "These young nobles have high tempers, and their blood's too hot. It takes a cool head to know when not to press."

Liam hung his head modestly. "Thank you, Peacemaker."

"Besides," the man continued, his smile turning patronizing, "if there'd been trouble, I'd have had to arrest all concerned—including you. You wouldn't want that, would you? A night in the cells?"

Liam managed a chuckle. "No, Peacemaker, I wouldn't want that at all."

"That's right. Another boat should be by soon enough. Godspeed to you, and keep a cool head." With an arrogant wink, the Peacemaker touched the brim of his hat and moved off along the Embankment.

Alone on the landing, Liam stood shivering, though whether from relief or anger he could not tell.

The Peacemaker was right: another boat came by soon enough, and responded to Liam's hail. He dropped onto the passenger seat, gave his destination, and then sank into a sort of stupor. The shivering past, he now felt numb, stunned by how close he had come to being caught. *A breath away.* He pressed the heels of his palms to his eyes.

"Tired, master?"

He blinked at the waterman. "Hm? Oh, yes. Tired." The man at the oars chuckled sympathetically and left him alone.

Gods, you were almost done for. Part of him knew that it had not been so desperate, not with the swordstick and Fanuilh to help and only one Peacemaker, but part of him marvelled at the narrowness of his escape. *You were that close. That close.* He stirred, resentment surfacing. *And all because of that bastard in the showy coat! And the arrogance of that Peacemaker! "You wouldn't want that, would you?" The pup. Why, I . . .* For a while he plotted spectacular revenge on both, before sinking back into amazement at his escape. *That close.*

Gradually, the shock wore off and his thinking cleared. Warden would spread his description to her men, so he could not count on going unrecognized again; further, it was possible that when the description was released, the Peacemaker might make the connection. *Which means new clothes and a new bag, and some kind of disguise.* He rubbed his chin, felt the sparse stubble; he could begin a beard, and possibly dye his hair. *Marcade might help me there.*

Worse than being able to tell what he was wearing, though, was the fact that the Peacemaker could tell Warden that he had been trying to cross the river. *It'll cut the area she has to search in half.*

Assuming that she could not connect him with Marcade—a safe bet, he decided, since he himself had not thought of his old schoolfriend in ten years—he tried to figure out how Warden would continue her pursuit. His description first, given to each of the thousand Peacemakers, and the round of the inns she had managed to avoid by finding the Sober Student so quickly. *But I won't be going anywhere near an inn, so that'll be fruitless. What else?*

In Southwark, with its twisting streets, irregular geography, and small constabulary, he would have run out of options. In Torquay, however, with a thousand Peacemakers, he would post men at the two river crossings—Halfcrown Bridge and Falls Walk—and at the major boat landings, as well as by the Grain Climb, the Flying Stair, and the road that wound up the valley of the Royal to the holy Vale of Rentrillian. That would leave the Embankments, which were too long to cover completely, and boats on the river. The watermen were a tough lot, independent and notoriously cantankerous, numbering in the hundreds; he would not bother approaching them in the same manner as the innkeepers until he had seen his other methods fail.

So, if she thinks like you, you can use the river for at least another day, maybe two. After that, he would be stuck on one side of the Royal or the other. *What else?*

Down in the City Below, he would search among the ships until he found the *Trade's Increase,* and interrogate the crew. Warden would probably see to it first thing in the morning, but as far as he could recall, nei-

ther the crew nor the captain knew anything that would
help her. *A nice little dead end. You know how much
fun those are.* He had run across more than his share
during the course of his investigations in Southwark, and
allowed himself a smirk at the thought of the Pacifex
wasting her time.

"The Processional," the waterman announced, and the
boat bumped into the steps, jarring Liam from his picture
of Warden gnashing her teeth.

*Wake up, idiot. If she catches you tonight, she won't
have any dead ends tomorrow.* He made a business out
of paying his fare, using the time to survey the landing
and the riverfront. The prayerful still gathered at the columns, fewer in number now but praying louder to make
up for it; he saw no Peacemakers, and Fanuilh reported
that there were none within a hundred yards in either
direction. He handed over his coins and stepped out onto
the landing. *Marcade lives west of the Processional,* he
projected to Fanuilh. *Her street shouldn't be far.*

Yes, master.

Privately, Liam thought, *I hope she remembers me.*

Stable Lane was not hard to find. He only had to ask
directions once, after working up his courage to approach a stranger, irrationally sure that the man he
chose—a servant in livery, loitering outside a
wineshop—would somehow recognize him, denounce
him, and call out the Peacemakers. The man did not; he
pointed out the entrance to Stable Lane a few streets up
and made a joke about the weather.

A small, crooked street, steep and hilly, lined with
narrow-fronted stone houses, Stable Lane was an alto-
gether less impressive part of King's Vale than the one
he had visited earlier. Many of the houses bore crests
with the royal chevron on them, but these were clearly
not the king's most important servants. Making his way
up the lane's first big hill, Liam projected, *I guess there*

isn't much money in being a companion of the House-hold, eh?

It would seem not, master.

He passed a couple, the man in a fur-trimmed robe and the woman in a heavily embroidered cloak, and decided against asking them which was Nennius's house. He wanted another servant, a maid or a groom; they always knew more than their masters.

Master, Fanuilh asked after a few minutes, *what will you do if she is not in?*

Liam shrugged. *Wait, I suppose. Leave a message, and go find some dark corner in a tavern.*

There was a pause. *And what if she is in, but does not want to help you?*

The question stopped him; he stood in the street and looked up at the sky, though the dragon was flying somewhere out of sight. *What do you mean? She'd have to—we're friends—were friends—she knows me.*

From ten years ago. And the old woman said she was very ambitious at court. Harboring a fugitive is not a stepping-stone to royal favor.

No, Liam admitted. *But you don't know Marcade.* He remembered her as adventurous, often impetuous, game for anything that offered excitement. And they had been good friends at Pauper's, close, often in each other's company; Old Becca had even commented on it. *She'll help.*

Still, he could not dismiss the doubt. He found the servant he wanted, a groom waiting with a horse outside his master's door, and found the house the man indicated, a short way down the street, but felt none of the relief he had expected, none of the feeling of imminent safety. *What are you going to say? "Good to see you again, Marcade. I'm being chased by the Peacemakers; can I stay the night?"* He shook his head to clear it. *She has to help.*

Nennius's house was the same as the others, except

that the chevron was exaggerated on his crest, far out-
weighing the other elements. Frowning, Liam studied it
for a moment, then stepped forward and raised his hand.

She has to help, he thought. *Something has to go my
way today.*

Then he knocked.

A servant left Liam outside while taking in his name,
and a few moment's later he heard it coming back toward him, repeated several times and punctuated by disbelief.

"Liam Rhenford? You must have misheard. Liam
Rhenford? It cannot be! Liam Rhenford? Never in life!"
Rapid footsteps and Marcade's unmistakable voice, a little deeper than he remembered, but still able to combine
excitement and cynicism in the same breath. He smiled
his relief, and the door opened again.

Marcade was somewhat rounder, her always full face
a trifle fuller, and she wore her black hair in a more
elaborate style than she had as student. Otherwise she
was the same as his memory of her, red-cheeked, snub-
nosed, her lips curved in a familiar half smile. She tilted
her head to one side and bit her lip, the expression she
wore when she was choosing a joke.

"This cannot be Liam Rhenford. He's a giant of a
man, near ten feet tall. Who are you, dwarf, to claim my
old friend's name?"

This, too, Liam remembered: the rivalry of insults. He
grinned. "I'm sorry, I must have the wrong house. I was
looking for Marcade Vulgus, but she would be a great
fat person with gray hair and no teeth."

"I've heard the name, but you are mistaken in the
description."

"Am I? All right—no hair and gray teeth. Is that better?"

She laughed her old laugh. "Better, better, but not
quite right. Get in, you," and she grabbed his arm and

pulled him over the doorstep, abandoning insults for the moment. "You must meet my husband—I've married—a companion of the Household, one of Nicanor's intimates." She shooed the servant away and shut the door herself, circling Liam at the same time and looking him up and down. "You haven't changed a bit, you bastard, while I've grown fat—you shouldn't have said it, but you were always cruel—come meet Ancus. Leave your bag and cloak there—the man will get them. Have you eaten? We dined at the palace, but our man can arrange something—come on, Ancus is just in here—our parlor, we call it, though it's little more than a closet, like the rooms at Pauper's—"

She tugged at his hand, drawing him into the entrance hall, a dark cubicle dominated by a steep, massive staircase that made three sharp turns before disappearing into the ceiling, with bannisters as thick as his thigh. He tugged back, made her stop.

"Hang on a minute," he said. "You may not want to introduce me to your husband just yet. Or at all."

Tilting her head, Marcade bit her lip again. "Have you come to make love to me, Rhenford? To spirit me away? I warn you, I'll need a few minutes to pack my bags."

He winced, and sought a way to explain. "I'm in trouble, Marcade. Wanted for murder."

"Oh, only murder," she scoffed, then noted his serious expression and frowned. "Have you not heard, then? The price was lifted some years past. The Lords gave you amnesty."

"Not that murder."

She took one last stab at humor. "Rhenford, have you gone and killed someone else?"

"Two," he said, which sobered her. "But I didn't kill them. I saw one of them being killed, and now I'm to be blamed for both deaths. I've been chased halfway across the city, and the Peacemakers are after me." He was beginning to babble, to blurt the story of his miserable day, and reined himself in, drew a deep breath. Marcade's eyes had glazed over, not from boredom, he knew, but in protection from news she did not wish to hear. *How many times did you see her do that at Pauper's? Sink away into a trance and block out the world?* "Look, I need your help." *No, don't plead. She has no patience for that.*

"Oh, Rhenford, Rhenford, what is this? I don't see you for ten years, and then you burst in out of the rain with wild stories of murder!" She shook her head, denying the whole situation. He took her by the arms and pitched his voice low, urgent but not desperate.

Make it interesting. Make it an adventure. "Marcade, listen to me. I was supposed to deliver a special package from the Duke of the Southern Tier to a servant of the king's, but the man has been murdered and the murderers are after me."

One word caught her attention and drew her back to him. "The king?"

"A servant of his, but yes, I believe the package was meant for the king." *Yes.* He suspected it, though he could not be sure, so it was not a lie; and suddenly a new idea sprang to mind. *Nennius is a companion of the Household. Why didn't you think of that before?* "I believe there may be a plot against Nicanor. These men, these murderers, are trying to keep me from delivering the package."

"A plot against the king?" Her eyes had cleared, and she was catching up to him. "But who? Some pretender?"

"Not that I know of, so far, but I know that—"

Taking his arm, she leapt ahead of him, tugging him toward the parlor. "You must tell Ancus this minute."

Again, he resisted. "You have to understand, Marcade: I'm being hunted by the Peacemakers. If they find me here, you'll be in trouble too."

She waved his warning away. "Trouble me no troubles, Rhenford. You must tell us all, Ancus and I, and we shall think what to do, we three!"

Somehow, Liam found her newborn enthusiasm less than encouraging.

Bursting in on her husband in the small parlor, Liam in tow, Marcade announced: "Rhenford has uncovered a plot to kill the king!"

He takes it well, Liam reflected, a blush rising to his cheeks, *but then he must be used to how excitable she can be.*

Ancus Nennius rose slowly from his chair by the fireplace, looking from his wife to the stranger in his parlor with an expression of mild curiosity. He was a tall man with a handsome, florid face, and had obviously been very fit in his youth; now, in his late thirties, he was beginning to go soft at the edges, and his pale brown hair lay fine and thinning against his pink scalp.

"Sir," he said, and made a small bow in Liam's direction.

Liam responded with a bow of his own, unsure what to make of the man's polite greeting. "Quaestor Liam Rhenford, at your service."

Marcade threw up her hands. "Oh, this is grand! Would you two dance, as well? The king, you fools, the king!"

Nennius clasped his hands behind his back and spoke wearily. "There are a dozen plots against the king every week, my dear. Most of them are no more than idle talk, or drunken boasting."

To Liam's surprise, Marcade's mouth twisted bitterly and she glared daggers at her husband. *There's a history there,* he guessed. *Maybe I'm not the first plot she's brought home.* He cleared his throat. "I'm afraid this is neither, Sir Ancus, though I wish it were. Two men are dead of it already."

Marcade crowed, "Ha! See you?" and Nennius flinched.

"I see. I see." He dropped his chin to his chest for a moment, musing, then raised his head and spread his hands in surrender. "Then you had best tell us all."

Between questions and outbursts from Marcade, it took almost an hour.

"I am a quaestor in the service of Vespasianus, Duke of the Southern Tier," Liam began, when the servant had been sent home for the evening and they were seated— or when he and Nennius were seated, since Marcade remained standing, the better to pace the small square of carpet in front of the fireplace.

He gave a brief history of his service with the Duke and his position as a merchant in Southwark, hoping to convince Nennius that he was a respectable man, not some raving crackpot. It seemed to work: the knight said he knew Vespasianus by reputation. "A noble lord, I believe. Widely respected, loyal to the throne—and wise."

"And very far away," Marcade said. "Get on with it, Rhenford."

"Very far away," Liam agreed, and told them about the package he took to Cade. He did not mention how strange his conversation with the scholar had been. To Nennius, he thought, it would look like paranoia. *But Cade was anxious about where I was this morning, and whether I had seen anyone. And he wanted me to send Fanuilh away, so as not to draw attention to myself.* The conclusion seemed natural: *He was afraid I had been, or would be, followed.*

All that he kept to himself, saying only that he had met the scholar and agreed to go to the house in King's Vale. He told the rest quickly, without details—the man pretending to be Master Bairth, his refusal to hand over the package, the fight, and the real Master Bairth's death, his flight, and the discovery of Cade's murder. He down-played the corruption of the Peacemakers; since it was incredible to him, it would be doubly so to Nennius and Marcade. "They say I committed both murders, and are chasing me because of it."

"I must confess that I do not see the king in this," Nennius murmured doubtfully.

"Hush, he's coming to that," Marcade said, and gave Liam a look that begged him to come to it quickly.

"The king is involved because the package belongs to him." He described the phial and gave them a brief outline of what Tollerdig had told him about true metal and image-glass. "How the Duke came to have it, I don't know, but by rights it should be Nicanor's. As for what it contains, I can't say."

Before he could explain his guesses, Marcade burst out, "Oh, some cure for his illness, I'd wager—some potion!"

Nennius looked skeptical, and Liam blushed and hurried on, "There's also the house. It's high up the vale, not far from the palace itself, and from the crest, the owner is in royal service."

"Could you find it again?" Marcade demanded.

"Yes, easily," Liam said, and named the street. "The crest bore four porpoises, and there was a mounting block out front shaped like a wave." The silence that followed surprised him, and he glanced back and forth from Marcade, whose mouth hung open, to Nennius, who was wincing and rubbing his forehead as if he had a headache.

"Could you describe this Master Bairth again?" the knight asked.

Marcade finally closed her mouth, only to open it immediately: "It's Severn!"

Waving her to silence, Nennius repeated his question, and when Liam had described the murdered man, asked, "And the other man—the impostor?"

Liam described the man in yellow, including his clothes, and watched Marcade's face light up and her husband's grow pale. *They know these men,* he realized. *And they're more important than I thought.*

"It is Severn," Marcade insisted, almost admiringly. "Oh, the bold villain!"

Nennius studied the tips of his house shoes and said, more to himself than anyone else, "He was in yellow at court this morning."

"Severn," Marcade marvelled, "plotting against the king!" Her husband could only shake his head.

Growing impatient, Liam said, "Excuse me, but who are they?"

Still contemplating his shoes, as if their upturned toes held a denial, Nennius said, "Your Master Bairth would seem to be Lord Bairth Severn, Steward of Nicanor's Household."

Liam frowned, confused: the king's steward held one of the most powerful positions at court, and his murder would explain Nennius's distress. *But didn't she just call Severn a villain?*

"And your man in yellow," Nennius went on, "would be his co-steward, Lord Auric Severn."

"His brother," Marcade stage-whispered, and then gave a judicious nod, as if she had expected it all along.

CHAPTER 6

"HIS BROTHER?" *WHAT in the Dark are they talking about?*

Marcade ignored his question, and looked to her husband. "Auric Severn plots against the king," she said, as if it proved some point she had tried to make before. "Even his Steward does not wait on his death!"

Nennius was still unsure, and held up a hand for time.

"Hold on," Liam said, "can someone explain this to me?" Of the four great titles held under the king, the Steward of the Household was the least public. The Prince of the Hosts, the Prince of the Mint, and the Royal Hierarch exercised their functions out among the people, but the Steward operated strictly within the palace, in the shadows of the court. "There are two of them? And they're brothers?"

Still working things out for himself, Nennius explained in a distracted voice, "Their father filled the position for Nicanor's father, and for a time under Nicanor himself." When the elder Severn died, the king split the position between the brothers, ostensibly because there was too much work for one man. "It was considered wise —Auric was the older, and thus the natural successor, but Bairth was the king's intimate, his friend since childhood, as well as trusted by Queen Ierne."

"Ierne the Childless," Marcade muttered, then told Liam, "More, it's known that Lord Auric is strong for Corvialus." Cimber Corvialus was a pretender to the throne, one of the scavengers Cade had mentioned. "His

claim's the best, through his mother, and when the king
dies—"

Nennius interrupted with an exasperated cry: "He is
not dead yet, Marcade!"

She sniffed and lifted her chin, disdainful of the cor-
rection. "No, he is not. But the great lords are beginning
to act as if he were."

They were obviously continuing a conversation begun
well before Liam arrived on the scene, and he needed
to bring them back to the issue at hand. "Then we have
to stop them. Or at least stop this Auric Severn." A chill
ran up Liam's back at the thought. *Gods, his own
brother.* "We need to get the phial to the king, and to
expose Severn for the murderer he is."

"Impossible," Nennius said flatly. "He controls access
to the royal apartments, determines who the king sees,
examines all gifts sent to him. It is impossible." He
brightened momentarily. "Unless the Queen . . ."

Both men turned to Marcade, the unspoken question
in their eyes. She tossed her head and said, "Don't look
to me. I can't approach the queen."

"But you must see her at court," Nennius pointed out.
"You said you saw her just the other day."

She sniffed and drew herself up. "You are mistaken.
She sees none but her ladies-in-waiting, and them rarely,
now that the king is ill and she is by his bed night and
day. They say she barely sleeps, the emptyheaded fool,
and must be reminded to eat."

Bitterness laced her comments, and Liam remembered
Old Becca's talk about her ambition. *She wants to be a
lady-in-waiting, and now the queen she has tried to cul-
tivate may not be queen for long.* "Well, we have to get
it to him somehow," he said, and for Marcade's benefit
added, "If it is a cure for his illness, we won't have to
worry about the queen being secluded by his bedside—
or about Auric Severn or Cimber Corvialus or any other
pretender." She gave a small shrug, half-convinced.

Her husband spread his hands. "I can only suggest that we take this to the Pacifex."

"No!" Liam and Marcade said simultaneously.

Surprised by their vehemence, he flinched back in his chair and blinked up at his wife. "Whyever not?"

Marcade blinked back for a second before answering. "Were you not listening? The Stone Cripple's after Rhenford—wants him for the murders!"

"The Stone Cripple?"

Making a moue of distaste, the knight explained: "A cruel nickname they have for her at court."

"The first for her heart," Marcade went on, with none of her husband's distaste, "and the second for her arm."

While it was cruel, Liam could not argue with it. *"I will find you."* With a sword at her throat. That is stone. You've certainly found a nice bunch of playmates. "It's not just that she wants me for murder," he said, and told them about Aldyne. "So we can't trust her at all."

Groaning, Nennius covered his eyes with his arm. "The Pacifex, too!"

"There must be someone else at court we can approach," Liam suggested. "What about the Prince of Hosts?"

"He's away in Caernarvon," the knight said.

"Giving his allegiance to Silverbridge, no doubt," Marcade said sourly. Rhaedr Silverbridge was the other main pretender, more popular than Corvialus but with a weaker bloodline.

"All right then—the Royal Hierarch, or the Prince of the Mint."

From behind his upraised arm, Nennius sighed. "The priest is in seclusion, praying for the king's life, and Catiline is down the coast, trying to collect taxes from one of the petty lords. He won't return until tomorrow evening."

The situation astonished Liam. "If they're all away, and the king is ill, who's ruling?" Then he answered his own question: "Auric Severn." He cursed, and shook his head. *This is impossible.* He cursed again, bleakly, and noticed that Marcade was looking at him out of the corner of her eye, her head tilted, biting her lip.

"Rhenford," she said tentatively. "This phial—you have it with you?"

He frowned, and realized that they had never seen it. *For all they know, you're making this up.* "Yes," he began, and then Fanuilh's thought crashed through his, a heavy block, a silent shout.

MASTER, THE PACIFEX IS COMING DOWN THE STREET.

Panic came first. Liam jumped to his feet, shouting, "What?"

Frightened, Marcade backed away, and Nennius glanced up in alarm.

Disbelief, then. *That's impossible,* he projected, the words shaky in his mind. *She couldn't have—there's no way!*

She is only a few houses away, master, with five Peacemakers in attendance.

A moan rose in his throat, and he clenched his fists. "It's not possible!"

Wary, as if she were dealing with a dangerous animal, Marcade took a step toward him. "Rhenford? Are you ill?"

An angry retort leaped to his tongue; he bit it back. "Warden's coming. She's coming here." He tore at his hair, trying to concentrate, to figure out what to do: he knew it was true, but he could not believe, and the constant refrain—*It's not possible!*—wrecked his thoughts.

"Here?" Nennius blanched. "Here?"

Only Marcade kept a clear head: frowning, no longer wary, she grabbed Liam's elbow. "Rhenford, how can you possibly know that?"

"Trust me," he snapped, and swallowed a deep breath,

trying to calm himself. The simplest explanation, though it was not true: "I'm a—a wizard. Of sorts. I have spells, magic. Trust me, she's coming here right now." *Which is absolutely impossible!*

Marcade accepted it and took command. "Then you must hide. Ancus, take him upstairs, all the way upstairs, to the garret. If they search, there's the trap to the roof." When the man did not move she clapped her hands. "Go! Don't just sit there!"

Liam moved first, running to the parlor door. He threw it open, sure Warden would be on the other side, and saw that the small entrance hall was empty. His dunnage bag sat on the floor by the front door; he snatched it up—there was no sign of his cloak—and ran for the massive staircase. Nennius caught up to him after the second landing and pushed him farther, shoving insistently and hissing, "Go go go!" in his ear.

The stairs were steep and unlit; Liam ran past a dark hallway on the second floor with Nennius urging him farther, pushing, and he launched himself up another set of steps to the third floor, almost pitch black.

Master, the Pacifex is at the door.

He missed his footing on the last riser, tripped, and fell heavily to the floor at the top of the stairs. Nennius landed on top of him, making frantic hushing noises.

Warden's knock echoed through the house and froze the two men in place, tangled together in the darkness.

Gods, how did she do it? Nennius's breathing was loud in his ear; the knight was heavy and lay without moving, a lead weight on Liam's back and legs. Down below there was another knock and the knight twitched, startled.

An inane thought passed through Liam's mind: *This is embarrassing.* He ducked his head and bit his lip to keep from laughing, knowing it was panic. *But it is embarrassing.* He bit harder, and heard Marcade speak.

"Yes? Oh—good evening, Pacifex Warden. What brings you here at this hour?"

Her voice sounded too bright to Liam, too artificial, and he strained to hear, the manic laughter that had threatened a moment before forgotten.

"My husband is abed, I fear—"

Warden interrupted her, but spoke so low that Liam could not hear what she said, only Marcade's response.

"Me? Whatever for?"

It sounded better to him, less forced.

"Liam Rhenford? Yes, I know a Liam Rhenford. Or, rather, I did. We were students together at Prosper's Tower."

Even better. Just the right note of genuine confusion, with a hint of suspicion. It was better, but he wished he could see her face. That was the best way to judge a person's sincerity—to watch their eyes, and the corners of their mouths.

"No, not in a dozen years or so, no. Why? Is he in Torquay?"

All wrong, Liam decided, and lowered his head to the floor, wincing. *If the Pacifex comes to your door late at night asking about an old friend, you assume something is wrong. You don't ask if he's in town, you worry that something might have happened to him.* The floorboards were cold and rough against his forehead.

Suddenly Marcade laughed. Liam's head snapped up and Nennius convulsed briefly, as if he had been struck by lightning. "Murder? Oh come, Pacifex, there was an amnesty for that years ago!"

What in the Dark is she doing?

A gasp, a pause, another gasp, and finally: "No, he has not been here at all. Do you think he will come? What shall I do if he does? Will he try to hurt me? Oh, I must rouse my husband!"

Better, much better. But will it fool her?

Warden apparently tried to reassure Marcade, because

when she next spoke, she sounded doubtful. "Well, if you are sure. It is so strange, though—he did not seem a murderer when I knew him." She managed a laugh bordering on hysteria that made Liam want to applaud. "But then, he was before, wasn't he? In the Midlands." Warden must have asked her to explain: "His father was killed in a duel with another lord, and that very night he slipped into the man's bedroom and slit his throat from ear to ear. And his wife's, too, they said."

Liam grimaced. *His wife didn't even sleep in the same wing of the castle. She hated him as much as I did.*

"Did I?" Marcade asked, her voice jumping, and then prattled on, sounding less and less convincing. "I suppose I was. He didn't seem a murderer when I knew him—and there was the amnesty. I assumed he must have been innocent, but now that you say he's done it again—" She stopped abruptly and Liam ground his teeth, wondering what the Pacifex had asked to rattle her so.

"You can't just leave, though! Shouldn't you stay, in case he comes? Or leave some of your Peacemakers? If he's so dangerous, and he's been asking after me—" Again she cut off in mid-sentence, then said, "Oh, that is very good to hear. They will be close? But couldn't they stay here? Inside?"

Liam held his breath, both awed and terrified by Marcade's boldness. *If Warden accepts—if she posts men here—*

She did not. "If you think so," Marcade said, skeptical. "Though I should feel safer if they were in the house. I know I shan't sleep tonight."

Let it go, Liam prayed. *Let it go and get her out of here.*

"What? Yes, yes, of course, if I hear from him at all or get a message, I shall inform you directly. Yes, I understand—you directly. But why not one of your men? They will be on hand, won't they? Oh, as you say,

Pacifex, as you say. Yes, Pacifex, good night, good night. Yes, directly to you, of course."

A moment of silence, and then the blessed sound of the door being slammed shut. Liam waited a few seconds, sweat prickling his back and soaking his armpits, then looked over his shoulder at Nennius, a blur in the shadows.

"I think you can get off me now, Sir Ancus."

While they waited for Marcade to join them on the third floor—by tacit consent, neither man made a move to descend—Liam told Fanuilh to follow the Pacifex.

How far, master?

As far as she goes. No, wait: follow her as far as the river, if she goes that way.

Yes, master.

Marcade arrived breathless from the climb and her own excitement, wearing a gleeful grin. The candle in her hand jumped and flickered as she hopped from foot to foot, casting grotesque shadows on the landing.

"Did you hear all that? I fooled her properly!"

Nennius made a choking sound; Liam put his hand on her shoulder to force her to stand still. "Did she say how many men she's leaving behind?"

"Only four, two at either end of the lane. You didn't hear it then? I fooled her properly!"

"We could only hear you," Liam said, and he could tell from the way her face fell that she was disappointed. *Gods, it's not some masque-game.* Still, she had lied to the Pacifex on his behalf, and a little praise seemed scant reward. "It was well done, very well done. But tell me, when you said that you assumed I was innocent before— because of the amnesty—what had she asked you?"

"What had she asked me?" Marcade frowned, then brightened. "Oh yes: she asked why I had sounded so excited when I thought you might be in Torquay. But I

got past her, I think, the withered little thing with her
rude questions."

Her quick questions, Liam thought. *Her very quick
questions.* He was not sure if he would have thought of
it. *Probably not. And she'll make something of it. She'll
know I'm here.*

Seeing his expression, Marcade frowned again. "What
is it, Rhenford? Why do you make that face? She's
left—gone. She believed me."

He shook his head in a distracted way, trying to work
it out for himself. "No, she just doesn't have reason
enough to search the house." Which made no sense to
him, but he believed it nonetheless. "She knows I'm
here, though, or suspects it." He could not say why he
was so sure. *Could it be because she's tracked you all
over the city without breaking a sweat?* "Or at least we
have to assume that. It's safest. Are there any ways out
of here beside the front door?"

"There's the way to the alley," Nennius offered, recovered somewhat from the shock of the whole thing
but still a little shaky. "Through the kitchen shed."

"You can't be thinking of leaving now," Marcade protested.

"She'll have the back way watched. Anything else?"

"Rhenford, you're plainly exhausted, and it's foul out,
and they're looking for you. You should hide here."

He ignored her, focused on Nennius. "Anything else?"

"A trap in the garret," the knight said, "but it only
leads to the roof."

"Rhenford, this is madness! You cannot leave tonight!
You're done in!"

She was right: he was exhausted, and he needed to
rest before going out on the roofs. "I'm not going to
leave now," he told her. *Not until Warden is far away.*
"Not for a while, at least. In the meantime, do you think
I could have something to eat, and a look at this trap?"

•   •   •

Feeble moonlight did its best to illuminate the roofscape through the thinning mist and clouds. A cold wind blew through the little hatch in the steeply pitched roof. At Liam's side, Nennius shivered; Marcade, annoyed at being left out of the exploration of the garret, had grudgingly gone downstairs to get food and blankets and only after making Liam promise to stay the night.

"You see?" the knight asked. "It's useless. You'd fall."

Liam took one last look at the roof, at the roofs all around. They were a perfect road. He shut the trapdoor, cutting off even the weak moonlight. "No," he said in the total darkness of the garret. "No, it's fine." *Well, not fine, exactly.* The roof tiles would be lead or slate or clay, slippery and dangerous, but he had done worse. "Good enough. Come on."

They groped their way back to the garret door and opened it on the steps, which led down to the third floor. Marcade's candle stood on the top step, and Nennius let out a pent-up breath at the access of light.

"Look," Liam said, "I can't stay here very long. I know what I told Marcade, but I'm going to go in a few hours." *Where?*

Nennius swallowed hard. "If you need to stay longer," he began, and Liam cut him off with a curt head-shake.

"No, I'm putting you two in danger. I'll go in a few hours. But I need you to do something, if you will."

Not bothering to hide his relief, Nennius nodded. "Of course. Do you want me to contact Publius Catiline for you?"

"Yes, exactly," Liam said, surprised that the man had caught on so quickly. He had to admit that he had not formed a very good impression of Marcade's husband. *For a knight, he has pretty weak nerves.* "Tell him what I told you, and see if he'll meet with me." *But then, if a wanted murderer dragged you into a conspiracy against the king and brought the Pacifex to your door in the middle of the night, you'd be nervous, too.*

Nennius moistened his lips and shook his head. "But where will you be? How will we get word to you?"

Liam thought a moment, then told the knight to leave a mark on the trapdoor if he could arrange a meeting with the Prince of the Mint. "Warden won't look for it up there, and I have a way to check." No need to say that the way would involve his dragon familiar flying over the house—and Nennius did not ask, just nodded and moistened his lips again.

They stood together by the candle, and the silence between them quickly grew oppressive. Liam could not shake the feeling that he owed Nennius an apology, that whatever duty the knight owed his king did not extend to harboring fugitives and defying the Pacifex of Torquay. *Not that you owe the king any more than he does. But then, it's your problem, isn't it? It's square in your lap.* He had the phial, he had been ordered to deliver it, he was going to take the blame for the deaths of Bairth Severn and Master Cade, and he was the one for whom Warden was searching.

With a nervous cough, Nennius said that he would go see what was keeping his wife, and disappeared down the stairs. Liam watched him go, feeling a certain guilty relief. *I've got to get out of here. She'll come back soon enough.* He sat stiffly on the top step, brooding over Warden. *Soon enough. How does she do it?* His feet were sore; he pulled off his boots and wiggled his toes gratefully. *How? No one knew you were coming here.* That was not exactly true—Old Becca and her son knew that he had asked, but they had no way of knowing that he was sought by the Peacemakers, and though he racked his brain, he could think of nothing in his behavior at Prosper's Tower that would have given him away. It was the same with his inn; only Cade had known he was staying there. *And Cade isn't telling anyone anything.*

He scowled at the joke, wishing he had not made it, and heard Marcade coming up the stairs. She had a blanket slung over each shoulder, and carried a plate covered by a napkin in one hand and a jug in the other.

"Your dinner, my lord," she said, a mock serving girl. "Where would you have it?"

Liam gave a tired smile, climbed to his feet, and took the candle into the garret. "In here, wench," he said, halfheartedly entering into the game. "And mind you're careful of my linens." The garret was unfinished, just a cramped space beneath the roof, all exposed beams and dust; he could barely stand in the center. "You may make up my bed in the west wing."

Letting the blankets fall in a heap, she sat on the floor, setting the plate and jug down in front of her. Liam sat across from her, removed the napkin, and started eating, hungrier than he had realized. It was only bread and cold meat but he ate as if it were a feast, taking a sort of comfort from the mechanics of chewing and swallowing. The meat looked as if it had been torn off the bone. *Marcade never was the domestic sort.*

She watched him as he ate, biting her lip, and when he finally pushed aside the plate—having left some meat for Fanuilh—and reached for the jug, she chuckled. "You were hungry." She made it sound like a weakness.

"Nothing like being the fox to build an appetite," he said, and sampled the jug: cider, on the verge of turning. He drank anyway.

"Rhenford," she said, bending forward to touch his knee, not bantering now, "what are you going to do?"

"Do?" The weight of the day pressed in on him, his full stomach a drain. He wanted to lie down, and he did, stretching out on his back and lacing his fingers behind his head. "Do? Your husband's going to try to get me in touch with the Prince of the Mint. If he can, then I'll give him this damned phial, he'll give it to the king, and I can go home."

She dropped her eyes to her hands, her fingers twining idly. "This phial—will it cure the king, do you think?"

Liam sighed. "I don't know. I don't know what it is, or what's inside. But it must be pretty important, since the good Steward thinks it's worth killing for."

"Severn." She shook her head. "He's cast his lot with Corvialus, you mark me. When Nicanor dies, Corvialus will have the throne."

"If Nicanor dies," Liam corrected, then chuckled, remembering how Old Becca had scolded her son for suggesting that there might soon be a new queen. "He's not dead yet, Marcade. It's not a good idea to vow fealty to the new king before the old one's been taken to Rentrillian. You read the same histories I did—men like Severn usually end up with their heads on pikes."

She bit her lip. "Or they end up steward to the new king."

"He's a murderer," Liam said, sounding harsher than he meant to. "He had his own brother killed, and for all we know he's trying to kill the king." A picture of the man in yellow appeared in his head, and he sat up and levelled a long forefinger at her. "If he ends up profiting from this, you mark me, I'll make him pay personally."

Marcade returned his glare with a look of skeptical amusement. "Of course you will." She laughed at his scowl. "Rhenford, you poor country rustic, you're in far over your head, aren't you? You have no idea what these men are capable of. They live and breathe plots and counterplots; they are weaned on treachery. The rest of us must just stay out of the way, curry favor when we can, and take what we may when the opportunity offers."

Ambitious! Gods, Old Becca didn't know the half of it. She had been cynical at university, but then there had been a freshness to it, as if she were cynical about everything but cynicism. Now even her world-weariness had a jaded edge. "I'll tell you what," he said. "When we hand the phial over to Catiline, you can have the reward. If there is one. And you can tell everyone at court how you saved the king's life."

The sarcasm was lost on her. "The phial—you have it with you? May I see it?"

"It's not here. I hid it somewhere safe."

"Where?"

"Somewhere safe." He sounded peevish even to himself, and she laughed at him.

"Poor Rhenford. You may have your secret if you wish. Only tell me this: is it nearby, your 'somewhere safe'?"

"Near enough. I can lay my hands on it when I need to."

She nodded her approval, then rose. "Good. You'll need it tomorrow, when you go to see Publius Catiline. And don't think I won't hold you to your promise. With rates what they are, I think that's a fair exchange for a night's room and board."

He started to say that he would not be there the entire night, then decided against it. *No sense having that conversation again.* He managed a smile. "Fair enough, though your cider tastes suspiciously like vinegar. Do you turn it yourself?"

"I whispered your name over it," she shot back, "and it turned on its own." They grinned at each other, back on familiar territory, and then her grin softened to a sad sort of smile and she went to the door. "Get you to bed, Rhenford, such as it is. I'll see you in the morning."

No you won't. "Marcade." She stopped on the top stair. "Thank you."

She waved the thanks away, and left.

Guilt pricked Liam a thousand different ways, and every time he refuted one pang, another took its place: that he had lied to Marcade; that he had thought her ambitious and cynical when she had taken him in without question, and stood off the Pacifex for his sake; that he had dragged her into the whole mess in the first place. Worse, he felt guilty because a part of him would be glad to get out of the house and away from her. She was not the person he remembered.

How would you know? Gods, you didn't even think of coming to see her until you needed help. If you weren't being chased, you'd have left Torquay without looking her up. And she was one of your closest friends. The thought—and what it might say about him—did not bear inspection. He growled and paced as well as he could in the tiny garret, focusing his mind to project.

Fanuilh! Where are you?

At the river, master. The Pacifex is here, at the landing, with a number of Peacemakers. She is giving orders. I am close enough to hear, if you would.

Sharing his familiar's senses was the benefit of their relationship he liked least; it made his skin crawl, and often left him disoriented. He was feeling penitent. *Yes. Your eyes, too.*

Closing his own, he envisioned himself putting on a great bell of a helmet, the visor fashioned like a dragon's snout. He imagined a clap of thunder, and then pictured pulling down the visor, which had no eyeslit. When he opened his eyes again, he was looking down on the Pacifex Warden from the top of the canvas covering of the public water stairs at the foot of the Processional. The shift in perspective made him wobble; he could feel himself sway, though what he saw did not move. His stomach fluttered, and he swallowed hard and planted his feet firmly. The Pacifex was speaking.

"He may be a wizard, but I do not suspect a very powerful one. Nonetheless, you will not approach him." She was shorter than all of the twenty Peacemakers who surrounded her, and had her cloak open, revealing the withered arm bound to her side. She was small, crippled—and the constables watched her and listened to her crisp commands with the quiet trust usually reserved for battle-scarred veterans. "You will patrol in pairs, and if you see him abroad, you will follow him wherever he goes. At the first opportunity, the junior man will report to me—directly to me, and no one else—while the senior man keeps him in view. Am I clear?"

As one, the Peacemakers said, "Yes, Pacifex."

Alone in the garret, Liam shivered. *She wants to capture me herself. So I don't have a chance to talk to anyone who's not in on it with her.*

Warden paired them off and gave them posts; he listened, marking the spots in his memory as best he could, wishing he knew more about the streets in King's Vale. When she was done, there were two men left over; she beckoned for them to follow her down the stairs to a small punt.

"We'll cross," she said, climbing into the boat with some difficulty. Neither man offered to help. "And once there, you two will go to the barracks and fetch twenty more for extra duty." She settled herself on the seat in the bow and the two men climbed in.

"On the far bank?" asked the man who took up the oars. "Your pardon, Pacifex, but I thought our fellow had gone to ground this side of the river."

"Our fellow," Warden replied, with the slow, careful speech of a patient teacher, "has murdered a Steward of the Royal Household, bested Lieutenant Aldyne and myself, and evaded a thousand Peacemakers when they knew every step he took. I do not think he will scruple at crossing a mere river."

Chastened, the man hung his head and applied himself to the oars.

Liam lifted the imaginary visor, pretended thunder, and looked once more on the garret with a sour grin. *Your fellow may have done all that, but he nearly messed himself doing it.* The grin faded, his lips twisting unhappily as he wondered what she meant about knowing every step he took.

Master, shall I follow her?

No. Come back here. We need to figure out a plan.

She did know every step he took. More, she seemed to know all about him: his inn, his collegium, his friends. *It's as if she's heard about me, or met me before. As if we had been introduced.*

All at once he cursed and put his head in his hands. *Introduced. Gods, you're an idiot.*

CHAPTER 7

IN HIS LETTER of introduction, the Duke had written that Liam attended university in Torquay; Master Cade had written down the name of his inn on the same letter.

"She's not omniscient," Liam muttered bitterly, "she just knows how to read." And how to follow up on it, he knew; he was not denigrating her, but berating himself. *She went right to the inn, and almost caught you there. When that failed, she picked up the very next thing she knew about you and sent men to Gown Street.*

Two questions sprang to mind: why had she given up so easily at Marcade's door, and what else might she know about him? He could not guess at the first, unless she wanted to avoid creating too much of a stir in her pursuit. The answer to the second worried at him, because he decided that it was everything. *Or everything useful, at any rate. Where I'm from, and thus my accent; the name of my ship. My history, my skills, such as they are, my business interests.* All that and a general summary of his character would be called for in a proper letter of introduction, and he had no doubt that the Duke would have written a very proper letter.

So she's read all about me. Small wonder she knows every step I take. He cursed again and sat down next to the blankets Marcade had brought him, dragging one around his shoulders. *If you could get just a glimpse of it. . . .* His shoulders sagged and he let his head fall, wishing he had the letter, wishing he had been nosy enough to read it during the journey from Southwark. *A week you carried the damned thing. A week.*

Every breath deflated him further, drawing his chin toward his chest, dragging his eyelids down, draining the strength from his arms and back. He was tired, so tired his aches and bruises seemed distant and dull. A dangerous apathy threatened, and Liam shrugged off the blanket and climbed slowly to his feet. He stretched, trying to drive blood to his limbs and his sluggish brain.

Master, I am on the roof.

He did not bother to respond, just went to the trapdoor and pushed it open long enough for Fanuilh to come through. Too late he remembered the candle, and then shrugged. Warden knew he was there, he was sure. *What's it matter?* He looked down at the dragon, sitting on its haunches at his feet, waiting to report. "I saved you some meat. Cooked, I'm afraid."

Thank you, master. It rose and padded to the plate, considered the cold meat for a second, and snapped up a large chunk. *There are two Peacemakers stationed at either end of the lane.*

"Where else would they be?" He sank down next to his familiar and grabbed a blanket again. The phial was still tied to the dragon's back; he reached out toward it, then let his arm fall. "What should I do, do you suppose?"

Fanuilh looked up from its dinner. *Do? Find out what this is*—it wriggled its back and the phial wobbled a little—*and what it does. If it belongs to the king, return it to him.* It bobbed its head once for emphasis, and resumed eating.

Liam chuckled and lay down on his side, tucking the blanket around him. "Can I do that from here, do you think?"

The dragon did not look up. *You are joking.*

"Oh yes. Yes, I am."

You are tired.

"Not at all." His eyes closed on their own.

If you will let me outside to stand watch, you can take a nap.

"No," he murmured, "I have a big mistake to make. And I should get out of here anyway." The cynical voice in the back of his head pointed out that he would not get far lying on the floor wrapped in a blanket. He agreed completely, but could find neither the strength nor the will to rise.

Since the Pacifex has not chosen to invade the house, I think we may conclude that she does not intend to. She may not even be sure that you are here; she posted men elsewhere, in case you were not. You should be safe for an hour, or perhaps two.

"You have a nap too, then." His voice barely rose above a murmur. Sleep tempted him. There was no point in staying awake, since Warden would come or not as she chose. There was something wrong with that logic, but he could not find the fault. "You sleep, too."

I am not tired.

"Good boy." He was stupid now, confused. "A little nap."

Liam dozed.

Time passed, and Liam could not be sure if he was asleep or awake. He saw things that could not be in the garret—a burning castle, a woman's face framed by auburn hair, the Flying Stair rising in its daily course beside the falls of the Royal—but he could not tell if they were memories or dreams. All the while he was aware of his situation, of the foolishness of sleeping, so he berated himself for thinking—or dreaming—of the woman, and the castle. It was worse than sleep, and when Fanuilh roused him he felt even more disoriented than before.

Master, there is a man on the stairs.

Liam struggled up to a sitting position, his eyes full

of sand. The candle had burned halfway down. "What?" His voice was scratchy; he coughed and tried again. "What? Who's there?"

I do not know. He stopped just outside the door.

The blanket had twined itself around him, he fought free and staggered to his feet, wincing. Stiff and sore, stupid with unsatisfactory sleep, he trudged over to the door and threw it open.

Nennius was crouched on the top step, his florid face all circles of surprise: wide eyes, gaping mouth.

"What is it?" Liam demanded.

"Rhenford," he stammered, jumping to his feet. "You—you must go."

Liam blinked several times at the knight, still trying to rouse his sluggish brain. Images from his dreams vied for his attention. "Yes, yes, you're right. Soon."

"No," Nennius blurted. "Now—this minute." His face screwed up in misery. "I fear Marcade has done something irretrievable."

"Everything she does is irretrievable." The fog was gradually lifting, driven by the knight's palpable anxiety.

"Please, you must go," Nennius begged. "They may come at any time. I tried to convince her it was madness, but she would not listen."

For the first time, Liam noticed that the other man was wearing a long nightshirt. He knuckled his eyes, shook his head. "What are you talking about?"

Master, I believe Lady Marcade has betrayed you.

Nennius drew a deep breath, closed his eyes, and plunged in. "She's gone to Severn. She means to strike a bargain with him."

Liam goggled for a long second, and when he found his voice, it rapidly grew to a shout: "A bargain? She's selling me to him?"

Cringing before his anger, the knight protested, "No, no, not that—not betrayal, never—but she thinks that the king is—that the king is lost, and that Severn is the

coming man. She means to make a bargain for you—
for your life."

Master, you should leave at once.

"My life," Liam spat, "and your advancement."

The knight blushed, miserable, and dropped his eyes
to his bare feet. "She is too ambitious, I know it, but I
swear that she would not let them harm you. She thought
that when you saw you were caught, you would surrender the phial and Severn could let you go."

"She thought nothing of the kind, the bitch. She
thought they'd kill me and then Severn would owe her
a debt. That's what she thought."

Aghast, Nennius made patting motions in the air. "Oh,
no, Rhenford, no! She'd never let harm come to you.
She's foolish and mad, but she does love you as a friend.
If you knew the times she spoke of you, and your days
at Pauper's! If I thought she meant you harm, I'd never
have let her go."

His head was clear now—too clear. "But you let her
go all the same, didn't you? Didn't have the courage to
go yourself." He glared disdainfully down at the knight,
then spun on his heel and went to the trapdoor, beckoning Fanuilh to join him. *Scout around. See who's out
there.*

"She would not be stopped," Nennius whined, then
gasped when he saw the tiny dragon jump through the
trapdoor Liam held open.

I will not be long.

Good. Come back when you're done. He shut the trapdoor and turned back to Nennius. "How long ago did
she leave?" The knight was still dumbstruck by the sight
of the dragon, and Liam had to repeat his question before he stammered that it had been about half an hour.

"I should have come sooner, I know—but she seemed
so sure it would work, that you would be safe, and we
should have friends in the court. I sat, and thought and
thought. She seemed so sure, and she told me to stay

put, not to interfere. She is so much wiser in these things than I."

While he rambled on, justifying his hesitation, Liam gathered the blankets, his bag, and his sword-stick. *Half an hour.* She would have arrived at Severn's by now, and was probably talking to him right then. *If she's not on her way back with him, the stupid bitch.*

Nennius was still explaining himself; Liam cut him off. "Do you have bars on your doors?"

"Y-yes. Why? You can't mean to wait here for them?"

"No. Come on." He shouldered past and started down the stairs at a trot. The knight followed, chattering questions, which Liam ignored. He barred the front door and did the same for the door that led out to the kitchen shed. He turned then and thought, *Now what?*

Nennius stood wringing his hands. "Please, Rhenford, what are you going to do?"

Liam put his back to the door and considered the man. He was barefoot, in his nightdress, with his arms clutched around his middle. "Do?" *You should kill him.* The thought was unwelcome, but would not be denied. Nennius knew he meant to escape by the roof, and that he meant to contact Catiline. *And he'll tell, too. He won't want to but they'll make him, or Marcade will.* For a wild moment, Liam considered asking if the knight wanted to come with him, then rejected the idea: Nennius would never accept. *Too scared. He'll say they'd never hurt him. You should kill him. You have to kill him.*

The wood of the stick was smooth in his hands; handle and sheath would slide apart like silk on silk. *Easy.* Liam saw it, the two quick thrusts, one in the stomach, since the blade was too slim to punch through the bones over the heart, and the second in the throat to finish him. *Easy.*

Instead, he paused. "Why did you warn me?"

Nennius blushed and averted his eyes. "That potion you have—will it save the king?"

"It may." *It just saved you.* "Come on." Again he ignored the knight's questions, leading him up to the second floor and into the first door he came to. It was a bedroom, with a big four-poster bed that, in the orange glow of the tiny coal fire in the grate, looked like a curtained catafalque. He handed Nennius one of the blankets, and the knife from his belt. "Cut it into strips. I'm going to have to tie you up, or else they'll know you helped me."

With shaking hands, the knight did as he was told. "But where will you go? What will you do? Will you still try to reach Catiline?"

"No. Marcade knows about that, and she'll tell them." He opened the stick a short way and used the edge to cut into the tough border of his blanket, then tore it the rest of the way.

"She did not mean—"

"I know, I know," Liam snapped. "She didn't mean me any harm. That's not the point. She's caused me harm. They'll have Catiline watched. I can't go to him." *Or you could—if they thought you wouldn't.* "No," he went on, "no, Catiline is out of it entirely." *What to tell him?* "I'll go to the priests, I think. Up in Rentrillian. They're loyal, and maybe one of them can get word to the Royal Hierarch."

"Rentrillian?" Nennius ripped dutifully, but looked doubtful. "There are not many places to hide there. Only temples and tombs."

Liam faked a grin. "Which means they won't look for me there. No, Rentrillian it is. The priests will help me. Now, I think we have enough. Lie down next to the bed."

The knight acquiesced so readily that Liam felt a pang of guilt as he bound the man's legs with the strips of blanket, and then his hands behind his back. "Too loose," the knight advised, and grunted when Liam yanked the strip tight around his wrists.

"Sorry about this," Liam said, holding up a last piece for a gag.

"It is I who must apologize to you," Nennius said, sounding wretched. "Do what you must, and save the king if you can."

Poor bastard. Swallowing around the unexpected lump in his throat, Liam gagged the knight, made sure he could breathe through his nose, and shoved him far under the bed. "You can thump around when they come in, and say I took you by surprise."

Nennius grunted through the cloth, and Liam hurried out of the room.

Without a candle this time, Liam held the trapdoor open and gazed out at the roofscape. There were fewer clouds and less mist. The moon, however, was fast going down, so the visibility was no better. *Can't help that.* He looked down at Fanuilh, perched on the roof outside, its reconnaissance finished.

I have seen a way you may get past them, though it will require a long jump from one house to the next.

"Let's do it, then," Liam muttered, and climbed out onto the roof.

Lead and wet, the tiles gave him almost no purchase; he had to brace his feet against the hinges of the trapdoor to boost himself up to the roofpeak. He straddled it, the pitch on either side so steep it was like riding a knife edge. *Which way?*

The dragon flapped its wings once and alighted beside him. *Behind you, master. After six houses, this row ends. The house across the way is not too far to jump, and if you wait until the Peacemakers are not looking, you should escape unseen.*

They won't look up, anyway. It was a common axiom among the thieves Liam had known, a sort of vertical blindness ascribed to constables and thieftakers across the kingdom. He hoped it still held—he had run with the thieves almost ten years before, when he was outlawed for the murder of Lord Diamond, and only for a year, never rising far above apprentice. *All right,* he projected, squirming around until he faced the other way, *get where you can watch the street. I want to know when Severn arrives.*

Fanuilh took off, and Liam took a deep breath.

Easier without the boots. Thieves who regularly did this kind of work went barefoot, or wore special slippers. *They also stay at home when it's wet and cold.* He swiped his hand across the tiles, and wiped cold water in his eyes to clean out the last of his nap. Another deep breath and he rose smoothly to his feet. He hesitated for a second, checking his balance, compensating for the dunnage bag slung over his shoulder—it was an awkward bundle, with the sword-stick jammed into it—then ran forward on the peak.

He kept his toes pointed ahead and out, the way the thieves had taught him, put each foot down firmly but briefly. Dancing a razor, they called it, and it worked, bringing him within a foot of the next roof, his boots holding on the slick tiles.

It was the bag that almost killed him, swinging in an unexpected way at the last second, the weight shifting him so he wobbled and slipped and fell right where the roofs met. His feet disappeared and he threw himself forward, the upper half of his body slamming down on the neighbor's roof, striking the edge with his ribs just below his heart. The air burst from his lungs and he scrabbled for a hold, palms and fingernails scraping on the wooden shingles of the new roof. His feet were nowhere, flailing in a black gulf with no purchase on Marcade's lead tiles.

Master, Lord Severn has arrived, with Lieutenant Aldyne.

He barely registered the thought, gripping with hands and elbows, folding up his legs until he could gather them beneath him and hook a foot over the peak of the lower roof and heave himself into a steady position. He hung there, not daring to breathe, sure that even his heartbeat would upset his balance.

They are coming down Stable Lane. They have the servant with them, but no other Peacemakers.

Finally, Liam breathed and hauled himself up to the next roof. The shingles gave better footing, and after settling his bag more securely in the middle of his back he scuttled across to the next house. There was a chimney at the far end, and he clutched gratefully at the solid bricks for a moment, getting his breathing under control, taking stock. His legs were water, and there was a new pain in his ribs. *Bruised, certainly, probably cracked. But not broken.* He offered a broadcast prayer of thanks, and then cursed Marcade.

Master, they are almost at the door.

Craning his neck, he tried to peer over the edge of the roof into Stable Lane, but the street was too narrow, and he could not see below the second floor of the houses opposite. The roof looked almost vertical, and he saw himself sliding down it, unstoppable, shooting over the gutters and dropping to the cobbles below. There was no wind but he felt something tugging at him, trying to pry him away from the chimney, the force and lure of the steep angles, the inevitability of falling. *Don't move.* His body seemed to lean into it, his blood drawn like the outgoing tide, yearning for depth. His heart beat loud in his ears, each pulse a tremor, and he clung desperately to the chimney. *Don't move.*

Master, Lieutenant Aldyne is trying the door.

It was vertigo; he knew it, but the gap at the end of the roof held his eyes, the dark canyon of the street, and he was sure that if he moved, he would fall. Second thoughts fluttered through his head: he should have

taken off his boots, he should have gotten gloves, he
should never have come to Marcade's in the first place.

Master! The thought swelled, forcing away his doubts,
crushing the disorder in his mind. *You must move* NOW.

He started, blinked, the spell of the fall broken, and
slowly began to inch his way around the chimney. With
his eyes fixed on the bricks it was easier, though the
chimney was wide and he had to let himself down onto
the slant of the shingles. He was all fingers and knees,
pressing the wet, gritty bricks, sliding down and around
until he could sense the drop on the far side. He risked
a quick glance—it was only a few feet to the next roof—
and lowered himself until his toes touched, then stayed
there for a few seconds, unwilling to release the chimney.

You used to be better at this. He laughed, a thin, shuddering sound, and forced a hand away from the comforting solidity of the bricks, twisted around to face the
direction he had to go.

Lieutenant Aldyne is putting his shoulder to the door.

This roof was better, wooden-shingled too but flatter,
and it met flush with the next. *The door will hold a
while.* He took a deep breath, winced at the flare of pain
from his ribs, took a smaller breath, and made his way
across. At the juncture of the houses he crouched down
for a moment to steady himself, listening. A muffled
thud rose up from the street, then another: Aldyne forcing Marcade's door. Liam rose and ran to the fourth
house.

More confident with the panic behind him, he swung
himself up to the new roof—an expanse of clay tiles
broken by a number of small chimney pots—and hurried
along the peak to the fifth house. He could think now,
wonder what it meant that Severn had not brought Marcade.

*She's probably had her throat slit, damn her. Always
so damned smart. Now who has no idea what these men*

are capable of? He snarled, set the thought aside. *I didn't make her go to them. I didn't make her betray me.*

The fifth house had no peak, just a gentle slope from front to back, and he crossed it in a flash. The sixth— and last, according to Fanuilh—was a story taller, and he had to jump to catch hold of its projecting eaves, then scramble with his feet, bootheels slipping erratically on the party wall, to hoist himself up.

Master, Lieutenant Aldyne has broken into the house.

The barred door had not gained him as much time as he had hoped, and he took the peak of the sixth house faster than any of the others, dropping down to hands and knees at the far end to survey the jump Fanuilh expected him to make to the next block.

With his head out over the edge, he could see all the way to the street below, which ran into Stable Lane at an angle. Two Peacemakers stood with lanterns at the corner, looking down toward Marcade's house, no doubt watching their lieutenant break in.

Are you crazy? Liam projected. The house opposite seemed miles away. *I can't jump that!*

It is not far.

Indistinct in the dying moonlight, he could just make out what looked like a pair of dormer windows. *There's no place to land!*

Aim in between the gables. There is more than enough space. I checked.

Liam ground his teeth. *I don't know if you noticed, but I don't have wings, Fanuilh. I'm not a little butterfly, like some of us.* Down below, the two Peacemakers stood talking in their circle of lanternlight. He could not hear what they were saying. *But you can bet they'll hear me when I thump down on that roof.*

I will watch them, and cast Sleep on them if they notice you.

The gap from house to house was perhaps six or seven

feet wide, which was, to Liam, more than enough space to miss. *Why can't you just do it now? Then I could climb down like a civilized person.* He knew the answer before Fanuilh replied.

I could, it projected, *but then when Lord Severn and Lieutenant Aldyne come out of the house, they will know that you have passed by. If you make the jump, they will wonder how you escaped, and your trail will be cold.* There was a pause, during which Liam remeasured the gap with a skeptical eye. *I did not say it would be easy, master.*

No, you just didn't say I was likely to break my neck doing it. The dragon was right, though: if he could get away without having to use its magic, Aldyne and Severn would be left with a cold trail. *A lukewarm trail, really. They'll find Nennius soon, and then they'll be after you in a flash.*

Worming back from the edge of the building, he stood and backed farther off, gauging the distance. *All right,* he projected, *keep an eye on the Peacemakers.* He tensed, folded into a sprinter's crouch and ran for the gap.

In the air for little more than a second, he had almost no time to be afraid—and then he hit the other roof, right between the dormers. The wave of joy that swept through him lasted no longer than the leap: the noise of his landing had sounded shockingly loud, like the kettle drums they used in the Storm King's temples to simulate thunder.

The Peacemakers have not moved, Fanuilh reported, but Liam was not interested in them. Beneath the shingles on which he lay, he heard someone grumble sleepily, and the creaking of rope springs, as whoever he had disturbed turned in their bed. He should have frozen, waiting for them to fall back asleep, but he could not wait: he reached out and pulled himself up one of the dormers, and from there up to the roofpeak. *Fanuilh, get up here. If anyone pokes their head out, put them to sleep.*

From the peak, the roof sloped gently back until it touched the rear wall of the building beyond. He ran to it and hoisted himself up to that roof, chose the direction that seemed easiest, and started off at a trot.

No one emerged from the dormers, and after Liam had put several houses between himself and the Peacemakers, he sent Fanuilh back to watch for Severn and Aldyne. *Let me know when they come out.* He continued on across the roofscape.

Occasional pigeons cooed their anger at him, and once an owl questioned his passing from a tree set incongruously in a hidden garden surrounded by four high-walled houses; otherwise he had the heights to himself. They were a road as good as any below, and since he could choose his own path, he never had to make a leap like the one by Stable Lane. Twice he had to cross gaps, but the biggest was only three feet wide, and he simply stepped to the far side.

He climbed chimneys or sought out particularly tall roofpeaks to check his bearings, heading as much as possible down King's Vale and toward the river, avoiding the posts he had overheard Warden setting up.

What he would do when he reached the Royal occupied his mind as he ran and climbed—climbed more often than not, up and down, until his arms trembled and the sweat ran down his face despite the cold. *Maybe not as good a road as any below,* he thought, and decided to take a brief break, perched atop the stone gable of some rich courtier's home. *Figure out what you're going to do.*

Catiline remained a possibility, his only one, as far as he could tell, in spite of what Nennius would tell Severn. *Marcade thought he could help.* He frowned and spat, thinking of her foolishness. *She probably didn't mean*

for me to come to any harm. She just didn't think. What
that had cost her he did not want to guess; it bothered
him that Severn and Aldyne had come without her. He
thought briefly about sending the dragon up to Severn's
house to see if Marcade was there and safe, then rebelled
against the idea. *The Dark with that. She betrayed you,
whether she meant you to get hurt or not. Let her get
herself out of it. You need to figure out your next step.*

There was Catiline, but the man would not be back
in Torquay until tomorrow, and Liam had no idea what
time he would arrive. *Warden will be out in full force
at dawn, you can count on that. Particularly when Aldyne tells her how close she came to getting you.* Her
failure to press in when she had him cornered puzzled
him more and more. He did not believe she had been
fooled by Marcade's lies, and niceties such as proof and
evidence had not stopped her lieutenant from breaking
down doors. So why had she balked at it? *Some deep
reason,* he granted her. *Some deep and clever trick. Aldyne may be all brute force, but she's all cold cunning.
She's better at this than you are.* And she knew everything she could want to know about her quarry, from
the Duke's letter of introduction.

Oh, I'd love to read that. Not just because he would
then know exactly what she did, but also because he
guessed it might tell him more about the phial. It might
give him another name, someone the Duke or Master
Cade knew whom he could trust. For that matter, five
minutes in Cade's study might be useful, even if the
Pacifex had removed the Duke's letter. The scholar had
not trusted the name of Liam's inn to his memory; there
was no telling what else he might have committed to
paper.

Five minutes, Liam thought, warming to the idea. *Why
not?*

Given what he hoped to find, crossing the river again
seemed a small price to pay, and breaking into Cade's

house would not be difficult. *Open window,* he thought, using the thieves' slang for an easy job, *especially for one who's danced the razor all over King's Vale.* He grinned wryly, but meant it nonetheless. Breaking in would be easy, and he did not think Warden would expect it. That decided him, in the end.

The Duke may have written a lot about you in that letter, but there's no way he would write that you were mad enough to return to the scene of a crime.

CHAPTER 8

LIAM DESCENDED FROM the rooftops a street away from the Embankment, and summoned Fanuilh to join him.

Severn and Lieutenant Aldyne have not come out yet, master.

I can't wait around for them all night, he projected. *We have things to do.* As the dragon made its way down to him, he explained his plan to break into Cade's house and rifle through his papers. Fanuilh disliked the idea.

You cannot be sure there will be anything there of use, it pointed out. *And anything you find, Pacifex Warden will have found before you.*

Liam had to admit both arguments. *But what else can I do?*

Leave Torquay, the dragon advised. It had obviously been considering the idea for some time, because it had reasons ready: Warden would expect him to try to stay in the city to deliver the phial, so she would be guarding against attempts to reach the king or those loyal to him, not to flee the capital; and while the *Trade's Increase* might be watched, she could not watch all the other ships in the City Below. *You could take passage on any of a dozen ships, and be back in Southwark within two weeks.*

He let his familiar finish, then projected a question. *And what about the king? What if he dies while I'm saving my own skin?*

You do not know that the phial will cure him, master.

118

That was true, but Liam had meant the question rhetorically: he could not flee Torquay, and he was surprised that Fanuilh had even suggested it. *It might save him, and if there's a chance, I have to try.*

He stood in the mouth of an alley, rubbing his arms to stay warm, and waited for the dragon to respond. Finally, as he was growing impatient, it asked, *Why?*

Why? Because he's the king. Why else?

There are others to follow him—Silverbridge, or Corvialus. They might be better than Nicanor. He is a weak man, and childless. You yourself have said that he is not a very good king, and that Taralon needs a stronger one.

He had said that, and believed it, and he winced. *That doesn't mean I can just let him die. Besides, if I go back to the Southern Tier now, how do you think the Duke would take it?*

Ah. Yes, he would be very displeased. That is true.

Displeased isn't in it, familiar mine. He'd have my head.

The prospect of the Duke's displeasure served to silence the dragon's objections, but it did not satisfy Liam. He was afraid of the Duke—a stern man, with little patience for failure or disobedience—but his refusal to leave was based on other, more obscure reasons.

Loyalty to the king was foremost among them, but Fanuilh's simple question made him wonder at it. Nicanor IV was a weak king, his rule ineffectual, and the land suffered for it: trade and travel were dangerous and slow; pirates infested the sea lanes; bandits, the roads and forests; petty lords fought wars among themselves. *So why not let him die, and hope a stronger man takes the throne?* He could not say why, except that it felt wrong.

Besides, you can do it. You can beat them. It was pure bravado, stubborn defiance in the face of Warden's manifest skill. She was better at this game than he could ever hope to be—or so he thought—but he refused to

back down. *You can beat them.* All he needed to do was
surprise her, to move where she and her allies would not
expect, to confound what they thought they knew of
him. *And stay alive. Simple enough.*

Fanuilh arrived, landing across the street and padding
up to him. It shook like a dog shedding water, and Liam
knelt down to check on the phial. Satisfied, he scratched
beneath the phial for a moment, at the spot between his
familiar's wings.

All set?

It bobbed its head at him.

"All right then. Let's surprise and confound."

Warden had men stationed on the Embankment but they
could not cover the entire riverfront, and in the gaps
between them Liam hoped to find a boat. He paralleled
the Royal one street inland as much as possible—moving closer or farther away as the twisting, unruly roads
required—while Fanuilh flew directly over the river,
noting the points of lantern-light that marked out the
Peacemakers, and scouting for an available boat.

Late as it was, he did not expect much luck. The
places he might steal a boat, the few small inlets and
sidewaters off the main stream where richer men kept
their private skiffs, would be watched, as would any
place where watermen gathered to wait for fares. Fanuilh
could cast a spell on the constables, but its Sleep cantrip
lasted only a few minutes, and they would awake knowing Liam had tried to cross the river.

Distant bells began to peal a few minutes after Liam
started his walk, the tones rolling across Torquay, and
he could tell that it was past midnight by the diminished,
forlorn sound: between twelve and six many of the towers did not toll the hours. He counted those that did
through to thirteen, and allowed himself an hour to find
a quiet way across the river. After that, he would let
Fanuilh loose and get a boat however he could.

Scarcely had he made up his mind when Fanuilh reported a remarkable windfall: an unwatched boat, moored at a ladder in the darkness almost exactly between two Peacemakers. Whispering a prayer to Luck, Liam made his way to a small alley that opened onto the Embankment, and slipped across to the bank. To his right and left, comfortably distant, the Peacemakers' lanterns shone out. Far up the river he could see another lantern bobbing along, and a few lights on the opposite bank; otherwise, the city was dark.

The ladder was wormy with age but sturdy. Liam found the rungs with his hands and went down blind, felt for the boat with his feet, wincing when it knocked against the ladder, and managed to climb aboard without falling into the river. Settled, he untied the painter, pushed off from the ladder, and unshipped the oars. Only then did he think about the fact that he was stranding someone on the south bank.

Better him than me, he thought. *He can use the bridge.* Cautious experiment discovered an awkward method of rowing that produced the least squeaking from the oarlocks, and he stroked out into the Royal. After a time, he heard Fanuilh's claws click on the seat opposite, and though he raised his head, he could not see the dragon. The lights on the south bank were farther away, and a quick glance over his shoulder showed him that he was being drawn downriver with the current, toward the shallow bend where the Royal turned before its approach to the falls.

The Peacemakers do not seem to have taken notice, Fanuilh thought at last. *And now you have your own boat.*

He hunched his shoulders, anxious to be off the river, away from the dark, deep water.

"My own boat," he muttered, feeling exposed. "Grand."

●　　●　　●

Arithmetic helped distract Liam as he pulled for the
northern bank, seeking a safe spot to land. One thousand
Peacemakers: how many off-duty, how many at regular
posts that could not be abandoned, how many stationed
in the City Below—and thus how many free to search
for him, divided by the rough length of the Embankment, cut in half for each side of the river, and then
halved again because Warden had them patrolling in
pairs. Many of his figures were pure guesswork, but he
came up with a rough estimate of two men for every
hundred yards, if the Pacifex used absolutely every man
she could spare.

Tight, but not too tight. And with darkness on his side,
he had the advantage.

Fanuilh scouted the bank and found several suitable
landing sites, ladders, or small stairs that were not
guarded by Peacemakers. Liam chose one almost at random, letting the boat glide silently into shore. He
grabbed hold of the moldy wood of the ladder and
groped with the other for the painter, tied the boat fast,
and climbed up as quickly as he could, not feeling safe
until he was firmly on dry land.

Bag slung over his shoulder, sword-stick in one hand,
a lantern hanging from the other—provided by the
thoughtful boat owner, stowed in a small locker at the
stern—he slipped across the Embankment and set a
quick pace for Artisans' Vale.

Cade's house was dark and unguarded. Fanuilh circled
it, reporting no windows at the back of the house on the
ground floor, three on the second floor, and a small alley
by which the place might be approached.

Liam stalked down the alley and chose his window:
the third, separated from the others by the bulk of the
kitchen chimney. The house was stone, like many in
Torquay, with the usual coat of ivy. He hid his dunnage
bag and the sword-stick at the foot of the wall, then took

off his boots and stowed them awkwardly beneath his tunic, wincing as his stockinged feet touched the cold ground. With the wire handle of the lantern in his teeth, he started climbing.

Even in the darkness, it was easy: the kitchen chimney projected out from the house, giving him some leverage, and beneath the ivy the stones of the wall were rough and unfinished. His fingers and toes found plenty of holds, and although he went slow to avoid rustling the leaves overmuch, he reached the second floor before his stockinged feet grew too cold. Wedged into the angle between the window and the chimney, he held himself with both feet and one hand; with the other he drew the knife at his belt.

Fanuilh, come up here. He imagined himself opening the window and crawling into the bedroom of Cade's dour serving woman. *If I wake anyone up, I want you to put them to sleep again.*

Yes, master.

His jaw and teeth were beginning to ache, as well as his toes; he inserted the blade of his knife between the halves of the window, then slid it up, found the latch, lifted. The twin halves of the window parted and ghosted inward, mercifully silent.

Ready, he warned the dragon, resheathing his knife, placed the lantern on the sill to one side, and heaved with his arms and legs, executing a slow, graceless somersault through the window, to finish crouched on the floor in the utter darkness of the room, listening.

Nothing stirred.

He waited for a slow count of five, sensed more than heard Fanuilh's entry, a movement just in front of his face, and then pushed the window halves closed.

All right, he projected, *the jewelry will be upstairs; you get that. I'll go downstairs and round up the candlesticks.*

Master?

Never mind. He had not found it funny either.

There were no curtains on the window, so he did not dare risk the lantern; instead, he inched blindly across the floor, eyes closed, raising and setting down his feet with elaborate caution. He found the far wall without encountering any furniture or sleeping serving women, and worked his way to his left, toward the center of the house, until he found the door. Holding the knob firmly, he eased it open and slipped through.

When Fanuilh said that it was through as well, he closed the door, opened his eyes, and waited, hoping he would be able to distinguish windows. On a better night, with a moon or at least fewer clouds, windows would have shown up a dark but curiously vibrant blue. This night, the darkness was so complete it was as if he had never opened his eyes. Kneeling, he guided lantern and familiar together with his hands. *Light this,* he projected, and waited while the dragon cast its spell.

Done, Fanuilh announced after a moment, and Liam opened the slide of the lantern a fraction.

The light was like a loud shout to him, and though it showed only an empty hall and the narrow staircase to the first floor, he cringed and had to restrain himself from cutting it off. *Come on, come on. Stick would laugh at you.* Stick was the nickname of the thief who had taught him; he had never learned his real name. *No, not laugh; weep, for his wasted lessons. Come on.*

He paused to tug on his boots, then went down the stairs at the edges of the treads, where they were less likely to creak. As best he could remember, there were no windows in Cade's narrow entrance hall, only doors; still, he kept his hand on the slide, watching the dim light spread from the foot of the stairs as he descended.

At the bottom he paused to breathe his relief: there were no windows to let his light shine out onto the street, a beacon to the Peacemakers. Even as he relaxed, however, a memory surfaced of rain like molten gold run-

ning down panes of glass in Cade's study. He stepped
across the hall to the study door, thought, *Wait here,* and
closed the slide.

In darkness again, he opened the door and stepped
inside, closing it behind him. He remembered the layout
of the room—the scholar's desk, the chairs by the now-
cold fireplace, the single window on the front wall—and
moved around with more confidence, finding the edge
of the desk and following it around with his hip and
fingers. When he was behind the desk, he turned to the
wall, groped for the window, the edges of the window—
and the shutters. He closed them, offering a prayer of
thanks to his luck, and turned again to the room, his
hand on the lantern slide.

An odd question occurred to him then: what had they
done with Cade's body? *What if they just left it here?*
He was not squeamish; it was simply better to be prepared, better not to be surprised. He squared his shoulders and trained his eyes on the spot where he imagined
Cade's chair had been, and lifted the slide, ready to see
the scholar's corpse.

Liam shouted and jumped, staggered into the wall behind him. Pacifex Warden rose from Cade's footstool,
blinking her faded-blue eyes against the light.

"Thief, traitor, murderer—and now housebreaker.
You are truly a man of parts, Quaestor Rhenford."

Liam reeled for a moment, disbelieving, then snarled and
made a move for the door. Warden was already there,
however, in a smooth step so casual, so certain, that he
froze. She wore an outsized black-and-white tunic, her
crippled arm bound to her side, and from her good hand
dangled what looked like a riding crop.

Master, who's there?

So strong was her hold on his imagination that he
actually stopped, as if she—more than a foot shorter, far
weaker, crippled—could block his way.

"I was not certain you would come," she said.

His snarl slipped to a sneer. "I don't think I'll stay," he replied, and stepped toward her.

Master, is that the Pacifex?

Warden raised the crop in a negligent gesture—it was a slim rod of dark wood, with a few small tassels at one end—and lightning exploded between them, lanced into Liam's chest, flung him back into the wall.

The considerable pain paled before the fact that he could not breathe, and that his heart refused to beat properly. He could feel it jerking in his chest like a landed fish, rhythmless and desperate, and try as he might, he could not draw breath. He gaped, throat working, but his lungs refused to fill. Grabbing at his chest, he slid down the wall.

"It will not last," Warden said. All the muscles in his chest and throat strained to quiet his runaway heart, to reflate his slack lungs. Strained over and over, his face going red, his nails digging into the floor. "When it passes, you will kneel with your hands on top of your head, fingers interlaced. Do you understand?" She gazed at him as if she expected an answer, but he could only stare at her, sure that his heart would stop in a moment. Out of the corners of his eyes he saw darkness, and sparks like lazy tadpoles swam in the air in front of him. "Do you understand?"

And then his lungs opened, and he breathed in a hoarse, shuddering gulp, sweet despite the pain as his chest expanded and he became aware of the circle burnt directly over his sternum.

Master, that was magic.

Liam panted what might have been a laugh, cobbled together a thought. *Think so?*

"Are you recovered?"

He held up a hand, palm out, and let his head flop from side to side. His heart still felt weak.

I have tried the cantrips on her, master, but they are

not working. Is she wearing a ring, or an amulet?

He looked up and saw, next to her seal of office, a tear-shaped stone on a thin silver chain. She waited patiently while he got his breathing under control, and it was that—her patience, her readiness to wait—that convinced him he was finished. *She's smarter than you.* Instead of anger or despair, he felt an odd mix of disappointment and relief.

Hide, he told the dragon, hauling himself to his knees at the same time. *Get out of the house if you can.*

Master, I should stay.

"Hands on your head." She sounded like a teacher bored with the lesson.

Hide. Don't let them get the phial. Bringing his hands to his head, he let one brush his chest: the cloth there was crisp and stiff, the flesh beneath tender. *Do it.*

"Fingers laced."

Yes, master.

He did as she commanded, then indicated the wand with his chin. "Useful thing, that."

She ignored the comment and considered him for a moment, eyes half-lidded, weighing. "You came back for the letter, yes?"

He shrugged with his upraised elbows. *Vanity. She wants to know if she guessed right.* He knew the urge, the desire to validate the conduct of the hunt. "The letter, yes. And anything else I could find."

"I confess I was not sure you would. I assumed you knew its contents—that you had read it while on your way here."

He resented the implication, and showed her a snide smile. "I'm sure that's what you would have done in my place." It was a petty insult. *But why not? Pettiness is all you've got left, idiot, now that you've walked right into her hands.*

As if he had not spoken, she said, "Then I thought,

'Perhaps he hasn't read it. Perhaps he doesn't know what he carries.' Do you know?"

"Enlighten me," he suggested, and she entirely missed his sarcastic tone.

"The King's Cure."

Warden said it as if she expected astonishment, and was clearly disappointed in his simple shrug. "The King's Cure," she repeated. "One of the Seventeen Treasures of Taralon. The key to His Majesty's health."

His continued indifference annoyed her, which was fine with him. *What's it matter? It could be all seventeen, with the crown and Strife's Sword thrown in for good measure, but I can't do anything with it.* If he had seen any hope in his situation he would have cared. "Well," he said, "it's mine now, and you can't have it."

"You've hidden it, then? In that, at least, you do not disappoint me."

"I do my humble best."

Again, his sarcasm went unnoticed. In fact, she seemed caught up in some internal debate; not distracted—she held the wand ready, and kept her eyes on him—but as if he represented a riddle that only she could see. "It does not hang together," she said at last. "You kill Cade and Lord Bairth for the Cure, and yet you say you did not know what it was."

The riddle became clear: how best to blame him for the murders Aldyne had committed, what story to concoct that would cover up their plot. "While you're at it," he said, "you may as well add the three widows I strangled. Oh, and a round dozen orphans."

Her eyes narrowed.

"The orphans were just for fun, though." He gave a mean smile. "They've nothing to do with the Cure."

For the third time his barb went awry. Warden shook her head, disgusted. "To make light of it so. You certainly fooled the Duke—from his letter, one would think he had sent a hero, not a vicious traitor. I wonder what he will think when he hears."

Liam dropped his smile. "He won't believe it."

"No, he will not." She twitched her shoulders, a delicate shiver, then recollected herself. "Now, I want to know if Sir Ancus and his wife were your co-conspirators."

"Co-conspirators?" He shook his head. "That's good. Co-conspirators. Yes, they were—that's why she betrayed me to Severn, because we're such close co-conspirators." He hoped she understood the sarcasm this time: he did not want to get Marcade and Nennius in any more trouble. "They knew nothing about it."

"To Severn?" She frowned. "Why Severn? Why didn't she just tell me?"

"Probably didn't think you were important enough." He grimaced in mock sympathy. "Sorry, but I guess the Steward of the Household is more important than the Stone Cripple."

Finally, she reacted: jerking her head back, her lips twisting and then pressing into a thin line. "Better men have said that. And I have sent better men to the gallows."

"Will I get to the gallows? I thought a private execution would be more in keeping. Say, in Severn's study?"

"There is no poetry in justice," she said coldly. "You'll hang for your crimes where all may see."

"As soon as you make up an appropriate story, that is."

"Pacifex!" They both looked up, recognizing Aldyne's voice calling from the street. "Pacifex!" They heard him try the front door.

Master—

Hide! Hide and stay hidden!

"In here," Warden called, and opened the door of the study.

"Your faithful hound," Liam said, and a moment later Aldyne appeared in the doorway, flushed and excited.

"Pacifex, that Rhenford—" He cut himself off, seeing Liam. Expressions flitted across his face—astonishment, fear, anger, and at the end, relief. "You have him! You have him!"

Warden frowned, as if Aldyne should have expected it. "He came for the letter."

"But I stayed for the company," Liam added.

Aldyne glared daggers at him. "I take it you didn't like the company at Nennius's, then?" He turned to Warden. "We found the knight, Pacifex. Just as with Cade and Lord Bairth—murdered in his own home."

CHAPTER 9

LIAM GROANED AND sagged as if he had been punched in the stomach, but his eyes stayed fixed on Aldyne. "Dead?" *You tied him up for them.*

Aldyne ignored him, giving the Pacifex the details. "We saw him on the roof, sneaking away. We gave chase, but he's cunning, and gave us the slip."

He saw the man talking, but was unable to take in the words. *You tied him up for them. Trussed him up and left him.*

"We knocked but no one answered, so we broke in." Aldyne's face darkened. "He'd cut the knight's throat, just like Cade."

Meaningless buzzing, infinitely removed from him: he stared at Aldyne but saw Nennius, bound up, shoved beneath the bed. *You're so clever. You may as well have killed him yourself.* The cynical voice in the back of his mind disagreed: he had done what he had to, it had seemed reasonable at the time, he had no reason to think they would kill the knight—it even hinted at Marcade's betrayal, as if that excused him. He ignored the voice, let it drown in the rising guilt.

"There was no sign of the woman, though. We searched the house, but she's not there. Completely disappeared. We've no idea where she went."

The corners of Liam's mouth turned down, his face crumpling as if he would cry, but his sorrow and his guilt were not the sort that ended in tears. Barren and unforgivable, they paralyzed him, sapped his will, sub-

131

jugated his hatred of Aldyne and Warden to an even greater hatred of himself. *You left him for them.*

"Or what he did with her," the Pacifex said, with a dark look.

When Aldyne grabbed him by the throat and shook him, he could not respond. His arms flopped down from his head and he let the man shake him until his teeth rattled. He deserved it.

"Where is she? What have you done with her, you bastard?"

His strength was gone; when Aldyne released him he sprawled to the floor. *You left him for them, and then you came here and let yourself get captured.*

"He'll not speak here," Aldyne spat, and turned to the Pacifex with a gleam in his eye. "Let me get him to a cell. He'll speak there. After I've worked him. Let me do it. You should look for the woman. She may not be dead."

Warden thought a moment, then agreed. "Yes, I'll go to the house. It may be that he's merely hidden her away. You searched?"

"Not very well," Aldyne promptly admitted. "When we saw the knight I came to find you, and the men on watch said you were here."

They worked out their plans, as oblivious of Liam as he was of them, wallowing in his misery. *You killed Nennius as surely as if you put the knife in him yourself. And Marcade, too. She'd never have done anything if you hadn't brought this down on her.* The cynical voice started to object, but he would not hear it. If he had gotten away, if he had not blundered into Warden's simple trap, he thought he might have been able to live with the mistake, if not to excuse it. *You didn't though. You're caught, and even if they don't have the Cure, the king doesn't either, and that's what they want, after all.*

Warden wrenched him out of himself, grabbing his chin and forcing his head up. "Do you see my amulet?"

He did not, at first—he looked at her and saw only her seal of office, dangling from her neck—and then she redirected his gaze to Aldyne. The tear-shaped stone hung on his chest, and he flicked it with one finger. "It is proof against your familiar's cantrips. You understand?"

He managed a nod and she let go of his chin, wiped her fingers on her tunic. "Take him, discover what you can of the Cure and Lady Marcade. Torture is permissible in cases of treason. I'll go to King's Vale, and see what I can learn at Nennius's."

Aldyne hauled him to his feet, his body slack and unresisting. "You hear, wretch? Torture is permissible."

Bewildered, ashamed of himself, Liam allowed Aldyne to prod him out of the house, shambling ahead of the man's shoves. Two Peacemakers waited a short way down the street, and took up position ahead of him at Aldyne's command.

"Keep a sharp eye out," he said. "This one's got friends abroad."

They marched toward Craft Street, Liam at the center of a triangle, staring with blank eyes at the black-and-white backs of the men ahead. They carried their truncheons in their hands, prepared for trouble; one held a lantern high. Liam shook his head from time to time, an involuntary expression of his hopelessness. *Torture is permissible. And then they hang what's left.* He was dead, and felt it: curiously distant, almost numb, his aches and pains those of another man.

Master, where are they taking you?

His head snapped up. *Where are you?*

I got out when Lieutenant Aldyne came in. I am on the roof of the third house on your left.

Behind him, he heard Aldyne drawing his sword, and then the point pricked right between his shoulderblades.

"Remember the amulet," the man said, and laughed.

"I am proof against your creature's spells, but you aren't proof against steel."

Liam dropped his eyes to the ground. *You heard that? Get out of here. Go to the palace and try to deliver the phial to the king.*

His voice dropping to an insinuating whisper, Aldyne went on, "Or do you wish to prove it?"

Master, I will never get into the palace, let alone see the king. You must escape.

They turned onto Craft Street, heading downhill now, toward the river.

Forget it. He's got the amulet. Leave me, and get to the king if you can.

The point dug into his back. "Do you, Rhenford? Eh? I'm curious to know what's inside." He jabbed the sword, cutting cloth and skin. Liam cried out and stumbled forward, a few steps out of reach. The Peacemakers ahead looked back over their shoulders, ready for trouble. "What do you think, boys," Aldyne said, "he has the gallows walk already, doesn't he?" They smirked at the grim joke and faced forward again.

You see? Liam projected. *I'm dead. Go to the king. I order you.*

Yes, master.

The speed with which Fanuilh agreed took away the last of his heart. Aldyne stepped close and spoke in his ear: "You'll hang."

"I know" was all he could think to say.

"Hanging's hard," the man continued, a private whisper. The Peacemakers marching in front could not hear. "And before the hanging, the torture. I'm good at it."

Liam saw what the man was doing—trying to spook him, to make him run. *So he can cut me down. Much simpler than a public execution, less chance of my talking to someone.* For a moment he was tempted; it would spare him the torture. *Get it over with.* Sheer fatigue held him back. He was tired, bone-tired; lifting his feet was so enormous an effort that he shuffled, scuffing his boots over the cobbles. Fatigue first, and then a thought: *Why does he want to torture me?* That Aldyne would kill him made sense; torture did not. They knew where Marcade was, and they did not care where the King's Cure was, as long as it was not with the king. *Maybe he just doesn't like me.*

"Go on," Aldyne whispered, his whisper tinged with impatience. "Run for it. You've your spells, and your familiar. You can get past us."

The goading made sense; he wanted Liam to run so he could be killed while escaping. Which meant that the two Peacemakers up ahead probably were not part of their superiors' plot. *So tell them all about it. They'll believe you, I'm sure.* His lips stretched, almost a smile. The constable on the right used the tip of his baton to scratch between his shoulder blades, exactly the same spot where Aldyne's blade had cut Liam.

"Go on," the voice in his ear urged. "Use your spells."

Liam shook his head. "You've got the amulet."

Abruptly, the constable on the left burst out laughing. *But they don't.*

Aldyne screamed in his ear and jerked away; the laughter of the man on the left spiraled up into a hysterical cackling and he doubled over, grasping his sides; the Peacemaker on the right wailed and threw himself to the ground, clawing at his body. For a long second Liam stood stunned, goggling at the men in front of him; then Aldyne screamed again and he spun on his heel.

Master, run.

The laughing man held the lantern; it swung wildly as he howled, tears gushing down his cheeks. By its wavering light, it looked as if a shadow writhed around Aldyne's head, a stormcloud. Liam heard a leathery rustle.

"Fanuilh?"

Aldyne's sword clattered to the ground and he tore at the snapping, clawing dragon.

Run!

"Oh, no," Liam said slowly, bending to pick up the discarded blade. As he rose, Aldyne got hold of the dragon and ripped it from his face, threw it aside, and staggered back, blood streaming through the fingers he clasped to his head.

"Oh, no." Strength flowed into Liam, seemingly from the hilt of the sword, and he snapped his teeth together. Fanuilh rebounded, rolling and coiling as soon as it hit the ground, tensed to spring.

Run, master! Now!

The Peacemakers were both on the ground now, one begging even as he scratched himself bloody, the other choking out hoarse laughter. Aldyne groaned and held his face, staggering.

"I don't think so," Liam said, hefting the sword, and then the street lit up with lightning. He threw up a hand against the glare, expecting the pain and the suffocation he knew from Cade's study. When it did not follow, he lowered his arm and saw the lightning far up the street—twining forks of it, like half a dozen whips wielded all at once, and Warden wielding them, waving the wand over her head.

They won't reach, he realized. The whips hissed and sizzled, crackling against one another, and none was longer than six feet. He grinned crazily.

Master, now!

Warden was a clumsy runner, the shoulder of her withered arm swinging forward with each step, but she held the wand and she was bringing it closer.

"Right," Liam said, and took a few steps backward before saying, "Right," again, pivoting, and running full-out down Craft Street. Behind him, lightning crackled, men screamed, and then a whistle shrieked. To him, the piping sounded desperate.

• • •

Flying down Craft Street, he felt good, his feet pounding the cobbles, and all he could think was that he was alive. An idiot's grin broke out on his face. *You were dead, and now you're alive.* An image of Aldyne, blood running through his fingers, made him bark a laugh, and he felt as if he could run all night. There were a few lights on Craft Street, candles in windows or the occasional lantern over a doorway, and they lit the way down to the river.

Master, turn right.

A small road just shy of the Embankment: he veered into it, running full tilt, and had to slow down because there was no light here. He jogged now, his breath coming a little harder, and then slowed to a fast walk, Aldyne's sword held out in front of him.

I can't see a thing, he projected. *I need to be on a bigger street.*

There are Peacemakers on all of them, Fanuilh reported. *Answering the Pacifex's call.*

Whistles were sounding all over Artisans' Vale, moving, converging on Craft Street. Liam grinned. *They should stay where they are, but they won't. They'll know where she was, and know it's her, and go rushing off to her aid.* He barked another laugh, triumphant, as if he had just won a race. *Can we get to the boat?*

I will check.

Liam walked on while the dragon scouted the Embankment. His initial elation wore off in stages, the energy of his escape fading as he realized that he was cold, still tired, and still in the same situation as before. *But you're free.* The sword-stick and his dunnage bag, his clothes, and the food were lost. *You've got money. Buy more tomorrow.* He made a pass with Aldyne's sword and grinned, though not as fiercely as before. He needed a sheath, and a place to hole up for the rest of the night. *Someplace she won't think of.*

Fanuilh reported that the Peacemakers had abandoned the section of the Embankment near the vale. *You can come out safely.* It guided him from above, down an alley he would have missed in the darkness.

Climbing down the ladder to his stolen boat, his joy diminished to nothing as he remembered Nennius gagged beneath the bed. *Cruel things,* he thought. *You've done cruel things.* He was free and at large, however, and he settled himself at the oars with a certain grim satisfaction. Free and at large, which meant he might still justify whatever he had done—he could get the King's Cure to the palace, perhaps even find a way to punish Warden and Severn and Aldyne. *You can make up for it.*

He rowed upstream, angling out to the middle of the Royal where he would be invisible from the banks. *Fanuilh, come down here.*

Yes, master.

A minute or so of steady rowing later, he heard the dragon's wings and then the click of its claws on the planks of the boat. He stopped rowing, shipped the oars, and reached down to pick his familiar up and settle it in his lap. It was warm despite the chill of the night, and its scales were soft beneath his fingers, ridged like moired cloth, not metallic. The disparity between the way they looked and how they felt never ceased to fascinate him.

"You're a fool and an idiot, you know that? I told you to go away."

Fanuilh shifted slightly: it did not like to be held, but submitted meekly now. *Yes, master.*

"And attacking Aldyne like that—that was the crowning foolishness of all."

Yes, master. I am sorry.

Liam smiled down on the dragon, then chucked under its drooping chin. *It was also brilliant. My first thought was to sell you off to a menagerie, but I'm willing to give you one more chance. Provided that, from now on, you promise to disobey any of my stupider commands.* The dragon lifted its head, and he added, *That wasn't entirely a joke, in case you're wondering. But don't let it go to your head.*

Several seconds passed before the dragon lowered its head. *As you say, master.*

Unless what I say is stupid, Liam countered, then went on, *Enough fulsome praise, you little monster. Let me just make sure you didn't lose our treasure in your heroic rescue, and then we'll figure out where to go from here.*

The phial was still attached to the dragon's back, the string that bound it in place secure. He touched it, feeling the gaps in the true metal where the mage-glass showed through, moving up to press the pad of his index finger against one of the points of the stopper-crown. It was not sharp, but he yanked his finger away nonetheless.

That it was the King's Cure, one of the Seventeen Treasures, did not change his plans—he would still try to get it to the king—but it changed his perception of it. *One of the Treasures!* They were mentioned in countless stories, a name everyone in the kingdom had heard a thousand times, even if, as Master Tollerdig had complained, most people could identify no more than a few of them. *And you've got one right here!* For a moment he wondered if it was safe to entrust it to Fanuilh, and then discarded the worry with a wry smile. *Safer with him than with you.*

He took up the oars again and started stroking upstream. Safety, for himself, Fanuilh, and the phial alike, meant finding a place where he could rest for a few hours: the borrowed energy from his escape was gone, and he was close to exhaustion. Options occurred to him, but as soon as an idea occurred to him, he rejected it. *She's sharp. Anything you can think of, she can too.* He allowed the dilemma to revolve around in his head, his oarstrokes weakening, the blades more and more often just scraping the surface of the river rather than biting deep. Finally, he put the question to Fanuilh. It suggested all the things he had already considered, allowing him to reject each in turn, and then gave its last possibility.

You could sleep in the boat.

"The boat? I'll freeze!" He had no coat, no cloak, no blankets. "I'm freezing now—and what if it rains? And where would I moor it?"

There are many places you could tie up. The central piling of Halfcrown Bridge would be best, I think. And while you would be cold, I do not think you would freeze to death.

Liam tried to object, opening his mouth or formulating the beginnings of thoughts several times, but he eventually had to concede that it was the best possibility. There was a certain appeal to the idea—hiding right out in the open, with the river between him and every Peacemaker in the city—and he did not think it would occur to the Pacifex. *No, it definitely won't.* As soon as he thought that, he stopped rowing long enough to fork his fingers against the Dark and touch his knuckles to the wood of the boat for luck. *You've thought that before.*

He hung his head for a moment, recruiting his strength, and then started rowing with more determination, aiming for Halfcrown Bridge.

The central piling of the bridge was a slim trefoil of stone, so slender it seemed impossible that it could support the structure that rested on it, its length decorated with carvings of leaves and sea creatures. The Royal barely objected to its presence, forming an almost imperceptible eddy, not enough to make approaching difficult or to rock a moored boat too much.

When Liam finally reached it, his strength was start-

ing to flag alarmingly. His strokes were sloppy, and he
had to throw his whole body into each, rather than just
his shoulders. He grasped the wet stone with splayed
fingers, and used his other hand to loop the painter
around the head of a sea dragon. When it was tied, he
did his best to stretch out, lying on his back in the bottom of the boat and propping up his knees and lower
legs on the passenger seat.

"I'm giving up feather beds entirely," he murmured,
feeling the keel dig into his back. "This is wonderful."
Not moving, though, had a charm all its own, and despite the discomfort he began to relax. The bridge and
the piling and the wales of the boat kept him out of the
cold winds that skated across the river; the gentle rock-
ing lulled him. *You should get some sleep as well.*

I will keep watch.

Too tired to argue, Liam shrugged, vaguely recalling
the hours the dragon spent sleeping at home, curled up
nose to tail like a dog. *Probably stores it up,* he thought
privately. And then he began to doze.

Snippets of dreams, fragments so truncated they were
little more than pictures, flashed through Liam's mind.
He was aware of them as dreams, aware that he lay in
a boat beneath Halfcrown Bridge, and harbored the suspicion that he should not be dreaming at all—he should
be sleeping, resting, gathering his strength.

He tried to tell this to each scene but they came anyway, random and frustratingly pointless. The rakes were
handed into a boat by a waterman who complained that
his boat had been stolen; Warden sat sharing a cup of
wine with a woman with long auburn hair whose face
Liam could not see, but whose identity he guessed at—
and objected to; Fanuilh dug a hole and buried the phial
in it; he himself dropped the phial and a loaf of bread
into a river, and reached frantically to recover the bread;
Aldyne killed Master Bairth. They came and went, some

hinting at deeper meaning, most just bizarre.

Wake.

He knelt in prayer in a temple to Fortune, and turned to Fanuilh. "Hush! I am awake!"

The dragon butted its head into his knee. *You are not. Wake.* WAKE.

Brushing at his knee, Liam opened his eyes. The sky was the royal blue of predawn. Fanuilh perched at the far end of the boat, not touching him. *Are you awake?*

Unfortunately. Liam sat up slowly, stiff in every joint, his accumulated bruises protesting every movement. *The question is, am I alive?* A twinge in his neck gave conclusive proof of that, and he groaned, then coughed. Something felt loose in his chest, the beginnings of a cold, and he shook his head. "Just the thing. Just what I needed. I have to get a coat or a cloak."

Yes, master. Shops should open shortly. It rang six a few minutes ago.

"Grand." He crawled to the side of the boat and scooped up a mouthful of icy water. His fingers went numb almost at once but he managed two more mouthfuls, enough to settle his cough, and then splashed cold water into his eyes and dried his hands by slicking his hair back. "That's refreshing. Let's never do it again." He was wide awake, though, his mind clear and surprisingly alert, alive to the many discomforts that clamored for his attention. He stretched with great care, working out what kinks he could, massaging warmth into his muscles. Apart from the occasional blunt pain in his ribs when he breathed too deeply, he decided he was as well as could be expected.

Only lightly battered, he projected. *Speaking of which, I nominate breakfast as our first priority. Breakfast, and then saving the king's life. What do you say?*

Fanuilh either missed his attempted joke or chose to take it seriously. *The Prince of the Mint may not return to Torquay until evening. We will have all day.*

Liam smiled. *Too true, familiar mine. Shall we take in a play?* He untied the boat, pushed off from the bridge piling, and started rowing upstream with leisurely strokes. *They have a play on the Row that's been going on for years. It never ends—each night is a new part of the story. And if I sneak you in under my coat, we'll only have to pay for one.* He would not have called his mood lighthearted, but he definitely felt better, less overwhelmed by his situation. *That'll pass,* he promised himself. *You'll be miserable by dawn.*

The rowing warmed him up, and before his mood could evaporate, he began to think through his day. A quick reconnaissance of Catiline's house first, then food and something warm to wear. The Prince of the Mint would live in King's Vale, presumably, close to the palace, and Liam wanted to learn the lie of the land. Once he knew that, he would find a quiet place to write his message, arrange to have it delivered, and then kill time until Catiline contacted him.

The theater might be just the place, once the Row opened at noon. In the dark, hidden among the audience, he could spend the hours of waiting both safe and warm. If he took a private stall, he could arrange to receive messages from Catiline; such luxuries had been out of his reach as a student, but between his pouch and the notes-of-hand in his boot, he had plenty now.

His rowing had brought him close to King's Vale. He could see lanterns all along the waterfront there, and brighter fires by the pillars that marked the entrance to the Processional; the density of light was greater than it should have been. Backing water, he frowned up at the sky and judged he had half an hour or more before sunrise. *Fanuilh, fly over there and see what's going on.*

The dragon sprang into the air and spiralled out of sight. Liam turned the boat and stroked once, letting it drift toward a spot on the bank east of the vale where there were no lanterns. He corrected his course once or twice, compensating for the current, and waited. *Too many men. If she tries to block off the vale. . . .* He shook off the thought. *You can send the letter by Messager, if you have to. They're practically sacred—even she wouldn't dare stop a Messager.*

Fanuilh was not long in reporting, and its news was exactly what he had feared. *They have cut off the vale, master. There are Peacemakers on every street that leads in, and other men, soldiers, I believe. They are wearing scarlet cloaks and armor.*

Those would be King's Men, the royal bodyguards. *And why not? Severn's Steward of the Household. He can do what he wants. So, forget the vale. Come on back.*

Yes, master.

Disappointed, he took up the oars again and rowed back to midstream.

Other boats were out on the Royal now. Most had lanterns hung, but not all, and these others glided out of the predawn darkness like ghosts. Fanuilh rejoined him and he gestured for the dragon to sit beneath the wales of the boat, out of sight.

Below Halfcrown Bridge the river curved, exposing a crescent of muddy beach on the northern shore; beyond the curve the river straightened out again, set on its last run to the falls. The noise was like distant thunder and the current picked up appreciably, strong enough to pull the boat along on its own. Liam rowed nonetheless, eager to get ashore before the sun rose. He could make out individual buildings on the banks and the eastern sky was lightening, gray at the notch where the Royal cut the coastal mountains, blue and bluer higher up.

Once past Artisans' Vale he turned inshore, looking for a likely place to land. There did not seem to be any lanterns on the Embankment, which might mean that Warden had called all her Peacemakers to the blockade of King's Vale, or simply that they had put them out as dawn approached. He prayed for the former and chose a landing place at random, a small set of mossy, neglected steps.

Last stop, he projected. *You should get up in the air, on the rooftops, before the sun rises.*

Yes, master. Fanuilh climbed up to the prow and launched itself into the air. *I will stay close.*

Liam jumped to the stairs. *Do that.*

The Embankment was empty, and he risked walking along it for a while. Side streets would be safer but he did not know them well; once he got to Stair he would risk getting lost. *Or if you spot a Peacemaker.* He did not, however; the Embankment was quiet, and he walked east at a brisk pace.

Stair was the least homogeneous of the vales, the only one not dedicated to a particular class. It was the unofficial entryway to Torquay—though more people actually arrived by the Grain Climb, which came out on the southern bank—and as such it catered to the varied needs of people without a fixed place in the city. It had the most inns, the most taverns and wineshops; it had the theaters on the Row, a Messager House, and it had the most bakeries, here where the wind could carry the smoke out to sea.

The smell of baking bread filled Liam's nose as he reached the outskirts of the vale, and his stomach grumbled. A yellow square fell on the cobbles up ahead—light from a window—and he jogged toward it, hoping for a bakery. As soon as he saw the signboard—a cutout of a man sitting tailor-style, sewing together what looked like two sheets of gold—he knew it could not be a bakery: the rents on the Embankment would be too expensive. *You do need a cloak, though.* Promising himself that he would track down the source of the good smells afterward, he went into the shop.

At first the tailor was none too pleased. He kept a

respectable shop and had a face made for deference, but the sight of Liam, dishevelled, cloakless and carrying a naked sword, made his eyes start from his head. A quick lie—a gambling party, his fur-lined cloak and cloth-of-gold sheath the stakes—and the jingle of Liam's purse restored his natural deference, and he proved more than willing to lighten the purse considerably in return for a hooded cloak of dove-gray wool. At no additional cost, he threw in directions to the nearest bakery, and bowed Liam out of the shop as if he were a lord.

The sky had gone completely gray while Liam was in the tailor's shop, and he jogged the few blocks to the bakery the man had told him about. The smell could have led him there, woodsmoke and fresh bread thick in the air: the whole street was lined with bakeries, and small carts stood in front of nearly every door, with servants and delivery boys at the ready. None of the shops bore signs, so Liam simply chose the first one he came to that did not have a cart waiting. Inside, the bakery seemed wonderful to him, warm and dry and filled with the odors of yeast and baking. His mouth watered.

"Any chance of a loaf?" he called over the abandoned counter. Behind it, the enormous beehive ovens stood unwatched, radiating a searing heat.

A scrawny, nervous woman appeared from behind the ovens, flour up to her elbows, her skin brick-red from the constant heat. "A minute, sir," she promised, opening one of the oven doors and poking her head into a furnace blast that made Liam wince and shield his eyes.

"Just a minute or two more, sir," she said, after closing the door. "Will you wait?"

Anxious as he was to get on with his busy day, the smell held him. At his nod, the baker smiled and started pulling wicker baskets from beneath the counter and arranging them by the ovens, ready for the next batch.

"Terrible the Steward, eh, sir?"

Liam tore himself from thoughts of bread. "What's that?"

If he had spoken more sharply than he intended, the woman did not seem to notice. She came to the counter. "The Steward, sir. Did you not hear? He was murdered just last night!"

"Murdered?" He could not think of an appropriate thing to say—could only hold back the one question he wanted to ask: *How does she know already?*

"In cold blood," she affirmed, with a solemn nod. "And in his own house."

"By who?" He stammered on the first word. *And how did the news get out so quick?*

"They'd not say. Very close they were. Though I'd guess it was that Corvialus, if you want my opinion. It's well known he hated Lord Bairth. Oh—did I say that it was Lord Bairth? Lord Auric is beside himself with grief, they said."

He glanced down at his hands and saw that he was gripping the edge of the countertop. "Who told you all this?"

"The Peacemakers, of course," she said. "They were in a little while ago, for a bite." Then, as if she had heard some signal he had not, she whirled away from the counter to the oven, and used a long-handled wooden board to draw out a round loaf, which she deposited on the counter. "Give it a moment, sir. It's too hot."

Liam looked down at the loaf as if he had never seen one before. "Did they say—did they say what they're going to do about it?"

The baker tossed her head and rolled her eyes. "What won't they do about it? They said the Pacifex—that's our chief constable, I suppose you'd say in the Midlands—the Pacifex's been up the whole night, hunting the murderer down. I don't know where she got the wizards to do it, but they'll be hanging his portrait soon."

Portrait? What does that mean? More important, at

the moment, was her aside. He cocked his head, trying to appear bemused. "Why did you say that? About the Midlands, I mean?"

Beneath the brick red, the woman blushed. "Your pardon, sir. Your accent is—that is, you don't seem a Torquay man—and you sounded a Midlander. I think you may take that loaf now, sir."

The crust was too hot; he picked it up anyway, bouncing it on his palms, and smiled to show that he was not annoyed. "I'm not from Torquay, as a matter of fact, but I'm not from the Midlands, either. I'm from Harcourt."

"As you say, sir." Embarrassed by her gaffe, she wanted to finish their business and hurry him along. "It's two barons."

He fished the copper coins out of his pouch. "Where will they hang this portrait you were talking about?"

On the Landing by the Stair, she told him, and then added Tall Gate, the Processional, Pamphlet Square, Halfcrown Bridge, the Row and Temple Vale, each location confusing him further. "Anywhere people will see it. I suppose there'll be a few down Below, but the rogues there rarely pay any attention to them."

"I see," he said, though he did not. *How can you hang a portrait in more than one place? And where did they get a portrait of me?* It made no sense, but she had mentioned wizards, and they did not always have to make sense. He decided that he had to see it—that he could not risk not seeing it. Thanking the baker, he tossed his coins on the counter and hurried out.

The Landing was the closest place she had named, only a few streets away: the broad plaza where the Stair stopped its ascent. The sky was all gray now, the sun minutes away, and people had begun to come out, scattered in ones and twos around the expanse of white stone, waiting for the first Stair of the day.

Liam kept his head down, pretending absorption in

his breakfast, though he hardly tasted the bread. *What has she done now? How is she ahead of me this time?*

He found out soon enough, on a sort of wooden frame set up in the northwest corner of the Landing. The frame looked like a diminutive gallows, and hanging from its crossbar, at eye-height, were a few dozen sheets of paper. Some were old, wrinkled and torn from exposure; five in the middle, however, were new, the paper stiff, the ink still shining. Liam sidled along the frame to them, unaware that he was making a low, despairing sound in the back of his throat.

Each sheet was a foot square; the older ones bore pictures of men he had never seen, limned in charcoal by an expert hand, their crimes in large block letters above their heads. There were two crimes listed on the five new sheets in a uniform, clerkly hand:

TREASON. MURDER.

And beneath them, Liam's face.

CHAPTER 10

TREASON. MURDER.

And his face, black and white and gray but his face nonetheless, the long blade of a nose, the thin, angular face—the artist had even caught the paleness of his blue eyes, if not the color. Beneath the picture was his history, a truncated version of the Duke's letter of introduction with everything flattering cut out.

Liam stared at the page in front of him, dumbstruck. *How?* He knew how, though: he was too stunned to think, but the cynical voice told him. *The wizards in Pamphlet Square.*

Not the drawing itself—Warden must have a talented artist in her pay, one who could make a perfect likeness from a description—but the copies. It was a simple spell, a training tool for apprentices, that took a page and reproduced it exactly. Would-be wizards were sent to Pamphlet Square several times a week to practice the spell and earn a little spending money, copying books and play scripts and pamphlets in a fraction of the time it would take a scribe. Liam had bought pages from them himself when he was a student, marvelling at the way the ink never ran or smudged.

And she figured this out. This—pictures of wanted men, in quantities large enough to spread around the city—was brilliant, a stroke of genius, an inspiration. He tore his eyes from his own likeness to glance at some of the others, eerily lifelike, with MURDER and RAPE and THEFT and ARSON hanging over their heads.

150

It's brilliant. And you're dead.

The whole city would know his face before the morning was out, and they would quickly guess what lay behind the charges. *They'll know it means Bairth. You're dead.* He jumped back from the frame and his portraits as if they had stung him, then forced himself still, held it for a moment, and slowly surveyed the square around him.

Buildings lined the Landing on two sides, inns and taverns to the west, an arcade of shops to the north, along with a Messager House, a small marble structure like a temple. To the south, far across the squares of white stone that floored the plaza, the Royal swept past and over the falls, the noise of which suddenly impinged on his ears, the muted thunder rising from the Pool. And to the east was—nothing. The white stones simply stopped, and beyond was the three-hundred foot drop to the City Below. There was no balustrade, no railing; it looked as if the Landing had been cut off with a sharp knife, the excised part left to fall into the blue gulf.

Four Peacemakers stood at the edge, perilously close to the drop, gathered in a knot around a low rostrum. They talked among themselves, paying no attention to the square, and he knew they could not recognize him at that distance.

But anyone else can.

Anyone else—the two old men strolling in companionable silence, the woman setting up her barrow to sell pies, the ink-stained clerk who paced back and forth by the rostrum. Anyone who had seen the portraits, and even as it sank in, penetrated so deep he could not deny it, the two old men started over to the frame, squinting, their faces alive with curiosity, wondering if those were new portraits, or if their poor eyesight had deceived them.

More people were coming into the plaza every second

and the sun was finally rising, pinking the sky as it peeped above the horizon.

Liam ducked his head and turned away from the frame, taking long strides for the arcade of shops. *You're dead.* He stepped beneath an arch in front of a shop that had not yet opened, leaned against the cold stone, put his hand to his brow as if he were massaging away a headache, and panicked. *Dead.*

He could not stand in the archway all day, shielding his face; he could not leave it. The theater was out, and the temples, and even just walking around. The Peacemakers were avoidable, with care and due precaution, but he could not avoid everyone. *And that's who it is,* he thought, his breath starting to come in shallower and shallower gasps, his fingers digging into his forehead. *Not anyone—everyone. I'm dead.*

The panic swelled, a force within him that ringed his heart and constricted his lungs. He panted, feeling as he had when Warden struck him with the lightning, knowing it would get worse. *Fanuilh she's got pictures of me all over the city now everyone knows what I look like what am I going to do?* The thought came out as one long string of words, as if forced from his head by the pressure of his fingers, which seemed to threaten to crush his skull. *What am I going to do? I'm dead.*

You are not dead yet, master. Where are you?

A grunt escaped him, the need to concentrate to project stemming the tide of panic for a moment. *In the arcade, near the Messager House. Fanuilh, everyone knows what I look like.*

You should pull up your hood.

My hood! A few clouds wandered the sky, not enough to justify covering up. Wearing his hood would mark him out, make him look suspicious. Forget it. *I need to get out of here, and fast, and I need a place to hide, a real place, where she won't look and people won't see me.*

Where, master?

I don't know! He mouthed the words as he thought them. *I don't know what to do.*

A stir from the Landing, a purposeful murmur and then a hush. "It's coming," someone called, loud enough to be heard across the plaza. Liam slatted his fingers and peered through them, distracted.

More people had arrived, two hundred or so now—a small crowd for the first arrival of the day—they did not fill the plaza; there were gaps and pockets and room to circulate. No one was circulating: they were watching the clerk of the Stair mount the rostrum, a large ledger under one arm, a pouch full of tokens slung around his neck. He handed the ledger to an assistant, who stood below the rostrum and held it open so the clerk, a mole-like little man with a ruff around his neck, could read from it.

"Form a line," the clerk shrilled, and a straggling line coalesced from the crowd. Perhaps half joined; the rest were waiting for people coming up, including a phalanx of men and women wearing identical blue sashes. They all held candles, and busied themselves passing a taper back and forth to light them, shielding the fragile flames.

When the line was of sufficient length, the clerk raised his head and twitched his nose. The first man on line stepped up next to the assistant and spoke his name to the rostrum, from which the clerk checked to see that it was in the ledger, produced a token from his pouch, and dropped it into the man's outstretched palm.

Liam's mouth was dry with envy, and sudden speculation. *The Stair. The City Below.* The baker had said something about the City Below and the portraits. *They don't pay attention to them there. And why would they?* The sailors and longshoremen and stevedores of the port were cousins to the watermen on the Royal, dangerous and independent. A whole other city of empty warehouses, slums and run-down neighborhoods, where he could go to ground far more easily than in Torquay. *I have to get down there. I can hide there, and she'll never find me. Yes.* His breath came easier, his heart slowed. *Down there.*

Only four Peacemakers guarded the Stair. Before the portraits, he would have considered that four too many; now they were hardly an inconvenience. *Can you take them?* he projected.

Take who, master?

Liam's thoughts had leaped ahead, though. *No—a distraction. Something to draw them away.*

Draw who away? The Peacemakers?

He looked around the Landing, at the buildings on its fringes, then down the length of the arcade. *Something to burn.* Less than ten feet away was a stall filled with scarves and cheap cloaks; many new arrivals from the City Below found Torquay much colder than they had expected. Beside the stall, swinging from one of the poles that held up its awning, a boy dawdled, the ragged sort who lingered in droves around markets, ready to run an errand or carry a package. Liam's thoughts leapt again. *You'll need a token.*

"Boy," he called, and his voice was a hoarse croak. He cleared his throat and tried again, terrified that everyone in the Landing would hear him, and would know that his voice belonged to the man in the portraits that said TREASON, MURDER. "You there! Boy!"

No one noticed except the boy, who let go of the awning pole and shuffled unhappily over to stand in front of Liam.

"Wait on line for me," Liam said, inexpressibly grateful for the boy's sullenness, the way he stared at his sprung shoes and mumbled something incomprehensible. "I'll pay you a prince." It was far too much, but the boy shrugged.

"Need a name," he muttered, hitching at his ragged, too-short pants. "And the fare."

Liam counted out coins. "Three crowns, isn't it?" The boy shrugged in a way that conveyed agreement. Liam handed over the gold, and held back the silver. "The name is Coeccias." It was the first that occurred to him. "And remember, I'll be watching you, so don't think you can make off with my coin. You'll have this when you come back with my token."

He held the silver coin out so the boy could see it. The boy shrugged and headed out into the crowd, muttering as he went, "If you're going to watch, go yourself."

Liam watched until the boy was gone, then turned back to the shadows of the arcade, seeking his diversion again. The scarves and cloaks would burn nicely, but he was not sure if a fire would draw the Peacemakers away. *Something that strikes a little closer to home.* He glanced through the arches and saw the edge of the frame with the portraits—there were a dozen people pressed around it, avidly scanning the new addition—and projected his idea to Fanuilh.

But they will see me, master.

That's the point. They'll see you, and they'll see the flames. As long as they don't see me. Everyone in the square would see the dragon, and with any luck panic would ensue. *A stampede,* he prayed. If it came at the right moment, no one would have time to connect his face with the portraits.

Fanuilh was dubious, but when challenged could provide no alternatives, and finally agreed to the plan.

Hidden behind the arch, Liam waited for the boy to return and let his mind race, seeking refinements and things overlooked. He kept his head down, and monitored the people who entered and left the arcade out of the corner of his eye. No one came to open the shop opposite him, but still he held his breath every time someone approached those to either side, or came down the length of the arcade, waiting for the one quick enough to connect him with the portrait of the murderous traitor. The man—for some reason Liam imagined it would be a man, a beefy, stupid ox who on any other day could not be counted on to remember his own name—the man would stop, and frown, and tilt his head the better to examine Liam's face. *Then he'll start shouting. And what will you do?*

As he pondered that, a young woman came along the arcade, toting an empty basket and humming under her breath. She gave him a brazen look as she passed, sizing him up, and he averted his eyes, glancing past her, lifting a hand to his mouth as if to smother a yawn. The flirt made an indignant noise and stalked off; Liam refused to watch her go, his eye caught anew by the stall filled with scarves.

Scarf—and a hat. A hood was mysterious, its depth and shadows drawing the eye, inflaming curiosity. A hat was protection from the elements, or simply stylishness; half the heads on the Landing bore a hat, male and female alike. *And anyone might wear a scarf on a chilly fall day. So buy a hat and a scarf.*

A simple proposition: walk up to the stall, pick out a scarf and pay for it, then go down the arcade until he found a stall selling hats. There had to be one, and he could afford it. His pouch was beginning to feel light, and he would soon have to change one of the notes in his boot, but he certainly had enough for a scarf and a hat.

He could not do it. *They'll see you.* A person selling hats looked customers full in the face, to watch the change the hat rendered, to pretend it was perfect, just the thing. *"So nice with your eyes, sir. I saw Lord Such-and-such wearing the same sort of thing the other day, and you're twice as handsome in it, if I may say, sir." They look at you, damn their eyes.* He scowled, wanting the protection, too afraid to go get it. He shifted his feet, meaning to go, to force himself a few yards down the arcade—and could not do it.

"Hey! Coeccias!" The boy had returned, bearing a token for the Stair. "Where's my prince?"

Liam held up the coin, warm from being clenched in his fist, and held out his other hand for the token. The boy held out his free hand in the same manner, and they made the exchange simultaneously, each dropping what the other wanted at the same time. Liam's fingers closed around the token—a wooden disk two inches across with a crude rectangle meant to represent the Stair carved on one face—as if it were gold.

The boy did the same with the silver, and before he ran off, sneered, "You're a clown and a rustic, Coeccias!"

As if a door had been opened on a storm, a blast of wind swept across the Landing, overwhelming the reply that sprang to Liam's mind. All across the plaza, talk stopped for a moment as the first, fiercest part of the blast swirled cloaks, threatened hats, flapped the portraits on the frame. When it had settled into a steady breeze, talk resumed, and a line began to form in front of the Peacemakers on the eastern edge of the Landing.

The Flying Stair was arriving.

In earlier days, wizards wrought miracles across the length and breadth of the kingdom. The Seventeen Houses had just arrived, and they and their newly established king imposed order on the land with cities and roads and fortresses. Springing up seemingly overnight, the cities of the conquerors amazed the conquered, and nothing more so than the works the wizards made—Tear Bridge and Cobweb Bridge in Harcourt; the famed triple arch of Carad Llan; the Lighthouse of Caer Urdoch; the mile-long galleries hewn with magic from the rock of Caernarvon; and finally, the capstone, the last great public magic, the Flying Stair of Torquay.

The last, and the most necessary: the capital in its high valley was too difficult to reach, isolating the king and his court. A courier could spend half a day on the Grain Climb from the City Below—if his heart or his horse's did not give out on the steep, switchbacked road. So the wizards cleared a space north of the falls, at top and bottom, and spent a month enchanting the Stair.

A square platform of mottled stone a hundred feet on a side, with a balustrade all around, it nested by night on a ledge above a pool at the base of the falls. Six times a day, on a schedule more regular than the tides, it rose in a slow, smooth motion three hundred feet from the City Below to the Landing in Torquay. Seen from below, the Stair seemed to rise on a column of storm and cloud, a turbulent, seething mass of water and rippling air, a thousand tortured waterspouts.

The ignorant claimed that the Storm King himself lifted up the Stair, or a water giant, or a sea dragon exhaling from the pool over which the platform rested when it was not moving. Some even claimed that it was the power of the falls themselves, the falling weight of the Royal reflected back up the cliff.

Countless other more or less fantastic legends accrued to the Stair, and none were true. Liam had come to Torquay believing one—a hazy idea about the spiritual power of the monarchy keeping the kingdom in order, regulating the tides and the moon and the seasons and the Stair—and been disabused of it by a scornful tutor. "It is Elemental magic," the tutor had sneered, "gathered and shaped by the wizards. Water and Air, in this case, though they can work as easily with Fire and Earth." There was power in the sea and sky, he went on to explain, and the wizards harnessed it, drew it out, and tied it to the pool. "The sea was dead for miles around when they were finished, black with rotting fish, all the life drained into their toy. It recovered, of course, within a few months." He made a gesture, as if to indicate that the recovery did not necessarily justify the initial destruction, then added with a somber look, "It's slowing down, you know. Someday it will stop completely."

He let this dramatic statement hang in the air for a long moment, savoring his students' expressions of dismay before explaining that a group of scholars and wizards with waterclocks and hourglasses and infinite patience had measured the time it took the Stair to rise, and discovered that it grew by a grain of sand or a drop of water every decade or so. "That's almost a minute in the thousand years since it was built," he said, and snickered at their relief. "The Elemental force is escaping slowly, to be sure, but surely nonetheless. Some day thousands of years from now, it will sink to the bottom of the cliff and never rise again. You'll want to get in a ride now, while you still can."

Useless advice for students: at three crowns, the Stair was beyond their meager means. It was for the king's convenience, and his court's, and that of the merchants and pilgrims and lords who could afford such extravagance.

And desperate criminals, Liam thought, the breeze that announced the Stair ruffling his short-cropped hair. He clutched the token, watching the line form at the far edge of the Landing. The crowd was too thick to see the platform as it rose—the candle-bearing, blue-sashed phalanx had taken up position directly in front of his section of the arcade—but he heard the clerk and his assistant warn people to stand back, to wait for it, threatening dire consequences to those who tried to anticipate the final stop.

"Wait for it! Wait for it!" the clerk called. "You'll lose a leg in the gap, there!"

And then the crowd released a collective sigh, and Liam knew the Stair had stopped. The phalanx began to sing, a bright hymn to some lesser god, and he started down the arcade, head bowed, toward its eastern end.

He passed the scarf-and-cloak stall without a second glance. Through the arches he saw the crowd shift to let the passengers off, the phalanx's hymn swelling as they were joined by a group of similarly dressed men and women stepping off the Stair.

Master, the Pacifex is here.

He flattened himself behind an arch. *Where?*

She is approaching the Peacemakers. She has two with her, and a third man who may be Lieutenant Aldyne. He wears the uniform, and has bandages on his head.

For some reason that detail—the idea of Aldyne's face swathed in bandages—steadied Liam. *You hurt him, I guess.* He reined in his panic, stood more naturally against the arch, out of sight of the square. *How do they look? Urgent?*

No, master. Though the Pacifex does not seem pleased. She is pointing at the Messager House. Now two of the Peacemakers are going there. They do not look happy.

They shouldn't, he replied. *I shouldn't either, come to think of it.* There had been no men on guard at the temple-like building; if he had not been so frightened by the portraits, he could have gone in and written his letter to Catiline. *Too late.* He could take care of that in the City Below. *So there are five of them now?*

Six, if you count the Pacifex.

Which we definitely do. In fact, we count her as two. Privately, he counted her as many more than that. She had the amulet, so Fanuilh's spells would not affect her, and Liam knew she could keep her head. He could not decide if she would be taken in by the diversion he planned, and he hid behind the arch, torn.

From its perch above the square, Fanuilh reported that the last of the passengers from the City Below were leaving the Stair, filtering through the gap in the balustrade that ran around the platform. Warden and her men stood by the gap, paying only desultory attention to those coming off: they knew he was still in Torquay.

With her present, he figured his chances of getting on the Stair were halved. If he waited until she left, the Stair might descend without him, leaving him stranded in Torquay, where the portraits would soon make his face infamous. *And she'll probably come back to watch the next one, and the next one, and the next one. She'll know you're desperate.*

Master, they are starting to let people on for the descent.

He ground his teeth, trying to parse the odds. If she did not respond to the diversion as he hoped, he could abandon the plan and run. *She'll know you're nearby, but maybe you can lose them in the crowd.* Again, though, that would keep him in Torquay when he had to get to the City Below, an imagined paradise of hiding places and people indifferent to crime.

We'll try it, he announced. *Same as we planned, only be careful not to let Warden get near you with that wand.*

Yes, master. I will wait for your command.

Drawing courage from the dragon's precise, uninflected thoughts—drawing it from wherever he could—he took a deep breath, emerged from the arcade, and started across toward the Stair.

Brighter than Liam had expected, the morning sun dazzled him a little, and he shaded his eyes as he passed through the crowd toward the eastern side of the Landing, where the balustrade of the Stair marked the line between the square and the platform. The railing was waist-high; it would have been easy to jump it and ride for free, except that the clerk's watchful eye maintained a cleared space on the near side—and the passengers, those who had paid and already been let aboard, would not allow it.

The Stair was filling up, the line waiting to have their tokens taken growing shorter, by the time Liam had covered half the distance to the clerk. There he waited, head bowed and eyes downcast, pretending to examine the pear-shaped balusters. Fanuilh kept him apprised of Warden's movements, or her lack thereof: she stayed by the gap where the clerk was collecting the last of the tokens.

No one else seems to want to board. The Pacifex is still with her men. She is talking with Lieutenant Aldyne.

It was a small crowd, the platform only two-thirds full. The passengers on the Stair milled around, the brave moving to the far side to admire the view of the sea and the City Below. The clerk stood in the gap in the balustrade and tapped his foot impatiently. Warden, according to Fanuilh, was examining the clerk's ledger.

The breeze, the updraft from beneath the Stair, abruptly stopped, paused, and then reversed itself, the column of storm beneath the platform preparing for its descent. "Clear away from the edge," the clerk ordered, though no one was near the edge. "Stand ready!"

No one controlled the Stair; it rose and fell on its own schedule, the sudden change in wind the only announcement of its imminent departure. Liam had roughly a minute.

Now.

Yes, master.

He raised his eyes from the baluster and looked toward the clerk, who was shooing people away from the gap. Beyond him were two Peacemakers. Liam fixed them in his gaze, intent on their faces, and started moving toward the clerk. The Peacemakers looked bored. He hefted the token like a rock.

A shrill scream cut through the babble on the square, and then confused shouting. Liam ignored it, working his way closer. It was easy—everyone was turning, looking inland to the source of the shouting—he slipped through the crowd, keeping the Peacemakers in sight. They were confused and hesitant, eyes shuttling back and forth from the Stair to the rostrum. Liam could not see Warden, but he knew they were looking to her, waiting for orders.

Master, the portraits are all burning.

He risked a glance over his shoulder and saw weak flames and thin spirals of smoke rising over the heads of the crowd, heard screaming. *Good.* He turned back to the two Peacemakers and slipped even closer, now less than ten feet away. The clerk was between him and the constables, craning his ruffed neck like everyone else to see what was going on.

Two Peacemakers are coming for me.

Put them down.

A groan came from the crowd closest to the burning frames, and out of it rose more screaming—the men who had come at Fanuilh, in the grip of the spell it called Itch.

The two Peacemakers in Liam's vision finally decided to move, running off into the crowd, leaving the clerk alone in the gap.

Master, the Pacifex is coming for me. She has her wand.

Keep away from it, Liam projected, moving as he did so, trotting up to the clerk and holding up his token. "Is there still time?" He had to raise his voice to be heard over the noise of the crowd.

"Eh? What?" The man glared at him, incredulous.

"Can I still get on?" He leaned close to shout in the clerk's ear and pressed the token on him, forcing him to close his fingers around it.

"Gods, man, there's a battle going on!" The clerk pushed him toward the Stair, where the passengers were crowding the balustrade, trying to see what all the commotion was about. As Liam stepped across the hairline crack onto the platform, lightning flared behind him. He squared his shoulders against the impulse to turn, and forced his way deep into the crowd, pushing against the tide of bodies. *You all right?*

Yes. I will try to—

Another burst of lightning, a flash of bright, actinic light accompanied by a vicious crackling sound and the smell of ozone. Liam cursed and shoved his way forward, saw an end to the mass of people ahead of him, lunged and broke into the clear on the far side of the platform. He reached the balustrade, a glimpse of the sea all the way to the horizon, the blue bowl of the sky, then turned to watch.

Unannounced, unheralded, the Stair had begun its descent; they were already a foot below the Landing. Whips of lightning played above the heads of the passengers, above the heads of the people in the square, and out of the skein of twisted bolts he saw Fanuilh mounting the sky, a scant foot away from the lightning. Liam gasped as the energy reached and reached, the dragon's wings beating, its body lunging up and up.

The moment stretched out, and it seemed as if Fanuilh could not climb any higher, as if it were fixed in place despite the convulsive sweep of its wings, while the crackling whips stretched closer, closer—and then failed, curling back on themselves, evanescing with a snake's hiss. The lightning disappeared, leaving faint traces in his vision, and Fanuilh shot up, dwindling in what seemed an instant. The crowd groaned its disappointment, and Liam hid a smile of relief behind his hand.

That was brilliant.

Thank you.

Aboard the Stair, the passengers were turning from the Landing to speculate among themselves, voices raised in excitement over the thunder of the falls to the south. The platform had sunk below the top of the cliff and the stone face was now visible, the smooth expanse slowly growing. Liam faced about, the better to cover the exultant expression that threatened to break out at any moment. *It worked!*

There was no sensation of movement, but he could measure his progress by watching the City Below: it came closer in tiny increments and he stared down, arms braced on the balustrade, picking out the features he knew as if he were returning to a favorite spot from childhood. The rough water of the Pool, where the falls crashed amid great billowing banks of spray; the placid oval of the inner harbor; the mole and the outer harbor; the profusion of masts along the many docks; the spot where the *Trade's Increase* was moored, though he could not be sure which ship it was; and, most important, the sprawl of warehouses and wineshops and disreputable houses all along the waterfront. It was like a vast forest, into the dark heart of which he could run and never be found.

He grinned down at it, counting the seconds as he came closer, minutes crawling past. Behind him, the other passengers buzzed about what they had seen. He heard one man in particular holding forth at great length in a loud, nasal drawl that pierced the din of the falls, pronouncing the disturbance the work of factions at the court, alluding to a shadowy conspiracy against the king but refusing details.

It was nonsense and Liam ignored it until they were some fifty feet into the descent, when he heard the man say, "Why, we'll ask him then. Call him over, why don't you?"

The skin on his back crawled, expecting the nasal drawl to single him out.

Instead, the man said, "Lieutenant! Your pardon, Lieutenant Aldyne, but may we ask what that was all about?"

• • •

Liam spun on his heel, reacting without thinking, and his eyes met Aldyne's even as the lieutenant opened his mouth to answer the question.

Both men cursed, Aldyne in wonder, his bloodshot eyes bulging, Liam bitterly, scrabbling under his cloak for the sword at his belt.

Fanuilh, come to me now.

The sword snagged in his cloak, then on his belt, but he still had it out before Aldyne drew his. Bandages ringed his face, as if he had a toothache, and padded the entire right side of his head, an inch thick over his ear. He was a good ten feet away, too far for Liam to gain any advantage from having drawn first, so Liam jumped forward, grabbed the nearest person, and dragged the man—a faintly protesting merchant in a green cloak—back to the balustrade, where he put his blade to the man's throat.

Scattered shouts from the passengers, and a few half-hearted halfsteps forward, which Aldyne quelled with a wave of his sword.

"Stand back," he commanded, stepping into the empty space in front of Liam and his hostage. "I'll handle this."

"Like you handled Master Bairth?" Liam spat. The point of the Peacemaker's sword hovered a foot or so from the hostage's trembling chest. "Going to kill him to get at me?"

Aldyne's eyes narrowed. "I can't see why you spew these lies, Rhenford. No one believes them. Everyone knows you murdered Steward Bairth. Did you really think the Pacifex would believe otherwise?"

The crowd vented a collective gasp, dimly perceiving who was being held at bay, and why. "That's the man!" someone shouted, "Kill him!" another urged.

Liam shook his head, confused. *The Pacifex? What's that mean?* To recover himself, he took a firmer grip on his hostage. "How's your ear, Aldyne?"

The Peacemaker laughed and began to rotate his wrist, the point of his blade describing circles in the air. "Give it up, Rhenford. There are a dozen men waiting at the bottom. You won't get off the Stair alive."

"I like your sword," Liam said. "Do you miss it?" Futile jibes, but they were all he could think of. Aldyne was right—between the passengers and whatever Peacemakers were waiting below, he would never make it off the platform.

"Lay it down," Aldyne advised. "You're done for."

He said nothing, mind racing.

"Funny," the other man continued, "I was just going down to deliver your likeness to the City Below." With his free hand he touched a scroll of pages thrust through his belt—copies of the portrait. "And instead I find the original, sharing the Stair with me."

The City Below: the Pool and the inner harbor and the outer harbor. *All that water.* Before he could reflect on the idea, Liam said, "Not sharing for long," and stepped backward, raising one leg over the balustrade.

"Rhenford," the lieutenant warned, and Liam shoved his hostage away and dropped his sword, straddled the balustrade for a split second and then brought his other leg over.

Master, what are you doing?

For a dizzying moment he clung to the Stair, gazing down at the toy city beneath him. *So much water. You have to hit some of it.*

He jumped.

CHAPTER 11

SO MUCH WATER—the mirror of the outer harbor winking in the rising sun, the still-dark inner harbor, the cauldron of the Pool—and for the first long seconds of Liam's fall, he knew that he would miss all of it.

He squeezed his eyes shut.

A giant hand grabbed him, yanked him backward, and his eyes snapped open as he was sucked into the storm that supported the Stair. He flipped end over end into the heart of the column, legs and arms wrenched in different directions, passing through conflicting currents of air. His cloak leapt out behind him, caught and dragged by a stronger current; the clasp dug into the underside of his chin, trying to rip his head off—and then the cloak came back and crashed into him, heavy with water. Raindrops fat as slingstones stung his face and thudded against his clothes; gales tore at him. He tried to draw in his limbs, to curl into a ball, but the storms would not let him, wrestling for possession among themselves.

Storms, more than one, a thousand, thrashing throughout the column—he passed from an updraft of hot, dry air to a freezing, ice-laden band, into a broad, powerful river of clear cold, whistling downward. He could not think, buffeted back and forth, the transition from storm to storm like breaking through walls, tumbled boneless, whipped from one weather to another, a dozen in a second. Each breath tasted different, scorched his throat

168

with steam and ozone, filled his mouth and lungs with water.

The noise was tremendous, as powerful a force as the wind, each band of storm with its own tone, muttering, thundering, growling and screaming to the others. They tortured his ears, driving against his eardrums, resonating in his guts, blasting like the wind.

Wrenched, torn, senseless, he fell through the column, all idea of up and down gone, until finally he slammed to a halt, stopped for the second it took to register that he had stopped, before falling again into a zone of clear air. Then he hit the water.

He opened his mouth, thinking it was another storm, and water poured in. Coughing, he thrashed and got his head out, back into the clear air, but the clear air did not want him—it pressed down, shoving him under the water, which he finally realized was the pool beneath the Stair, flattened by the vast downdraft cushioning the storm column.

The air pressed down and the water pulled, boots and cloak weighing on him. His head went under while he tore at the cloak, and when it came free he forced his head up for a gasping breath. He caught a glimpse of shore—a black bar separating air and water—and tried to swim for it, but his boots were like anchors and he had to tug and kick them off, frantic seconds underwater as they caught on his heels.

Even when they were gone swimming was almost impossible; the water plucked at him and the downdraft tried to dunk his head. He lunged toward the dark bar, throwing his whole body at it, fighting the downward pressure, the need so great it overwhelmed even panic.

His hands struck something hard and he cried out, swallowing water before he knew it was the sloping bottom of the pool, and started dragging himself up it, crushed by the downdraft. He got his feet down and crawled through the shallowing water, chest and stomach pressed flat against the stone bottom. The water was only inches deep now but the downdraft was like a hand on the back of his head, forcing his face into it. He twisted away as he crawled, cheek and ear scraping on the stone, water sloshing in his mouth and nose.

He crawled into inch-deep water, the very edge of the pool, and dully wondered why the pressure did not let up, why it was getting harder to move forward.

And then willing hands caught his arms and dragged him from the pool.

Master, you must get up.

Voices surrounded Liam, a babble of concern, and he could not distinguish them from the dragon's thought.

"Sweet Mother Pity, man—that was a miracle!"

"You fell, brother!"

"From the Stair!"

He coughed, brought up water, and flopped onto his stomach to retch. When he was done, the same willing hands rolled him over and helped him sit up.

Master, Lieutenant Aldyne will be here soon.

"Fanuilh?" he mumbled, and opened his eyes, his head lolling weakly on his neck.

Men were staring down at him. They broke into smiles and laughter.

"He speaks!" They cheered.

By gestures, he indicated that he wanted to get up and they hoisted him to his feet, steadied him when he swayed on weak legs.

"Easy there," said the man on whose shoulder he leaned, a sun- and windburned fellow with a brightly colored headcloth. "You've had the fall of the world, brother."

Master, you must go now.

They were sailors—he knew the earrings, the tattoos, the sleeveless vests, the breeches worn without stockings even in cold weather—six of them, and all grinning. He said the word, and they all smiled and bobbed their heads.

"Aye, so we are," said the man with the headcloth. "Just come off the *Tiger,* out of Caer Urdoch. Rafe here wanted to show us the Stair."

"I didn't think we'd see such a show," Rafe said, and they all started in at once, marvelling at his fall. Liam shook his head to clear it and managed to stand on his own, to take in his surroundings. He was on the eastern side of the pool, opposite the lower landing of the Stair, the sailors had carried him well clear of the storm column. He looked up, and saw the platform a hundred feet overhead.

Master, can you move?

"I'm all right," he said, though his legs trembled, and he could not seem to marshal his thoughts.

"You're alive," Headcloth said. "Much beyond that I wouldn't go."

There are Peacemakers coming around the pool. I will stop them, but you should go if you can.

"I can." He saw the puzzled looks the sailors exchanged, and fumbled for his pouch. "I'm better," he began, then stopped, seized by a sudden chill. When his teeth stopped chattering, he went on, still trying to open the pouch with numb fingers. "Thank you, brothers. I have to go."

"You can't!" they chorused.

He got the pouch open, saw the meager contents, and groaned when he remembered the notes-of-hand in his boots.

"You've no shoes," Rafe pointed out.

Two gold crowns, some silver, a scattering of coppers. He took out three silver coins and turned to Headcloth. "Say, brother, I can't meet up with any Peacemakers, if you know what I mean. I've got to go."

They caught on instantly, and reacted with even broader grins.

"Constables, eh? Put that away then," Headcloth said, pointing to the silver. "Give him your shoes, Weevil." The sailor indicated kicked off his wooden clogs with the alacrity of a man more accustomed to bare feet, and Liam stepped into them. "You fly, brother," Headcloth continued. "We'll see to the constables."

Liam's eyes grew moist with a weak, jittery kind of gratitude he could only ascribe to his recent battering, and he forced the coins on Headcloth. "For the shoes. You're grand, brothers. Thanks."

Master!

"I'm going," he said, saluted the sailors, and started off at a shuffling trot into the City Below.

After the towers and hills of Torquay, the port seemed flat and low, the stone and brick buildings squat and mean, few rising above two stories, and naked as well, the ivy that coated the upper city unable to adapt to the salt winds off the ocean. It was a functional place, with none of the architectural pretensions of the capital it served.

Liam loved it nonetheless, as he clattered along in Weevil's loose wooden clogs. Soaked to the skin, battered and shivering, he grinned stupidly to himself. He had ten minutes before Aldyne arrived on the Stair—Fanuilh had reported the Peacemakers from the lower Landing safely sleeping—and it seemed an eternity. The streets of the port were alive with people, porters, and stevedores carrying chests or trundling barrows, clerks with ledgers and sheafs of paper, women hawking pies from trays balanced on their hips, sea-gaited sailors, some with elaborate tattoos on their bare arms and even their faces, and the occasional well-dressed merchant. A few looked askance at his dripping clothes, but for the most part he was studiously ignored. He revelled in it, his mind emerging from the stupor of his fall through the storm to figure out his priorities.

Dry clothes first and foremost, because the wind from the sea was cold and his teeth were chattering, and then a place to hide. There was enough money left in his pouch for a shirt and breeches and a coat, if he was not picky, but that would not leave him much, and he still had to send his letter to Catiline. *Not to mention eating.* His stomach felt hollow, despite the loaf he had eaten less than an hour before. He had no idea how much the Messagers charged to carry a letter.

You need money. His hand went to his belt, anticipating his thought—there were rich men in the City Below, merchants and sea captains with fat purses— and found an empty sheath. He cursed. *You can't cut purses without a knife.* There were other ways to steal, though.

He spotted the Exchange from a few blocks away, its needle-spired belltower a landmark in the landscape of low buildings, and gravitated toward it, eyes open for potential marks. In his short walk he counted five easy purses, and one he might conceivably have gotten without a knife. By the time he saw the last, however, he had reached the small square fronting the Exchange, and found that he could aim for bigger game.

The Exchange was a massive brick hall, with a single row of tiny windows set high in the walls between tall pilasters of a darker brick, the belltower rising from one end. Two Peacemakers loitered by the incongruously tiny entrance. Liam noted them without concern; he was not interested in the Exchange.

Arranged around the square were several taverns and a number of shops; the columned portico of a Messager House; a windowless, featureless stone building, the many chimneys of which were venting quantities of smoke; and an inn. The inn had promise: it would cater to the wealthy, men who wanted to be close to the

Exchange, where the city's merchants came to sell and buy, to work deals and gamble obscene amounts in the name of trade. A bold thief would find the servants' entrance, slip in, and ransack the rooms.

Liam was not a bold thief, but he was willing to allow desperation to take the place of courage. *If necessary. It might not be.* The smoking building held his attention, offering an intriguing possibility. He started working his way around the square toward it, keeping his distance from the Peacemakers. There was a portrait frame next to the entrance to the Exchange—he wondered how many he had not noticed, elsewhere in the city—but Aldyne would not arrive with the new pictures for some time.

Fanuilh, where are you? As he came closer, he saw the double doors that broke the blank face of the smoking building.

Atop the belltower, master.

Can you see the roof of the building on the south side of the square? Does it have an atrium or anything like that?

A man in an expensive slashed coat and fur-trimmed cloak pushed open the double doors and strode toward the Exchange. His hair was wet.

Yes, master. There is a pool at the bottom. I think it is a public bath.

Grand. He grinned briefly, a wolf's cold grin that made him feel dangerous and competent, then let it lapse and picked up his pace, covering the rest of the perimeter of the square until he reached the doors of the bath.

Plain on the outside, the bath was opulent within, clearly meant for the rich men who spent their days across the square in the Exchange. The entrance hall was a vast, echoing space with a vaulted ceiling, the floor tiled with geometric mosaics. Giant murals of historic scenes—the arrival of the fleet of the Seventeen Houses, the destruction by sea dragons of Carad Rhenyth, the Lord Protector's conquest of the pirates at Gallows Rest— dominated the walls. The clattering echo of his clogs made Liam cringe, as if he had disturbed the quiet sanctity of a temple.

The hall was empty, but the sound of his profane steps summoned the porter from his booth, hidden away beside the door. He took one look at Liam, wet and rumpled, in cheap wooden shoes, and assumed an unwelcoming politeness.

"Are you lost, sir?"

"Lost?" Liam snapped, finding it easy to counterfeit the outrage of a man unused to contradiction. "Do I look lost, man? I want a bath!"

The porter blinked and stammered, wondering if he had underestimated this customer. "Of course, sir. Are you a member?"

If the bath was private, he would have to try the inn— unless he could bully his way in. He swelled up, looming over the increasingly uncertain porter, letting his voice rise almost to a shout. "Member? Gods, no, I'm not a member. I don't want to be a member. I want a bath, damn your eyes. My idiot servant upset my skiff and dropped me in the harbor. I'm wet, I'm cold, my clothes are ruined, and I want a bath! Do you hear me? I—WANT—A—BATH!"

It felt good to shout, though there was a slight, giddy stir in his stomach that warned him he might be going too far. The porter thought so: he winced and cringed and fawned, patting the air in front of him to calm Liam down. "Of course, sir, of course, of course, of course. You needn't be a member to use the baths, not at all, it's only that I must ask you for the fee, sir, and then we'll get you dry and warm, sir, as soon as ever we can."

With a sulky snort, Liam grudgingly let go his pretend anger. "What's the fee, then?"

"Only a crown, sir," the porter said, as if it were a very reasonable price.

Liam covered his surprise with a grunt, and produced one of the remaining gold coins from his pouch. The most expensive bath in Southwark charged less than a tenth of that. *But then, it doesn't have such pretty paintings. And you have to watch your belongings all the time.* He tossed the coin at the porter. "Where are the changing rooms?"

"Here, sir," the porter said, and hurried to show him the way, down the echoing hall and through a tall arch to a set of swinging doors. "Through there, sir. Old Cimber will take care of you." He bowed himself away, and Liam pushed through the doors.

The changing room was long and narrow, lined with wooden cubicles for bathers' clothes. Three men stood halfway down the length of the room—a fat, middle-aged man whose body was covered with curling black hairs, being undressed by a servant while chatting with a younger man who was undressing himself—and in the corner beside the door an old man with sad, rheumy eyes sat on a stool. He climbed creakily to his feet as Liam entered.

"Any shelf you like, sir," he said, indicating the rows of cubicles, roughly half of which were empty.

"I won't need a shelf. I'll need these dried." He plucked at his tunic to show that it was wet, and the old servant nodded as if customers came into the baths this way all the time.

"Not to worry, sir. I'll take them to the furnace room, and they'll dry like that." He snapped his gnarled fingers, not entirely successfully. "Have them brushed, too. You can swim or steam, as you like, sir, or take some exercise, or read in the library, as you wish, and I'll give you the word when they're ready. My name is Cimber, and you need only call on me for whatever you may

need. Shall I?" He made a vague gesture to indicate his
willingness to help Liam undress.

"No thanks, old fellow. I'll do it myself." He moved
a little way into the changing hall, close enough to hear
the conversation between the fat man and his friend,
kicked off the clogs, and started peeling off his wet
clothes.

The two men were discussing the king's health, and
how much worse it had become. "It's a shame," the
younger one was saying. "And no heir to follow him. If
he should fail . . ."

"Oh, he'll fail, all right," the fat man said. He held
his chins high, staring at the ceiling and letting his servant deal with his clothes. "You mark me, he'll fail, and
that within the week."

Liam dawdled, surreptitiously sizing them up. The fat
man was too short, and his shirt, breeches, and hose
were a bright, eye-catching blue. The younger man, on
the other hand, was only an inch or two shorter than
Liam, and his clothes were a more sober green. *They'll
do.*

"Pity forbid," the young man said.

The fat man scoffed. "Pity's got nothing to do with
it."

Master, Lieutenant Aldyne is here.

Liam willed down a sudden surge of fear. *What's he
doing?*

*He is talking to the Peacemakers. He has set a man
to putting up your portrait.*

It did not mean Aldyne had followed him; he did not
think the man capable of it. Warden might have figured
it out, but not Aldyne. *Keep an eye on him. Let me know
what he does.*

The other men had finished changing. "I heard the
king plans to go to Rentrillian for a sacrifice," the young
man said, folding his clothes and depositing them in a
cubicle. "As soon as Catiline returns."

"Much good it'll do him," the fat man muttered, counting coins out of a purse. He handed the money to his servant. "Fetch us a jug of Alyeciran red. We'll be in the steam room." The servant bowed and hurried past Liam and out the swinging doors, while his master and the young man headed to the far end of the changing room. The wall there was a thick wooden grille, through the interstices of which Liam could see a group of men fencing in a gymnasium. The two men went through a door set in the grille.

Liam stared after them for a moment, then finished undressing and carried his clothes in a sodden heap to the attendant by the door. Now that the moment was upon him, he was anxious, keyed up, and wondered if his nerves showed. "Will it take long, do you suppose?"

"An hour at most, sir," Cimber said, taking the wet bundle as if it were precious. "You make yourself at home, sir." He bowed and went out.

For a moment Liam hovered by the door, wondering if there had been some extra meaning in the attendant's last comment, a certain knowing spark in his sad eyes, or if they had widened just a touch at the sight of Liam's body, the many scars on his chest and legs. *He knows what I'm about. He knows I don't belong here.* His stomach fluttered—and then he shook his head fiercely. *The Dark with that. You don't have much time.*

Theft was fairly common in the cheaper baths he was used to, so much so that many posted warnings to that effect, and it was normal to tip the attendant to watch the clothes one left behind. In such an expensive place, frequented by rich merchants and gentlemen, the honor of the customers was relied on—that, and the fact that a man with a gold crown to spend on a bath was unlikely to need to steal. *He's also unlikely to be wanted for murder and treason, though, isn't he?*

Liam ran to the young man's cubicle and yanked

out the clothes. They did not fit well—the waist of the
breeches too big, the sleeves of the tunic an inch too
short—and they smelled of some sweet oil or perfume,
but he pulled them on anyway, cinching the belt tight,
grimacing at the way the wool stuck to his still-wet skin.
The young man's stockings and low, soft shoes were
a closer match, though Liam preferred boots. *Maybe
he'll buy some before you rob him again.* There was a
good cloak in the cubicle, and beneath it a purse and a
dagger.

With the cloak over his arm, the dagger thrust through
his belt, and the purse in his hand, he started toward the
door, then turned back and found the fat man's cubicle.
His purse was bigger and Liam snatched it up, as well
as a floppy hat of black velvet and a matching scarf.

Dressed and moneyed, he ran to the swinging doors,
slipped through, and poked his head out of the arch to
peer down the entrance hall. It was empty, the porter out
of sight in his booth. Liam's stomach fluttered again; he
lifted his head, squared his shoulders, and marched out
into the hall, toward the outer door.

*Master, Lieutenant Aldyne has left the square, headed
west.*

That was a relief, as was the soft whisper of his stolen
shoes, a far cry from Weevil's noisy clogs. *Then why
are you so nervous?* His stomach jumped and sweat
beaded on his forehead as he made the long walk to the
outer doors, eyes fixed on the porter's booth. *You're
wanted for murder and treason; what's a little petty
theft?*

Still, by the time he reached the doors he was holding
his breath—and then he was outside, free, wanting to
bolt, to put as much distance between himself and the
bath as he could. *Hold on.* He kept to a steady pace,
willed himself to act naturally: to put on his hat as a
normal person would, even if he pulled it down lower
over his eyes than most, to tie his two new purses to his

belt, to shake out his cloak before throwing it around his shoulders, to turn onto the first side street off the square as if it were his destination. All as if he did not expect men—porters, attendants, robbed and indignant bathers—to spill out into the street after him, shouting down the city on him.

One block, and half of another before he could not take it anymore. Then he started running.

Liam fetched up close to the waterfront of the outer harbor, in an area dominated by busy warehouses and factors' offices. Clerks and messenger boys and gangs of stevedores bustled through the streets. The morning sun was unseasonably bright and warm, particularly after the rain of the day before, and the people he passed seemed unusually, irritatingly cheerful.

It was not the sort of neighborhood he wanted to hide in—too full of activity, entirely lacking shabby tenements, sailors' dives and abandoned buildings—but he still needed to send his letter to Catiline, which meant paper and pen and ink, and someone to deliver it. He wandered the area for a few minutes before he found a small, decent-looking wineshop and stepped inside, praying for luck.

He found it: the place was empty, and if the proprietress, a wizened woman with a wan, hopeful expression, had been warned by the Peacemakers about a man answering his description, she gave no sign of it. She seemed instead too happy to see him, desperate for business and willing to accommodate. "Paper? Ink? Why, of course, sir, of course. Let me just send the lad to fetch it." She called a young boy out of the back room of the wineshop, and sent him scurrying.

While they waited, she told him the story of her life—a sea-widow, her husband lost on a voyage to the Suevi Principalities, all her poor means tied up in this failing shop—and though Liam was wondering whether she had in some subtle way communicated to the boy that he should fetch the Peacemakers, the main thrust of her tale got through to him. He ordered a cup, specifying only that it should be her best.

Flustered and grateful, she brought him a cup of red wine, which he sipped and found sour and near-undrinkable. The return of the boy with paper, ink, and quill saved him from having to comment, and he retired to a table in the corner of the shop to write his letter.

Seated, quill in hand, he tried to compose his thoughts. They would not come to order: confronted by the blank page, they scattered to the far corners of his mind, and the only thing he could think to write was the word HELP. *In block letters, underscored several times.* He did not write it, however, since the boy had brought only one sheet of paper. Instead, he leaned back in his seat and blew out a heavy breath.

Catiline'll think you're a madman. Severn killing his own brother, with the help of the Pacifex and her faithful lieutenant? You don't even believe it, and you were there. He sighed, and then remembered something odd, something Aldyne had said about trying to make Warden believe lies. He sat up, puzzled and disturbed, and sent a question to Fanuilh.

I am on the roof of the warehouse next to you, master. There are a great many gulls here.

Forget the gulls. Help me figure something out.

Step by step, they recreated the events of the past day and night, paying particular attention to Warden's part in everything. She was not present when Lord Bairth was murdered. She and Aldyne were at Cade's when he arrived; the lieutenant had to be there, because he had brought Liam's dagger from Severn's house, but there was no proof that Warden was there when it was used to kill the scholar. She had tracked him to his inn and then to Pauper's, and from there to Marcade's house, but it was Aldyne who broke down the door, some hours later: she had declined to force the issue, and gone to lie in wait for him at Cade's.

*And Aldyne was awfully anxious to get me away from her, once he got there. Wanted to send her off to look for Marcade, when he knew perfectly well where she was—that she was—*He cut the thought off, not willing to speculate on where, or in what state, Marcade was. *The point is, why did he want to separate us?*

There was a long pause before Fanuilh supplied the obvious conclusion: *Perhaps she is not working with them. Perhaps it is only Lieutenant Aldyne who is Severn's creature, and she does not know about it.*

Liam frowned, disliking the idea even though it had occurred to him as well. *Then why is she chasing me so hard? Why is she trying to catch me?*

She does not know you are innocent. Your knife was used to kill Master Cade, you have the King's Cure, and you have tried very hard to resist arrest. You have all the appearance of guilt.

Thank you.

Fanuilh ignored this. *It is her duty to capture you. You would pursue her in the same manner if this were Southwark.*

"Hunh." The dragon was right: just because it seemed as if the Pacifex was not on Severn's side did not mean she was on his. The realization—if realization it was: he might have misheard Aldyne on the Stair, or simply misconstrued the whole thing—was his alone. Warden would continue to chase him, and if she caught him he might well fall into Aldyne's hands. He looked down at the sheet of paper and thought of writing her a letter, then immediately rejected the idea. He might be wrong about her innocence, and even if not, she would be far more likely to trust her lieutenant. He could imagine her showing Aldyne such a letter, and laughing over what would seem a feeble pack of lies. There was nothing to do but follow the plan he had already begun, and to keep treating Warden as if she were his enemy.

It is funny.

Deep in thought, Liam was startled by the sudden intrusion of Fanuilh's comment—and by its content. *What?*

This situation. It is funny. You have frequently wondered what I find funny, master.

That was true: the dragon rarely understood his jokes, and never found them amusing; he had often accused it of lacking a sense of humor. *What's so funny about it?*

Everything. She is the Pacifex; you are a quaestor. Both of you are dedicated to tracking down and punishing criminals, and yet you are opposed to one another in this. It is as if two foxes were to fight, while the—No, that is not right. It is as if two lions—No. It is as if two fishermen were to try to catch one another in their nets, while a shark ate up all the fish.

Liam shook his head, incredulous. *That's not funny.*

Better yet, it is as if two shepherds were to fight, while a wolf made off with all their sheep. That is better. You are both like shepherds, in your way.

Fine, but it's not funny. He frowned up at the ceiling, wishing he could see his familiar. *It's not.*

There was a long pause. *It is to me, master.*

But it's just not. Maybe if it was someone else, but this is me we're talking about. It's not funny because it's me.

Another pause. *I just thought you would be interested to know that I do have a sense of humor.*

Liam sat up in his chair and pulled it close to the table, picked up the quill, and addressed himself to the blank sheet of paper. *If that's what you call a sense of humor, fine. Congratulations.* He dipped the quill and wrote Catiline's full name at the top of the paper.

You don't find the situation funny at all? Even though it is you?

No. Now leave me alone. I have to write this stupid letter.

Yes, master.

CHAPTER 12

THE LETTER CAME much easier now, though Liam had to stop every few minutes to frown up at the ceiling, wondering at his familiar's newly revealed sense of humor.

He told the Prince of the Mint very little: that Lord Bairth had been murdered to prevent the delivery of the King's Cure, that he had it and wanted to make sure it got to the king, and that there were those who wished to stop him. He deliberately left out any mention of Auric Severn, Aldyne, and the Pacifex, though he did make a suggestive reference to being unable to use the "natural and obvious ways of approaching the palace." By way of proof, he suggested a visit to Master Tollerdig; the scholar could at least confirm that the phial belonged by rights to the king, if he had discovered nothing more by the time Catiline contacted him. Finally, Liam wrote that he was wanted for two murders, and promised to turn himself in to Catiline once the Cure had been delivered to the king.

He read it over, and then signed his name.

While blowing on the ink to dry it—the boy had forgotten blotting sand—Liam realized that he had not given Catiline any way to contact him. Rolling his eyes, he spread the paper flat and started a postscript.

Should you perceive the truth of this, my lord, he wrote, *and wish to contact me, send a trusted servant to the City Below by the earliest possible*

*Stair. Have him go to the base of the mole by the
inner harbor, and wear a white feather in his cap.
I will give my name as Othniel Fauvel. I beg you,
my lord, to treat this matter seriously, and to make
all haste. The King's life may depend on it.*

The false name, the feather, and the location were all
plucked from the air and struck him as quite possibly
inadequate, but he could think of nothing better at the
moment, and he wanted the letter sent immediately. He
blew it dry, folded it, and wrote "PUBLIUS CATILINE,
PRINCE OF THE MINT, KING'S VALE" on one side,
along with "URGENT" several times. Then he went to
the counter, where the sea-widow had been having great
difficulty pretending not to be deeply curious.

"A love letter?"

"Something like," he said, with a wink. "Have you
any wax?"

She did, from the seal of a now-empty jug of wine,
and lit a candle for him to melt the wax across the fold.
He impressed the lump with the bottom of the ink bottle,
and let it cool.

"Now, do you think your boy could take this to Messager House for me? There's one by the Exchange, I
think."

"There is," she said, aflame with curiosity, and
shouted for the boy. He seemed more impressed than
curious, particularly when Liam dropped two gold
crowns in his hand.

"That should more than cover it. And if you're back
before nine, you may have the balance."

The bells had rung eight while Liam was writing. The
boy was gone in a flash, the letter clasped to his chest.
With an indulgent smile, Liam turned back to the sea-
widow. "Your excellent wine has gone to my head, ma-
dam. I think I'll take a short walk while he's off. Let

me settle up now, and start a new score when he returns."

A little disappointed, she tallied up his bill in her head and announced a figure that, he had no doubt, included the wax, the candle, and the air he had breathed while sitting in her shop. He paid the inflated amount cheerfully, however, with the last coins from the young man's purse, and added a hefty tip from the fat man's.

Outside, he made his way toward the sea and ended up on the waterfront. He kept his stolen hat pulled low and hid his face in the collar of his cloak—not entirely out of fear, since the wind was sharp, and flung cold spray into the air; he was at first not very worried about discovery. This was the City Below, after all, and while not the roughest part, it had its fair share of rough men, the sort who spat and forked their fingers against the Dark when a Peacemaker passed by. He saw someone do just that, after spotting two black-and-white tunics strolling the waterfront and putting a group of sailors between himself and them. One of the sailors, a bald man with a tattoo of curling ivy running from the bridge of his nose to the back of his skull, hawked loudly and spat at their retreating bootheels. They turned, their faces offering trouble if it was wanted—and Liam hurried on in the opposite direction, reassured as to the local love of authority.

Tattoos were more in evidence than he remembered from his days at sea; nearly half the sailors he saw sported them. More important, he realized that to blend into the neighborhoods in which he proposed to go to ground, he would need to buy a coat. Though it had seemed plain and serviceable in the bath, his stolen cloak would stand out among the poor, who almost never wore cloaks. *A cheap quilted jacket,* he thought, and patted the purse at his belt, blessing the fat man for his generosity.

After a while, he decided that he had given the boy enough time and returned to the wineshop by a different route. He stopped at the nearest corner and surveyed the street on which the wineshop lay, while Fanuilh flew among the shrieking gulls to scout out the far corner.

I see no Peacemakers, master.

Nor do I. He walked past the shop, glancing in at the window, saw the sea-widow at the counter with the boy, doubled back, and went in.

"You beat the bells," he told the grinning boy. "And so the change is yours. How much was it to send the letter?"

"A crown," came the reply, the boy suddenly fearful, knowing that a gold coin was worth a hundred such trips. "But you promised—"

"You did promise, sir," the sea-widow began at the same time.

"I know what I promised," Liam said, with a reassuring smile for both of them. "Was there any receipt?"

The word puzzled them, until the boy remembered the slip of paper crumpled around the coin in his hand. He disentangled it from his crown and handed it over.

Liam took the paper, thanked them, and left before they depleted his purse any more.

The slip of paper—the fresh ink a little smudged from the boy's sweaty palms—acknowledged the Messagers' receipt of his letter, and promised delivery within the day. Liam read it with relief, then folded it carefully in quarters and stowed it in his purse.

That's done, he thought, and started walking north.

His letter would reach Catiline by the end of the day. The Messagers were an odd institution, a family of couriers whose devotion to the reliable delivery of letters approached the religious. They had achieved their reputation and position in the earliest days of the coming of the Seventeen Houses, when the great lords were politicking amongst themselves to choose a king to rule over them all in the new capital. Servants carrying messages back and forth between the factions were frequently waylaid, and forced to divulge the secrets entrusted to them. The founder of the clan was a man named Gnaeus, a retainer of the lord eventually chosen as king, who withstood torture to keep his master's doings secret from his enemies. The grateful king gave Gnaeus the surname Messenger, granted him the right to carry royal correspondence within the city, and proclaimed his person and those of his family inviolate. Most important, he gave the much-scarred servant a permanent space on the Stair.

Gnaeus Messenger parleyed his royal prerogatives into a dynasty; he and his children, untouchable on penalty of death, offered their services as couriers to any who could pay. In the thousand years since, the family had become a widespread clan, with houses throughout the city and their own temple, in which, it was rumored, they held strange, stern ceremonies where young Messengers swore soul-blasting oaths that guaranteed their adherence to the family virtues. In their blue tabards, with their winged sticks, they were a symbol of purity and incorruptibility.

But then, Liam thought, *so are the Peacemakers.* He shuddered as he walked, and refused to consider the comparison anymore. *The letter will get there. I hope.*

The Royal, falling into the Pool and then spreading out through the inner and outer harbors to the sea, split the City Below just as it did Torquay. The vast majority of ships docked on the south side of the harbors, the better to send their cargos up the Grain Climb; it followed that the worst neighborhoods—the ones Liam wanted—would be to the north, far from the focus of the city's trade.

And it was true: the farther he got from the harbors and the area around the Exchange, the more dilapidated the buildings became, the shabbier the shops, the poorer the people. He passed through an area of boarded-up warehouses, emerged into a neighborhood of shanties and tumbledown tenements, and smiled ruefully to himself. *I bet there hasn't been a Peacemaker down here in ten years.* He could not imagine one of the proud black-and-white tunics in these dirty streets, where all the buildings were stained gray from the salt breeze, and the air stank of fish.

There were people abroad, mostly women, gossiping in the streets or fetching buckets of water from the public cisterns. Children played in ragged bands, chasing each other in complex, rule-less games, and it was only when a group of these stopped to watch him go by, with much whispering and nudging, that he remembered his decision to buy a cheap coat. Suddenly he was aware that everyone was looking at him, and felt exposed, his illusion of safety stripped away.

He kept his eyes open after that, and when he had come to a block of fishermen's shacks—the women were mending nets, and the gutters were heaped with fish guts—he finally spotted what looked like a rag shop. Otherwise indistinguishable from the shacks around it, it had clothes hung on poles outside the door, far too many to be washing. He knocked and a few moments later a young woman with a pinched, vulpine face and a baby on her hip came out. She looked him up and down, and pursed her lips skeptically.

"Lost, are you?"

"No." He indicated the assortment of clothes on the poles, which on closer inspection proved to be only a step away from rags. "I was hoping to find a coat."

She barked an unpleasant laugh. "There's coats, sure and there are."

"For sale?"

"Oh, yes, yes. All for sale. Please, my lord, help yourself." She spoke with heavy-handed sarcasm, but he could not see what she was being sarcastic about, and started browsing through the clothes. They were dirty, some so stiff with accumulated filth and salt that they felt as if they had been made from wood rather than cloth, but he managed to find a quilted coat such as he had imagined. *I didn't imagine all these stains, but better to be filthy than have some local tough try to cut my throat because I'm wearing too nice a cloak.*

When she saw he was serious, the woman shifted the baby to her other hip, put her hand on his arm, and shook her head. "You don't want these, my lord," she said, the sarcasm gone. "These are dead men's clothes."

He yanked his hand back. "What?"

"The men who go out and don't come back—their women or their families bring their extra clothes here. None'll wear them. After a time, we sell them, when the man's forgot. When none remembers who the clothes belonged to."

Liam grunted, not sure what to think. It seemed a macabre custom, and he wondered how a man's family could forget him when his clothes were on display. "Still, they are for sale, right?"

"Yes, but they're not for such as you, sir. These are dead men's clothes."

"That's fine," he said, taking the quilted coat down from a pole, and muttered, "I was a dead man myself, this morning."

She heard him and took offense. "You shouldn't, sir. You can buy better elsewhere." She reached out to take the coat away.

In the face of her disapproval he felt an urgent desire to explain—to tell all about the past day and night, why he really had been a dead man. The words boiled up in him, crowded onto the tip of his tongue. *I'm being hunted. People are trying to kill me.*

With the baby, the young woman could not pull the coat from his grasp, but she tried nonetheless. He resisted her tugging without being aware of it, struggling with the story that wanted to be told. *And what would she say? That you came down here to hide because it's so miserable the Peacemakers would never think to look for you here. That you want the clothes from their dead because they're so filthy Warden could never imagine you stooping to wear them.*

He let go of the coat. "Look, I'm sorry. I didn't mean to sound light. I need it, honestly, and I'll pay."

She tossed her head scornfully, clutching the coat close, and for the first time he noticed that her eyes were bright with tears. "Pay? You could buy a thousand such for the price of your hat alone. You don't need it."

"Fine." He bowed his head. *Just take it. She can't stop you.* "Fine. I'm sorry."

He hurried back the way he had come.

Dissatisfied, a sour taste in his mouth, Liam walked back through the shanties and tenements to the abandoned warehouses. Many of them had attracted squatters; furtive wisps of smoke rose from within boarded-up buildings, and Fanuilh, flying above, spotted traces of habitation through dust-smeared windows and half-collapsed roofs—a woman nursing a baby on an upper floor, invisible from the street; a family gathered around a makeshift hearth in a courtyard rank with waist-high weeds; an entire warehouse divided into illicit apartments by walls of sailcloth. With the dragon's help he found a building that looked to have stood truly empty for years. It had been solidly constructed of a dark red brick, and the entrances closed up with a lighter brick to keep out even the most determined; there was, how-

ever, a small window high up on a side wall, overlooking a narrow alley.

*This is where you should have come in the first
place,* Liam thought, as he sized up the wall beneath
the tiny window. *Shouldn't have wasted time looking
for a coat.* The courses of brick would make the climb
easy. *Why offer them for sale,* he wondered, *if you're
just going to get upset when someone tries to buy?*
Lurking beneath the question was the suspicion that
the pinched-faced young woman might not have forgotten a man—that she still remembered, perhaps even
remembered the coat Liam had picked out—but he
shook his head fiercely to drive the suspicion away.
You have your own problems.

Once Fanuilh reported that the streets nearby were
clear, he pulled off his shoes, tucked them into his belt,
and started up the wall. *Fingers and toes,* he thought,
fingers and toes. You're nothing but fingers and toes.
They were cramped and cold by the time he climbed the
twenty feet to the window, but not yet trembling, and
he hooked his forearm over the recessed sill and caught
his breath. There was no glass, only a shutter hung on
the inside of the wall; he found the hook with his dagger
quickly enough, released it, and wormed his way into
the warehouse.

The window gave onto a small sort of porch fixed
under the rafters, from which the owner might once have
overlooked the main floor of the building. Liam hooked
the shutter open and crossed to the interior edge of the
porch to survey his hiding place.

A vast space, silent and empty, smelling of salt and
mold, lit by dirty gray light from a grimy cupola in the
center of the roof. A steep, ladderlike staircase descended from the porch into a storage bay; there was
another bay at the far end of the building, the two separated by a sunken lane running from the bricked-up
entrance. Two rows of thick posts supported the ceiling

on either side of the lane, with appropriate gaps where cargo could be loaded from the bays onto wagons and carts driven into the lane. In the far bay he could see some odds and ends of lumber; otherwise the warehouse was empty.

Perfect.

He put on his shoes and climbed down the steps. Fanuilh flew ahead, swooping across to the far bay and then returning to perch on the crosstrees of a post. Liam followed across the floor of the bay, jumped down into the lane, and gazed around again, hands on his hips, nodding.

It was perfect: secluded, abandoned for years, in a neighborhood where squatters were common. Unless the Peacemakers decided to search every building in the area, he would be safe. He knew he should have been pleased, and he was, insofar as he had found what he wanted, but as he gathered scrap wood from the second bay and dumped it into the lane, he was aware that his mouth was set in an unhappy expression, and a vague dissatisfaction lurked at the back of his mind.

When he had enough wood he jumped down after it and started cutting shavings from the splintery boards, piling them on the unmortared bricks that paved the lane. The dissatisfaction puzzled and irritated him, because he could not discover its origin. He was safe, indoors, would soon have a fire, and his letter was on its way to Catiline. He had been hungry earlier but that had faded, leaving him only tired.

So what's wrong with you? You should be dancing for joy. He arranged boards over the neat pile of kindling and beckoned to Fanuilh. "Light this up for me, would you?"

The dragon fluttered down from its perch. Liam wondered if he was still annoyed at the dragon's strange sense of humor, and then, watching it crouch by the makeshift hearth, decided that was ridiculous. *Without him you'd be dead,* he thought privately, and knelt down beside Fanuilh while it cast its spell. A core of flame flared up amid the shavings; they crackled and curled as they burned, and the larger boards caught quickly. He reached out and untied the various knots that held the phial to the dragon's back.

"We can take this off for a while."

Fanuilh wriggled and stretched, flaring its wings and snaking its tail back and forth. There was something doglike about its relief; Liam smiled and scratched its back, prompting it to flatten itself against the bricks and bury its snout in its paws.

"Is it that uncomfortable?" Still scratching, he gazed at the Cure in his other hand. The fire, burning well now, glowed through the red glass, and he had the strange impression that the phial was filled with blood.

The dragon raised its head. *Only a little.* It stood out from underneath his hand, and padded a few steps away from the fire. *I will go outside and watch for the Peacemakers.*

Liam sat tailor-fashion by the fire, bouncing the phial lightly in his hand. "Don't bother. We're good for a while." Then he added silently, *I'm sorry I got angry about your joke.*

We have different ideas about humor.

Liam chuckled. *That we do.* Staring at the phial, with the fire warming him, he could see a certain irony in the situation, and said so. *But that's as far as I'll go. Irony. Not humor.*

As you will, master.

And yet he usually enjoyed irony, and its poor cousin, sarcasm. Most of his jokes, he knew, aspired to the former and achieved the latter. *So why are you so gloomy? This whole thing is irony writ large, the sarcasm of the gods.* He frowned at the fire even as he drew closer to it. It was not his situation that was bothering him, the unfairness of it, nor the way his body ached and his eyes drooped, the leaden weight of his arms. For a few moments he wondered if it might be a perverse jealousy—the knowledge that Warden was, in his estimation, a far better investigator than he—then decided against it. *She is better, but she hasn't caught you yet.* It was not Warden's superiority that nagged at him. He remembered the woman who sold dead men's clothes and decided it was not her, either, though he wondered briefly about her tears, and who might have fathered her child. It was a depressing life, certainly, waiting each day for the fishing boats and not knowing if your people would return from the sea, but it did not account for the itch at the back of his mind, the sense that something was wrong, something undone, or that he was missing some important point.

He growled to himself and lay down, wrapped in his stolen cloak. The fire was warm and cheerful, and he could feel his body slipping toward sleep.

Waiting. That, in the end, was the source of his gloom. The Messagers had his letter, and there was nothing he could do until Catiline received it and responded, which would not be until the next morning, at the earliest. *If he responds at all.* Matters were out of his hands, and he did not like it. For the rest of the day and the night to follow he was limited to waiting, hanging on Catiline. *That, and staying alive, out of Warden's hands.*

So thinking, he fell unaware into sleep.

The fire burned down while Liam slept; when he awoke it was reduced to smoking embers, and the warehouse was dark. He had not dreamed, but he came awake with a premonition of imminent danger, and jumped to his feet, glaring wildly into the black depths all around him.

Fanuilh!

I am outside, master.

What are you doing? He could see the window far above him, a pale gray square of sky that did nothing to illuminate the warehouse.

Watching. Two Peacemakers passed by in the middle of the afternoon, but they took no special notice of this building.

The middle of the afternoon? What time is it now?

The sun has just set, master.

He had slept the day away, which was not a bad thing—it brought him that much closer to the next, and the message he hoped to receive from Catiline—but he was not sure he felt any better for it. Blinking and yawning, he sank back to the floor and laid more boards on the embers, then poked the fire to life again. His aches and bruises clamored for a comfortable bed and a proper rest; his stomach growled. He pulled his cloak tight around him and hunched close to the heat.

A whole day gone. And now you're awake. He stared dully into the fire, hypnotized by the dance of the flames. *Which is a good thing, since this is all you have to do until tomorrow.*

Tomorrow he would have to go to the mole by the entrance to the inner harbor, and wait for Catiline to send a man with a white feather in his cap. From there, the Prince of the Mint would be in charge, and welcome to it.

And if no one comes? If he ignores your letter? Or worse, what if he turns out to be on Severn's side? The idea had not occurred to him; now it struck him as a possibility he should have considered long before. *What if he is? And he tries to capture you? Or tells Severn and Aldyne?* There were precautions he could take—a careful reconnaissance of the area around the mole, to start with, and leaving the Cure with Fanuilh when he met with the messenger—but they did not entirely set his mind at ease. He had taken Catiline's loyalty to the

king on faith, as he had taken the Peacemaker's incorruptibility, without any real evidence of either. If the
latter proved unworthy, the former might as well, and if
the former, so might anyone in Torquay: the priests, the
lords, the people, even the queen. *You might be the only
person in the whole damned city who cares if he lives
or dies.*

Once begun, such thoughts overwhelmed him. He
thought of the praying crowds on the Processional and
imagined them hypocrites, secretly snickering and hoping for Nicanor's death; he thought of Old Becca at Pauper's, chastising her son, and did the same. *That fat
bastard in the baths was ready to see him dead. Why
shouldn't Catiline?*

His unruly mind jumped from subject to subject, from
the disloyalty he suspected to the question of its end, to
the men who stood to benefit. Severn would not act so
on his own; the risks he had run required the support of
one of the claimants to the throne, Corvialus or Silverbridge. Marcade—his thoughts shied away from the
name—had assumed it was Corvialus, but now, in a
mood to doubt everything, he wondered, and tried to
make a judgement of his own.

Silverbridge, a prince from a cadet branch of the royal
family with ancestral holdings in the mountains around
Caernarvon, was the more popular man, so much so that
he was commonly called the Pretender, and highly re-
garded by many. Popularity, however, did not preclude
scheming and treachery, and his claim to the throne was
tenuous.

Corvialus's was better, his connection to the ruling
house stronger, and he was considered the more legiti-
mate contender. He was not as popular, however, and
while his personal reputation was unblemished, he was
widely believed to be a puppet for his mother, whose
ambition and ruthlessness were bywords.

Liam could not choose between them. *They could be*

*working together, for all you know, and since when do
you know so much about politics?* Smarter men than he
had spent their entire lives trying to comprehend the in-
trigues of the court.

This is ridiculous, he thought, and stood suddenly,
irritated at his own ignorance and the pointlessness of
trying to fathom the dark depths of the situation into
which he had been thrust. *Time to get something to eat.*

Up in Torquay there might be an hour or more to the
day; dusk had settled in the City Below, hastened by the
mountains beneath which the port lay. With his hat
pulled low, Liam slipped away from the abandoned
warehouses toward the more populated areas to the
south, looking for a tavern or a pie vendor. Fanuilh
trailed him overhead, watching for Peacemakers. The
dragon did not object to his going out, but it had been
surprised.

Where are you going, master? it asked, when he appeared at the little window of his warehouse.

Dinner, he projected, *and I may as well get a look
at the mole.* The building across the way was lower
than his window, and only a few feet away; he jumped
to it and walked across the roof, the slope of which
was much less steep than that of the houses in King's
Vale.

I flew around earlier, the dragon told him. *Your portrait has been posted in several places.*

Duly noted, he replied, and climbed down to the street
at the far end of the building.

Now, despite the thickening dusk, he wondered if he
had not been overly nonchalant. People walked by him
in the streets, sailors and workmen on their way home,
and though none seemed to pay any special attention to
him, he could not help feeling that they did, that when
they were past they turned around to stare. He developed
an itch between his shoulder blades and worried that he

might give himself away, that his anxiety not to be noticed would make him noticeable.

Constant checks with Fanuilh kept him from bolting back to the warehouse; from its high vantage the dragon reassured him that no one was staring, no one suddenly running for the Peacemakers once they were out of his sight. *I'm fine,* Liam told himself, and managed to control his nerves until he reached a tavern that, according to its sign—twin sailors, one reeling as he upended a jug and the other stuffing a whole fish into his gaping mouth—sold both food and drink. He gathered his courage and went in.

Smoke hung in thick banks throughout the low-ceilinged room, curling off the few tapers and billowing out from the fire in the hearth. Though it stung his eyes, it also wrapped him in an obscuring cloud, and he blessed all tavernkeepers who bought cheap tapers and poor-quality coal. Men sat drinking all around the tavern; confident in the poor visibility, he ducked his head to avoid the beams and crossed to the counter at the back.

The barkeep was a surly man in a stained apron. He grunted at Liam as he put his hands on the counter, grunted when Liam ordered something to eat, and grunted again when he produced what he had from beneath the counter: bread, cheese, and pickled fish.

Mold dotted the stale bread, and a waxy rind surrounded the cheese; Liam cut these away with his knife and ate what was left, softening the bread in his beer. *You're spoiled,* he thought. *Been eating too rich.* The fish were fine, and he was hungry enough to overlook the shortcomings of the rest.

As he ate, he looked around the tavern. Most of the clientele were young men engaged in serious drinking, downing beer with the concentration of philosophers. Many were sailors, by their sleeveless vests and innumerable tattoos; near the hearth an older man was scraping the last line of a crude mermaid into the razor-stubbled scalp of a glassy-eyed youth. Clippings and clumps of hair littered the far end of the bar, where the tattooist's assistant had just shaved a similarly liquid young man, and was now tracing out a design in ink on his nodding head.

They're going to regret those in the morning, Liam thought, and then, after a quick glance at the other customers, decided that they might not. He quickly finished the bread and cheese, scooped up the last three fingerlength fish, and headed for the door.

The cold air was nice after the smoke and heat of the tavern, and, with his hunger assuaged, he felt much less on edge. *Will you eat pickled fish?*

I can, Fanuilh answered.

But will you? I have some, if you want them.

Yes, thank you, master.

He met the dragon in an alley behind the tavern, and laid the three fish out for it to eat. While he wiped his briny fingers on his breeches, his familiar sniffed at the meal, picked one of the fish up in its teeth, and lifted its head to let the whole thing slide down its throat. It dispatched the other two, its serpent tongue flicking out to wipe brine from its muzzle. *Salty.*

Liam grimaced. *I know.* His fingers were sticky and smelled of brine; he scrubbed them harder on his breeches to no avail, and then gave up. *Come on. Let's go see the mole.*

Dusk was gone; night had fallen, and stars had begun to wink in the eastern sky. Fanuilh took to the air again and Liam started south, to reconnoiter the place he hoped to meet Catiline's messenger. He had gone less than two blocks when the dragon reported that he was being followed.

Two men, master. Not Peacemakers—they are not wearing uniforms, and are being very careful not to make noise and to stay in the shadows. That would not be hard: the few shops in this rough neighborhood were closed, and the only light in the street came from the occasional upper-story window.

Liam cursed to himself. *Are you sure they're following me?*

Not absolutely, but they are taking great pains to make sure you don't know they are there.

He cursed again, a small flutter of fear in his stomach, and prayed that they were only thieves. His clothes would have stood out in the tavern, and they might have seen his fat purse when he paid. *Please, let them be just thieves.* Walking at a normal pace he turned into an alleyway and then ran to the far end where he stopped short, struck by an idea. *If they're thieves—proper thieves, Guild thieves—they might help.* He ducked around the corner, out of sight, and thought quickly.

Fanuilh reported that they had started running as soon as he entered the alley, and were now hurrying down it.

Fine. Let me know when they're almost at the end. There was a little patch of light there, the weak shine of a candle from the second floor of the building overlooking the alley. He thought it through, gave Fanuilh its orders, and waited, fingers playing with the hilt of his dagger.

Now, master.

He stepped into the mouth of the alley, letting his cloak flare dramatically. The two men, advancing shadows in the darkness, skidded to a stop; one yelped in surprise.

"Well, well," Liam said, as Fanuilh dropped out of the air at his side, careful to pass through the square of candlelight from the window.

One of the men started to speak, but his words

were cut off as he slumped to the ground, snoring. Liam stepped into the light and beckoned to the other man.

"Avé, brother. Hie close."

CHAPTER 13

THE THIEF SQUEAKED, shaking in the shadows, and Liam crooked a finger, beckoning him again.

"Hie close, brother. Are chanter?"

Fanuilh jumped to Liam's shoulder, claws gripping his cloak for balance. The thief squeaked again, and Liam let an edge into his voice. "Hie close! Are chanter?"   •

After a convulsive step forward around the snoring bulk of his partner, the thief stammered, "*D-d-doh.* This one chants."

"This one as well," Liam said with a smile, genuinely happy. "This one is a chanter." He was naming himself a thief, a practitioner of the chant, the secret language of Taralon's professional criminals.

"No chanter this one connits," the thief said, cringing a little, as if surprised by his own boldness, and added, "Not in this carad." He was saying he did not know Liam, which meant he could not be a thief—each carad, or guild, kept careful track of its members, and they were vicious in putting down nonmembers.

"This one's not of Carad Torquay. Not operanding momenta, sola larking." He admitted not being enrolled in the city guild, but he was not working—"larking" covered many things, from visiting to loafing to retirement, anything but active thievery. *No need to mention the little escapade at the baths this morning.* "This one would drink the princeps of Carad Torquay," he said. "Drink the Banker."

The thief came forward another step, cocking his head to scrutinize Liam. He was a foot shorter, a hunched figure in the darkness of the alley. Liam let him stare for a few seconds, then repeated his request: "This one would drink the princeps. This one has a split for him." Princeps was the title of the head of the guild; in Torquay he always went by the nickname of the Banker, regardless of which man actually held the post.

At first, he thought the thief's low whistle of astonishment was in response to his request, and then the man spoke. "Connit your banner! From the pamphlet dance! Oh, brother, this one connits your banner!"

"How—" Liam began, and then cut himself off. *How could he know my face?* The answer came immediately, though it took him a moment to puzzle out the chant: his was rusty, and the slang changed frequently. A dance was a gallows tree, but pamphlet meant nothing to him until he remembered that the apprentice wizards did their work in Pamphlet Square—and that the frames on which Warden's portraits were hung had reminded him of gallows. He grimaced, cursing the Pacifex and her brilliant innovation.

"Oh, doh," the thief said, sounding both pleased and more sure of himself. "This one spied your banner in the Magnum Dog's dreams. 'Treason. Murder.' The Checkers howl for you." He nodded significantly.

Magnum was great, and dog, thieftaker; the great thieftaker would be Warden, her dreams the men in the portraits, whom she wished to catch, and the Checkers her Peacemakers, from their black-and-white uniforms.

Liam did not like the other man's tone; he sounded cocksure and superior, his earlier fright gone. *Time to bring it back.* He let a cold smile slide across his lips. "My trumpets blare, my opus is heralded in the glare and the omber." His reputation preceded him; his deeds were known by day and night, and thus by extension among both regular people and thieves. He directed the other man's attention to Fanuilh. "My vitae is mortissim, my modus green." His work was murder, and his methods magical. He narrowed his eyes, still smiling, and asked, "Would add your cognom to my opus?" Did he want his name on the list of Liam's achievements?

"No, brother, no," the thief stammered, suitably cowed.

"Cognom?"

"Slippery Cinna, brother."

"This one is Rhenford," Liam said, and allowed his smile to soften. "Connit that from the paper dance. Will wing my split to the Banker?" He wanted the man to take his deal to the Banker, but he was not entirely sure what the deal entailed. *Help. I need help.* Men to watch his back while he went to meet Catiline's messenger, or maybe even someone to go in his place. *If he can recognize your face in a dark alley, your hat isn't going to do much good in broad daylight.* "Will?"

"What's the split, brother?"

"Sola that this one would drink his banner. This one splits with none bar the princeps."

Cinna shook his head regretfully. "None bar the Banker? When chanters are praised, brother." In other words, it would never happen. "The princeps drinks no rogues."

The snoring man stirred; Fanuilh arched its back and hissed, a dry, whispering cough. The man subsided, and Cinna gulped audibly.

Thanks, Liam projected, and then spoke in a low and dangerous voice. "An wing him my opus, he will. Wing him my opus, brother, and he'll drink my banner." It was an arrogant assertion, that his deeds would impress the Banker enough to guarantee a personal meeting, but thieves respected arrogance—and threats. "Wing him my opus, Slippery Cinna, or your cognom joins it."

Fanuilh hissed again for effect, and the thief hastened to agree.

"Unum, unum. As say, Rhenford. This one'll abet. Mortissim. This one'll wing it."

"Momenta?" *Now?*

"Doh, momenta, momenta. As say."

Liam nodded, satisfied. "Fair split. Shine your brother."

Cinna slapped his friend awake and helped the groggy man rise. He groaned and started to speak, but Cinna hushed him. "We're croakers momenta, brother. Be golden." Croakers were messengers; golden was silent. The man grunted but said nothing, rubbing his head and squinting at Liam in the weak light of the faraway candle. He was much taller than Cinna, and wore a shabby coat.

"Your coat," Liam said, dropping out of chant because he could not remember the right word. He lifted the hem of his cloak. "I like it. Would you trade?"

"What the Dark is he talking about?" the second man demanded, and Cinna hushed him again, frantically urging him to make the exchange. Reluctant, but impressed by Cinna's obvious fear and the sight of Fanuilh, he took off his coat and accepted the cloak, inspecting it to see what was wrong with it.

"Tell the Banker," Liam said to Cinna, putting on his new coat, which stank of sweat and barely reached his wrists. "I'll wait for you in the tavern with the two men on the signboard."

"Doh, brother. The Two Gluttons." He tugged at his friend, anxious to be gone. "This one'll abet."

"Fair split," Liam said. "Cinna? Connit that your cognom would go well on my opus, and my brother will be spying." *Follow them for a while.*

Fanuilh had jumped to the ground while he took off his cloak; now it rose into the air, flapping its wings to hover directly in front of Cinna. The thief and his friend

backed away, nodding, then turned and retreated down
the alley, casting frequent glances over their shoulders
at the dragon behind them.

Master, is this wise?

Liam walked slowly back to the Two Gluttons, wondering much the same thing. *I'm not sure.* The idea had
come to him suddenly, and in general he trusted such
flashes of inspiration. If he could convince the thieves
to help him, he would be immeasurably better off. *You
could lounge around your warehouse, giving orders and
dispatching men around the city.* Not just ordinary men,
either: professional thieves, Torquay Guild thieves, respected throughout the kingdom. With the prospect of
their help, he could even consider what he had earlier
deemed unthinkable: the possibility that the Prince of
the Mint would turn out a traitor, too. *I'll bet a Torquay
thief could drop the Cure in the king's lap and be back
for breakfast without breaking a sweat. They're supposed to be the best.*

The best, perhaps—but still thieves, and that was why
he could not immediately answer his familiar's question.
The remarkable organization of the guilds was not a reflection of their innate desire for order, or of respect for
institutions; it was enforced by fear and violence, and
supported by a code of ruthless vengeance. Slippery
Cinna had responded to threats, but they would not work
on the Banker; a man in his position would stand up to
threats, and Liam could not back them up. *"My vitae is
mortissim." You clown.*

Loyalty and threats were useless, leaving only money.
He could promise that, and if things worked out, he
might even be able to deliver. *Or not, depending on
what you can get away with.*

He reached the Two Gluttons and leaned against the
wall, just outside the pool of light from the lantern that
hung over the signboard. Hugging himself in the cold

night air, he decided that he could pursue the idea a little further. *I'm not committed to anything,* he told Fanuilh. *If they go for it, fine. If not, I lose nothing. Cinna already knows who I am, and I don't plan on telling them too many details.*

I could kill Cinna. I could kill his friend as well.

Liam's jaw dropped. *Are you serious?*

They have seen your face, and know who you are. They might tell people. It could lead the Peacemakers to you.

He could not deny the logic of the suggestion, and he knew Fanuilh's sole concern was his own safety, yet he could not help but shudder. *No. Definitely not.*

There was a long pause. *Yes, master.*

The door of the Two Gluttons banged open and two drunken men stumbled out in a blast of hot, smoky air. They glanced at Liam as they lurched by, but without any special interest. He watched them go, face sunk in his scarf, hat pulled low, and thought bitterly about the way Cinna had recognized him. *In an alley at night, with this stupid hat and scarf.*

Thieves would have more reason than most to study the portraits Warden put up around the city; nonetheless, he knew that his poor excuse for a disguise would not serve in daylight. While he had slept the day away, though, thousands of people could have seen his portrait, noted his features, described him to friends. *For all you know, you might not be able to take a step tomorrow without gathering an angry crowd.*

Apart from his natural reluctance to murder Cinna and his comrade, that was another reason to let them go: the real problem was not that they had recognized him, but that anyone might recognize him. His face was all over the city.

You need to change it. He took a deep breath and blew out his cheeks, willing the stubble to grow. After a few seconds he exhaled, and chuckled sourly. *A few more*

weeks of that, and you'll have a beard. No one'll rec-
ognize you. The king will be dead by then, but no one
will recognize you. Under his breath, he muttered curses
at Warden and her invention. A man could change almost anything but his face.

The door of the tavern opened again, this time in a
storm of shouting, and the barkeep threw out the two
youths who had been getting tattooed. Both sprawled on
the street, mumbling incoherently to themselves. The
head of one looked like it was covered with blood—
smeared ink from the pattern the tattooist's assistant had
drawn. It streaked his face, too, black smudges on his
nose and down one cheek.

Liam stared for a moment, registering that it was indeed ink and not blood, and then cocked his head, trying
to trace the few lines that had not been smeared, the
remains of a series that were probably meant to represent
waves.

He ran his fingers through his own short-cropped hair.
Why not?

The barkeep raised an eyebrow when he reappeared in
the Two Gluttons with a different coat, but Liam tipped
him a wink and shrugged. The man shrugged back. No
one else seemed to notice.

He bought another mug of sour beer and went over
to the hearth, where the tattooist and his assistant were
sitting side by side, drinking in silence. They looked up
as he approached, identical expressions of disinterest,
and he decided against a smile.

"You mark the two outside?"

The tattooist, a stringy weather-beaten man with
greasy gray hair pulled back in a tail and bared arms a
solid blue-black with his own work, glanced significantly down at the tools at his feet: scrapers and fine-
pointed awls, a number of sharp quills, and two pots of
muddy pigment. "Why should you care?"

Liam shrugged again. Indifference was a badge of manhood in places like this. "I want to try one." The tattooist smirked and opened his mouth, so Liam added, "Just the ink. To show my girl. See if she likes it."

Disgruntled at not being able to cut him down, the tattooist shrugged and jerked a thumb toward his assistant, a younger, plumper version of himself. Liam turned to the man, who shrugged. "Whole head? Shave?"

Liam nodded, and the assistant sighed, as if put upon. "A prince."

"Done."

With another sigh, the assistant gathered his own tools—straight razor, inkpots, brushes—and led the way to the bar. He sat Liam on a stool, stropped his razor two or three times, and held the blade out for inspection.

"Sharp enough?"

Liam shrugged.

"That's right. It's sharp enough. We were finished for the day, but it's sharp enough." He started in shaving, drawing the cold edge up from the back of Liam's neck. "She won't like it, you know," he continued. "Not at all. Women don't like a clean man to come back with art. If he has it to begin, that's all right. But if she knows you pale and clean, she'll hate you colored. You shouldn't waste my time, or your money."

Liam repressed a shudder at the cold scrape of the blade. "My money to waste." Hair trickled beneath his collar, and he developed a violent desire to itch. "And it's too late now. Can't go back to her bald."

The assistant stood back a minute, wiping stray hairs off the razor with his thumb. "You'll be bald when the ink comes off. First rain, or if you sweat too much. Waste of time." He moved in again.

Hair pattered on Liam's shoulders and knees, the raspy scrape of the razor loud in his ears. He had to work to keep himself still, to ignore the itching and the impulse to shiver that rose up each time the cold metal touched his skin. Eyes fixed on the floor and the drifts of hair gathering around his feet, he focused on the assistant's voice, his continuous discouraging patter.

"It's not for most. You're no sailor—why do it? Look foolish on you. And your lady won't like it, you mark me. Waste of time." For all his attempts to dissuade Liam, he did his work well, shaving close and clean with deft strokes. It was a dry shave, but he did not cut Liam even once, and he bent each ear gently out of the way when he reached that high.

Master, the thieves have reached their destination.

Liam closed his eyes. *Where?*

A house not far from the inner harbor. They have gone inside, and I cannot follow them.

It was not the Banker's house, that he knew. *Wait for them.*

Yes, master.

The assistant spent a great deal of time touching up before proclaiming himself finished. "You've an odd head," he said, cleaning the razor and setting his inkpot on the bar, readying his brush. "Wipe it off."

Liam brushed the hair from his clothes and ran his fingers over his bare scalp, marvelling at the irregularities of his skull. He had expected it to be round and smooth. "How's it odd?"

"Narrow," the assistant said, and shrugged. "Nothing wrong. But your lady won't like it. I won't give you waves; you want a rounder head for that. Lightning, then." Without waiting for Liam to agree, he inked his brush and started drawing. The brush was strangely soothing, the cool, wet bristles tracing lines on his skin. He closed his eyes and waited while the man worked, silent now, concentrating on his art. The tattooist came over.

"Think you can draw the king?"

Liam tensed, but kept his eyes shut.

The assistant grunted and continued painting long jagged lines on Liam's head.

"Tar over there wants him," the tattooist explained. "Big doings on Godsday, seems. Carrying him to Rentrillian for prayers and magic, ceremony for his health. Going to be big crowds, they say. If you could draw the king, we could offer it. Crowns, too—can you do a crown?"

"Crown, I could," the assistant said, and the tattooist muttered something and went back to the hearth.

Liam relaxed, pondering. *The day after tomorrow.* With any luck he would have given the Cure to Catiline by then, but if he had not, the ceremony in Rentrillian might give him an opportunity—at least it would mean the king was out of the palace, where Severn controlled everything. He made a mental note to have Fanuilh fly by the entrance to the Pilgrims' Way, south of the City Below, and see how heavily it was guarded.

A thought appeared in his head then, as if the dragon knew he was thinking of it. *Master, they have come out again, with a third man.*

Let me see. He imagined the helmet and the dragon-snouted visor, lifted it, and saw three dark figures walking down a dark street. He frowned and closed the visor, took his own sight back. He did not need to see the third man's face to know this was not the Banker. Cinna and his friend had found him too easily, and he had come too quickly. *A lieutenant, then, or a local gang leader. What did you think, that the most important thief in Torquay would drop everything and come at your bidding?*

While the thieves made their way to the Two Gluttons, the assistant finished his design, drawing patterns of clouds and lightning down over Liam's forehead and around his eyes. The ink had already begun to dry on the back of his head, making the skin feel as if it were shrinking, pulling tight to his skull.

"Done."

Liam opened his eyes and looked at his face in the battered tin mirror the assistant held out. His right eye was centered in a black cloud and a serrated bolt ran across his left; a storm played itself out on his forehead. Crude and simplistic, it nonetheless changed his face completely.

"Good you only want the ink," the assistant said. "That'd take hours to dig in, and'd hurt to beat the Dark."

"It's fine," Liam said, understating. "My lady'll hate it, but I like it."

The assistant shrugged, and accepted the coin Liam took from his purse. "Don't get wet, and don't touch it for a bit."

Liam nodded, lowering his hands, which had risen in natural response to the cold ink on his forehead and cheeks. Feeling fierce and different, he went outside to wait for the thieves.

Slippery Cinna and his friend followed a half step behind the man they had brought, as if they were ready to hide behind his imposing bulk. He was tall and broad, with something in his stride and the swing of his clenched hands that indicated both authority and impatience.

Fanuilh flew ahead of them, out of sight, and warned Liam of their imminent arrival. *Master, what have you done to your face?*

Don't you like it? He heard the thieves' footsteps and stood out to intercept them as they approached the Two Gluttons, stopping them well outside the circle of light in front of the tavern door. "Avé, brothers." He wagged a finger at Cinna. "This one said the Banker. Sola the Banker."

The big thief studied Liam for a second, and then glared at Cinna as well. "Said Rhenford, pickit. From the pamphlet dance. This is not the banner this one saw."

Cinna gulped. "That one flies a new banner, uncle."

"A new banner?" the big thief growled. "In a quarter hour?"

"Vertas," Liam said, interceding for the little thief. Among other things, the word meant "true." "It's vertas. This one switched banners in the temple." He nodded over his shoulder to indicate the tavern. "And this one is Rhenford. Cognom?"

The big thief faced him. "Rhenford vertas? And a chanter?"

"This one chants. Cognom?"

"A pretty banner it is," the man said, crossing his arms belligerently.

Liam shrugged. "It suits. Cognom? A chanter should part his cognom to a brother."

Master, I heard them call him Ringer on their way here.

The man ignored the request. "Torquay Carad plays no rogues, Rhenford. Hic away. Too much in the glare, Rhenford, and—Oh, the Dark with this!" He shook a finger under Liam's nose. "I'll not chant with a traitor. You're hot, Rhenford, and you'll bring the Checkers down on us in an instant. They want you bad—and I don't blame them. We've no business with traitors. Get you gone before I turn you in myself."

This is not what I had in mind at all. "That wouldn't be wise, Ringer."

The thief let his hand drop, doing a poor job of concealing his surprise. "We've no business with traitors or wizards, Rhenford. Get you gone!"

Cut your losses. "Fine. Forget it—and me, Ringer. If I find you've talked to the Checkers about me, things will become unpleasant." *Fanuilh, come down here, please.* He snapped his fingers.

Ringer began to bluster, then cut himself off as the dragon dropped down to the street. He cursed and spat. "We're not traitors, as some are."

Protests rose at the back of his mind, but Liam decided not to waste them. "Right. You're upstanding men, with nothing to fear from men or gods. Just forget my face, or you'll wish you had. Unum?"

Eyeing Fanuilh, reluctantly Ringer agreed. "Unum."

With a mocking bow, Liam turned and walked away, Fanuilh trotting at his side. He listened for the sound of footsteps behind him, the skin of his exposed back crawling, but the thieves did not try to rush him. When he was out of sight around a corner, he sent the dragon back to watch them and went on alone, taking a street that led away from his warehouse.

Follow them for a bit, see where they go.

The dragon lifted into the air and disappeared. A few minutes later, it reported that they were still standing outside the Two Gluttons, having an argument. Ringer wanted the two lesser thieves to follow Liam, and they were refusing. *They are frightened of you, master.*

No, Liam replied, *they're frightened of you. You have that effect.*

There was no immediate answer and he walked on, brooding now. *Who would have guessed thieves would have scruples?* He thought of Ringer refusing to chant with him, calling him a traitor, and clenched his fists. *And he a thief! A thief calls me a traitor!* As he walked through the dark streets, he growled to himself at the injustice of it, and wished he had taken the time to enlighten the man. *He might have helped, if you had explained it properly. Or if you hadn't come on so strong. "My vitae is mortissim." What made you say that? All you did was rile them up.* He consoled himself with the thought of his letter, no doubt in Catiline's hands by now.

Master, Ringer has convinced Cinna to follow you, and find where your "caster" is. What is that?

Chant for hideout. He frowned, though he had expected something like this. *Let him get a little way from*

*them, then block him. If he tries to double around you,
block him again. He probably won't, though; I imagine
he'll run. Chase him back to Ringer. Show yourself to
him, if you can, so he knows we know where he is.*

Yes, master.

The thieves had seen him go in one direction; he
changed his course, and headed back to his hiding place.
He had misread them entirely, and the disappointment
robbed him of his appetite for nighttime exploration.
Scouting the mole could wait until the morning.

In the night air, the ink had dried; his scalp began to
itch, and his ears burned in the cold. He picked up his
pace, jogging along, thinking of a fire in his empty warehouse, and maybe a nap.

By the time Liam was climbing into the warehouse window, Fanuilh had finished harrying Cinna back to
Ringer's house. *I showed myself every few blocks, and
he ran quite quickly. I waited outside the house until
Ringer came out, and let him see me. He did not seem
pleased.*

Nor should he be, Liam projected, smiling, *to see such
a fearsome creature at his door. Good work, familiar
mine. Now come back and help me light the fire.*

Yes, master.

Liam stepped down onto the little porch beneath the
window, and stared into the utter darkness of the warehouse. *I should have thought of this.*

The meager starshine merely served to outline the
window and the cupola, without lighting the vast, dark
space. Berating himself, he groped his way across the
porch to the stairs and descended them like a ladder,
feeling for each step. Once on the floor he paused, swallowed up in the enormous void, his imagination pestering him. Ghosts, demons, monsters—and Pacifex
Warden, waiting with a shuttered lantern.

Ridiculous. He started shuffling across the floor to the

sunken lane, hands stretched out before him like a blind man's. A searching wind found the hooked-open window and whistled through, then blew cold air around the warehouse with a sound similar to whispering. He tried to whistle up some courage, had to wet his lips, and produced a stuttering version of a bawdy song he had learned long ago. It sounded weak and frail, so he gave it up and forced himself across the floor.

His hands brushed something in the dark, and he yelped before realizing it was one of the posts by the loading area. Laughing too loud, he felt his way around it and dropped into the lane. By touch, he found some of the waste lumber he had stockpiled earlier and, crouching down beside it with his back to the brick wall of the lane, started whittling kindling with his knife.

Fanuilh?

Yes, master?

You coming?

Yes, master.

Good. No hurry.

He tried whistling again.

Fanuilh finally arrived and, at Liam's urgent request, cast a spell that set fire to his pile of shavings. By the meager light, he built a decent blaze and then sat warming his hands at it, defying the revealed shadows of the warehouse. After a time he stretched out on the brick floor, staring into the fire, and decided he might sleep again. "Wake me before dawn, will you?"

Yes, master. The dragon sat a few feet from him; as he lay on his back with his hands clasped behind his neck, it rose, padded close, and examined his face. *Master?*

"What?"

Is that permanent?

He rolled over and raised his eyes to meet the dragon's. "Of course. Don't you like it?"

Fanuilh lowered its head, humbly defiant. *No, master.*

Liam chuckled and rolled over again. "Well, get used to it. It's very much in fashion. I think you should get one to match." He closed his eyes, as warm and content as he could be in an abandoned warehouse in a hostile city.

After a time, as he was drifting off, Fanuilh sent another thought. *Master?*

"It's just ink," Liam murmured. "Wake me before dawn."

CHAPTER 14

IN A CHILDHOOD field, in midsummer, Liam lay back in the warm, high grass and listened to the insect hum as it swelled and swelled around him.

Wake, it said. *Wake.*

Rolling over, he turned his face from the brilliant blue sky, blinked, and woke blind. The fire had died out.

Good morning, master. Fanuilh was somewhere nearby; he could hear the click of its claws as it shifted on the brick floor. *The sun will rise in half an hour.*

"Grand," Liam grumbled, missing the warmth of the dream in the chilly warehouse. He rose, hugging himself against the cold and feeling weak. "Just grand." For a few moments he turned and turned in the darkness, irresolute and confused by sleep.

Master?

"Right, right." He stretched irritably, cataloguing his bruises, then dragged himself to the edge of the loading area and climbed out. Somehow the lightless void was less frightening than the night before, and as he shuffled glumly along, his only thought that he should have bought a candle. He bumped into the far wall, cursed, groped to the stairs and up them, found the window, and opened the shutter. Cold air washed over him; he stood for a moment and let it clean away the cobwebs, smelling the salt sea. The sky was a deep blue.

Fanuilh came and perched on the windowsill beside him. *When will the first Stair arrive?*

"An hour," Liam said, rubbing his stubbled jaw. "And

if Catiline's man is on it, then we're almost done."

And if he is not? If Catiline does not send a man at all?

Liam frowned and shot a sour glance at the dragon. "Rentrillian, I suppose. Try to see the Royal Hierarch, or the king himself. We can't wait too much longer to deliver this. Speaking of which." He pulled the Cure and the string from his shirt. "Time to resume your burden."

The dragon submitted patiently, and while Liam tied the phial to its back, he described its tasks for the day. *The mole first—I need to know what streets lead up to it, side streets, alleys, dead ends, that sort of thing, and a good place to wait. After that, when I'm in place, I want you to wait by the Stair, and tell me who gets off.*

I will look for a white feather?

White feathers and Peacemakers.

Of course.

"Of course." He sighed, wishing to skip the morning entirely, to jump to the time when it would all be behind him. Sighing again, Liam put his hands on the windowsill, ready to climb down. "Come on; long day ahead of us."

Flying ahead, Fanuilh reached the mole before Liam had covered half the distance, and flew in wide circles above it, relaying the street plan to him and picking out sheltered spots where he could wait for Catiline's messenger. When Liam was satisfied that he knew all he needed to, he sent the dragon on to the Stair. *A white feather and Peacemakers, remember.*

Yes, master.

The City Below woke earlier than Torquay, and as Liam walked, the streets began to fill up with men and women beginning their day's work, some bearing lanterns or torches but most finding their way by habit and the lightening sky. Twice he passed lines outside bakeries, and his grumbling stomach urged him to join in.

Later, he thought, striding on. *After I've seen Catiline's man.*

His head was cold, the skin of his scalp prickling beneath the ink. He saw sailors heading for the harbor, and was relieved to note that many had similar tattoos; none, however, wore hats, so he kept his in his hand, trusting to his disguise. *It'll do until you hear what Catiline wants to do. After that you can wear the hat, or a hood, or a dress. It won't matter.*

He walked quickly, noting the changing shade of the sky, the gray in the east over the sea. The Stair was on its way up to Torquay—he could see the flat-topped column of storm, rising slowly beside the falls—and he prayed to his luck and Fortune that when it came back down it would bear a man with a white feather in his cap.

Six streets converged at the landward end of the mole that separated the inner and outer harbors, running into a wide, circular plaza with a statued fountain at its center. From the plaza the mole extended south, a broad breakwater of mammoth stones, like a road cut through a forest of masts, the shipping massed on either side. A hundred yards separated its far end from the opposite bank; it was a dead end, and Liam realized that he should have been wiser in his choice of rendezvous.

He posted himself at the mouth of a small alley from which he could see the entire plaza and the three streets that entered it from the west—the direction a man coming from the Stair would take. Once Fanuilh guaranteed the man was not being followed, he would intercept him and lead him away from the mole. *Simple enough,* he thought. *Assuming he comes.*

Huddling in his quilted coat, he drove the gloomy possibility from his mind and resigned himself to waiting.

The plaza was alive with men, several hundred stevedores and longshoremen gathered around the central fountain in loose groups, talking among themselves and trying to keep warm. Pie-sellers and boys with trays of fresh bread circulated through the crowd, as well as a lonely talebearer in his motley cloak, but few of the men bought either food or stories. One had somehow climbed atop the statue in the fountain—a marble sailor shading his eyes with one hand and pointing into the dawn with the other, waves of stone rolling around his feet—and clung there, scanning the streets leading into the square. He was particularly interested in Liam's alley, and often seemed to be staring directly at him, to the point where Liam wondered if the man had penetrated his disguise.

From that distance? Nonsense. Nonetheless he frowned, and tensed each time the lookout glanced his way, considered moving, refused. *No one's looking at you.* He folded his arms and leaned against the corner, feigning confidence, almost defiance.

Master, the Stair has started down.

And then the lookout on the statue flung up his arm, pointing as the marble sailor did but in a different direction—at Liam. "There he is!" he shouted, and every man on the square turned toward the alley.

Liam gaped, tensing for flight, and a man walked past him, an elderly clerk in a dirty white hood with a high point in back, carrying a sheaf of papers. The clerk waded into the swarming laborers.

"And the others!" shouted the lookout, before leaping down from his perch.

Behind Liam, doors all along the alley opened and clerks poured out, greeting one another, sharing a joke or coming to a private accommodation before strolling into the plaza, where they spread around the plaza, each with his sheaf of papers. The stevedores and longshoremen surrounded them, and the clerks started calling out their needs.

"A dozen to load and escort four wagons up the Climb!"

"Seven on Rotten Pier, glassware from the *Dordrecht Prince!* No drunks, no cripples!"

"Water butts to six carvels in the roads! Ten men as can handle oars—a baron extra if you help fill the butts!"

"A score to shift flour sacks in the Goddard warehouses! All day work!"

Reading from their notes, the clerks formed gangs for chandlers, merchants, and factors; when they had filled an order they chose a man to lead, gave him a slip of paper, and sent the gang on its way. The men clamored for the choicest jobs, boasting or pleading as their circumstances required, and the gangs marched off one after another, in all directions from the plaza.

It was a brisk half hour, a common rite in seaports; Liam had seen it in Southwark and a half dozen other cities, but it never ceased to fascinate him—the bravado that masked desperation; the arrogance that indicated a worker with connections or a needed skill; the cruel laughter at the expense of the unemployable; the callousness of the clerks, as if they were buying cattle, and their rare kindnesses.

The sun was up and the last of the work gangs forming when Fanuilh sent word that the Stair was approaching the City Below. *It will be perhaps fifteen minutes, master.*

Fine.

The remaining day-laborers—the drunk, the lame, the sick, and those for whom there simply were not enough spaces—drifted out of the plaza, wandering disconsolate into the City Below. The clerks enjoyed a brief respite, chatting for a few minutes around the fountain before strolling back to their offices in the alley. One of them nudged Liam as he walked by, offering a wink and a nod.

"You'll find nothing here, tar—the market for berth is on the other side of the water."

His colleagues laughed and Liam managed a grin before bowing his head, heart racing. *At least you know it works.* His grin grew real then. *It works.*

The plaza looked empty, left to the pie-sellers and bread boys and the lone talebearer. They hawked their wares to the men passing through, and had better luck: as the day aged, the traffic grew wealthier, merchants going to their offices, sea captains to their ships, factors to their warehouses. Even the talebearer made money, reciting the latest news to three men in satin doublets for a copper coin. Liam strained his ears to hear, half fearing that his name would be part of the news, but the man spoke low, and was too far away.

As he tried to eavesdrop, a teenage girl with a basket of pies on her arm sidled up to him and asked in a desultory way, as if she did not expect a sale, "You hungry, Stormy?"

Liam looked sharply at her and she cringed, ready to back off, before he understood the nickname. His stomach grumbled. "I am, in fact," he said, smiling. "What've you got? And it's Lightning, not Stormy."

"I can't say what's in them, but no one's died yet." She grinned back, and added, teasing, "Stormy."

He rolled his eyes, drew a copper from his purse, and took one of the small pies from her basket. It steamed when he broke it open, and if there was no readily evident meat inside, it was at least warm, and the crust rich with butter. He ate quickly, considering the idea of a second.

Master, the Stair has landed.

The girl, having seen his purse, lingered, deliberately nonchalant. "So, you're waiting for someone?"

Stifling an impulse to stare at her, Liam concentrated on his pie and nodded.

"A girl?" She twitched her skirt with one hand, making the hem swirl over the cobbles, and cocked her head at him, a sly smile playing over her lips.

He nearly choked, and frowned down at her. She was no more than sixteen. "A friend," he said. "A mate's going to get me a berth out. Now go on with you, sell your pies."

The girl shrugged and moved off. Liam gulped down the rest of his pie and licked the crumbs from his fingers, waiting for Fanuilh's next thought, eyes moving restlessly around the plaza.

I do not see a man with a white feather in his cap.

Liam rubbed his eyes, schooling himself to patience. *That's all right. He may not have put it on yet.* Only then did he remember the ink on his face and check his hands, breathing a sigh of relief when he saw no smudges. *What about Peacemakers?*

There are two, but they appear to have come to relieve the men standing watch.

Come back. We'll just have to wait for him to get here. He'll put on the feather when he does. The Prince of the Mint would respond; he would send a man. *You just have to have patience. Wait. Someone will come.*

No one came.

The walk from the Flying Stair to the mole should take no more than fifteen minutes. Fanuilh covered the distance in five, and helped Liam watch for Catiline's messenger from the roof of the highest building overlooking the plaza.

Fifteen minutes passed, and no one came.

They marked every man who entered the plaza, scanning hats with hard-dying hopes. Feathers appeared now and again, four or five examples of widely-varying plumage, always the wrong color. The closest to white was dark gray, and the man wearing it was in company with his two young sons; they crossed the plaza without stopping, and never once looked at the mole.

After half an hour Liam sent Fanuilh down the length of the mole—the gulls were out in force, squabbling over the garbage that dotted the waters of the harbor, so it could fly without much risk of notice—but the dragon saw no white feathers on the heads of the few people taking the morning air on the breakwater.

After an hour, with the bells of the Exchange tolling eight and the City Below well launched on its day, Liam finally admitted that Catiline had not replied to his letter. He cursed under his breath for a full minute, pounding his clenched fist against his thigh, and then took a deep breath. *The Stair will come again in a couple of hours. You'll just have to wait for it.* There was a chance that Catiline had not received his message until this morning, and Liam clung to it. *He'll send someone.*

He pounded his fist again and hissed out a breath. He hated waiting; worse, he worried that he had been exposed in one place too long. Lurking in an alley for hours on end was a sure way to draw unwanted attention. He needed to move, or find a reason to stay.

The talebearer.

The man paced back and forth by the fountain, hands clasped behind his back, head bowed as if he was engaged in deep thought. His multicolored cloak trailed out behind him, flapping and snapping in the breeze, more banner than garment. It was a studied pose popular with talebearers who specialized in news rather than stories, an attempt to appear more serious.

Liam made up his mind and crossed the plaza to join him. "Hey, talebearer."

"Eh? What?" He was older, his black hair streaked with silver, his spade beard grizzled. On seeing Liam, he affected a condescending attitude. "What would you, sirrah?"

"None of that," Liam said, patting his purse. "I've money, and am as good a man as you. I'm waiting on my captain, who's due on the next Stair. I'll pay you a prince to entertain me till he comes."

Newsmongers pretended to pride, but did not make much money; the man's eyes bulged, though he managed to keep the eagerness from his voice. "Entertain? I'm no mere bard or jester, to entertain. However, for a prince I can inform and educate, and present you with the hidden secrets of the age, the city, and the court. A prince, in advance."

Liam laughed, produced a silver coin, and made it vanish up his sleeve. "After. Come on." The talebearer gave in, and let himself be drawn to the edge of the fountain. Liam sat on the stone lip and placed the older man in front of him as a shield. "All right—inform and educate me, brother."

The talebearer stiffened for a moment, reminded himself of the coin, and relented. He flourished his cloak. "You should know, sir, that I am Sir Tasso, and that I have advised the king himself—you are not from Torquay, I believe?—the king himself, I say, in his palace. Have you seen the palace?"

Liam shook his head, more intent on looking around the talebearer, hoping to see a white feather on the head of one of the passersby.

"Ah, it is a wondrous place, the work of mages and giants, and should be seen by all who visit Torquay. Though much troubled at the moment, with our good King Nicanor's illness. You are perhaps not unaware of his illness, sir? The ignorant ascribe it to many different causes, but I can attest, sir, that there are only three possibilities. You may forget all talk of demons and ghosts, of the displeasure of his royal ancestors, of malice on the part of the Freeport League. No, sir, there are but three possibilities, and I, as a frequent intimate of the court, happen to be in a position to elucidate them. Would you hear?"

Despite himself, Liam was interested, and nodded to show it.

Tasso bowed, and held up three fingers. "The first—the displeasure of the gods. This the priests argue, and demand sacrifices and acts of penance from both his majesty and his people at large. Hence, he will undertake a journey to the sacred vale of Rentrillian tomorrow morning, for purification, sacrifice, and penance. The priests, however, cannot say what his sin might be, which causes some to entertain the idea of other possibilities."

His two other possibilities were the workings of a sinister wizard unconnected with the Mages Guild, and a plot on the part of one of the rival pretenders to the throne. Liam scoffed at the first, and tried to get more information about the second, but though Tasso elaborated shamelessly and at length about Corvialus and Silverbridge, he could tell him nothing new on the subject.

"Mark me," the talebearer finished, laying his finger alongside his nose, "it is most likely the last. The court is a sinister place, and the king is beset by enemies who wear false faces, and call themselves loyal."

Can't argue with that. Instead, he scratched his cheek and asked, "Is there nothing that can cure the king? Some potion or magic?"

Tasso made a regretful moue. "Alas, the wizards have done their best, to no avail. The Magister himself came to the king's bedside, and worked divers enchantments and sorceries. That was in the summer, but all has come to naught. The king languishes, his illness proof against the intervention of leeches, surgeons, healers, divines and wizards. It is a passing woe."

"But what about—isn't there something else? Some artifact or antique or something they can bring in?"

"There seems to be no remedy for it," the talebearer said, shaking his head with a sad smile, as if explaining the hard facts to a child. "Neither ancient nor modern, artifact nor new-made thing."

"I'm sure I remember something in a story—isn't one of the Seventeen Treasures good for healing?"

The other man waved a dismissive hand. "Oh, well, if you would look to legend, there is the King's Cure."

Liam snapped his fingers and pointed. "That's it! Why don't they use that?" He bridled at Tasso's patronizing smile, but held his temper.

"In the first place, my good man, because no one has seen it in centuries. And in the second, because there is no proof it ever existed in the first place. A great many things are spoken of in tales and fables that do not exist."

It's flying over your head right now, idiot. "But it's in stories, right? Do you know any of them?"

Tasso frowned. "I deal in news, sir, not legend."

"Come on, you must know some of the stories. The Seventeen Treasures are famous. And it's my coin paying."

With a sigh, the talebearer admitted that he was somewhat familiar with the Treasures, and at Liam's urging agreed to dredge up what facts he could. These were few and far between: the King's Cure was not central to any of the legends, appearing instead in stories that revolved around other, more important Treasures. It had saved the life of King Cimber, when he was sorely wounded retrieving the Edaran Swords and the Quintine Shield after his father lost them in the wild lands of the north; and done the same for the twin knights Thabol and Theren, when they fought against the giants of the Trössus Mountains. In all it accounted for perhaps five miraculous battlefield cures; in a few more cases it was not specifically mentioned, but could be assumed to have been present. "However, those are all in the mists of the past," Tasso pointed out. "There have been no new wonders in hundreds of years. If it ever did exist, it may well have passed out of the kingdom with Quelen the Traveller, who is said to have carried several treasures with him on his ill-fated voyage."

"And that was two centuries ago," Liam said, pretending defeat.

The talebearer gave a prim nod. "Just so."

While he had been telling his legends, the bells tolled nine, and he had gone on some time after that. A glance to the west showed the Stair rising again. Liam decided he had had enough, and handed over the silver coin. "My captain'll be here soon. Thanks for the tales."

He got up, stretched, and, ignoring Tasso's profound bow, strolled back to his post at the mouth of the alley. *Should be about time,* he projected. *Why don't you go take a look at the Stair?*

Yes, master.

Leaning against the wall, he pared his nails with his knife and endured the wait, mulling over what he had learned. If it had done half the things it was credited with, the Cure was certainly powerful enough to heal the king. How it had come into the Duke's hands, he could not say, though gifts to loyal supporters were by no means rare. Several of the other Treasures were associated with important houses, and from the stories it seemed that the Cure worked on everyone, regardless of whether their blood was royal.

The wait was maddening. From where he stood, he could not see the Stair, and much as he wanted to, he refrained from pestering Fanuilh with questions. The dragon had plenty to do, and bothering it would not speed up the Stair.

Finally, when he had cleaned his nails thoroughly for the sixth time, a thought appeared in his head.

Master, the Stair is descending, and I can see a man holding a cap with a white feather in it.

He slumped against the wall, offering broadcast prayers of gratitude.

Lieutenant Aldyne is also aboard.

• • •

Liam could not seem to catch his breath. He made Fanuilh give him a glimpse through its eyes, and confirmed both the man with the feather and Aldyne with his bandages. *If he knows about it—if he's followed the man from Catiline's, then I can't approach him.*

The wait was interminable, the Stair crawled, and his breathing was all wrong. *If he knows—if he's followed.* It could be a coincidence, a routine visit to the City Below, something Aldyne did every day, for all Liam knew. *But if he knows—if he's followed.* He could not seem to get enough air into his lungs.

And then the Stair arrived, and Fanuilh reported that the man in the white feather went one way, and Aldyne the other. *He seems to be headed toward the Exchange, master.*

"Yes!" Liam hissed, and then looked around him to be sure no one had heard. There were fewer people in the plaza now, a knot of men gossiping here, a drudge filling a bucket at the fountain, a stubborn pie-seller crying her wares. *Follow Aldyne. Make sure he doesn't come anywhere near here.*

Yes, master.

One last wait, the fifteen-minute walk from the Stair. Liam counted the seconds, ticking them off on his long fingers. He closed his eyes from time to time, willing the minutes to pass more quickly; otherwise he glared at the street the man was most likely to take, remembering the drab gray tunic he had glimpsed through Fanuilh's eyes.

Master, Lieutenant Aldyne has reached the Exchange. He is talking with the Peacemakers on duty there.

Fine.

The man came striding into the plaza behind a trio of porters carrying sacks on their shoulders, so when Liam first caught sight of him it was as if he had materialized out of thin air. He put on his hat with a flourish, straightened the long white feather with a flick of his finger, and slackened his pace, seeming suddenly aimless.

Thank you, Liam prayed, and scanned the plaza quickly: no Peacemakers, no suspicious lurkers. *Except yourself.* He pushed away from the alley and bore down on the messenger. The man frowned at him as he approached, and then his eyes widened.

"I'm Othniel Fauvel."

"You? I—" He cut himself off, stared for a moment at Liam's face, and shook his head. "Never mind. I've a letter for you. You should read it now." He produced a folded piece of parchment from his tunic, the great seal of the Prince of the Mint on it in purple wax.

Liam broke the seal and opened the letter, fumbling in his haste.

I do not traffic with murderers or madmen, it read. *I suggest you surrender to Pacifex Warden immediately.*

A sprawling, illegible scrawl served for a signature.

Liam swayed, light-headed, read the letter again, and felt the messenger's hand on his arm. He looked up.

"Keep the letter," the man said, searching Liam's eyes as if he were afraid he were not listening. "Tomorrow morning at eleven o'clock, my lord's son will be praying in the shrine of Night in Rentrillian. He is Publius Cestus Catiline—do you know him?"

Numb, Liam shook his head.

"Never mind. He will be alone at eleven." He spoke slowly and clearly, freighting each word with significance. "The king will be in Rentrillian as well, you know that? A great many common people will be making pilgrimages there tomorrow, to pray for his health. The king will be there, and the court, and my lord and his son. At eleven, in the shrine of Night. Good day, Master Fauvel."

Catiline's messenger spun on his heel and strode off, leaving Liam to shake his head, bewildered, and stare

down at the letter. It was a brutal rebuff—and totally at
odds with the verbal message. The man had left no doubt
as to why he mentioned the place and time of the
younger Catiline's private prayers, his solemn manner
pointedly contradicting the cold, dismissive tone of the
letter. *So why send it at all?*

Shaking his head, Liam folded the paper and tucked
it inside his coat, then hurried away from the mole, puzzled.

Reasons—or possible reasons—occurred to Liam as he
walked, tentatively surfacing once he emerged from the
first shock and confusion of the meeting.

He fears a trap. To be caught in correspondence with
the man accused of murdering a Steward of the Royal
Household could be damaging for Catiline, all the more
so in these dark, suspicious days, when people saw plots
and conspiracies everywhere. *So on paper, he refuses to
see me, and arranges to have me meet with his son in
such a way that he can deny it was arranged at all.
Everyone will be at Rentrillian.*

The sacred vale was a good choice, and not least because so many people would be there. It was holy
ground, and weapons were forbidden there, even the
smallest dagger, except to certain of the priests and the
king's own guard. More important, Rentrillian lay outside Auric Severn's sphere of influence, and it would be
easier for Catiline to approach Nicanor with the Cure
there than in the palace. Finally, the shrine of Night was
perfect: on the outskirts of the vale, rarely visited, dark,
and offering a number of private chambers.

Clever. Through the cloth of his jacket, he felt the
crisp outline of the letter. *He's good at this kind of shadowy work. And you're not.* He tried to imagine what his
face had looked like when he first read the letter; it must
have been comic, but he was too close to the surge of

panic and fear to laugh. *Later, though. And I'm sure Fanuilh will find it funny.*

He did not laugh, but he was relieved; having an ally, however distant, had lifted a burden from him of which he had not been entirely aware. There was still work to be done, and more waiting as well, but the tasks seemed light compared to what he had already gone through, and he was almost looking forward to them.

Remaining at large until the next day would be easy, since he had the warehouse. Getting up to Rentrillian would be more difficult; he would have to go by the Pilgrims' Way, which would likely be watched by Peacemakers.

Fanuilh!

Yes, master?

Aldyne had disappeared inside the Exchange, and the dragon readily agreed to scout out the entrance to the Way. It did not mention if it found Catiline's dual messages amusing—but then, Liam did not mention how the letter had crushed him.

With his familiar dispatched on its mission, the rest of the day loomed before him. As he walked, he began to consider the warehouse and its many deficiencies. He stopped and counted out the contents of his purse. The fat merchant had amply endowed him with coins. *Why not?*

An hour later he arrived back at the warehouse, carrying a dunnage bag like the one he had lost outside Cade's. Inside were a couple of blankets, a cheap tinderbox, three candles, food for himself and Fanuilh, and, finally, a book. He had bought it all at different stalls and shops, the last on a whim he secretly mistrusted.

You shouldn't have done it, he told himself, as he slung the dunnage bag over his shoulder and kicked off his shoes. *Luck only lasts so far.* He tucked the shoes into his belt, checked both ends of the alley, found them empty, and scaled the wall to his window.

Once safe inside his hideout, the feeling that he had tempted fate dissipated. *You can hole up here for days.* There was enough wood for that long, if he did not make the fires too big; he started one with his new tinderbox, laying a single board on the shavings. Then he unpacked and arranged his purchases, spreading the blankets, setting out candles. He grinned at himself as he did so, and laughed out loud at the way he repacked the food in the dunnage bag, to keep it out of the dust.

Look at the blushing bride, setting up house for the first time.

When he was done, he stepped back to admire his little household. "This isn't the work of a dead man," he whispered, then raised his voice. "This is the work of an idiot." Chuckling, he went and sat by the small fire, picking up the book.

Fanuilh, where are you?

Above the coast road, master. I can see Pilgrims' Way ahead.

Grand. Have a look, then come back. I've got your dinner all ready, and I'm just going to curl up by the fire with a book.

A book?

Never mind. I'm an idiot. I'll see you later.

Yes, master.

The book was a famous collection of travelers' stories that he had read and reread as a child. He opened it to the first page, not really meaning to start, just to look, and saw the words he remembered:

In ancient days, the roads and byways of the kingdom were not so safe as they are now.

Written at a time when the king was stronger, the line made Liam laugh—*He should see how bad they are now*—but he was hooked, and kept his finger in the book as he stood to light the candles.

He had a long splinter in one hand, flame trembling

at its tip, and the book in the other when he heard his name called.

"Rhenford! You're a damned hard man to find!"

He spun around, and saw Aldyne standing on the little porch by the warehouse window.

CHAPTER 15

"OH YES," ALDYNE said, hooking the shutter closed. "A very hard man to find." The warehouse darkened, but not by much; sunlight still filtered in through the grimy windows of the cupola.

Liam goggled for a second, then looked wildly around, he was not sure for what—a weapon, a way out, an explanation. Aldyne laughed at him.

"But found in the end, eh? Though not in Rentrillian, as Nennius would have had us believe. Found in the end—and not expecting it, I see." Drawing his sword, he started down the steps.

Liam cursed and forced himself to move, to drop the book and the burning sliver of wood, to draw his dagger. He put his back to the wall of the sunken lane.

Casually, as if he were coming to greet an old friend, Aldyne slouched down the steps. "Not that it was easy. You should have let me do for you two nights ago. Or on the Stair. Saved us all a deal of trouble."

His sword bobbed as he walked, gripped loosely in his fist. Liam glared at his pathetic dagger, with a quarter of the reach. *Don't wait for him, idiot. Don't let him get close.* He cursed, snatched up his dunnage bag, and scrambled out of the lane into the far side of the warehouse.

Aldyne jumped over the last three steps, landing with a loud thump and flashing a smile through his bandages, as if he had enjoyed it. "A deal of trouble. Do you know how happy I was when I thought you were dead? When you fell?" He shook his head over the fond memory. "Happier than ever in life, I tell you. And then I hear you walked out of the Pool. Oh, I wasn't so happy then. And then you go robbing the baths, and sending Messagers to Publius Catamite. It was by Messager, eh?"

With the sunken lane a gulf between them, Liam wrapped the top end of the bag around his fist, tested the swing, and cursed. *A book, when you should have bought a sword. A book!* He was no great swordsman, but it would have been better than a slim dagger and a bag full of food.

"Not saying?" Aldyne wandered toward the lane, lazily swinging his sword back and forth, loosening his arm. "Well, no matter. Should have had him send word back by Messager, eh? Simple enough to follow his private secretary down to the City Below, where he meets a strange-looking fellow. Have I complimented you on your new face?" He reached the lip of the lane, and leaned against one of the posts. "It's most becoming."

"Thanks. I like yours, too. Think those'll heal?"

Aldyne touched the bandage over his ear, his smile dimming for a moment, and then recovered, recognizing the desperate edge in Liam's voice. "Sooner than yours will, I imagine." He jumped lightly into the lane.

In a straight fight, Liam knew, he did not stand a chance; he advanced cautiously toward the lane, dagger held out in front of him, bag trailing behind. Aldyne grinned and came to meet him, scooping up the book Liam had discarded in a single, smooth motion. "What are you reading, Rhenford?" He threw the book and, as Liam knocked the fluttering pages away with his knife hand, feinted at his ankles.

Jumping back, Liam swung his bag and batted the blade aside, then took up position again, crouching now. He wished he had taken one of the blankets instead of the bag: there was too much inside, too little loose cloth; it would not trap Aldyne's sword. *And if wishes were horses, beggars wouldn't die in warehouses.*

The Peacemaker stepped back, uncommitted. "We have something of an impasse, don't we? You up there, and me down here." The wall only came to his waist, but there was no way he could climb up without exposing himself. "I could starve you out, I suppose, though your dragon might come and make trouble. Or I could call my boys in, but I'd rather do this in private."

Dragon. Oh, gods, you are an idiot. He gathered his scattered wits and projected: *Fanuilh, get back here now. Now.*

"An impasse," Aldyne mused.

I am coming, master.

Not that it would do much good: the shutter was hooked. *Come as fast as you can.*

"Unless." The Peacemaker held up a finger. "Unless."

Liam watched as he picked up one of the blankets and dangled a corner over the guttering fire. The rough wool caught almost at once, and Liam cursed. Aldyne laughed.

Liam flipped his dagger and held it by the blade, lifted it to throw, but the balance was all wrong. *It'll bounce off.* He reversed it again, gripped the hilt, cursed.

Flames licked up through the folds of the blanket, and Aldyne suddenly whirled it over his head like a dancer's cape, fanning the flames. "To keep you warm," he explained, and moved closer to the wall.

Jump him, Liam thought, and backed away, imagining himself impaled on the Peacemaker's sword.

The blanket roared and crackled, blazing furiously, and Liam ducked back each time Aldyne whirled it toward him. Then it flew, lofting, a monster of fire, great-winged. He leaped away, swung his bag into the middle of it, deflating the monster—as Aldyne vaulted up from the lane.

His bag enmeshed in the burning blanket; he swung it at the Peacemaker, who rolled aside, came to one knee and swept the burning wool over his shoulder and away, to die out. Liam brought his bag back and caught Aldyne on the side of the head on the upswing. The man shouted a curse and flinched back, but it was too little too late, even with the sudden darkness beneath his bandages and the way he raised a hand to his opened wound as he stood.

"Hurts, I hope," Liam spat, winding the end of the bag more tightly around his fist, grim and watching the other man for signs.

"Dead man," Aldyne said, smiles and banter gone, and gave the signs—flexing his knee, turning his shoulder and hips, a slight readjustment of his grip—before lunging, a good pass; he was angry but well-schooled, and though Liam slid out of the path of the blade, he knew he would not be able to do it many more times. He tried to press close, swinging the bag high and coming in low with the dagger, but Aldyne would have none of it, parrying the dagger and dancing back, putting distance between them.

Both men paused, measuring, breathing hard, and the Peacemaker came in again with a shout, all point. Liam turned the blade with his dagger, twisting his wrist, and Aldyne clouted him in the face as they switched places, dust swirling around their feet.

Liam backed off now, dashing tears from his eyes with his knuckles, ears ringing, cheek numb.

"Hurts, I hope," Aldyne growled, came in again— they reversed without contact, Liam wise to the punch now—and again, Liam almost losing his dagger in the parry, twisting his whole body away, a terrible moment when his back was to the other man, wide open; he threw himself forward and stumbled down to one knee to get away, spun onto his feet, and faced off again.

You can't last, he thought, and saw Aldyne think the same, a cruel light in his eyes, a triumphant compression of his lips. *Get in close. Get in close.*

He came in first this time, swinging the bag wide at shoulder height, regretting the whole motion even as he let the sword in under his guard, turning toward it instead of away, committed, twisting only a little so the point scraped his ribs, the edge cutting his coat and his side—and the bag came around from one side and his knife from the other. He was getting in close.

Aldyne saw it, his sword arm trapped beneath Liam's, the dagger coming, raised his free hand in an awkward block and the short blade cut between his fingers and drove into his side. He grunted and Liam shouted, wrapping one arm around and pushing forward, tearing at the dagger.

They toppled together, fell to the dusty floor, and the air burst from Aldyne's lungs. He lost the sword and starting thrashing, kicking and bucking, clawing at Liam's face. He was gasping hoarsely and Liam tore at the dagger—it would not come, he could not believe it, he had got in close and the dagger would not come free—the Peacemaker's fingers closed around the back of his neck and he gave up on the dagger, grabbed the other man's head and slammed it against the bricks. The hand on his neck tightened convulsively, and he raised Aldyne's head and slammed it down again, again, again, the first sharp cracks going dull, until the other man stopped fighting, until he stopped moving at all.

Then Liam rolled away, pain burning his side, and dragged himself a few feet through the dust. He found the sword and grabbed it, used it to climb to his feet, where the pain made him cry out and lurch, like a sailor in a heavy sea. He almost fell, the point of the sword scraping against the bricks, and ripped open his coat, frantic, tugging his wet tunic up, groaning at the blood and the cut, a long, shallow slash, the blood on his hands and side.

Master, you have been hurt.

He laughed through the tears, weak, almost hysterical

laughter, and reeled toward the sunken lane, caught his
balance against one of the posts and clutched his wound.
His mind reeled as well, trying to handle the pain and
the overwhelming knowledge that he was still alive.

Master, how badly are you hurt?

His knees refused to hold him up, and he slid down
the post, whimpering at the jolt at the end. He clamped
his hand to his side and pressed his forehead against the
cold, rough wood of the post.

Master!

He ground his teeth and made himself still, as if the
pain could be fooled by immobility. *I'm . . .* , he projected, *all right.* The pain was not fooled. It pulsed
through his fingers, pounding like a second heart.

I will be there soon.

He closed his eyes and tried to fool the pain again.

After a time, the pain diminished from a pounding heart
to a thready pulse, and Liam's mind was able to move
around it, to skirt its edges. He dropped the sword into
the lane and carefully followed, gasping and groaning
when he hit the ground, reeling again. When he had his
balance, he peeled off his slashed coat and tunic, awkwardly trying not to move his wounded side. The pain
flared up, soaking him in sweat, but he struggled on,
bending at the knees to pick up the second blanket.

Lacking the strength to cut it into strips, he wound it
around his torso, pausing only a few seconds for a
glimpse of the cut—the lacerated flesh, more gouge than
cut, weeping blood—before wrapping it in rough wool,
bunching up the ends, and tying them off.

*Master, I am outside. There are two men here, with
a ladder. Are they looking for you?*

"Found me," he muttered. His tongue was thick in his
mouth; he leaned against the wall, and angled his back
until the soothing cool of the bricks was close to his
wound. The cold seemed to leach away some of the pain.

Master, are they Peacemakers?

Projecting was an effort. *Yes. Aldyne's here. Dead.*
The shutter is closed, master. I cannot get in.

He imagined himself gathering his sword and jacket,
climbing out of the lane and going to the window. Fanuilh would put the two Peacemakers to sleep and he
would climb down the ladder to slip away into the city.
He imagined it but did nothing, leaning against the wall,
dull-witted and suddenly sleepy.

Master, the Peacemakers are debating whether they
should come in.

The hook would keep them out. He could not think
very clearly about it. Sweat dripped into his eyes, trickled onto his lips; he licked them, the salt delicious, and
then swiped a clumsy hand down his face.

Shall I put them to sleep?

His hand was sticky with blood, both his hands; blood
slicked one side of his breeches, stained his purse. He
blinked and pushed himself away from the wall, bent his
knees again to pick up his coat. The pain roared back,
cutting through his haze, and he focused through it to
shrug into one sleeve; the other, by his wound, was a
red blur and a strangled shout, but then he had the coat
on and could shuffle across to the far wall of the lane.

They have decided not to wait.

"Grand." He stared at the bricks, his mouth twisting
miserably at the thought of the climb, childish tears
threatening. He hoisted himself up with just his arms,
not bending his torso at all, and fell into another red
haze, gasping and crying out when he pulled his legs
up, got his knees beneath him on the edge, and sagged
against a post, hugged it, weak. The steps to the porch
loomed ahead, and he was sure he could go no farther.

Master, can you move at all?

"I'm moving," he whispered.

Where are you hurt?

He recalled his glimpse of the gouge, and pushed feebly at it.

If you could open the window, could you use the Cure?

His immediate reaction was to refuse—it was not his to use; it was for the king—but it tempted. *Just a little. Sip.* His side throbbed, burned, and against it he saw the phial, the red glass and the black metal, tasted the sweet potion; it would be sweet, he felt, and cold, like a honeyed ice. *Just a sip.*

Crossing to the stairs was not so hard, and with a vision of the phial leading him on, he climbed them on hands and knees. Black clouds restricted his vision, and he saw only the step ahead and his trembling fingers. He hardly breathed until he reached the top. The pain raged, as if it realized how close he was, and he had to crawl to the window, afraid rising would strain his muscles. He fumbled twice with the hook before it came free.

Come in, he thought, and then hung his head, finished, on hands and knees. For how long, he could not tell—forever—and then Fanuilh was pushing through the shutter, wriggling through the gap and dropping down beside him. *Can you untie the knots?*

Liam let his head swing from side to side and the dragon arched its long neck, snaking its head over its shoulder, gnawing at the rope that bound the phial between its wings. *We do not have much time, master. The Peacemakers will wake up soon.* It savaged the rope like a dog hunting fleas, frantic chewing and snuffling. The knots parted in three places, but Liam had tied it well: the Cure was loose but not free, and Fanuilh could not reach any more of the rope. It pushed itself against his arm. *Can you get it?*

He shook his head again but nonetheless raised his hand, groping for the phial, and tugged it out of the rope. *It'll be sweet and cold.* He lowered his head to the Cure, pulled the crown-stopper out with his teeth, spat it to the floor of the porch, and managed a small sip.

In his side, a flare of heat so intense Liam bucked and collapsed to his elbows—but not pain, rather a burst of sunlight, a cleansing. He shuddered helplessly, feeling the flesh around the cut swarm through the heat, knitting together, the pain melting away. And not just in his side; there were lesser flares all over his body, aches and bruises sloughing off, burned out.

When it was done, he let out an awed breath, eyes wide with wonder. He still held the Cure—blessedly upright, liquid still left inside—reached out with a steady hand to find the crown and stopper the phial. A thought occurred to him: he could not remember how it had tasted.

Master, the Peacemakers.

He got to his feet, still awestruck, and absently lifted the shutter. Fanuilh jumped out; he let the shutter fall after it, staring at the red glass. *Gods, that's . . . that's. . . .* Words failed him. He felt better than he had in days, suffused with strength. A voice spoke in the alley outside, and he turned reluctantly to the shutter, slow to act, caught up in the miracle.

Master, Pacifex Warden is here. She says she wants to talk to you.

His mind cleared in an odd way—not to alarm, or panic, but to calm and an otherworldly confidence. He lifted the shutter and hooked it open, leaned on the sill to look down.

She stood at the base of Aldyne's ladder, his two Peacemakers sprawled at her feet, her pale face turned up to his. Fanuilh hovered nearby.

"Good day," Liam called. "Have you figured out yet that I'm innocent?" From above, she appeared even more insubstantial than he remembered, like a little girl; he almost laughed at her grave nod. "When did you figure it out?" He felt firmly in command, buoyed up by the effects of the Cure.

"When did I suspect, or when was I sure?"

He grinned—the conversation seemed absurd—but he wanted to know. "Either."

She saw nothing absurd in it, and pursed her lips, casting back. "I began to suspect at Cade's," she said at last. "You behaved very oddly, and said strange things. About Lord Auric in particular." Frowning, she looked down at her feet and shook her head. "No, I suspected before. When you recognized my lieutenant. And then his behavior was odd, as well. There were breaches of procedure—incomplete reports—the fact that he personally discovered every crime you had committed." She grimaced, closed her eyes briefly. When she opened them, she spoke more decisively. "I was sure this morning, when he came after you without telling me."

She stared up at him, waiting for his assessment of the trail that had led her to him. He thought about it, wondering if he would have done as well, then shrugged: it did not matter anymore. "Come up here. We've things to discuss in private."

Her lips twisted briefly, and she indicated her withered arm with a glance. "We do indeed. But I am not very adept at climbing."

"Ah, no. Of course not. I'll come down."

It was a joy: the ease and grace of his body as he swung over the windowsill and started down the ladder, the way his muscles moved together. He jumped the last few feet, landed lightly on his toes. Aldyne had jumped the same way; he stopped smiling.

"I had to kill him, you know."

Warden nodded. She wore a plain blue cloak with a hood over a gray dress; only the wand stuck in her belt indicated her power. "I assumed so."

"He killed Lord Bairth, and Master Cade." He stared at her, trying to find in the small figure the pursuer who had so terrified him. He could not—for a moment, with some surprise, he found her pretty, and a mad impulse to kiss her seized him—until she fixed her eyes on his. The washed-out gaze sobered him.

"So I have come to think." If she was troubled by the deduction, she gave no sign. "They lay in wait for you, yes? They learned what you were bringing, and when you came to meet Lord Bairth, they tried to murder you both. You alone escaped. You have the Cure?" He held it up for her to see. "And a way to deliver it? To Prince Publius, if not the king himself?" He nodded, seeing no reason to share his plan with her. "Then there is only Lord Auric to attend to."

"I thought I'd leave that to you. I'm going to hand over the Cure, and then put as many miles between myself and Torquay as possible. You can attend to Lord Auric."

She drew back, looking at him as if he had gone mad. "And how would you suggest I do that?"

"Arrest him," Liam suggested, his Cure-induced good mood waning just a bit. "You can start with treason and work your way down from there."

"I can't arrest him, Rhenford. I have no proof."

"Proof? You know he's guilty. Arrest him."

One of Aldyne's Peacemakers stirred; the Pacifex spared him a brief, bitter look. "Have your familiar ensorcel him again." Fanuilh fluttered down next to the man, who fell back into deep sleep a moment later. The interruption finished, Warden explained, none too patiently, "What I know is as nothing, only what I can prove. I do not know how you do things in the Southern Tier, but I must be able to prove my accusations. All the more so because the man is the Steward of the Royal Household. I must prove him guilty."

Liam frowned, frustration eroding his feeling of mastery, sapping his confidence. "You have proof—"

She cut him off with a gesture. "What I have, Rhenford, is you at the Severns' house when Lord Bairth was killed, and two witnesses to claim you did it. I have your knife at Master Cade's, and you at Sir Ancus Nennius's house just before he was murdered and his wife abducted. I have you fleeing my Peacemakers, committing arson, holding a man at swordpoint in front of my lieutenant and a hundred witnesses." He raised his hands, palms out, to show that he understood, but she continued, implacable. "I may point to irregularities in Aldyne's conduct—that he pursued you without keeping me informed—but that is very little, considering that you have admitted murdering him, and it is nothing with which to accuse one of the most powerful men in Torquay. Do you see?"

"Yes."

"I am no power here, no great man who may do as he sees fit, provided he has the force to support him. I am a small player, Rhenford, and may only do things that accord with the law. I command the Peacemakers on sufferance, because my father requested it of the king on his deathbed. I have only kept my post because I have never had to confront a power in the city. There are those who would be happy to remove me, a woman and a cripple. Auric Severn is among them, and he has the power to do so, if I cross him. I cannot jeopardize my position or the reputation of the Peacemakers on ungrounded accusations."

He waved his hands in irritable submission. "Fine, fine. I understand. Actually, I don't care—about your position or your Peacemakers. I have a pretty low opinion of them, at the moment."

"Because we pursued you?" she asked, indignation flashing in her eyes. "Because we did our duty, and tried to take you in when you seemed a clear murderer?"

That was why, but he would not say it; he found a better reason. "I was thinking more of the fact that your second was a murderer and a traitor who was trying to help a bigger traitor kill the king." He gestured to the two sleeping Peacemakers. "And not just your second, it seems. How many Checkers have gone bad, do you suppose? How many of your men are loyal, Pacifex, and how many in Severn's pay?"

She flinched, but met his eyes. "I cannot say. That is why you must work with me to find evidence against him."

Biting off a sarcastic reply, he made a disgusted sound and shook his head. In his plans, if he had thought of Severn at all, it had been in a vague, corollary sense: when he had delivered the phial to Catiline, the Steward would naturally be punished, though he had never considered how, or by whom. "Why me? You have a thousand men at your command." He shrugged. "Nine hundred and ninety-nine, now."

"I cannot trust them, as you have made clear." She indicated the two sleeping men. "I thought them incorrupt, as I thought Aldyne. Your loyalty, however, is certain."

Liam gave a wry laugh. "I'm honored, I'm sure. But my task at the moment is getting the king his Cure, and I don't want to risk mucking it up by going against Severn. Afterwards, perhaps."

"That will be too late for what I have in mind," she said, impatience evident in the brusque shake of her head, the clipped words. "It must be before."

He sighed. "What did you have in mind?"

She sighed, too, but in a different manner, as if he had at last seen reason. "It is simple. You need only arrange to meet Lord Auric in a place where I and an impeccable witness may overhear. Offer to sell him the Cure. He will buy, and when he does not give it to the king, I can arrest him. It is very simple. Do you think you could do it?"

Ill-concealed condescension lay behind the question; stung, he snapped, "Do you think *you* could?" She lifted her chin, indignant, and he went on, "You've left out an important part—the part where I sell the Cure to Lord Auric, and then he and the thirty or forty incorruptible Peacemakers he's bought off kill me."

"I will have reliable men nearby."

"That's comforting, really it is. There's also the part where he actually has the Cure, and destroys it. You arrest him, and the king dies. That doesn't seem very satisfactory, as both the king and I are dead at the end."

To her credit, she acknowledged the problems. "We will have to choose a suitable place, where he cannot bring men without our knowing it. You will have to make him speak of his treason before he has the Cure. Then I will arrest him. With the proper witness, he does not have to be in possession of the Cure."

"And who would that be?" Despite not liking the plan in the least, he had begun to see how it might be done.

Warden pressed her lips together for a moment, thinking. "Not a courtier," she said. "A priest, then. From a respectable temple."

"Laomedon," Liam suggested, and the Pacifex immediately agreed. The priests of the god of death and the Gray Lands had a good reputation.

"And the meeting could be in a temple!"

Why are you helping? "In Rentrillian, perhaps?" Seeing that it could be done, he also saw that, perhaps, it should be done. "Everyone will be up there tomorrow, won't they?"

"Yes!" she exclaimed, an excited smile lightening her face briefly—and then passing away, replaced by comprehension. "Ah, I see. That is where you will meet Catiline."

"At the shrine of Night."

"Catiline's idea, or yours? Never mind—it will do. I will be able to watch all who enter, and in the gloom it will be easy to overhear your conversation."

For her, he could tell, it was all settled. "Easy for

you," he pointed out. "Not so easy for me. How many men can you bring?"

She frowned, counting in her head. "A dozen, that I am completely sure of."

Now he calculated. "Leaving nine hundred and eighty-seven unaccounted for. I'll be cut to tiny pieces before you and your dozen can rescue me."

"You have your familiar," she said. "And no man is allowed to go armed in Rentrillian."

"Then I'll be beaten to tiny pieces," he replied, but he had already decided to do it. He gestured, wiping away his objection. "All right. I'll send him a letter, as I did Catiline. I'll arrange to meet him at ten. Ten o'clock in the morning, you understand?"

Warden repeated the time, nodding.

"Have your men ready, and the priest. If you can't find a priest, or aren't ready in any way, come into the shrine and find me, because if Severn shows up and you don't, I'll sell him the Cure, and happily blame the whole thing on you."

"You will not," she said, with a certainty he found annoying. "But I will be there, with my men and an honest priest."

"See you are."

One of the men stirred, and Liam asked Fanuilh to put him out again. When the dragon had finished, he knelt and began pulling off the man's coat.

"What are you doing?"

He paused to glance up at her. "I'm taking his coat. I'm also going to take his pouch and his knife. I don't know if you noticed, but mine's got a spot of blood on it." He held up the torn hem of his jacket to show the broad stain.

"That is theft, Rhenford."

Liam shook his head, incredulous, and went back to stripping the sleeping Peacemaker. Warden chewed her lip, restraining herself.

While he removed his ruined coat and unwound his blanket-bandage, he asked if she could help him get onto the Pilgrims' Way. "Can you reduce the guard there, or put in men you trust?"

It took her a moment to reply: she seemed more upset by his open theft than by any of the larger crimes they had discussed. "No—it will be too clear a sign. If Lord Auric has more of my men in his pay, they will report it to him, and it will arouse his suspicions. You should avoid inns and hostels, as well. I sent your description to all of them."

"Too bad." He paused in his dressing, intrigued by the sight of his side, where the wound had been. Apart from the dried blood, there was no sign—no scar at all. He ran his finger along where he thought the cut had been; the skin was smooth and soft, new. He gave a low whistle, and shrugged on the Peacemaker's coat. "I'll do it on my own. What about getting there? Any ideas?"

As he took the man's belt and pouch, she averted her eyes. "You may hire a boat to take you across the harbor. I have not posted any extra men there."

"Good enough." He poured the contents of his bloody purse into the new one, and cinched the belt around his waist. His hands were splotched with blood, and one leg of his breeches stuck to his skin. "I've got to wash, and get some new clothes. Is there any blood on my face?"

She inspected him. "None that I can see, though it is difficult to tell with the ink. It is ink, yes? Not a real tattoo?"

"Just ink. Though I was thinking of making it permanent."

"You should not. Tattoos are grotesque."

"Thanks," he said, with a wry grin, and then thought of something. "What about these two? They've seen my grotesque tattoo."

A cold light entered her eyes. "I shall take care of

them. They will be locked away in a deep cell, until they can be tried with Lord Auric."

"See to it." He took a deep breath, and decided not to bother about the things he had left in the warehouse. *Let the rats have it all.* "Then I'm off. I'll see you a little after ten tomorrow. Be there, or I'll sell the Cure."

She shook her head, her certainty annoying him again. "You will not."

He studied her for a moment. She had hunted him relentlessly, and yet now, after a mere five minutes of talk, she appeared to trust him more than men she must have known for years. "How do you know? What makes you think I won't just flee right now—get on a ship, disappear? Take the Cure with me?"

Warden shrugged. "I have read the Duke's letter. I know now that he was right about you. You are a man of parts, as the southerners say."

"Ah." He cleared his throat. "I'll want to see that letter, when this is all done." She said nothing—there was nothing more to say—but he lingered, dissatisfied. There was an unfinished quality to the moment, some gesture left incomplete. "I'm off, then," he said at last, and she nodded.

Frowning, he turned and walked down the alley, puzzling over his odd sense of anticlimax.

CHAPTER 16

SOME BLOCKS AWAY, Liam paused at a public fountain to wash his hands. Most of the blood came off, leaving only faint traces in the lines of his palms and beneath his nails. He clenched his hands at his sides, out of sight, and walked on.

The sun was high, nearing noon, and he lengthened his stride. He knew where he was going—to the harbor and across, to get as close to the Pilgrims' Way as he could—yet he felt unsure of himself at the same time, somehow lost. Partly it was the long hours that stretched before him, almost an entire day before he needed to be in Kentrillian, and all those hours needing to be filled. *You'll find another hideout. Get something to eat, new breeches, get your hands clean.*

That would not fill the day, he knew. More, though, he was unsure of the plans he had laid, and the people with whom he had laid them. Catiline was an unknown quantity, but Warden troubled him more: her coldness and her certainty, her strange priorities. *You tell her you've killed her lieutenant, and she shrugs; take a man's coat and she yelps. You want to help the king; she wants to arrest Severn. And she arrives at just the right time, with a ready-made plan for it.*

She had followed Aldyne, suspecting and allowing him to prove her suspicions. *At my expense. She was in no position to stop him from killing me.* He realized that she had done a similar thing the night he had been captured at Cade's: leaving him in Aldyne's hands, and following at a distance to see what happened. *She can play with my life that way, but she can't arrest Severn without proof. Because to her, I'm expendable.*

Fanuilh! The dragon had stayed behind to keep the Peacemakers asleep while Liam got away. *You can leave now.*

Yes, master.

Expendable—and perhaps he was, in the greater scheme of things, but that did not mean he had to act that way. He did not have to blindly accept her plans. *Wait. Find a hidden spot, and watch the Pacifex. Follow her when she leaves.*

Yes, master. There was a pause, then, *Do you have reason not to trust her?*

No. I just want to know what she does. Trust was not the issue. She had let him go, after all; he did not expect her to betray him. *Unless she's playing a far deeper game than I think, in which case I'd be in over my head anyway.* Having Fanuilh spy on her was a gesture of independence, a sign to himself that he was not expendable, and that he would not sacrifice caution and self-preservation either to save the king or to punish Severn.

As he walked, he listened to the cynical voice in his head say, *A petty gesture, a meaningless sign. You pretend you're independent, but you're going to go to Rentrillian nonetheless, and put yourself in harm's way while she stays safe. Petty and meaningless.*

Both, he acknowledged; but he felt better for it, and instructed Fanuilh to let him know when the Peacemakers awoke, and what Warden said to them.

Stiff, unpredictable winds chopped the outer harbor, which was alive with small craft: lighters and pinnaces and longboats dashing among the bigger ships anchored out in the roads. The piers were crowded and busy; it was a few minutes before Liam could hail a skiff to take him to the far side, but he saw no Peacemakers and was soon out on the water, settling into the bob and swell of the waves.

The waterman was an old sailor with a tan, wrinkled face, an earring, and three jutting teeth in his gums. He pulled the oars as if it were nothing. "Brawling, I suppose," he said, indicating the stain on Liam's breeches with his chin. "Bit of a hurt there."

Liam faked a cocky grin. "It's not mine, grandfather. It's the other fellow's."

That struck the waterman as funny; he wheezed merrily at intervals for the rest of the trip, and spoke no more. Brooding, Liam pretended to examine the ships they passed, most of them coasters, with a few of the larger, blue-water ships mixed in, and one or two of the great grain ships, towering hulks that rode high, empty now. While he was in the shadow of one of these, Fanuilh reported that Warden had woken the two men and hustled them away from the warehouse.

She refused to answer their questions, and said only that she would send men back for Lieutenant Aldyne's body. They seemed very nervous.

As well they should, Liam projected back. *You're following them?*

Yes. They are heading in the direction of the Exchange.

Fine.

Out of the shadow of the grain ship, Liam realized they were close to the mooring of the *Trude's Increase*. He shifted in his seat to look and spotted her a little ways off their path, a squat tub wallowing against the waterfront, an unwieldy pig of a ship, and he thought he had never wanted anything more than to be aboard.

"Put us in there," he said, pointing out an opening a few ships down from the *Increase*, and the old sailor happily obliged. Liam jumped lightly from the skiff to the waterstairs, climbed up to the stone quays, into the busy streams of traffic there, and worked his way slowly toward the *Trade's Increase.*

Four Peacemakers guarded the base of the ship's gangplank; the crew loitered on the deck, some sewing sails or braiding rope, but most just lay around, silent and inactive. Captain Mathurin, presumably, was below. *In his cabin.* Liam sighed and moved on, hidden in the crowd. *His very comfortable cabin.* His own cabin was very comfortable too, or so it seemed in memory.

Master, the Pacifex has reached her destination. It is near the Exchange, and looks like a jail—there are bars on the windows, and a few Peacemakers in front.

Liam acknowledged the information, then left the ship and the waterfront behind, plunged inland, looking for the right kind of tavern or wineshop. Several he ignored because they were too seedy, and he passed up one because it looked too expensive, before settling on a small, out-of-the-way place that had a discreet signboard—a ship's wheel—a well-scrubbed doorstep, and a sparkling clean bay window. Disapproving glances met his entrance. The customers were sober and plainly dressed, captains and officers and harbor pilots, too important to mingle with common sailors but not important enough to eat with owners and merchants. They saw his tattoo, scowled, and went back to their meals.

The man at the bar, too, was displeased with his appearance. "It's beyond you, tar. And we've no beer—only wine, and that watered."

"I don't want either," Liam said, mild and deliberately unoffended. "I want dinner, and something to write with. I can pay." He produced a silver coin from his pouch, but it was his quiet demeanor that won him a grudging shrug and a nod toward a table in the rear.

Stylus, paper, and ink were brought, as well as a broiled fish with bacon and a loaf of bread. The smell overwhelmed him, wakening a ravenous appetite, and he set aside the unwritten letter to concentrate on the meal.

First hot meal in—what? Two days? He left nothing but bones behind, and sat back for a few minutes afterward, picking his teeth, before sighing and pulling the blank piece of paper to him.

The letter came easily, far more so than the one he had sent to Catiline, and his thoughts dashed ahead of his neat, cramped handwriting.

I have the thing your lieutenant sought, he wrote, *which he will seek no more. If you will meet me alone at the shrine of Night in Rentrillian at ten bells tomorrow, we can discuss what it might be worth to you. If not, I am sure there will be others in the palace who will appreciate its value. I need hardly say that I will take amiss any attempts to interfere with or trouble me, as your lieutenant would attest, if only he could.*

A signature seemed unnecessary.

It was not perfect, but it struck the right note of greed, caution, and arrogance. *He'll come,* Liam decided on reading it over. *The question is, will Warden?*

Speculation was pointless; unless Fanuilh saw something suspicious, he would simply have to rely on her. He let the ink dry, toying with but ultimately rejecting the idea of a glass of wine, then folded the letter and addressed it to Severn. With a grin, he added, "From Lyndower Vespasianus"—the Duke's name. *That'll catch his attention.*

He checked his pouch, saw that the Cure was still safely in place, and left the tavern with the letter tucked inside his coat.

Finding an urchin who was willing to carry the letter to the nearest Messager House was easy. "I have to wait here for a friend," Liam told the grimy boy, counting out coins. "But I'll want the receipt."

While the boy was gone, Fanuilh reported that a large number of Peacemakers had set out from the jail in the general direction of the warehouse. *They are in a great hurry, master, but the two men who were with Lieutenant Aldyne are not among them, and the Pacifex has not emerged yet.*

Fine. Stay a while longer. I'm going to try to find a place to spend the afternoon.

Yes, master.

Breathless and beaming, the urchin returned in a quarter of an hour, and on receiving his tip for the receipt, besieged Liam for other commissions. "Carry your bags, sir? Run an errand?" Then, with a knowing look, "Find you a woman?"

Liam tried to shake the boy off. "I don't have any bags, you've run my only errand, and I'm not interested in your sister."

"Ah, my sister's a pig," the boy said. "I know a fine house, where the girls can . . ." He started in on a list of indecent accomplishments and Liam cuffed him on the side of the head.

"Get away with you, you little pimp."

The boy rubbed his ear, undeterred. "No girls, then?"

"No," Liam said, and held up a finger to forestall the inevitable offer. "And nothing else, either. Get away with you." He shooed the urchin off, saw him regrouping, preparing another siege, and left himself, outdistancing the boy with long strides.

South of the harbor, the City Below was far more jumbled up—warehouses and slums, sailors' dives and decent taverns, chandlers' shops and brothels all standing cheek to jowl. Liam walked for an hour without any definite purpose, gradually working his way closer to the coast road and Pilgrims' Way. He saw the occasional Peacemaker, but they were easy to avoid in the crowded streets and he blended well: sailors outnumbered everyone else two to one, and half of them had tattoos.

At a stall in a small market square he bought clean clothes, but there was no place to change, so he carried them draped over his shoulder. Stained clothing was

even more common than tattoos, and the blood on his
breeches had dried enough to be indistinguishable. It
was uncomfortable, however, the stiff cloth itchy, and
as he wandered he tried to think of a place where he
could have a few minutes of privacy.

Inns were out, a pun that brought him little joy. There
were countless sailors' dives, where a man ashore between voyages could sleep for a night or two, but they
ranged from the merely filthy to the outright dangerous,
and he could not risk being robbed with the Cure in his
pouch.

Remembering the persistent urchin, he briefly considered a brothel. They were as numerous as the dives, and
accustomed to men who wanted a few hours in private.
Not that I'd . . . , he told himself, his cheeks growing
warm at the unfinished thought. There was something
too shameful about going to a whorehouse in the middle
of the day, regardless of his intention to do nothing except hide; it indicated a depth of debauchery, and he
could imagine too well the winks and nods that would
meet his entrance. *Maybe later,* he thought, meaning
never.

A shrine saved him, a low stone building in a street
of tall, rickety wooden tenements. As he caught sight of
it, two sailors entered through the curtain that served as
a door, one carrying a jug, and at first he thought it was
a wineshop. As he came closer, though, he saw the two
sheltered candles that burned on either side of the door,
and the icon of a lightning bolt above it.

The Storm King. Intrigued, he pushed aside the curtain
and went in, pausing to let his eyes adjust to the gloom.
Nets and sailcloth lowered the already-low ceiling, creating the impression of a tent. *Or between-decks,* Liam
realized, as he stooped to go farther in. Two short rows
of rough wooden benches flanked a central aisle, at the
end of which stood a strange altar: an enormous irregular
block of coral that filled the back of the room, carved

with odd niches and shelves. Votive candles flickered in some of the niches, the light playing over the orange and pink and salmon of the stone, illuminating the varied gifts.

Under the benevolent gaze of the shrinekeeper, a young man missing an arm, the two sailors knelt before the altar to make their offering. They bowed and held up the jug together, mumbling prayers, then rose and poured wine into a bowl set in the coral. When they were done, they placed the jug in an empty niche, bowed again, nodded to the shrinekeeper, and strode out of the building.

Liam stepped aside to let them pass, then made his way up to the altar and knelt, more to admire the coral than to pray. The Storm King was chief of the pantheon and commanded the grandest temples, but this small shrine impressed him more than many larger ones. The offerings were more interesting and more beautiful, if not as rich: three separate ship models, carved with a wealth of detail that included each ship's individual figurehead and name; and scrimshaw work of fantastic intricacy, on bones and horns of all sizes. There were common offerings as well, jugs and loaves and cruets of sweet-smelling oil, all of which seemed to gain in mystery and beauty from their setting, the rainbow of colors in the coral, its complexity of branches and shelves and dark cavities. Above the whole hung a board with a simple saying burned into it: EVEN AS THE SEA.

"Even as the sea," Liam murmured, and finished the phrase in his head: *Even as the sea is the God, without depth or limit; even as the storm is the God, strong beyond man.*

"Even as the sea," murmured the shrine attendant in reply, and smiled when Liam looked his way. "Do you sail soon, brother?"

"I hope so," Liam temporized, unwilling to tell a lie in front of the altar. He did not have much use for organized religion, but he knew the gods existed, and it was better not to tempt them. "Soon, with any luck."

"Well, the king listens," the attendant said, massaging his stump. "Whether he'll act for you, none can say."

Liam gave a rueful nod; that was his problem with the whole apparatus of temples and priests—the gods were there but unreliable, and no amount of prayer and sacrifice could change that. He glanced at the benches. "I'd like to stay a bit, pray some. Is that all right?"

The attendant waved magnanimously. "As long as you like, brother. We're open through the night."

Liam drew a few coins from his pouch and placed them in a niche, then made his way to the last row of benches, the one closest to the door, and sat in the corner with his back to the wall. The light from the candles on the altar barely reached him, and only a little spilled in from the curtained doorway; he sat in shadows, warm enough in his stolen coat, and let himself relax.

Thoughts whirled in his mind—Warden and Severn, the Cure and the king, treachery and loyalty, duty and foolishness—clamoring for attention that he refused to give. Better to watch the play of candlelight on the convoluted structure of the coral altar, the shy colors flickering in and out of darkness. His eyes grew blank, mesmerized, and he fell into a sort of stupor that was a far more pleasant way to pass the time than dwelling on his troubles.

After an hour, Fanuilh reported that the Pacifex had left the jail in the City Below and was headed toward the Flying Stair. Without thinking too much about it, Liam ordered the dragon to follow her up to Torquay.

He watched the altar for the rest of the afternoon, without thinking too much about anything.

Supplicants came and went, sailors or their wives, to pray and leave offerings. None gave him so much as a look; nor did the attendant, who sat on his stool, as much entranced by the altar as Liam.

Fanuilh had a more active afternoon, following War- den up the Stair and through Torquay, visiting four Peacemakers at posts scattered throughout the vales, and several more at their homes. It reported each encounter, and Liam received them with scant interest. She was simply contacting those she knew she could trust, ar- ranging for the men who would protect him the next morning. *Living up to her end of the bargain,* he thought, and left it at that.

Six o'clock tolled by distant bells and the attendant slid off his stool, stretched, and gathered the loaves of bread that had been left as offerings. He had them under his arm when his replacement came in, a young woman on crude crutches, her legs twisted. They chatted for a minute and then he went out, with a nod and a salute for Liam. His replacement hoisted herself onto the stool, rested her chin in her hand, and stared at the altar.

The sun had set; no more light came from under the curtain, and Liam stirred on his bench. Listening to the attendants' banter—lighthearted, commonplace, the sort they undoubtedly exchanged every day at six—had lifted him out of his self-induced stupor, and for no real reason he felt it was time to go. He stood, stretched, started to leave, then turned and strode back to the altar to put down a few more coins. *For luck,* he half-prayed, nodded to the new attendant, and went out.

It was colder; he rubbed his arms as he walked. *A meal,* he decided. *And then a brothel?* The thought made him chuckle. *From shrine to whorehouse. "Where did you spend the night before you saved the king, Rhen- ford?" "Oh, in a whorehouse, of course. Where else?" Food first, though.*

For a while he walked aimlessly, rejecting several likely taverns just to draw out the time, and finally ended up in a noisy place called the Bulging Purse, which was

filled with sailors just back from a successful voyage to
the Freeports. They had pushed most of the tables in the
common room together, and were celebrating their return with endless toasts and dirty songs. The owner sized
Liam up and offered him a private room; he declined,
and took the last free table in the commons, in an out-
of-the-way corner.

While he ate, the sailors' celebration grew steadily
more riotous and by the time he was finished the first
man had already vomited, to thunderous applause.
They're as bad as students, Liam thought as he paid,
*except students don't spend months at a time in rigging
fifty feet off the deck, in freezing gales.* Concealing an
affectionate smile, he went to the door.

"We've driven him out," shouted a sailor. "Hey,
brother, come back! We've driven him away, boys!
That's not fair!"

Others took up the call, instinctively generous, begging him not to leave, to join in, to drink with them. He
shook his head. "Shipping out tomorrow early, brothers.
I wish you joy of your return."

They gave a mixed roar—"Well said!" and "Go
drunk!" in equal parts—and he had to shout to be heard
over the din.

"The king, brothers!" He raised a hand in salute. "His
health!"

The tradition sobered them; those who could raised
their mugs, and even the drunkest lifted their heads to
slur the response. "His health!"

He slipped out the door.

Brothels were everywhere, it seemed: red lanterns
gleamed down every street, pimps pandered on each corner, prostitutes called from upper windows. The prospect
was tempting, but not of a woman—he had recently
found a lover in the Southern Tier, a fellow quaestor,
and knew that after such a betrayal he would not be able

to meet her eyes on his return—it was the notion of a bed that drew him. *A real bed. With a canopy and soft blankets.* The trouble was that as soon as he began to think of beds and blankets, other ideas sprang to mind, and he wondered if he could trust himself.

In the end, he wandered for an hour before seeking refuge in the shrine of the Storm King again. Somewhat shamefaced, he slipped into the back row; the crippled woman on duty noted him with some surprise, and after a few minutes got her crutches and made her laborious way over to stand by his bench.

"You're one for religion, aren't you?"

"Bit of a vigil," Liam replied shortly. He had hoped to catch a nap, and there was a hungry expression on her face that suggested she was interested in conversation.

"Vigil?"

"Going up to Rentrillian tomorrow," he said, hoping to close off the discussion.

The young woman eyed him askance. "Rentrillian? Cance said you were looking to sail."

Liam sighed. "I was, but it seems we're not off for two days. So I thought I'd head up to Rentrillian."

"For the king," the girl said, with a sage nod.

"Yes," he agreed. "Now I think I ought to pray." He closed his eyes, folded his hands, and leaned his head back against the wall.

Skeptical, the girl said, "Looks like sleeping to me."

Liam did not open his eyes. "There's more than one way to pray."

"Just as there's more than one way to pay for a place to sleep," the girl said, and something in her tone made Liam sigh again, open his purse, and produce a silver coin. The shrinekeeper took it with a short laugh, spun on her crutches, and headed for the door. "Watch the place a moment, will you, pilgrim? I'm for the wine-shop."

Liam stared after her for a second, then took quick advantage of her absence to change into the new breeches he had bought—praying all the while to the Storm King that she would not interrupt him. She did not; was gone, in fact, for over a quarter of an hour, and by the time she returned, two jugs of wine stowed in the front of her dress, he was halfway to sleep.

Halfway was as far as he got for the rest of the night, dozing off and on for several hours. The young woman, well provisioned, drank her way slowly through the two jugs and left him alone. No one else entered the shrine, but he would not let himself slip all the way. *What if you snored?*

More important, he had decided to head up to Rentrillian early, around two in the morning. The walk to the Sacred Vale took four hours, and the earlier he arrived, the more time he would have to look over the shrine of Night. So he drooped, jerked awake, drooped, jerked awake, listened to the bells toll through ten, eleven, twelve, one. The thought that occupied his mind was that within a few hours he would be free of the Cure, and free to hold his head up. *Or lay it down. On a pillow.*

When the bells rang two, he shook himself and stood. The shrinekeeper gave him a bleary wave, and he saluted her before stepping out into the cold night. It was refreshing to a certain degree, though not as much as the fact that one way or the other, he would be done before noon. Warming to the idea, he called Fanuilh to him and steered south and west by the stars, toward the coast road.

On the southern outskirts of the City Below, the close-packed buildings gave way to open markets and marshalling yards where the wagons that brought goods up the Grain Climb gathered before starting out for Torquay. At two in the morning the yards and the streets around them should have been empty, or at best just beginning to fill up with teamsters and carters.

Instead, Liam saw signs of movement everywhere: knots of people with torches and lanterns and candles, ghosting through the streets and across the beaten earth of the yards, thin streams all heading silently to the south and west, to the coast road. He stared at them, puzzled and apprehensive. *Where are they going?*

He saw a bonfire in a marshalling yard up ahead, a bright splash of orange in the night, and around it a circle of men and women in blue sashes, their heads bowed in prayer. Blankets and packs lay on the hard ground; they had camped there, to be closer to the beginning of their pilgrimage.

To Rentrillian. They're all going to Rentrillian. He frowned as the blue-sashed pilgrims started singing an antiphonal hymn, wondering how many others would be going up to the Sacred Vale, and what it would mean for him. The streets seemed alive with solemn and purposeful people, all converging on the coast road. He saw families, children being carried or pulled along, sleepy and uncomprehending but uncomplaining, the young helping the old, a man carrying his lame father on his back. They looked like refugees, abandoning the city in the dark of night.

But they're going to Rentrillian, to pray for the king. And this is just the earliest, the most dedicated. Their numbers would swell as the day progressed; by ten, the vale would be full. He tried to guess how many would come, halfheartedly counting the groups around him, and then gave up. *Enough to fill every shrine and temple in the place.* They would bludgeon the ears of the gods with prayers for the king—and make it next to impossible to have a private meeting.

If any of them go to Night, he thought. *If.* Night was not a popular god, and did not even have a temple to himself, just a shrine charitably maintained by the priests of greater gods. *Let's hope he stays unpopular.*

It was too late to change his plans in any case, so he kept going past the marshalling yards to the coast road, joining the burgeoning stream headed for Rentrillian.

Wind and waves tore at the coast road where it ran out of the City Below, snaking between the ocean and the mountain spur that walled Torquay to the south. Liam and the other pilgrims endured the cold salt spray that slicked the paving stones, the gusting winds that played havoc with torches and candles. Flames whipped and guttered and flickered all up and down the column as it marched around the mountain spur to the beginning of Pilgrims' Way.

Master, there are Peacemakers ahead of you.

The constables were posted where the road turned inland to the Way, sheltered from wind and water by a seamount—though here, at least, the number of pilgrims worked in Liam's favor. He moved to the middle of the road and shuffled along, hidden in the mass. His heart beat faster and his stomach fluttered a little as he passed by the Peacemakers, but he could not help smiling: the way they pursed their lips and shook their heads at one another showed they were not bothering to check very carefully, and he entered the Way without any trouble.

The valley sloped sharply up; he looked over the heads of those in front of him and saw a line of winking lights ascending to the sky, thinning toward the top. Walking, he felt the incline in his calves, and after a few minutes saw people resting on the side of the Way, mostly the very old, sitting on the boulders that lined the road and watching the others go by with sad, determined eyes.

The farther he went, the more people he saw stopping to rest or to eat a quick meal, or simply to stare back down the valley, where the stream of lights was growing thicker by the minute. Here and there enterprising men

and women sold food and offerings and amulets and
luck wheels to the pilgrims, but they did not hawk their
wares: they stood and waited, made their exchanges in
quiet voices, and did not haggle. There was an aura
about the journey—a solemnity and a shared purpose—
that left Liam feeling both humbled and strangely superior.

They were going to pray for the king's health; he was
going to deliver the Cure that would ensure it. They
would ask the gods to help the king; he would help
expose and punish the traitor who was doing so much
to kill him. *No one knows,* Liam thought, glancing at
the pilgrims who surrounded him. *They haven't the
slightest idea.*

To his right, a woman came plodding along, dressed
in rags and carrying a sleeping child. He hung his head
and quickened his step, leaving her behind.

Halfway up the valley, Liam stepped out of the stream
long enough to buy and eat a cold loaf of bread. When
he was done, he joined the silent march of pilgrims
again. No one spoke around him, saving their breath for
the climb and perhaps unwilling to desecrate the valley,
as if it were all a temple. His calves ached, as did his
feet because of his inadequate shoes; he kept his hands
in his pockets, his head down.

As the sky flushed pink in the east, he saw the top of
the Way ahead of him, where the column turned north
into the mountains, over a saddleback pass into Rentrillian itself. In the gray light, the valley behind him looked
far longer than he would have imagined, stretching back
and down into the sea. He shuddered and turned forward
again.

*Master, there are both Peacemakers and some kind
of priests in the pass.*

Fine, he replied, thinking of the ease with which he
had entered the Way. *I'll breeze by.*

Yes, master.

The column bunched up near the pass, compressed by its narrow mouth, and he allowed himself to be jostled forward, pilgrims pressing close on either side. The road sloped steeply, slowing the march, and he could see the Peacemakers Fanuilh had mentioned—just two—at the very top of the pass. A few feet below them were the priests, a dozen men and women with shaven heads, all in plain brown robes. They carried no weapons, but they had the hard faces and scars of warriors, and they scrutinized the pilgrims, slit-eyed.

Strife's, Liam thought, and grimaced. He had recently had legal problems with the temple of Strife, and bowed his head as he approached them, though there was no way these priests would recognize him. *And they're not armed, anyway.* He remembered the dagger at his belt. *Not armed. And not just Strife—Strife Emptysheath.*

"You there!" A hawk-eyed priest pushed through the crowd toward him.

Emptysheath was the aspect of the god who looked over Rentrillian; his priests, chosen from the wider hierarchy of Strife, enforced the rule against bearing weapons in Sacred Vale. They were trained to fight unarmed, and it was said that no one could join their ranks before defeating a master swordsman with his bare hands.

"You there, with the tattoo!"

Liam lifted his head and laid a hand over his heart. "Me?"

The priest stopped in front of him and crossed his arms; he was young, and bore an expression of extreme disappointment. "Would you carry that into the vale?" He let his eyes drop for a moment to the dagger. "Eh?"

The crowd flowed smoothly around them.

Liam gasped. "Oh, gods, I forgot! Sorry, Hierarch—here." He fumbled the dagger from its sheath, and held it out to the priest. "I forgot entirely, Hierarch. It's just my eating knife, you know—I didn't mean to—"

"Don't worry," the young man said, taking the hilt of the dagger between his thumb and forefinger. "It's easy to forget. Do you want it back? We'll give you a token for it." He gestured to the side of the road, where two of his comrades stood by a basket half-filled with knives with numbered tokens attached to them.

"Oh, no," Liam stammered. "I'll get another, or go without, or something. I just forgot, you see—didn't think. You can keep it."

The priest gave him a forgiving smile and said with complete sincerity, "You may consider it an offering."

"Thanks," Liam said, struggling against sarcasm, and rejoined the moving stream of pilgrims, praying that the Peacemakers had not noticed.

They had not; nor had anyone else, since the confiscations were common. Liam saw the priests stop two more men before he reached the top of the pass. Then he dropped his eyes until he was beyond the Peacemakers, and inside the Sacred Vale.

CHAPTER 17

KINGS FLANKED THE Way where it descended into Rentrillian, twenty feet tall, carved
out of the rock wall of the pass. Beyond them the vale
spread out to the east and west, a park of copses and
lawns dotted with temples, tombs, and shrines, the Royal
running swift down its center. Roads and paths of white
marble twined through it, linking the buildings in loop-
ing arcs: from the towering granite mausoleum of Auric
the Great, its enormous friezes inscribed with his law
code in letters as tall as a man, to the tiny tomb of his
brother, the Lord Protector, tucked away in a circle of
evergreens; from the fountain-altar of Uris, topped by a
statue of the goddess-as-artist that made music when the
wind blew across it, to the Black Rock of the Storm
King, at the top of which his priests offered sacrifices in
lightning storms; from the open-sided rotunda athwart
the river where new kings received their crowns, to the
unornamented rostrum at the foot of the golden obelisk
of Ascelin Edara, from which they eulogized their pred-
ecessors.

There were a hundred other buildings, temples to
every god, tombs for every king, scattered among the
autumn-brown lawns and the leaf-dropping groves—and
there were priests and pilgrims everywhere, processing
from place to place, making obeisances and sacrifices.
Already plumes of greasy smoke were rising from altars
across the vale, a hecatomb for the health of the king.
Brown-robed priests of Strife stood at every intersection,

equally ready to offer guidance or quell disturbances, though they had opportunity to do neither: the pilgrims knew where they wanted to go, and went there quietly.

Liam peered across the breadth of Rentrillian to the northern side, trying to make out Night, but it was screened by two temples and a long line of plane trees, and he could not tell if people were making sacrifices there. *Best to find out now.*

Past the stone kings, the Way split off in a dozen directions and the pilgrims did likewise, heading for a favored temple or shrine. Liam chose the largest road, which ran fairly straight toward the Royal. The river was narrow this close to its source; four bridges spanned its swift flood. His road crossed on the lowest, a modest arch with a fine view of the descending course of the river to the bend that obscured Torquay. The sun was brightening the sky there, though it had not yet struggled above the cliffs.

Once across the Royal he found fewer people, and began to hope that Night might be ignored in the day's prayers. He skirted the fortress of Strife Emptysheath, where an old acolyte was barking orders at early supplicants, lining them up to enter the fane. "Groups of ten," the old warrior commanded. "Ten, and no more! There'll be time for all!"

Behind the fortress was a rookery, the harsh babble of a hundred holy crows; the eye-stinging smell of their massed droppings made Liam gasp. He hurried off on a smaller path, avoiding the hedge-maze that surrounded Arethusa's graceful temple and colonnaded observatory, and finally struck off on a gravel walk that looked to take him close to the line of plane trees. In the gaps between their trunks he could see the back of a row of small tombs.

The gravel walk brought him to an arch set in the line of trees; the keystone was a crest bearing two ships and a rising sun—the sign of House Maridianus, the original holders of the throne. A brown-robed priest stood beneath the arch; he nodded Liam through.

"You're the first," he said, and Liam smiled.

Modest kings, the Maridianii built modest crypts: twelve brick buildings the size of small cottages, windowless and undecorated except for the name of the king or queen within, engraved on a sandstone tablet set above the door. They were deep in the shade of the planes, facing the sheer north wall of the vale. Liam crunched along the gravel walk that fronted the tombs, thinking that it was an odd location for the men and women who had founded the kingdom. *They had the whole vale to choose from, and they picked this little corner. No wonder they lost the throne.* The walk continued past the last tomb for a hundred yards or so before curving toward a thick stand of tall pines at the edge of the vale. *Or maybe they liked Night.* He glanced back over his shoulder and saw he had the place to himself: long dead, eclipsed by their greater successors, the Maridianii did not attract supplicants.

The pines encroached on the gravel walk, and his passage set their bushy limbs swaying until he reached the cleared space behind them, a half moon of bare stone at the base of the rock wall. It was colder in the shade of the tall pines, and Liam shivered a little. A brazier and a squat marble table stood off-center in the space, where Night's few offerings were left; most people avoided entering the shrine proper.

And I can see why. The entrance was a set of steps that pierced the wall, descending into an unlit tunnel beneath the mountains. Beyond was a system of caves, believed by some to extend into the heart of the earth, and by others to reach farther, to the Gray Lands of the dead. *No need to go as far as that,* Liam thought, squared his shoulders, and went down the steps.

Smooth at first, the walls and floor gave way to unfinished rock at about the same point the light from the entrance petered out. Liam paused for a moment on the threshold of blindness, then growled at himself and moved on, brushing his fingertips along the rough rock to either side. *Not that far.* The main rooms of the shrine were near the surface, and he did not intend to penetrate much beyond them. There was a slight downward slope to the tunnel, noticeable in a tendency to walk too quickly; he reminded himself of it, and took deliberate steps. *It's just darkness, you baby. And there's nothing Dark about Night.*

The rock grew colder beneath his fingers, as did the air in his lungs; he shivered again and quickened his pace. Luminescent swirls danced in his vision—and then there was one that held still, and seemed to swell slowly as he walked, until he realized it was light ahead. Sighing, he hurried toward it, and stumbled into the first room of the shrine.

On either side the tunnel fell away from his fingers, the walls curving outward into a large cavern, pillared with stalactites and stalagmites that had married over the ages. Around the edges, black-mouthed tunnels led farther into the mountains; some were marked with plaques of dimly glowing metal, but the main source of light was across the floor of the cavern against the far wall— the image of Night. It gave off a cold, white glow, and as Liam walked between the thin-waisted pillars toward it, he had the impression of wandering in a moonlit forest. His breath smoked.

Night sat enthroned beyond the pillars, raising his cloak to mask his face with one hand; in his other, palm down, he held a globe suspended. Two wolves crouched at his feet, and an owl perched on his shoulder, the whole group emanating an unearthly radiance.

An acolyte stood a few feet from the statue, a woman in the white robes of Mother Pity, detached for duty at the shrine. She raised her head at Liam's approach.

"Greetings, child."

She was easily ten years his junior. Liam bowed, hiding a smile. "Greetings, mother."

"Have you come to sacrifice?" She whispered, and he did the same.

"For my master, mother. He would come later, and told me off to explore the shrine. He's never been here before, and was worried about getting lost. They say the caves are deep."

The acolyte smiled, teeth flashing in the glow of the god. "They are, but it is a straight path here, as you see."

"He would pray in private, mother." He gestured at the tunnel mouths all around the edge of the cavern. "Is there someplace?"

"There is, I will show you." She led him through the pillars to a tunnel without a plaque and entered ahead of him, a wraith in her white robes. He could not hear her footsteps, only his own, the scuffle of felt on stone. The passage curved down and away until the light from the main cavern was no longer visible, and then there was a light ahead: a weak, sourceless twilight that lit up the curving tunnel, which widened imperceptibly to a broad natural step. The priestess waited on the step, smiling in the dimness. "I think this should suit," she whispered. "The Well of Night."

Damp sand covered the floor below the step, and the ceiling lifted away; otherwise the new cave seemed a continuation of the tunnel, with a more pronounced curve. At a gesture of invitation from the priestess, Liam walked onto the sand and into the new chamber. It spiralled in upon itself, like the shell of a nautilus; within twenty paces he was out of sight of the priestess. In forty more he reached the Well: the corridor stopped at a short flight of steps descending to a circular chamber with a small altar. Sand dusted the steps and the floor of the Well. He searched the walls and roof, but could not find the source of the soft light that illuminated the place.

Doesn't matter. Warden and her priest can follow

Severn in, and stay hidden in the curve while we talk.

"It's perfect for my master," Liam told the acolyte when he rejoined her. "Thank you, mother."

She smiled, and led the way back.

Outside again, Liam stood in the enclosure of the pines and filled his lungs with fresh air, grateful for daylight. *It's not perfect,* he projected. *I'd rather there was more than one way to get in and out. But it'll do.*

Are you sure it is safe?

No. Didn't I just say that?

Perhaps I should go in with you.

No. I've other plans for you. Speaking of which, why don't you come down here? He opened his pouch and took out the Cure, then frowned, remembering that he had no string. Groaning, he unbuttoned his jacket and pulled the lace from the neck of his shirt. *Idiot. For want of a nail...*

Fanuilh dropped from the sky in front of him. He closed up his jacket and knelt to tie the Cure in place. *You have to keep this safe and out of the way, in case something goes wrong.*

The dragon resumed its burden without objection, but complained that the phial did not feel as secure. *Are you sure it is tight enough, master?*

"It's a shirtlace," Liam said. "What more do you want? It should do, as long as you don't get into any fights. Or move much. Or breathe." He looked around the enclosure, at the dense pine branches. "Why don't you hide yourself up in the trees? Then you'll be able to see everyone who comes in."

But if you should be in any danger—

A tap on the dragon's head served to stop the thought. "The important thing here is the Cure. Remember that."

It looked up at him, its slit-pupilled eyes unreadable, and finally bowed its head. *As you say, master.*

Good. He chucked the dragon under the chin. From

far off came the blare of trumpets. *That'll be the king, coming up from Torquay. Get into the trees, and hide yourself well.*

Fanuilh spread its wings tentatively, peering over its shoulder at the Cure, and took to the air in a series of hesitant hops, like a fledgling just learning to fly. When it was safely up in the branches, positioned to watch the entrance of the shrine, Liam left the enclosure.

With all the holy sites in Rentrillian inundated by pilgrims, Night and the Maridianii had managed to attract only five: two beefy middle-aged men and their wives knelt before the first tomb of the extinguished dynasty, reciting prayers and oblivious to the trumpets; a teenaged boy stood behind them holding a wicker basket. The boy looked up as Liam walked by, a blank, incurious gaze, then glanced away.

Thousands more pilgrims had arrived while Liam was underground; they overflowed the roads and paths of Rentrillian, flocking onto the lawns to line the main road up from Torquay.

The sick king was coming.

Trumpeters marched ahead, stopping every hundred paces to blow a fanfare. Behind came the banners, snapping in the brisk morning breeze, and a contingent of priests bearing placards with images of Nicanor; then a troop of King's Own in scarlet cloaks. There was a discreet gap and then the king's litter, slung between two teams of white horses, the curtains closed, the gilded woodwork decorated with bunches of bright flowers.

Liam watched from the steps of an Edaran tomb, above and apart from the silent crowd. As the procession approached, winding along the road, a ripple ran over the pilgrims—hats coming off, heads bowing. The silver call of the trumpets echoed lonely across the vale.

Three men followed the king's litter: Liam was too far away to see their faces, but he knew the man in black

would be Severn, pretending to mourn his brother, and
the robed man beside him would be the Royal Hierarch.
The third, a slight figure, would be the Prince of the
Mint. Liam squinted, wishing he was closer but not willing to descend into the crowd.

Another gap, another troop of guards, and then a
block of officials and courtiers. He thought he saw Warden, a glimpse of yellow hair, but he could not be sure.
She'll be there. She'd better.

Trumpets rang out and the procession made its slow
way through the vale. It took the better part of an hour
to reach its destination: the Coronation Rotunda span-
ning the Royal. Three pavilions had been erected on the
bank next to it, and a sizable delegation of priests stood
outside the largest, awaiting the arrival of the king.
When his litter was brought up they waved censers of
incense around it, personally unharnessed the horses,
and then carried it inside the tent themselves. The Steward, the Royal Hierarch and the Prince of the Mint followed, and the trumpeters gave a last salute.

Preparations were being made inside the Rotunda—
Liam could see priests scurrying around inside, lighting
candles and arranging tables for sacrifices—and masses
of people had gathered on both banks to watch, hoping
to be as close as they could to the coming ceremony.
Others, the vast majority, headed back to the temples,
the crowd breaking up.

Liam decided to return to Night, to mull over his plan
and see how it might be bettered. *A weapon would be
nice.* Some of the priests were allowed knives with
which to conduct sacrifices and read omens; wondering
about the possibilities of theft, he left the steps of the
Edaran tomb and made his way through the dispersing
crowd.

Rounding Arethusa's hedge maze, he caught a
glimpse of a familiar face farther up the path and
stopped dead, frowning. A pilgrim bumped into him

from behind; he ignored the woman's apologies and jogged after the face, muttering curses. He wove through the crowd until he drew abreast of the man, confirmed his suspicion, and grabbed his arm.

"Avé, Cinna. I hope you're not looking for me."

The little thief squawked and quailed, his face going slack with fear. "I—I—I—"

Liam pulled him off the path, away from the pilgrims. "Now listen, Cinna, listen very carefully: I've important business here, and if you get in my way, the king may die. Do you understand?"

Trembling violently, Cinna swore that he did. "But it's Ringer! He's a madman! He made us come!"

Liam cut him off. "How many?"

Through chattering teeth, the thief said, "A dozen."

For a moment, Liam considered making his offer again—a dozen men would be a godsend—then realized it would never be accepted. *If Ringer's mad enough to chase me, he won't even listen.* "Forget what I said before. You go find Ringer and the rest of your boys, and tell them you saw me heading out of the vale, back to Torquay. Understand? I went back to Torquay."

"Back to Torquay, right. Back to Torquay. You're not here. You've gone."

"And remember, Cinna, if I see any thieves around here, it's you I'll come after. Understand?"

Near tears, the thief promised, and when Liam said, "Now go," he took off at a run. As soon as he was out of sight, Liam shook his head and started on his way to Night again.

Scanning the faces all around him, alert for Cinna's comrades, Liam saw no one suspicious before reaching the lane of Maridianii tombs. Once through the arch— the priest of Strife recognized him with a neutral nod— he breathed easier.

Just another pilgrim, Liam thought. *That's me.* The

two couples and the teenaged boy were gone; he had the Maridianii dead to himself. He went down the path and squeezed through the pines to the forecourt of the shrine.

You up there? he projected.

Yes, master. High in one of the trees, branches rustled. *Grand.*

The sun was well up, beaming warm and welcome on the cold fall day, but it barely touched the enclosure behind the trees. Liam paced back and forth, rubbing his arms and frowning. There were no bells in Rentrillian, so it was impossible to tell, but he guessed he had at least an hour to wait before he could begin to expect Severn.

If I can expect him at all. He decided that he would not be too disappointed if the Steward did not appear, and as he paced he wondered why he had allowed Warden to force him into this. *I'm just an errand boy. Let Catiline do it.* The Prince of the Mint would not let Severn go unpunished, once he had the Cure in hand and learned the details of the man's treachery. *Which I will be happy to provide.*

Severn was powerful, though, and it would be difficult to act against him without proof. Liam sighed and resigned himself to this last task. *Once it's done, you can go.* He occupied himself with daydreams of the time after—of a bath and a large, hot meal, of wearing clothes that were not stolen, of his cabin on the *Trade's Increase,* of the ship at sea on its way back to Southwark.

The minutes crawled by and Liam's daydreams paled, less and less able to distract him from waiting and worrying. *What will I say?* Extracting a confession was difficult enough when both sides knew that was the point; he needed to draw one out without raising the Steward's suspicions. The man thought he was a fugitive, which worked in his favor; Severn would not expect a trap. *I hope.* He growled low in his throat, assailed by a thousand doubts. *If I had this all to do again,* he thought, *I wouldn't do it at all. Failing that, I'd do it completely differently. To start, I'd have a weapon. And I'd have arranged some way to talk to Warden, and I'd have chosen a place with more than one way in.*

Fanuilh rustled in the branches. *Master, I see Lord Auric coming. He has his servant with him.*

Liam's mouth went dry. *Anyone else?*

No. Lord Auric has a walking stick.

He cocked his head, puzzled—then remembered. *Damn.* He rubbed his forehead, thinking. *All right. Stay ready. And when we go inside, keep an eye on things. Let me know when Warden gets here.*

Yes, master.

He went to stand by the entrance of the shrine, and a moment later Severn strolled in through the pines, whistling a low dirge.

CHAPTER 18

SEVERN STOPPED WHISTLING. They faced each other across the open space, the Steward planting his walking stick in front of him and resting both hands on it. He wore a coat of fine black wool, slashed to reveal black satin. A band of black crepe encircled his hat, and a crow feather jutted up from it. From a necklace around his neck hung a tear-shaped stone. He lifted a finger to stroke his goatee, and peered at Liam for a moment, pursing his lips in wonder.

"Can this be the same man?" As if Liam had lost weight, or changed tailors—as if this were just a chance encounter.

"It is."

"But so changed," Severn marvelled. "A new face. Interesting—but not necessarily pleasing, I'm afraid."

"Lieutenant Aldyne didn't like it either," Liam said, and then pointed over Severn's shoulder, at the thin servant hovering there. "We're going in for a few minutes. He stays out here, along with your stick."

Severn smiled. "Why, it would be sacrilege to bear a weapon in Rentrillian."

Pacifex Warden has just passed through the arch. She has several men with her, but they are not wearing the uniforms of Peacemakers. One is in robes.

"So it would be. Leave it with your man, or you can forget our business."

Severn tapped his lips with his finger. "Ah, our business. Why can't we conduct that here, I wonder?"

"Because I don't trust you," Liam snapped. "I want to do this in private."

The other man considered for a moment, then nodded. "Very well. But you should know, sir, that Pacifex Warden is not the only person who can arrange protection against magicks." He stroked the tear-shaped stone, then lifted the walking stick over his shoulder; the thin servant took it, squinting balefully at Liam. "Lead on, Master Rhenford."

Master, the Pacifex has sent a man into the enclosure.

She was being careful; that was good. *Fine.*

Behind him, Severn's bootheels tocked on the tunnel floor. Shoulders tense in anticipation, Liam concentrated on the sound, measuring the man's stride, waiting for it to change. *If he rushes me—what?*

There was no change, just a steady tocking, Severn matching his stride perfectly; then, absurdly, the man began to hum under his breath. Liam ground his teeth.

The servant is trying to tell the man he cannot enter the shrine.

Fine. Interminable, the tunnel stretched on and on, black and cold. Liam found himself panting, though he was not walking very quickly, and drew a few deep breaths to calm himself. Up ahead, the nacreous glow of Night swam out of the darkness.

They are arguing.

He reached the large cavern. Murmurous echoes filled the place, and as he crossed between the natural stone pillars to the tunnel leading to the Well of Night, he caught a glimpse of the two couples he had seen kneeling outside the Maridianii tombs. They were praying to Night now; the teenager waited behind them, basket on his arm. He turned his head at the sound of footsteps, his eyes tracking Liam through the pillars, and then hastily averted his face, as if embarrassed to be caught staring.

The priestess stood by the entrance to the curving passage, her head bowed in silent prayer; she looked up and smiled when she heard him approach.

Liam smiled tightly back, and jerked a thumb over his shoulder. "My master." He turned to make sure Severn was following, then started down the tunnel.

Behind him, he heard Severn say, "I would pray in private, mother. If you could see that I am not interrupted, I would be grateful."

"As you wish, my lord."

And then the tocking of bootheels.

The Peacemaker has seized the servant, master; he is calling out to the Pacifex that it is safe.

Liam closed his eyes for a moment as he walked, and breathed a quiet sigh. *Fine.* Then his eyes snapped open, and he panicked: she would not know which tunnel he had taken. *There are a dozen of them. She'll never find us.* His steps faltered.

"Master Rhenford? If you would go a little slower, please. It is difficult to see you." There was a smile in Severn's voice.

Master, the Pacifex has entered the shrine with the robed man. She has left her Peacemakers on guard.

All the strength had gone from his legs; his stride slackened. *She'll ask,* he hoped. *She'll see we're not there, and she'll ask the priestess.* Severn had requested privacy, but she could hardly deny the Pacifex. *She'll ask.* He took a deep breath.

Along the curve, he led the way deeper into the sand-floored nautilus with its sourceless light. At the end, on a sudden impulse, he hurried down the steps into the Well, knelt, and scooped up a handful of sand. With his fist clenched, he turned and waited.

Severn strolled down the steps into the chamber, hands clasped behind his back, directing a curious gaze at the roof of the cave. "Hm. Do you know, Master Rhenford, none can say where the light comes from? In all this shrine, I mean. I have studied it, but there is no answer." He saw Liam's startled expression, and made a dismissive gesture. "It is of no moment. This is a fine place to conduct our business. You have the item you mentioned in your letter?"

Liam shook his head.

"No? Then what business can we have together?"

"It's somewhere safe." He tried to estimate how long it would take Warden to reach the cave. *Drag it out.*

Severn arched an eyebrow. "You do not trust me?"

"Trust you?" Liam scoffed. "Trust you? You forget, Lord Auric, that I saw you kill your own brother."

"Ah. Yes. So you say—though the Peacemakers think you did that. As they think you killed that unfortunate scholar. You are much sought after, I believe."

Liam shrugged. "Much sought, but never found. Shall we discuss the Cure? I assume you are interested in it." *How long? Five minutes?*

"Oh, very."

There was something in Severn's manner that worried him—an ill-concealed amusement. "Very interested, right. After all, if your brother's life isn't too great a price to pay for it, what sort of price would you put on it in coin?"

Severn shook his head, mimicking sorrow. "You mustn't value it that way. While I was greatly saddened by my dear brother's shocking murder, I cannot in all honesty say that I miss him. Suffice it to say that we were not close, and while I deplore the manner of his death, the fact of it does not distress me. So we must find another value for this item."

Does that count? Is that enough for her? He frowned, trying not to look over Severn's shoulder to the steps. "Perhaps we should consider what it would mean if I delivered the Cure to the king. His recovery would be a great blow to you and your . . . allies."

"My allies?" The Steward affected confusion. "I fear

you misjudge me, Master Rhenford. I have no allies. I am simply considering the best interests of the kingdom."

"And yourself."

Severn acknowledged the fact with a modest shrug. "I flatter myself that they are the same. But let us consider your conjecture: should you deliver the Cure—your ability to do which is doubtful—and should it effect the king's recovery—which is not completely assured—I believe the best interests of the kingdom would suffer. It is on that basis that we should value this item."

That sounds like treason to me. Is she even out there? "On the basis of your desire to keep the king sick. Or, rather, to see him die of his illness."

Severn frowned, and rolled his fingers in the air, searching for a phrase. "Let us not say that. Let us say, on the basis of my considered judgment of what is best for the land."

Liam shook his head, disgusted. "Whatever you want. Here's the question: how much will you pay to keep the Cure away from the king?"

"No sum springs to mind."

Master, the thieves are coming.

"What?" The word burst out before he could think to project.

Eyes narrowing, Severn repeated himself.

The thieves are coming, master. A dozen of them, with Ringer in the lead.

"No sum," Liam stammered, torn between the two conversations. "You can't think of a sum."

"No, I cannot." The Steward frowned. "Are you quite well, Master Rhenford?"

They are coming through the trees.

"You can't put a price on the king's life." *What in the Dark are they doing here? And where's Warden?*

"No. You must do that for me. If it is reasonable, I shall pay it."

The Peacemakers do not want to let them in. Lord Auric's servant is calling them murderers. He is accusing them of trying to murder his master. I do not think the thieves realize they are Peacemakers.

"Sounds like treason to me," Liam said, raising his voice. *Damn her, is she even listening to this?* "That should raise the price."

"Ah, but you are also committing treason, which lowers it."

Master, the thieves are fighting the Peacemakers.

At the same time, the piercing shrill of a tin whistle reverberated through the shrine. Severn jumped and spun around, but Liam breathed a sigh of relief. It had to be Warden, summoning her men. Occupied with the thieves, they would not come, but as long as she was there, with her wand and the priest, it did not matter. A moment later the whistle cut off.

"What can that be?" the Steward asked.

"You'll find out soon enough," Liam said, and then Warden stumbled into view at the top of the steps. Blood trickled down her cheek from a cut above her eye and she cradled her crippled arm, biting her lip against pain. Behind her came the white-robed priestess, a bloody short sword in one hand and Warden's lightning wand in the other.

"She came after you, my lord," she said, tossing the wand down to Severn. "She had a hierarch of Laomedon with her. They meant to eavesdrop on you, I think."

Severn ran a finger down the length of the wand, made a sound of mild surprise, and then turned to Liam.

"Master Rhenford, it occurs to me that you are not dealing in good faith."

No reply came to mind. Mouth slack and gaping, Liam could only stare at Warden—at the suffering plain on her face—and think that she had killed him. The priestess shoved the Pacifex down the steps; she stumbled to her knees at the bottom, close by Liam, and he shied back, shaking his head in disbelief. *She got caught. She got caught.*

"You have allies, I see," Severn said, and then addressed the priestess as she came down the steps. "Thrasa, my dear. The priest?"

"Dead." From beneath her robes, she produced a second short sword and presented it to the Steward.

"The people praying?"

"Moved on to another chamber. And I saw no sign of the dragon."

Warden climbed to her feet. Liam moved belatedly to help, but she pushed him off. "You will not escape," she told Severn. "I have a dozen men waiting outside the shrine."

No, you don't, Liam thought. *They're fighting my thieves.*

The other man made a practice cut with his blade and frowned as if displeased by the balance. "Then Master Rhenford must murder you quickly." He nodded to Thrasa, who gripped her sword low and advanced, her other arm raised.

"Wait!" Liam shouted. The woman did not stop.

"You can kill me—" Warden began, but Thrasa was too close. Liam threw his fistful of sand at her face and rushed her. She cried out, spun away so he only clipped her shoulder, sent her crashing into Warden; he barrelled into the wall, spun in time to see Severn bearing down on him. He threw himself to the side, came down in the sand.

Warden's whistle shrilled through the cave.

Liam scrambled backward, desperate on his elbows. Severn caught him at the base of the steps, put the heavy point of the sword at his throat.

"Wait wait wait," Liam shouted, stretching his neck away.

"Shut her up!" Severn ordered. Thrasa, sobbing a

curse, backhanded Warden; the tin whistle spun across the cave and the priestess kicked her for good measure, then stooped to retrieve her sword, dashing tears from her eyes.

"If you kill us the king gets the Cure," Liam blurted. "And the whole story, too."

The Steward glared down at him for a moment, then dug the point in. "Speak."

Liam cursed and writhed away, feeling blood trickle down the side of his neck. Even if the Peacemakers could respond to Warden's whistle, it would never be in time. *Fanuilh! Listen!* "If I die, my dragon brings the Cure and a letter to the king."

"Nonsense." He jabbed the sword suggestively, without touching skin. "Your familiar dies with you."

"Not for an hour or more. It takes time for the spirit to fade." He blinked, licked dry lips. *Fanuilh! Are you listening?* "And he's sitting atop the Coronation Rotunda right now. If I die, he flies right down into the ceremony."

Master, what are you saying?

Severn hovered, one eye screwed up in calculation.

Shut up and listen! "I'm telling you, if I die, he brings the Cure right to Nicanor himself. And a letter." He closed his eyes. *Understand? Go to the Coronation Rotunda!*

Severn finished his calculations and smiled. "Nonsense." He changed his grip, held the sword with both hands, preparing to drive it down into Liam's chest.

Master, are you in trouble?

In a broken voice, Warden said, "My men will be here any moment."

"Shut up!" Liam snarled, and cupped his hands beneath the sword, pleading: "It's not too late. Spare us, and you can have the Cure. Just spare us. Forget the money, forget it."

Severn raised the blade and murmured, "Consider it forgotten."

Liam's eyes went round, and then he heard a new voice, high-pitched but calm and authoritative. "Lord Auric, stay your hand."

The blade came down, but Severn faltered and Liam twisted aside, lashed out with his legs and scrambled away, lurching to his feet.

The teenaged boy looked down on them from the top of the steps, the two couples a wall behind him, arms crossed over their chests, glaring at the sword in the Steward's hands.

"Lord Auric, that is sacrilege," the boy pointed out. He was pale and slender, his face composed. Silent and graceful, the two men and two women slipped past him and down the steps, fanning out to stand guard, one apiece, over the four in the Well.

"Ah, Cestus," Severn said, ignoring the burly guard at his elbow. "You are well come. I have just captured these two plotting treason." He waved the sword to indicate Liam and Warden. The man guarding him tracked the blade with hate in his eyes.

Catiline's son, Liam realized.

"Yet you commit treason yourself," the boy said in a matter-of-fact tone. He indicated the four guards. "These are Strife Emptysheath's. They do not like weapons in Rentrillian."

Thrasa made a sudden move, and—Liam did not exactly see how—a moment later lay on the floor of the cave, clutching her stomach and gasping. Her priest-guard did not seem to have stirred at all.

Severn's eyes flickered, and then he dropped his sword. "Of course. You must understand, Cestus: we took them from these two. They were plotting against the king."

Liam laughed; Warden cleared her throat. "Do not believe him, Prince Cestus."

Playing his new part, Severn whirled on her. "Silence, traitor!" He had raised his hand to strike her, but a priest of Strife stood in his way. He lowered his hand, smoothed the front of his coat.

Cestus ignored him in favor of Liam. "You are the man I was to meet?"

Liam nodded. "Yes, my lord."

"May I ask why you met with Lord Auric instead?" He was barely more than thirteen, and there was something both preposterous and eerie about his self-possession.

Master? What is going on?

Hang on a minute. I think things are all right.

"Not instead, my lord. Before. Pacifex Warden and I were attempting to procure evidence of his treachery."

"An obvious lie!" Severn exclaimed. "Cestus, you must not listen to this!"

The boy suddenly nodded, understanding. "The priest was to listen in, and confirm it."

"Exactly."

"And now he is dead. By whose hand, I wonder?"

Liam glanced significantly at Severn, who threw up his own hands. "Look at the man, Cestus! A wanted murderer! Who would you believe—a painted rogue, or a Steward of the Royal Household?"

The boy gave Liam an apologetic look. "You do look . . . disreputable, Master Rhenford. This is beyond what I was tasked to do. I suggest we all repair to the king's tent, and present this to him."

"That's what they want!" Severn blurted. "To get close to the king, so they may assassinate him!"

"If that is so," the boy said coldly, "then we shall go to my father instead. I hope that is agreeable to you, Lord Auric." Before the Steward could reply, he gestured to the priests. "Good acolytes, if you would escort these worthies?"

Cestus led them up to the surface, the priest-guards staying close to their charges. Liam walked directly behind the boy; when they had almost reached the main cavern of the shrine, he coughed to get his attention. "You should know, my lord, that there is a group of Peacemakers outside, waiting on the Pacifex Warden. They were fighting some thieves." *Are they still fighting?*

No, master, but the Peacemakers have had a very difficult time of it. Are you safe?

Yes. Stay where you are.

The boy looked at him for a moment, then nodded. "Very well."

They marched in line up the long tunnel to daylight; near the end, Cestus strode ahead to address the Peacemakers. They were formed up by the time Liam emerged: much bruised, some bloodied, but anxious for their commander. When she came out last, it was only the stern looks of the priests of Strife that kept them from rushing to her aid.

"I am fine," she said, though she winced with every step, and held her crippled arm gingerly. "Do as Prince Cestus commands."

He led them out of the enclosure, then set the Peacemakers to form a phalanx around the four prisoners and started off down the gravel walk.

Master, why are you under guard?

Don't worry about it, Liam projected. *When we're out of sight, come out of your tree and follow us to the tents by the Coronation Rotunda.*

The brown-robed priest at the arch bowed to Cestus, and fell in with them as they made their way through the vale toward the pavilions of the royal party. Their progress grew steadily more difficult: the closer they came to the rotunda, the thicker the crowds became, and before long the boy had to call for people to step aside. They pushed through the pilgrims, leaving a wake of murmurs and whispers and discreetly pointed fingers.

A dozen yards from the tents, the press was too much; Cestus wormed his way forward to the cordon the King's Own were maintaining, and got them to clear a space. The Peacemakers were separated and led aside, while the rest followed the boy and a sergeant of the guard to the smallest of the three tents.

Small is relative, Liam thought, gazing around Catiline's tent. Poles twenty feet tall supported the canvas roof, a dozen carpets had been laid on the grass, and four huge braziers struggled in vain to heat the vast space.

Four men stood waiting across the tent—two tall soldiers in gleaming silver breastplates, plumed helmets under their arms, a grizzled bull of a man in the brown robes of Strife, and the slight figure Liam remembered from the procession. Catiline was only an inch taller than his son, with the same thin chest and slender waist. Their faces were similar as well: unrevealing masks. The father's hair was gray, clipped a little shorter than the boy's; otherwise they might have been brothers. He wore a blue tunic and pearl gray breeches.

"Publius!" Severn called. "I have uncovered a plot against the king!"

The Prince of the Mint held up a finger for silence, and beckoned Cestus to join him for a quiet conference. If he was surprised by his son's report, he gave no sign; he asked several questions, received Cestus's answers, then paused, head bent, thinking. He might have been a statue.

"Publius! This is madness!"

Catiline's voice was surprisingly deep for so slight a man. "Captain, silence Lord Auric. If he ventures to move or speak again, you may gag him." The indicated soldier, baffled by the order, hesitated and received a mild look of reproof. "See to it, Captain. The man is guilty of sacrilege and high treason."

Still uncertain, the soldier went to stand by Severn's side. The Steward glared at him but the man refused to meet his gaze, and after a moment Severn dropped his eyes, frowning. Beads of sweat had appeared on his brow.

Catiline beckoned Liam close. All eyes in the tent lay on them, but the Prince of the Mint seemed oblivious, as if they were the only two people present. "You have the Cure?"

"It is nearby, my lord. I can have it in a minute."

"Do so." He turned away and called Warden to him. She came forward slowly, a greenish tinge discernible beneath her ordinary pallor. Catiline noticed. He found her a camp chair and sent his son to fetch a glass of wine. Cestus dashed off while his father and the Pacifex talked.

Liam hesitated for a moment, unsure how to proceed. There was a sense of anticlimax about the whole thing, whispered talk where there should have been rousing denunciations, murmured orders in place of a chorus of gratitude. *Isn't it always the way?* He shrugged, and projected: *Fanuilh, did you see which tent I went into?*

Yes, master.

Come to the entrance.

He glanced around, thinking he should tell someone what he was going to do, then shrugged and went to the tent flaps. No one stopped him, but his priest-guard fell into step beside him.

"Don't worry," Liam told him. "I'm not going anywhere."

The priest smiled as if he knew that already, and let Liam part the flaps and step outside.

Gasps and cries rose up from the crowd as Fanuilh descended from the sky; the royal guards stared and pointed, unsure what do, and were not entirely reassured when Liam said, "He's with me," and lifted his forearm for the dragon to land on. *Quite an entrance.*

Is everything all right, master?

Fine, Liam projected, ducking back into the tent. *I think.* He worked at the shirtlace as he carried his familiar over to where Catiline knelt by Warden's side.

"My lord," he said, and held out the phial. "The King's Cure."

The Prince of the Mint rose before reaching out, and met Liam's eyes briefly. Then he bowed, and took the Cure. "Our thanks, Master Rhenford—mine, and the king's, and the land's. You have served nobly. I must ask you to allow my son to take you to my home. You may rest there, and be refreshed from your trials. Cestus, take a dozen guards."

It was couched as a kind offer but meant as an order, and Catiline did not wait for thanks. He turned and knelt beside Warden again, speaking in a low, confidential voice. "It must be done without fuss," he told her.

Liam bowed to his back and went to join Cestus. *It's not a hymn of gratitude,* he thought, *but it's the best you're going to get.* To make up for it, he paused by Severn on his way out and muttered, "Is it so warm in here, Lord Auric? You seem to be perspiring."

He grinned at the Steward's hate-filled look, and followed Cestus out.

With a dozen red-cloaked guards to smooth the way, leaving Rentrillian was easy. The most difficult part was the first hundred yards; people in the crowd there had seen Liam with Fanuilh, and though the soldiers pushed and cursed, the pilgrims tried to press close, pointing and shouting questions.

Liam tucked the dragon under his arm and tried to conceal it as much as possible. *Let's keep you out of sight, shall we?*

I could fly, master.

*And start a panic? Thousands trampled? I don't think
so.* He opened his coat and lifted one side over the
dragon's head. *Just stay quiet.*

They finally got through the pilgrims and reached the
road down to Torquay, which was empty. The guards
spread out, six in front and six behind; Cestus walked
beside Liam. He spoke only once in the vale, the words
coming out as if against his will.

"Is it true you jumped from the Stair?"

Liam winced. "Not by choice."

The boy nodded, and the rest of the walk passed in
silence. At the bottom of the vale, where the Royal widened, were a set of stone piers, at which were moored a
number of lavishly decorated barges. Cestus led them
onto one, ordering servants to cast off and take them to
King's Vale, then showed Liam to a padded seat in the
bow.

"I'm afraid there's nothing aboard to offer you, Master Rhenford, but when we reach my father's house,
you'll lack for nothing."

Liam thanked him and slumped back on the cushions.
He set Fanuilh on his lap and closed his eyes.

Master, are you under arrest?

Of a sort. You too. Catiline's a very careful man.

He said you acted nobly.

He's wise, too. Despite the joke, Liam felt a twinge
of anger. Catiline had thanked him—and then bundled
him off, disposed of him, assuming that he would do as
he was told. Only a twinge, however: *You're just an
errand boy, after all, not a prince or a pacifex. And
you've completed your errand. The tip wasn't as big as
you might have liked, but at least you're finished.* It took
a few minutes for the realization to sink in: he was finished.

The sun was warm on his face and the cushions soft;
he sank deeper into them, and smiled to himself.

• • •

They landed at King's Vale and walked up to Catiline's mansion, a grand house a short block from the palace itself. Cestus showed Liam to a large suite. "My father was very specific," he said, when Liam commented on the number of rooms. "I will send servants to bathe you, and some food. Is there anything you would like?"

Memories of his daydreams outside Night's shrine came to mind; he shrugged them off. "Anything would be fine, my lord. But I would ask for some raw meat— for my friend." He nodded at Fanuilh; it was delicately kneading the mattress of the four-poster bed with its claws. "And something to read, if you wouldn't mind. Paper and ink, as well. I imagine I'll be here a few hours."

"My father will no doubt wish to speak to you, and he may be occupied for some time, yes. I will send up the things you asked for." He bowed and left Liam alone.

Servants came in short order, led by a tyrannical chamberlain. He organized the bath and the food and clean clothes as if Liam was not present, refusing to acknowledge the dirty, tattooed menace or the dragon on the bedclothes. When everything was in order the chamberlain clapped his hands and ushered the lesser servants out, waiting by the door until they were all gone, as if he were counting to make sure none were missing.

Two brass tubs had been set up in the tiled bath; Liam scrubbed himself clean in the first one, muddying the water with dirt, blood, and ink, then soaked in the second for a long while. He studied himself in a hand mirror afterward, noting the faint shadow of ink still visible on his face and head. His scalp was stubbled.

The hair will grow in, but will the ink ever come off?

"What would you think of that?" he asked, pulling on

a robe and joining Fanuilh at the table the chamberlain had set. "Just a hint of a tattoo."

The dragon had already eaten half a plate of raw beef. *Quaestor Casotte would not like it.*

"Oh, I don't know. If she loves me, she should love me with a tattoo."

No one likes it. Prince Cestus said it made you look disreputable.

"He didn't say that exactly. I think he was referring to the company I keep." There was a great deal of food on the table—a platter of cold meat, a mound of fruit, three wheels of cheese, two large loaves of bread—but Liam found he was not hungry. He pushed away from the table and strolled over to the bed. "I mean, dragons, after all. What kind of reputation do they have?"

He crawled on top of the soft blankets.

You are joking.

Liam nodded at the canopy above the bed, and had loving thoughts about sleep.

CHAPTER 19

LIAM WOKE MUCH later in darkness: the bed-curtains had been drawn while he slept, presumably by servants. He pushed the curtains aside and saw that they had also lit a fire in the large fireplace, cleared away his uneaten meal, laid out clothes for him and—he caught a glimpse of the empty bath through the door—taken away both tubs of dirty water. *And all on tiptoe, so as not to wake poor me. Very nice.* He yawned, stretched, and focused his thoughts.

Fanuilh?

I am in the parlor, master.

He was not sure which of the four rooms in his suite constituted the parlor, but as he tested the floor with his bare toes he heard a distant clatter of hooves. *What's that all about?* The tiles were freezing; the shoes he had stolen in the bath house were gone.

A troop of soldiers, master. They have been coming and going all night.

After a few moments of hopping he found the soft fur slippers that had been left as replacements and shuffled through the dark suite in search of the dragon. It was lying on a broad windowsill in the parlor—a long, narrow room of overstuffed divans and squat chairs with spindly legs—two stories above an interior courtyard lit with torches.

He sat beside it, staring down at a squad of red-cloaked King's Own led by a mounted officer. The officer leaned from his saddle to hand a scroll to Catiline himself; Liam quietly lifted the latch and eased the window open. Cold air and the officer's message flowed in.

"The weapons are secure, my lord, and the numbers match those from the list we found in—" He started to say where they found the list, then stopped. "They match the list we found. There was no sign that any had been removed."

Catiline dismissed the man with distracted thanks and turned away, unrolling the scroll. A servant ran after him, bearing another message; the officer wheeled his horse and led his squad out of the courtyard. Liam shivered and closed the window.

"Counting the palace armory, eh? He's not taking any chances."

Fanuilh rose and hopped down from the windowsill. *It has been like that all day. Couriers and Messengers coming in and out, soldiers, Peacemakers. Pacifex Warden has been here six times. She looks much better than she did before.*

Frowning, Liam followed the dragon back into the bedroom. It stretched out by the hearth and he lit a few candles from the fire—wood, he noted, not coal. "Do you know what time it is?"

It was one o'clock not long ago.

"One?" He gave a low whistle. *And while I've been dreaming the day away, they've been out there—doing what?* He tried to imagine what would have been necessary: securing not just the armory but the entire palace; seizing and searching Severn's house; rooting out his supporters. *What else?* Counting the weapons seemed a little extreme, but if Catiline was worried about an armed insurrection, he might well have started vetting the royal guards, using those he trusted to check the loyalty of the others. Warden, he knew, would have had to do something similar with her Peacemakers. Interrogations, arrests, quite possibly executions—he shuddered at the thought. *Be thankful you're just an errand boy.*

There were things he had to attend to, however, now that he was no longer an outlaw. He glanced around the bedroom. "Did they bring ink and paper while I was asleep?"

It is in the sitting room, with some books from Prince Cestus.

Taking up a candle, he went to the one door he had not yet opened. *What's the difference between the parlor and the sitting room?*

It is where they put the ink and paper.

He saw a large table with writing supplies and a stack of leather-bound tomes; the room reminded him of Severn's study, though it was not quite as richly appointed. A fire had been laid but not started in the fireplace; he lit it with his candle, and went to sit behind the table.

The books were philosophy, mostly from the stern School of Virtue, and not the sort of reading Liam had had in mind. He flipped idly through the well-thumbed volumes for a few minutes, noting the frequent notes in the margins, often in different color inks. *Cestus certainly goes in for philosophy.* Setting the books aside, he pulled a piece of paper close, uncorked the ink bottle, and picked up a stylus.

At the top of the page he wrote "Owed," and listed first the things he had stolen from the bath house, with rough estimates of their value. When he was done he leaned back in his chair and tried to remember if he had stolen anything else. *A sword each from Aldyne and Severn,* he thought, frowning. *I don't have to pay for those. And I don't know who the boat belonged to.* He wrote a note to make an offering at one of the river shrines that gave charity to the poor. Coats came to mind—the one he had taken from the thief, and the one from the Peacemaker outside the warehouse—but he could not muster any guilt over them. On the whole, he decided, he had done very little damage in his flight through the city.

His satisfied expression wavered then, and he grimaced. He dipped the stylus and wrote:

Marcade???

He underlined the name, stared at it for a long second, then threw down the stylus and stood. It was the middle of the night, and he was suddenly tired. After blowing out the candle, he shuffled back to bed and tried to sleep again.

Fanuilh roused him early the next morning, from a confused dream set in Rentrillian.

Master, there is a servant here. He is not sure if he should wake you.

Glad to be out of the dream, the unsettling details of which he could not quite remember, Liam stuck his head through the bedcurtains. "Yes?"

The servant yelped and jumped back, then recollected himself and bowed. "Master, Prince Cestus sends to see if you are available to receive him."

"Tell him I'm at his service."

The servant hurried off and Liam dragged himself to the bath, filled a basin from the pitcher there and scrubbed his face, washing away sleep and his dream.

When Cestus arrived Liam was waiting in the parlor, dressed in his new clothes: a slashed jacket with seed pearls down the front, short satin breeches, and fine wool hose. He stopped plucking at his legs—he hated hose— and rose to greet the boy.

"My father asked me to convey his apologies," Cestus said, after they exchanged bows. "He would have come to see you himself, but he has pressing business. He hoped you would understand."

"Of course. He need not bother himself with me."

Cestus held up a contradictory finger. "Ah, no, Master Rhenford. He asked me to repeat his thanks of yesterday, and to see if you would claim some reward for your services. There are commissions available in the King's Own, for instance." The boy misinterpreted Liam's frown, and added, "As an officer, naturally."

"That's very kind of him," Liam said. "There's nothing I want." He was sure Cestus had not meant to phrase the offer that way—as if he would expect payment, a fee for services rendered—but it irritated him nonetheless. "Please thank the prince for me."

Nonplussed, the boy cleared his throat. "I shall, certainly." An awkward pause followed, and then he blurted, "Did you get the books I sent?"

"I did, thank you."

"Perhaps they are too weighty," Cestus said, with innocent concern.

"Not too weighty," Liam said, bridling at the suggestion that the books were beyond him. *And from someone half your age.* "Too weighted. To the School of Virtue, I mean. Their arguments fall down in places, you know—in history particularly. It's not a very good guide to virtue. Or, if it is, it can also be a good guide to vice, as well. Present events, for instance, when the scholars write them down, will teach as much about treachery as loyalty. History is a mirror, not a sermon."

Cestus blinked, surprised. "Who said that?"

"I did," Liam replied, then laughed. "But I took it from Sallust's *Mirror of Policy*. You should read it. It's a good antidote to the Virtuists."

"Mm. Perhaps I should." He gazed at his feet for a moment, then shrugged away philosophy. "I almost forgot: Pacifex Warden is with my father at the moment. She asked if she might call on you when she is done." Liam said she might, and Cestus bowed. "I will have the servants bring you breakfast." As he left, he muttered the name Sallust under his breath.

• • •

Breakfast was laid in the sitting room; it was there that Warden found Liam, lingering over the demolished remains. He shooed Fanuilh off the table and drew up a chair for her.

Her eyes were puffy and underscored with dark bags; she winced when she sat, gently massaging her crippled arm. Her checkered tunic was stained and rumpled. They faced each other in silence until Liam thought to offer her something to eat.

"No, thank you," she said, and sat a little straighter, as if she had just remembered why she had come. From a pouch at her belt, she produced the Cure and held it out to him. "The king would have you return this to the duke." He hesitated, then took the phial. "In truth, it was Queen Ierne who gave it. The king is—gods, the king is worse than I had thought."

Liam glanced up sharply from the phial; she was rubbing her eyes with her good hand, and looked briefly like a desolate child. "But he's recovering, isn't he?" He recalled the single sip he had taken, and the immense feeling of well-being that followed. He gestured with the Cure. "I mean, after this. He's better, isn't he?"

She met his eyes, then looked away and shook her head. "He will die soon. In a matter of days, if not hours."

With an angry noise, Liam shoved back from the table and stood. "That's ridiculous! This—this was supposed to—" Words failed him.

Her voice was hollow. "It is proof against wounds only. Or perhaps disease as well, we do not know. In any case, it cannot save a man who has been poisoned."

"Poisoned?" Liam blurted.

She nodded slowly, her chin sinking lower with each descent. "We found the poison in Severn's house. He had been administering small doses for quite some time. It is a rare and unfamiliar type, and the scholars tell us there is no antidote."

"But if it didn't help, why did the Duke send it? And why was Severn so set on getting it?"

"He could not be sure. His plans were well advanced; he could not risk having them upset. The cost must have seemed reasonable to him. As for the Duke, he said in his letter to Master Cade that he was not sure the Cure would help. He sent it as a sort of last resort."

An image of Lord Bairth, blood welling around his fingers, sprang unbidden to Liam's mind. He ground his teeth, glaring down at the Cure. He wanted to throw it, smash it, but settled for a strangled curse. Then a different thought struck him. "Did you find out who Severn was working for? Was it Silverbridge or Corvialus?"

"None of his creatures knew. We are questioning several of them now— questioning them quite closely—and know that he promised them rewards under the new king, but he did not tell them which it would be, apparently." She drew a deep breath. "And we cannot ask him, as he committed suicide last night."

Liam gawked at her. "How did he do that?" he demanded. "Didn't you watch him?"

Her eyes flashed. "It was not my decision, Master Rhenford. Prince Publius set the conditions of his imprisonment. You may rest assured that I would at least have taken away his belt, but the prince forbade it."

Suicide was much favored by the School of Virtue, particularly for the disgraced. "Well, that's just grand. That's really wonderful. Now there's even odds that our next king will be a murderer."

"Perhaps it is best that we not know which, then." She sighed. "In any case, it is not for us to question the orders of princes."

"It is when the orders are stupid!"

She winced, but kept her voice calm. "You should know that what I have told you is not to be spoken of. That the king was poisoned, in particular. Prince Publius does not wish it known."

Liam made an angry gesture. "Then why are you telling me?"

"I am not sure," she replied honestly. "I cannot say." She quirked her lips. "Perhaps I thought you deserved to know. You risked your life—you faced great dangers." She shook her head. "I cannot say. I felt you deserved to know. It was nobly done."

"For nothing," he muttered. "Nobly done for nothing."

"Not for nothing. We exposed a vicious traitor and his creatures."

He could not argue with that, but he was thinking of the king—and Cade, Lord Bairth, Nennius, the hierarch of Laomedon. *All dead for nothing. And Marcade. Marcade, too.*

As if she had read his mind, Warden said, "You may wish to know that we discovered your friend, the Lady Marcade, imprisoned in Severn's cellars. Apparently he scrupled at killing a woman."

Or he was keeping her to help him later on, Liam thought, and was instantly ashamed.

"She was quite distraught," the Pacifex went on. "Some ladies of the court went to comfort her, but I understand that learning of the death of her husband distressed her further."

Liam squeezed his eyes shut. "That was my fault. I left him there—I tied him up—he helped me, and I thought they'd leave him alone when they saw I'd tied him up." Abruptly, he remembered the offer Cestus had relayed. "Catiline promised me a reward. A commission, I think, something like that. Do you think—could you ask him if he could help her? A pension, maybe, or an honorific at the court? Something permanent. Could you ask him for me?"

Warden studied him, then nodded. "I'm certain something can be arranged. I believe she is staying with one of the ladies-in-waiting at the palace, if you should choose to call on her."

"No," Liam said hastily. He could not imagine facing Marcade. "Just—if something can be arranged."

"As you wish." She rose with difficulty and started for the door. "We must all bear burdens, Master Rhenford. Actions we regret, plans that went awry, mistakes."

He crossed his arms and smiled bitterly. "I know, I know—don't let it weigh too heavily."

She paused by the door and shook her head. "No. They weigh what they weigh, and must be borne. The consolation lies in doing better in the future." She smiled then, a shy, fragile smile, as if she were unused to it, and unsure if it was appropriate. "Consider that I almost hunted you to your death, Master Rhenford. Think how that would have weighed on me. But for Fortune's blessing, you would have hung for murder, and I would have been to blame."

"Fortune's blessing?" Liam asked, raising an eyebrow. "Luck?"

Her smile, though still small, grew more certain. "Yes, Master Rhenford. Luck."

He could not think of a retort—he wanted something witty—but nothing came to mind, and he could not force his thoughts past the heavy knowledge of the futility of the last four days. He managed a smile. "Well, I pray for luck all the time."

"And I pray that I may never hunt a man as lucky again." Her expression turned serious, and she offered him a deep bow. "You are free to go, you know. I wish you a safe voyage back to Southwark."

He bowed in return, and she left.

A short while later Liam left Catiline's house with an escort of royal guards. The officer in charge insisted, quoting orders from both the prince and the Pacifex. At first he wondered if it was a sign of distrust, and only gradually realized that it was because of the portraits. *They're worried an angry mob will see my face and tear me apart.*

There were few people in the streets, however, and those hurried about their business, heads down. Rumors of the purge at the palace, as well as the king's continued illness, had combined to leave Torquay nervous and unsettled.

They boarded a barge at the royal landing and rowed downriver to the Flying Stair. Only a dozen people were waiting to make the trip to the City Below, and the four Peacemakers on duty stared with increasing suspicion at Liam until the guard officer pulled a scroll from his belt and took them aside to read it. The constables backed off after that, and the officer returned with a smug look.

Liam shrugged, and decided not to ask.

The guards escorted him all the way to the far berth where the *Trade's Increase* lay, and left him at the gangplank with a salute. The sailors saw him there and crowded around as he stepped aboard, welcoming him back and pestering him with questions.

"Where were you, Quaestor?"

"Wherefore were we arrested?"

"Wherefore wouldn't they let us part the barky?"

Liam claimed to be as baffled as they were, offering an unsatisfactory guess about customs troubles and mistaken accusations of smuggling. He maintained the same line when he was closeted in his cabin, alone with the captain.

"I don't know what it was all about, Captain Mathurin. The city is very unsettled at the moment. In all the confusion, someone made a great mistake, that's all I can think."

The older man squinted at Liam's shaved head, the lingering traces of ink. "Ah," he said, "well, there's that, to be sure. There were great doings up above, we heard.

Battles and murders and the like. To be sure. As you say, Quaestor."

Liam met his questioning gaze full on, refusing to be drawn out.

Mathurin coughed into his fist. "As you say, Quaestor. Shall we be shipping out, then?"

"Not right away," Liam said. "There are some things we need to take care of. I'm making a list."

Errands did not bother the sailors; they were happy for the chance to get ashore. Liam sent a man to change one of the notes-of-hand from his sea-chest, and then dispatched others with letters or sums of money or both to various locations around the city: a bath house, an inn in Stair, a ship called the *Tiger* out of Caer Urdoch, three separate shrines, and a collegium in Tower Vale.

By dusk, Liam watched the last sailor come up the gangplank, and Captain Mathurin joined him at the rail. "Would it like you to get under way, Quaestor?"

"Not just yet," he replied.

Frustrated but polite, Mathurin gave a resigned smile and headed off to his cabin. Fanuilh fluttered down from the rigging to take his place.

Master, what are you waiting for?

Liam told the dragon, and it cocked its head at him. *Is that necessary?*

"No," he answered, after a while. *But we may at least take the news back with us.*

It is unfortunate that the Cure did not work.

Liam gave a bitter laugh. *Yes, I would say that it was unfortunate. That's definitely the word I would use.*

But it is not your fault. You did everything you could.

Liam sobered, and reached out to scratch between his familiar's wings. *I know. So did you.* He stood at the rail for a long time, watching the sky darken and the first stars appear. Then he went below and climbed gratefully into his hammock.

• • •

He was up on deck the next morning to hear the bells toll six; so was Mathurin. The captain joined him at the rail, hope in his eyes.

"I would be the last to plague you so, Quaestor, but for that it would like the boys to part this cursed city. Would you know at all when we might sail?"

Liam glanced over his shoulder at the City Below, at the falls and the great cliffs. "I don't think it will be long, Captain. Another day at most."

Mathurin blanched at the idea of wasting a day, but said nothing.

It was not a day, however: only a few minutes later, the faint echo of bells in Torquay reached them, and slowly bells all over the City Below began to take up the tolling, wild, arhythmic peals that went on and on. Fanuilh trotted up from belowdecks and joined Liam.

Is that the signal, master?

I think so. He listened for a moment longer, then turned and called, "Captain Mathurin, we may cast off as soon as you are ready."

The sailors needed no urging, and they set to readying the *Trade's Increase* with a will. Later, when they were at sea, Liam told them what the bells meant and many of them wept unashamedly. For the moment, though, they worked happily, and soon enough the ship was making its way out of the harbor, trailed by the sound of bells tolling for the king who had died in the night.